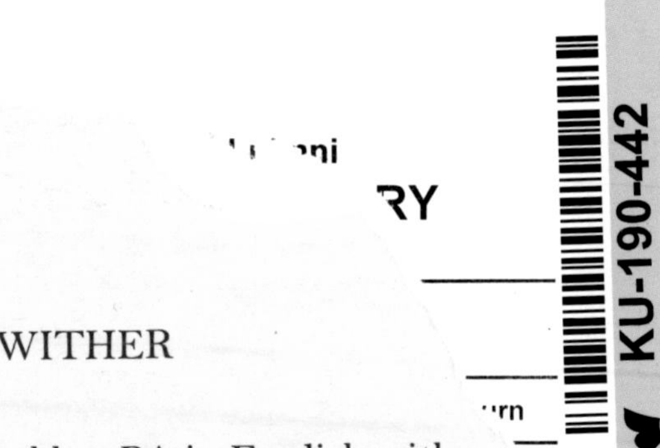

WITHER

Lauren DeStefano earned her BA in English with a concentration in creative writing from Albertus Magnus College in Connecticut. *Wither* is her first novel. She lives in Connecticut.

Visit http://www.LaurenDeStefano.com to learn more about Lauren.

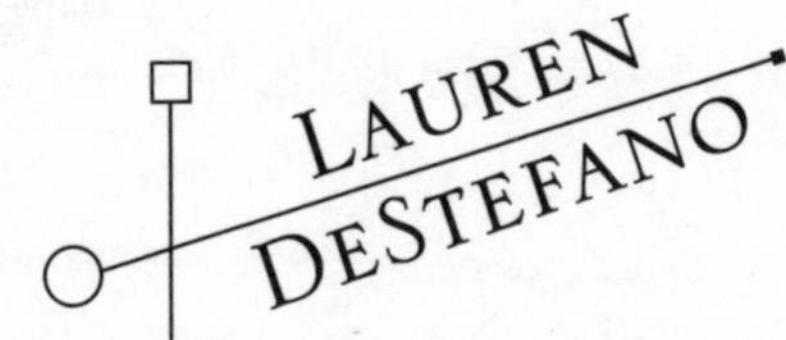

WITHER

THE CHEMICAL
GARDEN TRILOGY

BOOK
ONE

HarperVoyager
An imprint of HarperCollins*Publishers*
77–85 Fulham Palace Road,
Hammersmith, London W6 8JB

www.harpercollins.co.uk

Published by Harper*Voyager*
An imprint of HarperCollins*Publishers* 2011
1

A catalogue record for this book
is available from the British Library

ISBN: 978 0 00 738698 7

Book design by Lizzy Bromley

Printed and bound in Great Britain by
Clays Ltd, St Ives plc

FOR MY DAD,

WHO TURNED TO ME
AND SAID,

"ONE DAY, KID,
YOU'LL DO GREAT THINGS."

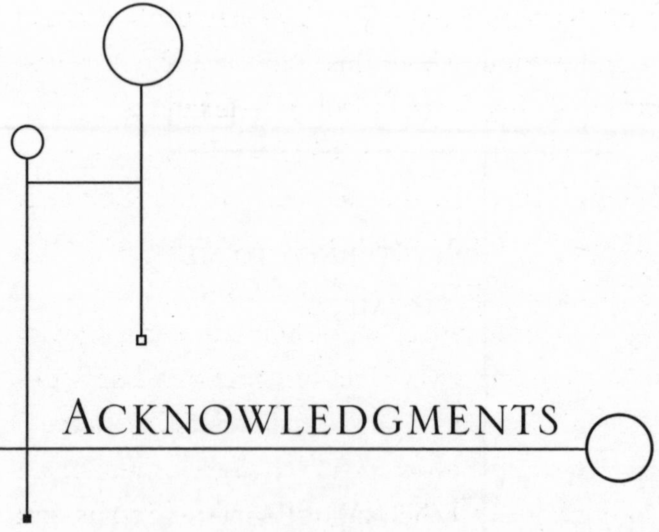

ACKNOWLEDGMENTS

Thanks to my wonderful family for all their support, love, and warmth. And an extra-special thanks to my little cousins for being so magical and for boosting my imagination and spirits when I needed it most.

Thanks to my fifth- and seventh-grade teachers for reading my earliest writing endeavors and not burning them, and for introducing me to the idea that I could publish a book.

Thanks to Dr. Susan Cole, Professor Charles Rafferty, and my former classmates at Albertus Magnus College for all of the writing workshops, and to Ms. Deborah Frattini and Dr. Paul Robichaud, who each introduced me to new authors that, to this day, influence everything I write.

Thanks to the dazzling, otherworldly creature that is my agent, Barbara Poelle, for all of her brilliance and optimism, and without whom this story would never have been realized. To my fantastic editor, Alexandra Cooper, for sharing this vision with me. To Lizzy Bromley for the heart-stopping cover. To the cast and crew at Simon & Schuster Books for Young Readers for all of the hard work and for being so wonderful and enthusiastic.

Thanks to Allison Shaw, who huddled over pages of my manuscripts in classrooms and restaurants and bookstore cafes, and who never gave a halfhearted critique—everything I write is better for it. To Harry Lam for all of those long phone calls helping me sort out details, and for being so logical and for always challenging me. To Amanda Ludwig-Chambers for being the ultimate and most poetic of fans. To April Plummer for reading the earliest draft of this story and offering up her suggestions and encouragement. To Laura Smith for being my fellow tortured artist and for cheering me on. And to everyone else who supported my pursuits and read snapshots of this story piecemeal in IMs and e-mail, offering their thoughts and advice. I could never have done this alone.

This is the way the world ends

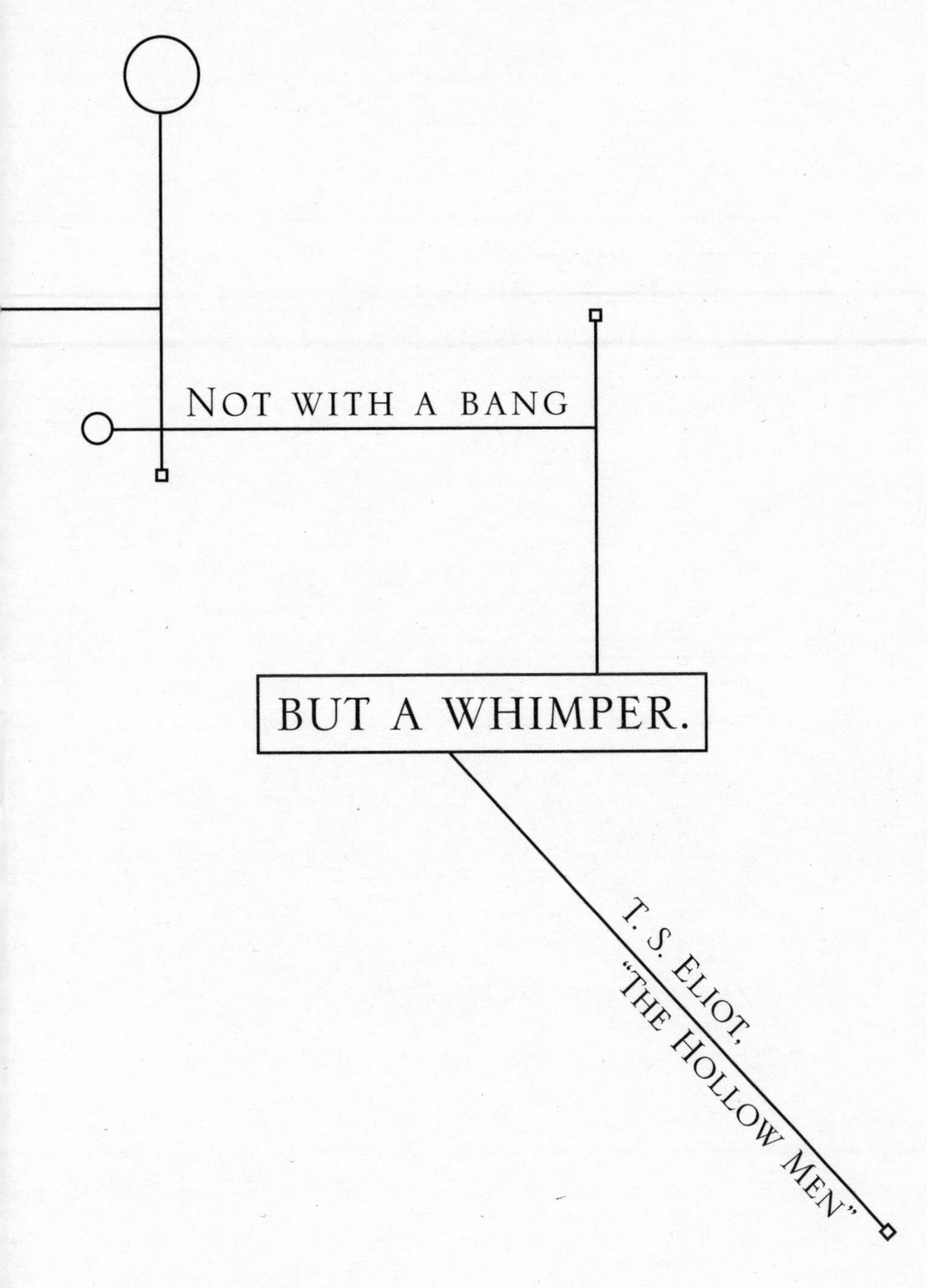

NOT WITH A BANG

BUT A WHIMPER.

T. S. ELIOT,
"THE HOLLOW MEN"

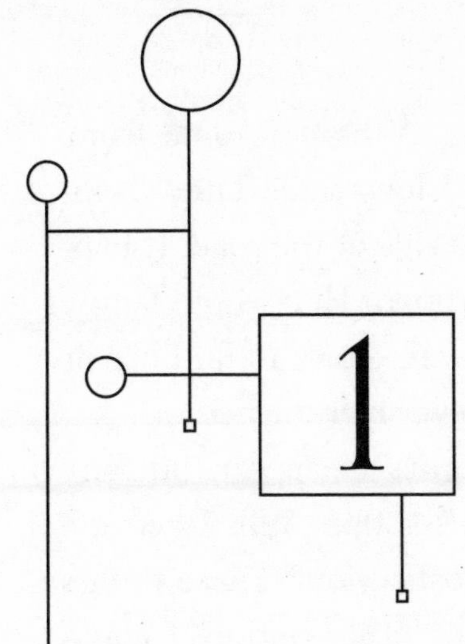

1

I WAIT. They keep us in the dark for so long that we lose sense of our eyelids. We sleep huddled together like rats, staring out, and dream of our bodies swaying.

I know when one of the girls reaches a wall. She begins to pound and scream—there's metal in the sound—but none of us help her. We've gone too long without speaking, and all we do is bury ourselves more into the dark.

The doors open.

The light is frightening. It's the light of the world through the birth canal, and at once the blinding tunnel that comes with death. I recoil into the blankets with the other girls in horror, not wanting to begin or end.

We stumble when they let us out; we've forgotten how to use our legs. How long has it been—days? Hours? The big open sky waits in its usual place.

I stand in line with the other girls, and men in gray coats study us.

I've heard of this happening. Where I come from, girls have been disappearing for a long time. They disappear from their beds or from the side of the road. It happened to a girl in my neighborhood. Her whole family disappeared after that, moved away, either to find her or because they knew she would never be returned.

Now it's my turn. I know girls disappear, but any number of things could come after that. Will I become a murdered reject? Sold into prostitution? These things have happened. There's only one other option. I could become a bride. I've seen them on television, reluctant yet beautiful teenage brides, on the arm of a wealthy man who is approaching the lethal age of twenty-five.

The other girls never make it to the television screen. Girls who don't pass their inspection are shipped to a brothel in the scarlet districts. Some we have found murdered on the sides of roads, rotting, staring into the searing sun because the Gatherers couldn't be bothered to deal with them. Some girls disappear forever, and all their families can do is wonder.

The girls are taken as young as thirteen, when their bodies are mature enough to bear children, and the virus claims every female of our generation by twenty.

Our hips are measured to determine strength, our lips pried apart so the men can judge our health by our teeth. One of the girls vomits. She may be the girl who screamed. She wipes her mouth, trembling, terrified. I stand firm, determined to be anonymous, unhelpful.

I feel too alive in this row of moribund girls with their eyes half open. I sense that their hearts are barely beating, while mine pounds in my chest. After so much time spent riding in the darkness of the truck, we have all fused together. We are one nameless thing sharing this strange hell. I do not want to stand out. I do not want to stand out.

But it doesn't matter. Someone has noticed me. A man paces before the line of us. He allows us to be prodded by the men in gray coats who examine us. He seems thoughtful and pleased.

His eyes, green, like two exclamation marks, meet mine. He smiles. There's a flash of gold in his teeth, indicating wealth. This is unusual, because he's too young to be losing his teeth. He keeps walking, and I stare at my shoes. *Stupid!* I should never have looked up. The strange color of my eyes is the first thing anyone ever notices.

He says something to the men in gray coats. They look at all of us, and then they seem to be in agreement. The man with gold teeth smiles in my direction again, and then he's taken to another car that shoots up bits of gravel as it backs onto the road and drives away.

The vomit girl is taken back to the truck, and a dozen other girls with her; a man in a gray coat follows them in. There are three of us left, the gap of the other girls still between us. The men speak to one another again, and then to us. "Go," they say, and we oblige. There's nowhere to go but the back of an open limousine parked on the gravel. We're off the road somewhere, not far from the highway. I can hear the faraway sounds of traffic. I can see the evening city lights beginning to appear in the distant purple haze. It's nowhere I recognize; a road this desolate is far from the crowded streets back home.

Go. The two other chosen girls move before me, and I'm the last to get into the limousine. There's a tinted glass window that separates us from the driver. Just before someone shuts the door, I hear something inside the van where the remaining girls were herded.

It's the first of what I know will be a dozen more gunshots.

I awake in a satin bed, nauseous and pulsating with sweat. My first conscious movement is to push myself to the edge of the mattress, where I lean over and vomit onto the lush red carpet. I'm still spitting and gagging when someone begins cleaning up the mess with a dishrag.

"Everyone handles the sleep gas differently," he says softly.

"Sleep gas?" I splutter, and before I can wipe my mouth on my lacy white sleeve, he hands me a cloth napkin—also lush red.

"It comes out through the vents in the limo," he says. "It's so you won't know where you're going."

I remember the glass window separating us from the front of the car. Airtight, I assume. Vaguely I remember the whooshing of air coming through vents in the walls.

"One of the other girls," the boy says as he sprays white foam onto the spot where I vomited, "she almost threw herself out the bedroom window, she was so disoriented. The window's locked, of course. Shatterproof." Despite the awful things he's saying, his voice is low, possibly even sympathetic.

I look over my shoulder at the window. Closed tight. The world is bright green and blue beyond it, brighter than my home, where there's only dirt and the remnants of my mother's garden that I've failed to revive.

Somewhere down the hall a woman screams. The boy tenses for a moment. Then he resumes scrubbing away the foam.

"I can help," I offer. A moment ago I didn't feel guilty about ruining anything in this place; I know I'm here against my will. But I also know this boy isn't to blame. He can't be one of the Gatherers in gray who brought me here. Maybe he was also brought here against his will. I haven't heard of teenage boys disappearing, but up until fifty years ago, when the virus was discovered, girls were also safe. Everyone was safe.

"No need. It's all done," he says. And when he moves the rag away, there's not so much as a stain. He pulls a handle out of the wall, and a chute opens; he tosses the rags into it, lets go, and the chute clamps shut. He tucks the can of white foam into his apron pocket and returns to what he was doing. He picks up a silver tray from where he'd placed it on the floor, and brings it to my night table. "If you're feeling better, there's some lunch for you. Nothing that will make you fall asleep again, I promise." He looks like he might smile. Just almost. But he maintains a concentrated gaze as he lifts a metal lid off a bowl of soup and another off a small plate of steaming vegetables and mashed potatoes cradling a lake of gravy. I've been stolen, drugged, locked away in this place, yet I'm being served a gourmet meal. The sentiment is so vile I could almost throw up again.

"That other girl—the one who tried to throw herself out the window—what happened to her?" I ask. I don't dare ask about the woman screaming down the hall. I don't want to know about her.

"She's calmed down some."

"And the other girl?"

"She woke up this morning. I think the House Governor took her to tour the gardens."

House Governor. I remember my despair and crash against the pillows. House Governors own mansions. They purchase brides from Gatherers, who patrol the streets looking for ideal candidates to kidnap. The merciful ones will sell the rejects into prostitution, but the ones I encountered herded them into the van and shot them all. I heard that first gunshot over and over in my medicated dreams.

"How long have I been here?" I say.

"Two days," the boy says. He hands me a steaming cup, and I'm about to refuse it when I see the tea bag string dangling over the side, smell the spices. Tea. My brother, Rowan, and I had it with our breakfast each morning, and with dinner each night. The smell is like home. My mother would hum as she waited by the stove for the water to boil.

Blearily I sit up and take the tea. I hold it near my face and breathe the steam in through my nose. It's all I can do not to burst into tears. The boy must sense that the full impact of what has happened is reaching me. He must sense that I'm on the verge of doing something dramatic like crying or trying to fling myself out the window like that other girl, because he's already moving for the door. Quietly, without looking back, he leaves me to my grief. But instead of tears, when I press my face against the pillow, a horrible, primal scream comes out of me. It's unlike anything I thought myself capable of. Rage, unlike anything I've ever known.

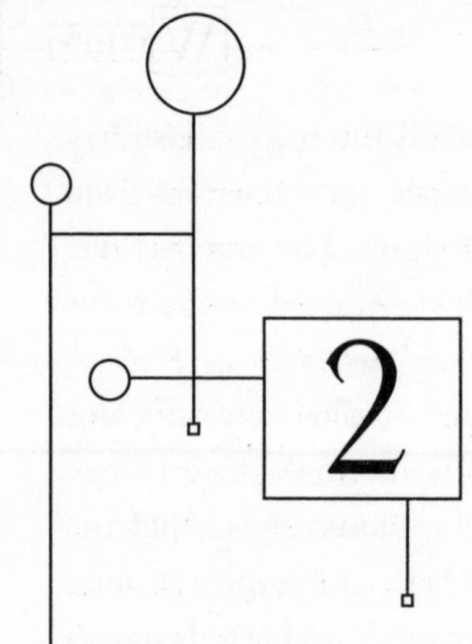

2

FOR MALES twenty-five is the fatal age. For women it's twenty. We are all dropping like flies.

Seventy years ago science perfected the art of children. There were complete cures for an epidemic known as cancer, a disease that could affect any part of the body and that used to claim millions of lives. Immune system boosts given to the new-generation children eradicated allergies and seasonal ailments, and even protected against sexually contracted viruses. Flawed natural children ceased to be conceived in favor of this new technology. A generation of perfectly engineered embryos assured a healthy, successful population. Most of that generation is still alive, approaching old age gracefully. They are the fearless first generation, practically immortal.

No one could ever have anticipated the horrible aftermath of such a sturdy generation of children. While the first generation did, and still does, thrive, something went wrong with their children, and their children's children. We, the new generations, are born healthy and strong, perhaps healthier than our parents, but our life span stops at twenty-five for males and twenty for females. For fifty years the world has been in a panic as its children die. The wealthier households refuse to accept defeat. Gatherers make a living collecting potential brides and selling them off to breed new children. The children born into these marriages are experiments. At least that's what my brother says, and always with disgust in his voice. There was a time when he wanted to learn more about the virus that's killing us; he would pester our parents with questions nobody could answer. But our parents' death broke his sense of wonder. My left-brained brother, who once had dreams of saving the world, now laughs at anyone who tries.

But neither of us ever knew for certain what happens after the initial gathering.

Now, it seems, I will find out.

For hours I pace the bedroom in this lacy nightgown. The room is fully furnished, as though it's been waiting for my arrival. There's a walk-in closet full of clothes, but I'm only in there long enough to check for an attic door, like my parents' closet has, though there isn't one. The dark, polished wood of the dresser matches the dressing table and ottoman; on the wall are generic paintings—a sunset, a beachside picnic. The wallpaper is made up of vertical vines budding roses, and they remind me of the bars of a prison cell. I avoid my reflection in the dressing table mirror, afraid I'll lose my mind if I see myself in this place.

I try opening the window, but when that proves futile, I take in the view. The sun is just beginning to set in yellows and pinks, and there's a myriad of flowers in the garden. There are trickling fountains. The grass is mowed into strips of green and deeper green. Closer to the house a hedge sections off an area with an inground pool, unnaturally cerulean. This, I think, is the botanical heaven my mother imagined when she planted lilies in the yard. They would grow healthy and vibrant, thriving despite the wasteland of dirt and dust. The only time flowers bloomed in our neighborhood was when she was alive. Other than my mother's flowers, there are those wilting carnations that shopkeepers sell in the city, dyed pink and red for Valentine's Day, along with red roses that always look rubbery or parched in the windows. They, like humanity, are chemical replicas of what they should be.

The boy who brought my lunch mentioned that one of the other girls was taking a walk in the garden, and I wonder if the House Governor is merciful enough to let us go outside freely. I don't know much about them at all except that they're all either younger than twenty-five or approaching seventy—the latter being from the first generation, and they're a rarity. By now, much of the first generation has watched enough of its children die prematurely, and they are unwilling to experiment on yet another generation. They even join the protest rallies, violent riots that leave irreparable damage.

My brother. He would have known immediately that something was wrong when I didn't come home from work. And I've been gone for three days. No doubt he's beside himself; he warned me about those ominous gray vans that roll slowly through city streets at all hours. But it wasn't one of those vans that took me at all. I could never have seen this coming.

It's the thought of my brother, alone in that empty house, that forces me to stop pitying myself. It's counter-productive. *Think.* There must be *some* way to escape. The window clearly isn't opening. The closet leads to only more clothes. The chute where the boy threw the dirty dishrag is only inches wide. Maybe, if I can win the House Governor's favor, I'll be trusted enough to wander the garden alone. From my window the garden looks endless. But there has to be an end somewhere. Maybe I can find an exit by squeezing through a hedge or scaling a fence. Maybe I'll be one of the public brides, flaunted at televised parties, and there will be an opportunity to slip quietly into the crowd. I have seen so many reluctant brides on television, and I've always wondered why the girls don't run. Maybe the cameras neglect to show the security system that keeps them trapped.

Now, though, I worry that I may never even have a chance to make it to one of those parties. For all I know, it will take years to earn a House Governor's trust. And in four years, when I turn twenty, I'll be dead.

I try the doorknob, and to my surprise it isn't locked. The door creaks open, revealing the hallway.

Somewhere a clock is ticking. There are a few doors lining the walls, mostly closed, with dead bolts. There's a dead bolt on my door as well, but it's open.

I tread slowly, my bare feet giving me an advantage because on this rich green carpet I'm practically silent. I pass the doors, listening for sound, signs of life. But the only sound comes from the door at the end of the hallway that's slightly ajar. There are moans, gasps.

I freeze where I stand. If the House Governor is with one of his wives trying to impregnate her, it would only make things worse for me if I walked in on it. I don't know what would happen—I'd either be executed or asked to join, probably, and I can't imagine which would be worse.

But no, the sounds are strictly female, and she's alone. Cautiously I peek through the slit in the door, then push the door open.

"Who's there?" the woman murmurs, and this throws her into a rage of coughs.

I step into the room and find that she's alone on a satin bed. But this room is far more decorated than mine, with pictures of children on the walls, and an open window with a billowing curtain. This room looks lived in, comfortable, and nothing like a prison.

On her nightstand there are pills, vials with droppers, empty and near-empty glasses of colored fluids. She props herself on her elbows and stares at me. Her hair is blond, like mine, but its shade is subdued by her sallow skin. Her eyes are wild. "Who are you?"

"Rhine," I give my name quietly, because I'm too unnerved to be anything but honest.

"Such a beautiful place," she says. "Have you seen the pictures?"

She must be delirious, because I don't understand what she's saying. "No," is all I say.

"You didn't bring me my medicine," she says, and drifts gracefully back to her sea of pillows with a sigh.

"No," I say. "Should I get something?" Now it's clear that she is delirious, and if I can make up an excuse to leave, maybe I can return to my room and she'll forget I was even here.

"Stay," she says, and pats the edge of her bed. "I'm so tired of these remedies. Can't they just let me die?"

Is this what my future as a bride will look like? Being so entrapped I'm not even allowed the freedom of death?

I sit beside her, overwhelmed by the smell of medication and decay, and beneath that, something pleasant. Potpourri—perfumed, dehydrated flower petals. That melodic smell is everywhere, surrounding us, making me think of home.

"You're a liar," the woman says. "You didn't come to bring my medicine."

"I never said I did."

"Well, then, who are you?" She reaches her trembling hand and touches my hair. She holds up a lock of it for inspection, and then a horrible pain fills her eyes. "Oh. You're my replacement. How old are you?"

"Sixteen," I say, again startled into honesty. Replacement? Is she one of the House Governor's wives?

She stares at me for a while, and the pain begins to recede into something else. Something almost maternal. "Do you hate it here?" she says.

"Yes," I say.

"Then you should see the verandah." She smiles as she closes her eyes. Her hand falls away from my hair. She coughs, and blood from her mouth splatters my nightgown. I've had nightmares that I'll enter a room where my parents have been murdered and lie in a pool of fresh blood, and in those nightmares I stand in the doorway forever, too frightened to run. Now I feel a similar terror. I want to go, to be anywhere but here, but I can't seem to make my legs move. I can only watch as she coughs and struggles, and my gown becomes redder for it. I feel the warmth of her blood on my hands and face.

I don't know how long this goes on for. Eventually someone comes running, an older woman, a first generation, holding a metal basin that sloshes soapy water. "Oh, Lady Rose, why didn't you press the button if you were in pain?" the basin woman says.

I hurry to my feet, toward the door, but the basin woman doesn't even notice me. She helps the coughing woman sit up in the bed, and she peels off the woman's nightgown and begins to sponge the soapy water over her skin.

"Medicine in the water," the coughing woman moans. "I smell it. Medicine everywhere. Just let me die."

She sounds so horrible and wounded that, despite my own situation, I pity her.

"What are you doing?" a voice whispers harshly behind me. I turn and see the boy who brought my lunch earlier, looking nervous. "How did you get out? Go back to your room. Hurry, go!" This is one thing my nightmares never had, someone forcing me into action. I'm grateful for it. I run back to my open bedroom, though not before crashing into someone standing in my path.

I look up, and I recognize the man who has caught me in his arms. His smile glimmers with bits of gold.

"Why, hello," he says.

I don't know what to make of his smile, whether it's sinister or kind. It takes only a moment longer for him to notice the blood on my face, my gown, and then he pushes past me. He runs into the bedroom where the woman is still in a riot of coughs.

I run into my bedroom. I tear off the nightgown and use the clean parts of it to scrub the blood from my skin, and then I huddle under the comforter of my bed, holding my hands over my ears, trying to hide from those awful sounds. This whole awful place.

The sound of the doorknob awakens me this time. The boy who brought my lunch earlier is now holding another silver tray. He doesn't meet my eyes; he crosses the room and sets the tray on my nightstand.

"Dinner," he says solemnly.

I watch him from where I'm huddled in my blankets, but he doesn't look at me. He doesn't even raise his head as he picks the sullied nightgown off the floor, splattered with Lady Rose's blood, and disposes of it in the chute. Then he turns to go.

"Wait," I say. "Please."

He freezes, with his back to me.

And I'm not sure what it is about him—that he's close to my own age, that he's so unobtrusive, that he seems no happier to be here than I am—but I want his company. Even if it can only be for a minute or two.

"That woman—," I say, desperate to make conversation before he leaves. "Who is she?"

"That's Lady Rose," he says. "The House Governor's first wife." All Governors take a first wife; the number doesn't refer to the order of marriage, but is an indication of power. The first wives attend all the social events, they appear with their Governors in public, and, apparently, they are entitled to the privilege of an open window. They're the favorites.

"What's wrong with her?"

"Virus," he says, and when he turns to face me, he has a look of genuine curiosity. "You've never seen someone with the virus?"

"Not up close," I say.

"Not even your parents?"

"No." My parents were first generation, well into their fifties when my brother and I were born, but I'm not sure I want to tell him this. Instead I say, "I try really hard not to think about the virus."

"Me too," he says. "She asked for you, after you left. Your name is Rhine?"

He's looking at me now, so I nod, suddenly aware that I'm naked under these blankets. I draw them closer around myself. "What's your name?"

"Gabriel," he says. And there it is again, that almost smile, hindered by the weight of things. I want to ask him what he's doing in this awful place with its beautiful gardens and clear blue pools, symmetrical green hedges. I want to know where he came from, and if he's planning on going back. I even want to tell him about my plan to escape—if I ever formulate a plan, that is. But these thoughts are dangerous. If my brother were here, he'd tell me to trust nobody. And he'd be right.

"Good night," the boy, Gabriel, says. "You might want to eat and get some sleep. Tomorrow's a big day." His tone implies I've just been warned of something awful ahead.

He turns to leave, and I notice a slight limp in his walk that wasn't there this afternoon. Beneath the thin white fabric of his uniform, I can see the shadow of bruises beginning to form. Is it because of me? Was he punished for making my escape down the hallway possible? These are more questions that I don't ask.

Then he's gone. And I hear the click of a lock turning in the door.

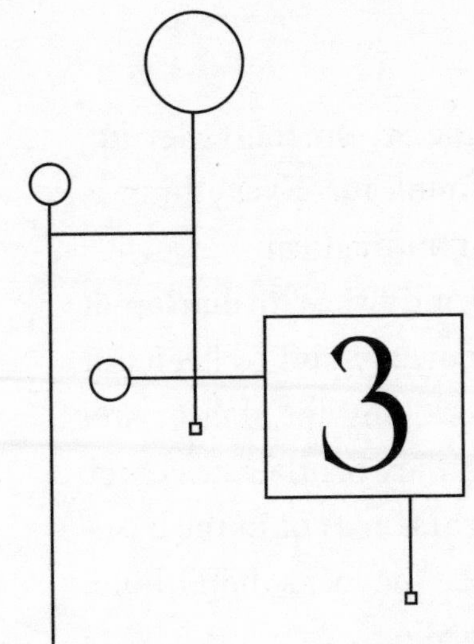

3

IT'S NOT GABRIEL who wakes me in the morning, but a parade of women. They're first generation, if the gray hair is any indication, though their eyes still sparkle with the vibrancy of youth. They are chattering among themselves as they yank the blankets from me.

One of the women looks over my naked body and says, "Well, at least we won't have to wrestle this one out of her clothes."

This one. After everything that's happened, I almost forgot that there are two others. Trapped in this house somewhere, behind other locked doors.

Before I can react, two of the women have grabbed me by the arms and are dragging me toward the bathroom that connects to my room.

"Best if you don't struggle," one of them says cheerfully. I stagger to keep pace with them. Another woman stays behind to make my bed.

In the bathroom they make me sit on the toilet lid, which is covered in some sort of pink fur. Everything is pink. The curtains are flimsy and impractical.

Back home we covered our windows with burlap at night to give the impression of poverty and to keep out the prying eyes of new orphans looking for shelter and handouts. The house I shared with my brother has three bedrooms, but we'd spend our nights on a cot in the basement, sleeping in shifts just in case the locks didn't hold, using our father's shotgun to guard us.

Frilly, pretty things have no place in windows. Not where I come from.

The colors are endless. One woman draws a bath while the other opens the cabinet to a rainbow of little soaps that are shaped like hearts and stars. She drops a few of them into the bathwater, and they sizzle and dissolve, leaving a frothy layer of pink and blue. Bubbles pop like little fireworks.

I don't argue when I'm told to get into the tub. It's awkward being naked in front of these strangers, but the water looks and smells appealing. It's so unlike the bleary yellowed water that runs through the rusty pipes in the house I shared with my brother.

Shared. Past tense. How could I let myself think this way?

I lie in the sweet-smelling water, and the bubbles pop against my skin, bringing samples of cinnamon and potpourri and what I imagine real roses must smell like. But

I will not be hypnotized by the wonder of these small things. Defiantly I think of the house I share with my brother, the house where my mother was born at the threshold of the new century. It has brick walls still imprinted with the silhouette of ivy that has long since died. It has a fire escape with a broken ladder, and on its street all the houses are close enough together that as a child I would hold my arms out my bedroom window to hold the hands of the little girl who lived next door. We would string paper cups across the divide and talk to each other in giggles.

That little girl was orphaned young. Her parents were the new generation. She barely knew her mother, her father fell ill, and then one morning I reached for her and she was gone.

I was inconsolable, that girl having been my first true friend. I still think of her bright blue eyes sometimes, the way she'd toss peppermints at my bedroom window to wake me for a game of paper-cup telephone. Once she was gone, my mother held the string we had used for our game of telephone, and she told me it was kite string, that when she was a little girl she would spend hours in the park flying kites. I asked her for more stories of her childhood, and on some nights she gave them to me. Stories of towering toy stores and frozen lakes where she would skate swanlike into figure eights, and of all the people who had passed beneath the very windows of this very house when it was young and covered in ivy, and when the cars were parked in neat, shiny rows along the street, in Manhattan, New York.

When she and my father died, my brother and I covered the windows with burlap potato and coffee bean sacks. We took all our mother's beautiful things, all our father's important clothes, and stuffed them into trunks that locked. The rest we buried in the yard, late at night, beneath the ailing lilies.

This is my story. These things are my past, and I will not allow them to be washed away. I will find a way to have them back.

"She has such agreeable hair," one of the women says, scooping warm cupful after cupful of frothy water over my head. "Such a lovely color, too. I wonder if it's natural." Of course it's natural. What else would it be?

"I bet that's what the Governor liked about her."

"Let me see," says the other woman, cupping my chin and tilting it. She studies my face and then gasps, letting her hand flutter spasmodically against her heart. "Oh, Helen, look at this girl's eyes!"

They both stop bathing me long enough to look at me. Really look at me, for the first time.

My eyes are usually the first thing people notice, the left eye blue and the right eye brown, just like my brother's. Heterochromia; my parents were geneticists, and that was the name they gave my condition. I might have asked them more about it when I grew older, if I'd had the chance. I had always thought the heterochromia was a useless genetic glitch, but if the women are right and my eyes are what the Governor noticed, heterochromia has saved my life.

"Suppose those are real?" one woman asks.

"What else would they be but real?" This time I speak aloud, and they're startled, then delighted. Their doll has a voice. And suddenly they're all questions. Where am I from, do I know where I am, don't I just love the view, do I like horses—there's a lovely stable—do I prefer my hair up or down?

I answer none of these. I will share nothing with these strangers—however well intentioned they may be—who are a part of this place. The questions come so fast that I wouldn't know where to begin anyway, and then there's a soft knock at the door.

"We're getting her ready for the Governor," one of the women says.

The muffled voice on the other side of the door is soft, gentle, and young. "Lady Rose would like to speak to her right this moment, please."

"We're only half done bathing her! And her nails—"

"Excuse me," the voice on the other side of the door says patiently, "I have a direct order to bring her now, whatever condition she may be in."

Lady Rose is apparently someone who has the final say in things, because the women are tugging me to my feet, patting me dry with a pink towel, brushing my wet hair, and slipping me into a robe that feels like waves of silk against my skin. Whatever was in that bathwater has heightened my neurons, left me feeling unpeeled and exposed. I still feel as though bubbles are popping against my skin.

When the door opens, I see that the voice belongs to a little girl, barely half my height. She is dressed like the older women, though, in the feminine version of the white blouse Gabriel wore, with a tiered black skirt, where Gabriel had worn black pants. Her hair is braided into a circle around her head, and her cheeks bloom into apple shapes when she smiles at me. "You're Rhine?"

I nod. "I'm Deirdre," she says, and puts her hand in mine. It is cool and soft. "It's just this way," she says, and leads me out of my room and along the hallway down which I made my brief escape yesterday.

"Now," the girl says, nodding seriously, her eyes focusing ahead. "Just speak if spoken to; she doesn't like questions, so you'd do best not to ask any; refer to her as Lady Rose; there's a button above her night table, a white one—press it if she becomes ill. She's in charge of things. The House Governor will do anything she asks, so be sure to stay on her good side."

We stop before the door, and Deirdre reties the belt of my robe into a perfect bow. She knocks on the semi-open door and says, "Lady Rose? I brought her like you said."

"Well, then, let her in," Rose snaps. "And go make yourself useful somewhere else."

As she turns to leave, Deirdre clasps both of her hands

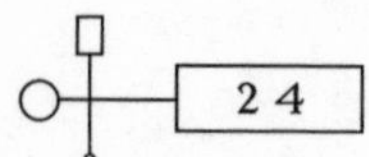

around one of mine. Her eyes are round as moons. "And please," she whispers, "try to avoid the topic of death."

When she's gone, I push the door open and step only as far as the threshold. From here I can smell the medications Rose complained of yesterday. I see the assortment of lotions, pills, and bottles on her nightstand.

She's sitting up today, in a satin-upholstered divan by the window. Her blond hair is tangled in sunlight, and her skin appears to be less sallow. There's color in her cheeks, and at first I think she's feeling better, but when she beckons me closer, I can see the unusual, almost neon pink of her cheeks, and I know it must be cosmetics. I know the red of her lips must not be real either. What are real are her eyes, incredibly brown things that stare at me with intensity, with youth. I try to imagine a world of natural humans, when twenty *was* youthful, when it was years from a death sentence.

Natural humans used to live for at least eighty years, my mother told me. Sometimes a hundred. I hadn't believed her.

Now I can see what she meant. Rose is the first twenty-year-old I've spoken to at length, and though she's stifling a cough that sprays blood into her fist, her skin is still smooth and soft. Her face is still full of light. She doesn't look very different from, or very much older than, me.

"Sit," she tells me. I find a chair across from her.

There are wrappers all over the floor around her, and

a bowl filled with candies on her divan. When she speaks, I can see that her tongue is bright blue. She fiddles with another candy in her long fingers, bringing it close to her face, almost looking like she'll kiss it. Instead she lets it fall back into the bowl.

"Where are you from?" she asks. Her voice has none of the peevishness she showed Deirdre at the door. Her thick eyelashes flutter up. She watches an insect spiral around her and disappear.

I don't want to tell her where I'm from. I'm supposed to sit here and be polite, but how can I? How can I when I'm made to sit and watch her die so I can be given to her husband and forced to bear children I never wanted?

So I say, "Where were you from when they took you?"

I'm not supposed to ask her questions, and as soon as I've asked it, I realize I have stepped on a land mine. She'll be screaming for Deirdre or her husband, the House Governor, to take me away. Lock me in a dungeon for the next four years.

To my surprise she only says, "I was born in this state. This town, in fact." She reaches up behind her, takes a picture from the wall, and holds it out for me. I lean in to get a look.

The photo is of a young girl standing beside a horse. She's holding the reins, and her smile is so bright that her teeth dominate her face. Her eyes are nearly closed with all the delight of it. Beside her, a much taller boy stands with his hands behind his back. His smile is more controlled, shy, as though he hadn't meant to smile but couldn't help himself in the moment.

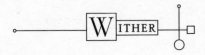

"This was me," Rose says of the girl in the photo. Then she traces her finger over the boy's outline. "This is my Linden." For a moment she seems lost in the sight of him. A little smile comes to her painted lips. "We grew up together."

I'm not sure what to say to this. She is so lost in this memory, and so blind to my imprisonment. But still I feel sorry for her. In another time, under different circumstances, she would not have needed to be replaced.

"See?" she says, still pointing to the photo. "This is in the orange grove. My father owned acres of them. Here in Florida."

Florida. My heart sinks. I'm in Florida, on the bottom of the East Coast, more miles from home than I can count. I miss my ivy-silhouetted house. I miss the distant commuter trains. How will I ever find my way back to them?

"They're lovely," I say of the oranges. Because it's true, they are lovely. Things seem to thrive in this place. I would never have suspected that the vibrant girl standing beside her horse in the grove could be dying now.

"Aren't they?" she says. "Linden prefers flowers, though. There are orange blossom festivals in the spring. That's his favorite. In the winter there are snow festivals, and solstice dances—but he doesn't like those. Too loud."

She unwraps a green candy and pops it into her mouth.

She closes her eyes for a moment, apparently savoring the flavor. The candies are each a different color, and this one, the green, has a peppermint smell that takes me back to my childhood. I think of the little girl who would throw her candies into my bedroom, how their smell would fill the paper cup into which I'd respond to her voice.

When Rose speaks again, her tongue has taken on the emerald color of the candy. "But he's an excellent dancer. I don't know why he's such a wallflower."

She sets the picture on the divan in a sea of wrappers. I can't decide what to make of this woman, who is weary and so sad, and who snapped at Deirdre but is treating me like a friend. My curiosity quells my bitterness for the moment. I think, in this strange world of beautiful things, there may be some humanity after all.

"Do you know how old Linden is?" she asks me. I shake my head. "He's twenty-one. We'd planned to marry since we were children, and I suppose he thought all these medicines would keep me alive for four extra years. His father is a very prominent doctor—first generation. Toiling away at finding an antidote." She says that last bit fancifully, letting her fingers flutter in the air. She does not think an antidote is possible. Many do, though. Where I come from, hordes of new orphans will file into laboratories, offering themselves up to be guinea pigs for a few extra dollars. But an antidote never arrives, and a thorough analysis of our gene pool turns up no abnormalities to explain this fatal virus.

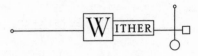

"But you," Rose says. "Sixteen is perfect. You can spend the rest of your lives together. He won't have to be alone."

I feel the room go cold. Outside there are things buzzing and chirping in the infinite garden, but they are a million miles from me. I had almost, for just a moment, forgotten why I'm here. Forgotten how I arrived. This beautiful place is dangerous, like milky white oleanders. The thriving garden is meant to keep me inside.

Linden stole his brides so he wouldn't have to die alone. What about my brother, alone in that empty house? What about the other girls who were shot to death in that van?

My anger is back. My fists clench, and I wish someone would come to take me out of this room, even if it means being imprisoned somewhere else in this house. I cannot bear another moment in Rose's presence. Rose with her open window. Rose who has mounted a horse and ridden beyond the orange groves. Rose who intends to pass her death sentence on to me once she's gone.

My wish comes true, to make matters worse. Deirdre returns and says, "Excuse me, Lady Rose, the doctor is here to prepare her for Governor Linden."

I'm led down the hall again, and into an elevator that requires a key card in order to work. Deirdre stands beside me, looking rigid and worried. "You'll meet Housemaster Vaughn tonight," she whispers. The blood has drained from her face, and she looks at me in a way that reminds me she's just a child. Her lips purse in—what? Sympathy? Fear? I don't know, because the elevator doors open and she returns to herself, guiding me down another, darker hallway that smells of antiseptic, and through another door.

I wonder if she has any advice for me this time, but she's not even given the chance to speak before a man says, "Which one is this?"

"Rhine, sir," Deirdre says, not raising her eyes. "The sixteen-year-old."

I wonder, briefly, if this man is the Housemaster or the Governor who's to be my husband, but I don't have the chance to even look at him before there's a stinging pain in my arm. I have only time to process what I'm seeing: a sterile, windowless room. A bed with a sheet, and restraints where arms and legs might go.

Keeping in theme with all the other things in this place, the room fills with shimmering butterflies. They all quiver, and then burst like the strange bath bubbles. Blood everywhere in their wake. Then blackness.

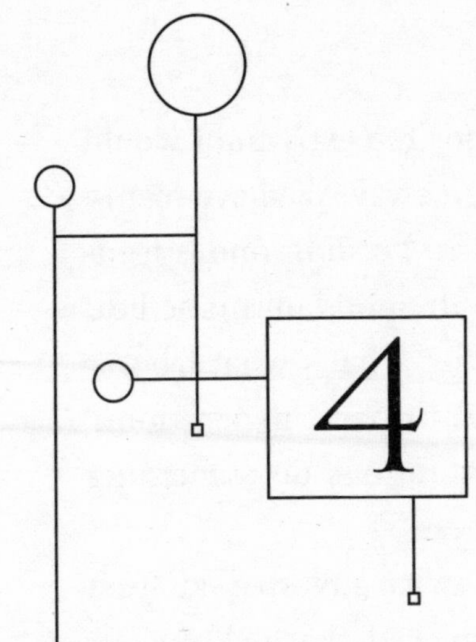

IT'S MY TURN to keep watch. We've locked the doors and windows and barricaded ourselves in the basement for the night. The tiny refrigerator hums in the corner; the clock is ticking; the lightbulb swings on its wire, doing erratic things with the light. I think I hear a rat in the shadows, foraging for crumbs.

Rowan is snoring on the cot, which is unusual, because he never does. But I don't mind. It's nice to hear the sound of another human, to know that I'm not alone. That in a second he would be awake if there were any trouble. As twins, we make a great team. He has the muscles, and his aim with the shotgun never misses, but I'm smaller and faster, and sometimes more alert.

We've only had one thief ever who was armed, the year I turned thirteen. Mostly the thieves are small children who will break windows or attempt to pick the lock, and they only stay long enough to realize there's nothing to eat or nothing worth stealing. They're pests, and I would just as soon feed them so they'd go away. We have plenty to spare. But Rowan won't allow it. Feeding one is feeding them all, and we don't own the goddamn city, he'd say. That's what orphanages are for. That's what laboratory wages are for. Or how about the first generations? he'd say; how about the first generations do something because they caused this whole mess.

The armed thief was a man twice my size, at least into his twenties. He somehow picked the lock on our front door without making a sound, and he figured out quickly that the residents of our little house were hiding somewhere, guarding what was worth taking. It was Rowan's watch that hour, but he'd fallen asleep after a full day of physical labor. He takes work where and when he can get it, and it's always arduous; he's always in pain at the end of the day. Long ago, America's factory jobs were outsourced to other industrialized countries. Now, because there's no importing, most of New York's towering buildings have been converted to factories that make everything from frozen food to sheet metal. I'm usually able to find work handling wholesale orders by phone; Rowan finds work easily in shipments and delivery, and it exhausts him more than he cares to admit. But the pay is always cash, and we're always able to buy more than we need in terms of food. Shopkeepers are so grateful to have paying customers—as opposed to the penniless orphans who always try to steal the essentials—that they give us deals on extras like electrical tape and aspirin.

So there we were, both asleep. I awoke with a blade to my throat, looking into the eyes of a man I did not know. I made a small sound, not even a whimper, but that was all it took for my brother to jolt back to consciousness, gun at the ready.

I was helpless, paralyzed. Small thieves I could handle, and most thieves did not want to kill us, not if they could help it. They only made meager threats on the hope of getting food, a piece of jewelry, and if they were smaller than you, they would just run away when you caught them. They were only trying to survive however they could.

"Shoot me, and I cut her," the man said.

There was a loud sound, like the time one of our pipes burst, and then I saw a line of blood roll over the man's brow. It took a second for me to realize there was a red bullet hole in his forehead, and then the knife went slack against my neck. I grabbed it, kicked him away from me. But he was already dead. I sat up, eyes bulging, gasping. Rowan was on his feet, though, checking to be sure the man was really dead, not wanting to waste another bullet if it wasn't necessary. "Goddamn it," he said, and kicked the man. "I fell asleep. Damn it!"

"You were tired," I said reassuringly. "It's okay. He would have gone away if we'd fed him."

"Don't be so naive," Rowan said, and lifted the dead man's arm pointedly. It was then that I noticed the man's gray coat. The clear mark of a Gatherer on the job. "He wanted—," Rowan began, but couldn't finish the thought aloud. It was the first time I'd ever seen him tremble.

I had thought, before that night, that Gatherers swept young girls from the street. While this is true, it isn't always the case. They can stake a girl out, follow her home, and wait for an opportunity. That is, if they think she's worth the trouble, if they think she'll get a good price. And that's what had happened. That's why the man had broken into our home. Now my brother refuses to let me go anywhere unless he's with me. He worries over our shoulders, peers into alleyways we pass. We've added bolts to the door. We've strung the kitchen floor in a labyrinth of kite strings and empty aluminum cans so that we'll be alerted—loudly—to any intruders before they can hope to break into our basement.

I hear something else now, something I at first assume is another rat scurrying around upstairs. It would be the only thing small enough to wind a path around our trap. But then the basement door begins to rattle at the top of the steps. The bolts pop open, one at a time.

Behind me, Rowan has stopped snoring. I whisper his name. I say I think someone has broken in. He doesn't answer me. I turn around, and the cot is empty.

At the top of the stairs, the basement door flies open. But instead of the darkness of our house, there's sunlight, and the most breathtaking garden I have ever seen. I barely have time to take it all in before the doors close in front of me. The doors of a gray van, a van full of frightened girls.

"Rowan," I gasp, and throw myself upright.

Awake. I'm awake now, trying to console myself. But reality does not offer a safe haven. I'm still in this Florida mansion, still the intended bride of the House Governor, and Rose is gasping for her life down the hall while voices try to soothe her.

My legs and hips feel sore when I stretch them against the satin sheets. I peel back the blankets, assess myself. I'm wearing a plain white slip. My skin is tingling and hairless. My nails have been rounded and polished. I'm back in my bedroom, with its window that doesn't open and its bathroom so pink it's practically glowing.

As if on cue, my bedroom door opens, and I don't know what to expect. Gabriel, beaten and limping as he brings me a meal; a parade of first generations coming to exfoliate, fluff, and perfume what's left of my skin; a doctor with a needle and another scary table, this time on wheels. But it's only Deirdre, carrying what looks to be a heavy white package in her tiny arms.

"Hello," she says, in a tone that's gentle as only a child's can be. "How are you feeling?"

My answer wouldn't be kind, so I don't say anything.

She flits across the room, wearing a wispy white dress rather than her traditional uniform.

"I've brought your gown," she says, setting the package on the dressing table and undoing the bow that was holding it together. The dress is taller than she is, and it drags luxuriously along the floor as she holds it up. It glitters with diamonds and pearls.

"It should be your size," Deirdre says. "They measured you while you were out, and I made some alterations to be sure. Try it on."

The last thing I want to do is try on what is clearly my wedding gown, just so I can meet House Governor Linden, the man responsible for my kidnapping, and Housemaster Vaughn, whose name alone made Deirdre go pale in the elevator. But she's holding up the dress and looking so sympathetic and innocent about it that I don't want to give her a hard time. I step into the gown and allow myself to be zipped in.

Deirdre stands on the ottoman at the dressing table to tie the choker for me. Her deft little hands make such perfect bows. And the gown is a remarkable fit. "You made this?" I ask her, not hiding my amazement. A blush spreads across her apple cheeks, and she nods as she steps down.

"The diamonds and the pearls take the longest time to thread," she says. "The rest is easy."

The dress is strapless, shaped like the top of a heart at my collarbone. The train is V-shaped. And I suppose, from an aerial view, I could be a satiny white heart as I make my way down the aisle. At least I can't imagine a lovelier thing to wear on my way to lifelong imprisonment.

"You made three wedding dresses by yourself?" I say.

Deirdre shakes her head and gently guides me to sit on the ottoman. "Just yours," she says. "You're my keeper; I'm your domestic. The other wives each have their own."

She opens a drawer in the dressing table, and it is lush with cosmetics and hair barrettes. With a rouge brush in her hand, she gestures to the buttons on the wall just above my night table. "Press the white one if you need anything, that's how you can reach me. Blue is the kitchen."

She begins to paint my face, blending and brushing colors onto my skin, holding my chin up to inspect me. Her eyes are serious and wide. When she's satisfied, she starts on my hair, brushing and weaving it around curlers, and prattling on about information she feels will be useful to me.

"The wedding will be held in the rose garden. It goes in order of age, youngest first. So there will be a bride before you and a bride after. There's the exchange of vows, of course, but the vows will be read for you; you won't be required to speak. Then there's the exchange of the rings, and let's see what else . . ."

Her voice trails off, into a sea of description; floating candles; dinner arrangements; even how softly I should speak.

But everything she says blurs into one hideous mess. The wedding is tonight. Tonight. I have no hope of escaping before it occurs; I haven't even been able to open a window; I haven't even seen the outside of this wretched place. I feel sick, winded. I'd settle for being able to open the window not to escape but to gasp in the fresh air. I open my mouth to take a deep breath, and Deirdre pops a red candy into my mouth.

"It'll make your breath sweet," she says. The candy dissolves instantly, and I'm flooded with the flavor of something like strawberries and too much sugar. It's overwhelming at first, and then it subsides, tastes natural, even settles my anxiety somewhat.

"There now," Deirdre says, seeming pleased with herself. She nudges me so that I'm facing the mirror for the first time.

I'm stunned by what I see.

My eyelids have been painted pink, but it is not the obnoxious pink of the bathroom here. It's the color between the reds and yellows at sunset. It sparkles as though full of little stars, and recedes into light purples and soft whites. My lips are done to match, and my skin is shimmering.

I look, for the first time, like I am not a child. I am my mother in her party dress, those nights she spent dancing with my father in the living room after my brother and I had gone to bed. She would come into my bedroom later to kiss me while she thought I slept. She would be sweaty and perfumed and delirious with love for my father. "Ten fingers, ten toes," she would whisper into my ear, "my little girl is safe in her dreams." Then she would leave me feeling like I'd just been enchanted.

What would my mother say to this girl—this almost-woman—in the mirror?

As for myself, I'm speechless. With her talent for color Deirdre has made my blue eye brighter, my brown eye nearly as intense as Rose's stare. She has dressed me and painted me well for the role: I am soon to become Governor Linden's tragic bride.

I think it speaks for itself, but in the mirror I can see Deirdre behind me twisting her hands, waiting to hear what I think of her work. "It's beautiful," is all I can say.

"My father was a painter," she says with a hint of pride. "He tried his best to teach me, but I don't know if I'll ever be as good. He told me anything can be a canvas, and I suppose you're my canvas now."

She says no more about her parents, and I don't ask.

She touches up my hair for a while, which has been curled into ringlets and pinned back with a simple white headband. This goes on until the watch on Deirdre's wrist begins to beep. And then she helps me into my un-sensible high heels and carries the train of my dress down the hallway. We descend in the elevator and weave through a maze of hallway after hallway, and just when I'm beginning to think this house has no end, we come to a large wooden door. Deirdre goes ahead of me, opens the door just barely, and pokes her head in. She appears to be talking to someone.

Deirdre steps back, and a little boy peers out at me. He's her size or close to it. His eyes sweep across me, head to toe. "I like it," he says.

"Thank you, Adair. I like yours, too," Deirdre says. There's such professionalism in her young voice. "Are we almost ready to begin?"

"All ready here. Check with Elle."

Deirdre disappears behind the door with him. There's more talking, and when the door opens, another little girl peers out at me. Her eyes are big and green; she claps her hands together excitedly. "Oh, it's lovely!" she shrieks, and then disappears.

When the door opens again, Deirdre takes my hand and leads me into what can only be a sewing room. It's small and windowless, cluttered with bolts of fabric and sewing machines, and everywhere ribbons drip from shelves and lay strewn across tables. "The other brides are all ready," Deirdre says. She looks around herself to be sure no one else can hear, and then whispers to me, "But I think you're the prettiest."

The other brides stand in corners of the room opposite each other, being fussed over by their domestics, all of whom are dressed in white. The little boy, Adair, is straightening the white velvet bodice on a willowy bride with dark hair, who stares despondently at her shoulder and does not seem to mind being prodded.

The little girl, whom I presume to be Elle, is adjusting pearl barrettes in the hair of a bride who could not tip the scale above a hundred pounds. This bride has her red hair done up in a beehive, and her dress is white with just a slight glimmer of rainbow hues when she moves. The bodice has big translucent butterfly wings in back that seem to be hemorrhaging glitter, which I realize is some sort of illusion, because none of this glitter ever touches the ground. The bride is wriggling uncomfortably in her bodice, though, a bit too small to fill in the chest of it.

On tiptoes the redhead wouldn't even reach my shoulder; she is clearly too young to be a bride. And the willowy girl is too forlorn. And I am too unwilling.

Yet here we are.

This dress is so comfortable against my skin, and Deirdre is so proud, and here I stand in the room where I suppose my wardrobes are to be constructed for the rest of my life. And all I can think of is how I can escape. An air duct? An unlocked door?

And, of course, I think of my twin brother, Rowan. Without each other we are only half of a whole. I can hardly stand the thought of him all alone in that basement at night. Will he search through the scarlet district for my face in a brothel? Will he use one of the delivery trucks from his job to look for my body on roadsides? Of all the things he could ever do, of all the places he could ever search, I am certain he will never find this mansion, surrounded by orange groves and horses and gardens, so very far from New York.

I will have to find him instead. Stupidly, I look to the too-small air duct for a solution where there is none.

The domestics summon each of us brides to the center of the room. It's the first time we've been able to look at one another, really. It was so dark in that van, and then we'd been too horrified to do anything but keep our eyes forward when we were assessed. Add the sleeping gas in the limo, and we're still perfect strangers.

The redhead, the little one, is hissing to Elle that her bodice is now laced too tight, and how can she be expected to stay still during the ceremony—the most important moment of her life, she adds—if she can hardly breathe?

The willowy girl stands beside me, saying and doing nothing as Adair perches on a stepladder and dots her braided hair with tiny fake lilies.

There's a knock on the door, and I don't know what I'm expecting. A fourth bride, perhaps, or for the Gatherers to come and shoot us all. It's only Gabriel, though, holding a large cylinder and asking the domestics if the brides are ready. He doesn't look at any of us. When Elle tells him we're ready, he lays the cylinder on the ground, and with a mechanical whirr it somehow unrolls a long red carpet that stretches out into the hallway. Gabriel disappears into the shadows.

Strange music begins to radiate, seemingly from the ceiling tiles. The domestics arrange us in a row, youngest to oldest, and we begin to march. It's amazing how in sync our footsteps are, for having no practice and considering we were all dragged to this place in unconscious heaps after the time spent in that van. In a few minutes we'll be sister wives. It's a term I've heard on the news, and I don't know what it means. I don't know if these girls will be my allies or enemies, or if we'll even coexist after today.

The bride in front of me, the redhead, the little one, seems to be skipping. Her wings flutter and bounce. Glitter swirls around her. If I didn't know better, I could swear she's excited about all this.

The carpet leads to an open door to the outside. This is what Deirdre called the rose garden, which is abundantly clear by the rosebushes that make up the high walls around us. They are an extension of the hallway, really, and despite the open sky overhead, I feel no less trapped than I did inside.

The dusk sky is full of stars, and absently I think that back home I would not dream of being outside at this hour. The door would be bolted, the noise trap laid out in the kitchen. Rowan and I would be having a quiet dinner and washing it down with tea, and then we'd watch the nightly news to see about available jobs and to update ourselves on the state of our world, hoping dismally that one day there might be a positive change. Since the old lab exploded four years back, I've been hoping a new lab will replace it, so that pro-science research jobs will be created, and so that someone can discover an antidote; but orphans have made a home for themselves in the ruins of the old lab. People are giving up, accepting their fate. And the news is nothing but job listings and televised events put on by the wealthier class—House Governors and their sad brides. It's supposed to encourage us, I guess. Give the illusion that the world isn't ending.

I don't have a chance to feel the oncoming wave of homesickness before I'm nudged into the clearing at the end of the rosebush hallway and made to stand in a semicircle with the other brides.

The clearing is sudden and gaping, and a relief. The garden at once becomes enormous, a city bustling with fireflies and little flat candles that seem to be floating in place—I think Deirdre called them tea lights. There are fountains trickling into tiny ponds, and I can see now that the music is somehow being amplified from a keyboard that plays itself, the keys lighting up as the notes radiate out, sounding like a full band of strings and brass. I know the melody; my mother used to hum it: "The Wedding March," the theme of weddings back in her own mother's day.

I'm led to a gazebo at the center of the clearing with the two others, where the red carpet becomes a large circle. There is a man beside us in white robes, and the domestics take their places opposite us, their hands clasped in front of them as though in prayer. The youngest bride giggles as a firefly spirals before her nose and disappears. The oldest bride stares into space with eyes as gray as the evening sky. I just do what I can to not stand out, to blend in, which I suspect is impossible if the Governor has taken a liking to my eyes.

I don't know much about traditional weddings; I've never attended one, and my parents, like most couples at that time, were married in city hall. With the human race dying off so young, hardly anybody gets married anymore. But I suppose this is how it used to be, more or less: the waiting bride, the music, the groom in a black tuxedo approaching. Linden, the House Governor, my soon-to-be husband, is led to us on the arm of a first generation man. Both of them are tall and pale. They part at the gazebo, and Linden takes the three steps that lead him to us. He stands at the center of the carpet circle, facing us. The little redheaded one winks at him, and he smiles adoringly at her, the way a father might smile at his young daughter. But she's not his daughter. He intends for her to carry his children.

I feel nauseous. It would be defiant enough just to vomit on his polished black shoes. But I haven't eaten any of the food Gabriel has brought me since my first day here, and vomiting won't win me any favoritism. My best chance at escape will be to earn Linden's trust. The sooner I can pull that off, the better.

The man in white robes begins to speak, and the music fades to a stop.

"We are gathered here today to join these four souls in this sacred union, which will bear the fruit for generations to come . . ."

As the man speaks, Linden looks us over. Maybe it's the candlelight, or the mellow evening breeze, but he doesn't seem as menacing as before, when he selected us from the lineup. He's a tall man with small bones that make him seem almost frail, childlike. His eyes are a bright green, and his glossy black curls hang like thick vines around his face. He is not smiling, and not grinning the way he did when he caught me running in the hallway. For a moment I wonder if he is even the same man. But then he opens his mouth, and I see the glimmer of gold in his teeth, way in the back molars.

The domestics have stepped forward. The man in white has stopped talking about how this marriage will secure future generations, and now Linden is addressing us each by name. "Cecily Ashby," he says to the little bride. Elle opens her clasped hands, revealing a gold ring. Linden takes this ring and places it on the small bride's hand. "My wife," Linden says. She blushes and beams.

Before I can process what's happening, Deirdre has opened her hands and Linden has taken the ring from her and slipped it onto my finger. "Rhine Ashby," he says. "My wife."

It doesn't mean anything, I tell myself. Let him call me his wife, but once I'm on the other side of the fence, this silly little ring will mean nothing. I am still Rhine Ellery. I try to let this thought sink in, but I've broken into a cold sweat. My heart feels heavy. Linden catches my eyes with his, and I meet his stare. I won't blush or flinch or look away. I won't succumb.

He lingers a moment, and then he's on to the third bride.

"Jenna Ashby," he says to the next girl. "My wife."

The man in white says, "What fate has brought together, let no man tear asunder."

Fate, I think, *is a thief.*

The music starts up again, and Linden takes each of our hands long enough to guide us down the steps, one at a time. His hand is clammy and cool. It's our first touch as husband and wife. As I move, I try to get a good look at the mansion that has imprisoned me these past few days. But it's too massive, and I'm standing too close to see more than one side of it, and all that register are bricks and windows. I think I see Gabriel, though, for a moment as he passes one of the windows. I recognize his neatly parted hair, his wide blue eyes watching me.

Linden leaves us after that, disappearing somewhere with the first generation man he'd approached with. And the brides are herded back into the mansion. There is ivy growing along it, though, and just before I'm inside, I reach out and grab a small piece of that leafy green plant and close it in my fist. It makes me think of home, even if ivy no longer grows there.

Back in my bedroom I hide the ivy in my pillowcase before Deirdre begins fussing over me. She helps me out of my wedding gown, which she folds neatly, and then begins to spray me with something that at first attacks my senses and makes me sneeze, but then recedes into a pleasant rosy scent. She makes me sit on the ottoman again and opens the makeup drawer. She scrubs my face clean and begins again, this time painting me in dramatic reds and purples that make me appear sultry. I like it even better than the earlier look; I feel like my anger and bitterness have been manifested.

I'm dressed in a fitted red dress that matches the color of my lips, with black lace around the collar and capped sleeves. The dress only falls to about midthigh, and Deirdre tugs at the material to be sure it drapes properly. While she's doing this, I step into yet another pair of ridiculous heels, and stare at myself in the mirror. Every curve of my body protrudes through the velvet material—my breasts, hipbones, even the ghost of ribs. "It's a symbol that you're no longer a child," she explains. "That you're ready for your husband to come to you at any time."

After that I'm led to the elevator and down more hallways, until we reach a dining hall. The other brides are dressed in black and yellow versions of my outfit, respectively. All of us are wearing our hair down now. I'm seated between them at a long table beneath crystal chandeliers. Cecily, the redhead, is looking excited, while Jenna, the dark-haired one, seems to be coming out of her melancholy. Under the table her hand brushes mine, and I'm not sure if it's accidental.

We all smell like flowers.

Bits of glitter still fall from Cecily's hair.

House Governor Linden arrives, with the first generation man again. They make their way to us, and Linden raises each of our hands to his lips for a kiss, one at a time. Then he introduces the man, his father, as Housemaster Vaughn.

Housemaster Vaughn also kisses our hands, and it takes some effort for me to keep from squirming at the feel of his lips, which are papery and cold. It makes me think of a corpse. As a first generation, Housemaster Vaughn has aged well; his dark hair has only sparse flecks of gray, and his face is not horribly wrinkled. But his skin is a sickly pallid shade that would make even Rose appear vibrant by comparison. He does not smile. Everything about his touch is chilled. Even Cecily becomes subdued by his approach.

I feel a little better when Linden and Housemaster Vaughn are seated at the opposite end of the table, with Linden facing us and Housemaster Vaughn at the head. We brides sit in a row beside one another, and the other table head is left vacant. I suppose it's where Linden's mother would have sat, but since she's not here, I assume she's dead.

When Gabriel enters the room balancing a stack of plates and utensils, I find that I'm relieved by his presence. I haven't spoken with him since last night, when he limped out of my room. I've been worrying that my actions led to his punishment, and that Housemaster Vaughn will decide to lock him in a dungeon for the remainder of his life. My worries always lead to dungeons; I can't imagine a worse thing than to be imprisoned for the rest of one's life, especially with so few years to enjoy what little there is.

Gabriel seems well enough now, though. I look closely for signs of bruises beneath his shirt, and find nothing. His limp is gone. I try to catch his gaze, hoping to give him a sympathetic or apologetic look, but he doesn't raise his eyes to me. Four others in the same uniform follow him in, with pitchers of water, bottles of wine, a cart of extravagant foods—whole chickens basting in caramel sauces, pineapples and strawberries cut and shaped like pond lilies.

The door to the dining room is propped open as the attendants come and go. I wonder what would happen if I ran—if Gabriel or one of the others would stop me. But ultimately it's my fear of what my new husband might do that keeps me in place, because surely if I ran, I wouldn't make it far before I was caught. And then—what? I'd be locked in my room again, probably, forever marred as the one who can't be trusted.

So I stay, participating in a conversation that is strained and sickeningly pleasant. Linden doesn't talk much himself; his mind seems to be elsewhere as he brings spoonful after spoonful of soup to his mouth. Cecily smiles at him, and she even drops her spoon, I think, just so he'll look at her.

Housemaster Vaughn is talking about the hundred-year-old gardens and how sweet the apples are. He even makes fruits and shrubbery sound ominous. It's his voice, low and raspy. I notice that none of the help looks at him as they bring new dishes and clear away the old.

It was him, I think. He's the one who hurt Gabriel yesterday when my door was left unlocked. Even with his smiles and harmless chatter, I can sense something dangerous in him. Something that hinders my appetite and drains the color from Deirdre's pleasant face. Something, perhaps, more dangerous than heartsick Governor Linden, who stares past us, lost in love with a woman on death's door.

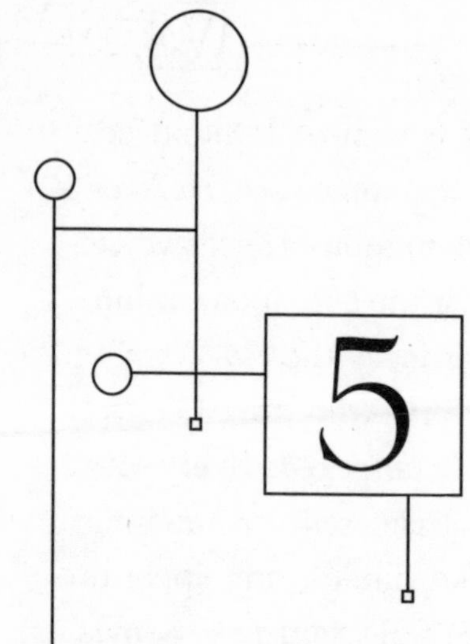

WHEN THE EVENING is at last through, I languish on the bed in my white slip while Deirdre rubs my sore feet. I might stop her if I weren't so exhausted and her touch weren't so relaxing. She's kneeling beside me, so light that she scarcely even makes a dent in the fluffy comforter.

I lie on my stomach, hugging a pillow, and she begins to work my calves; it's just what I need after so many hours in those high heels. She has lit some candles too, filling the room with the warm scent of obscure flowers. I'm so relaxed that I just let the words come out, so beyond worrying about being classy at this point, "So how does this wedding night work? Does he choose us in a lineup? Drug us with sleeping gas? Pool the three of us into one bed?"

Deirdre does not seem offended by my crassness. Patiently she says, "Oh, the House Governor won't consummate his brides tonight. Not with Lady Rose . . ." She trails off.

I push myself up just enough to look over my shoulder at her. "What about her?"

A tragic look is on Deirdre's face, her shoulders moving as she rubs my sore legs. "He's very in love with her," she tells me wistfully. "I don't believe he'll visit any of his new brides until she has passed on."

It's true that Governor Linden doesn't come into my bedroom, and after Deirdre has blown out the candles and is gone, I eventually drift off to sleep. But in the early hours of the morning, I'm awakened by the turn of the doorknob; in recent years I've become a very light sleeper, and without any sleep-inducing toxin in my system, I've returned to my usual alertness. Still I don't react. I wait, eyes wide open, watching my door open in the darkness.

The curly hair of the shadowy figure identifies Linden for me.

"Rhine?" He says my name for the second time in our short marriage. I want to ignore him and pretend that I'm still asleep, but I think the terrified pounding of my heart must be audible across the room. It's irrational, but I still think a creaking door will mean Gatherers coming to shoot me in the head or steal me away. Besides, Linden has seen that my eyes are open.

"Yes," I say.

"Get up," he says softly. "Put on something warm; I have something to show you."

Something warm! I think. This must mean he's taking me outside.

To his credit, he leaves the room so I can get dressed in private. The closet illuminates when I open it, revealing rows of more clothing than I bothered to notice earlier. I choose a pair of black pants that are warm and fleecy, and a sweater that has pearls worked into the knit—Deirdre's handiwork, no doubt.

When I open the door—which is no longer locked from the outside as it was before the wedding—I find Linden waiting for me in the hall. He smiles, loops his arm through mine, and leads me to the elevator.

It's distressing how many hallways make up this mansion. Even if the front door were left wide open for my escape, I'm certain I'd never be able to find it. I try to make a note of where I am: a long, plain hallway with a green carpet that looks new. The walls are a creamy off-white, with the same kind of generic paintings that are in my bedroom. There are no windows, so I can't even tell that this is the ground floor until Linden opens a door and we're on the path to the rose garden, down the same familiar hallway of bushes. But this time we pass the gazebo. The sun has yet to come up, giving the place a subdued, sleepy feel.

Linden shows me one of the fountains, which trickles into a pond populated by long thick fish that are white, orange, and red. "Koi fish," he tells me. "They're originally from Japan. Heard of it?"

Geography has become such an obscure subject that I never encountered it in my brief years of schooling, before my parents' deaths forced me to work instead. Our school was held in what was once a church, and the students barely filled out the first row of pews in full attendance. Mostly we were the children of first generations, like my brother and me, who had been raised to value education even if we'll die without a chance to use it. And the school had an orphan or two with dreams of becoming an actor, who wanted to learn enough reading to memorize scripts. All we were taught of geography was that the world had once been made up of seven continents and several countries, but a third world war demolished all but North America, the continent with the most advanced technology. The damage was so catastrophic that all that remains of the rest of the world is ocean and uninhabitable islands so tiny that they can't even be seen from space.

My father, however, was a world enthusiast. He had an atlas of the world as it appeared in the twenty-first century, with full-color images of all the countries and customs. Japan was a favorite of mine. I enjoyed the painted geishas with their penciled features and puckered lips. I liked the pink and white cherry blossom trees, so unlike the meager things that grow in fences along the Manhattan sidewalks. The whole country of Japan seemed to be one giant color photo, glossy and bright. My brother preferred Africa, with its floppy-eared elephants and its colorful birds.

I imagined the world outside North America must have been a beautiful place. And it was my father who introduced that beauty to me. I think of these long-gone places still. A koi wriggles past me and disappears into the depth, and all I can think is that my father would have been so happy to see it.

The grief of my father's loss is so sudden that my knees nearly buckle under the weight of it; I force tears back down my throat, past the lump that's forming there. "I've heard of it," is all I say.

Linden seems impressed. He smiles at me, and raises his hand as though to touch me, but then changes his mind and continues walking. We come to a wooden swing that's shaped like a heart. We sit for a while, not touching, rocking slightly and staring at the horizon over the edges of the rosebushes. The color comes slowly, bits of orange and yellow, like with Deirdre's makeup brush. Stars are still visible, fading away where the sky blushes with fiery color.

"Look," Linden says. "Look how beautiful it is."

"The sunrise?" I ask. It is lovely, but hardly worth getting out of bed so early. I'm so used to sleeping in shifts, taking turns keeping watch with my brother, that my body has been trained not to waste whatever sleep it can get.

"The start of a new day," Linden says. "Being healthy enough to witness it."

I can see sadness in his green eyes. I don't trust it.

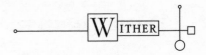

How can I, when this is the man who paid the Gatherers so he could have me for the last years of my life? When the blood of those other girls in the van is on his hands? My sunrises may be limited, but I will not view all the rest of mine as Linden Ashby's wife.

It's quiet for a while. Linden's face is lit up by the early sun, and my wedding band burns in a twist of light. I hate the thing. It took all my willpower last night not to flush it down the toilet. But if I'm to earn his trust, I have to wear it.

"You know about Japan," he says. "What else do you know about the world?"

I will not tell him about my father's atlas, which my brother and I hid with our valuables in a locked trunk. Someone like Linden has no need to lock anything precious, except for his brides. He would not understand the madness of poorer, more desperate places.

"Not much," I say. And I feign ignorance as he begins to tell me about Europe, a tower clock called Big Ben (I remember the image of it glowing at twilight amidst a London crowd), and extinct flamingos whose necks were as long as their legs.

"Rose taught me about most of these things," he admits, and then, just as the sunlight is awakening the reds and greens of the garden, he looks away from me. "You may go back inside," he says. "An attendant will be waiting to take you up." His voice catches at the end, and I know that now is not the time to sit and pretend to adore him. I find my way back to the door, leaving him to his new day so he may think of Rose, whose sunrises are numbered.

In the days to follow, Linden barely acknowledges his brides. Our bedroom doors are unlocked and we're mostly left to ourselves, allowed to wander about the floor, which has its own library and sitting room, but not much else. We aren't permitted to use the elevator unless he invites us to dinner, which happens rarely; usually our meals are brought on trays to our bedrooms. I spend a lot of time in an overstuffed chair in the library, thumbing through brilliant pages of flowers that no longer grow in this world, and some that can still be found in other parts of the country. I educate myself on the polar ice caps, vaporized long ago by warfare, and an explorer named Christopher Columbus who proved the earth was round. In my prison I lose myself in the history of a free and boundless world that's long dead.

I don't see my sister wives often. Sometimes Jenna will take a couch beside me and look up from her novel to ask me what I'm reading. Her voice is timid, and when I look at her, she flinches like I might hit her. But beneath that timorousness there's something more, the remains of a broken person who had once been assured, strong, brave. Her eyes are often bleary and misting with tears. Our conversations are measured and brief, never more than a sentence or two.

Cecily complains that the orphanage didn't do a good

job teaching her to read. She'll sit studiously at one of the tables with a book and sometimes spell a word out loud, waiting impatiently for me to pronounce it and sometimes tell her what it means. Though she is only thirteen, her favorite reads are all about childbirth and pregnancy.

But for all her shortcomings, Cecily is something of a musical prodigy. I can hear her sometimes as she plays the keyboard in the sitting room. The first time, I was drawn to the threshold well past midnight. There she sat, this tiny body with flame red hair, trapped in a hologram of flurrying snow that was projected from somewhere on the keyboard. But Cecily, who is so dazzled by the false glamour of this mansion, played with her eyes closed. Lost in her concerto, she was not my little sister wife in a winged dress, or the same girl who throws silverware at the attendants who cross her on the wrong day, but rather some otherworldly creature. There was no ticking time bomb inside of her—no indication of this horrible thing that will kill her in a few short years.

She'll play more clumsily in the afternoons, tapping the keys in nonsensical patterns to amuse herself. The keys won't work unless one of the hundreds of hologram slides is inserted into the keyboard to accompany the music: rushing rivers, a sky full of glittering fireflies, speeding rainbows. I have never seen her use the same hologram twice, and yet she scarcely acknowledges any of them.

There's no shortage of illusions in the sitting room. The television can, at the press of a button, simulate a ski slope or an ice rink or a racetrack. There are remotes, steering wheels, skis, and a whole assortment of controllers to replace the actual world. I wonder if my new husband grew up in this way—trapped within this sprawling mansion, with only illusions to teach him about the world. Once when I was alone, I tried my hand at fishing, and, unlike with the real thing, I excelled at it.

In my abundance of time alone, I've wandered the entire length of the wives' floor several times, from Rose's bedroom on one far end of the hall, to the library on the other. I've inspected the vents, which are bolted to the ceiling, and the laundry chutes, which are too small to fit anything larger than a small load of laundry. None of the windows budge, except in Rose's room, which is always occupied by her.

The fireplace in the library is entirely fake, with a hologram flame that makes crackling sounds but provides no warmth. There's no chimney, no way for the air to reach the sky.

And there's no staircase. Not even a locked emergency exit. I've felt along the walls, peered behind bookshelves and under furniture. And I wonder if the wives' floor is the only part of the house without a staircase, and if there's a fire and the elevators stop working, Linden's brides will be burned to a crisp. We're easy to replace, after all. He didn't think twice about the lives of the other girls in that van.

But that doesn't make sense. What about Rose, with whom Linden is so madly in love? Isn't her life worth something more to him? Maybe not. Maybe even first wives, favorites, are disposable.

I try opening the elevator, but none of the buttons will work for me without a key card. I try prying it open with my fingers, and then with the toe of my shoe, pretending that there's a fire, pretending my life depends on an immediate escape. The door doesn't budge. I search my bedroom for a tool that can help me, and I find an umbrella hanging in my closet, and I try that. I'm able to wedge the point between the metal doors, and they part just slightly, enough for me to fit my shoe between them. And then—success!—they slide open.

Immediately I'm blasted with the stale air of the elevator shaft, and the darkness that intensifies when I look up or down. I study the cables, with no way to tell where they begin or end. I don't know how many floors are above or below. I reach out and touch one of them, get a firm grip on it. I could try climbing it, or just hold on to it and slide all the way down. Even if I only got as far as the floor below me, I might be able to find an open window, or a staircase.

It's the word *might* that makes me hesitate. Because I *might* not be able to open the elevator doors from the inside. I *might* be crushed to death if the car comes before I'm able to escape.

"Contemplating suicide?" Rose says. I flinch, retract my arm from the elevator shaft. My sister wife stands a few feet away, arms folded, in her wispy nightgown. Her hair is tousled, her skin pale, her mouth an unnatural candied red, and she's smiling. "It's all right," she says. "I won't tell on you. I understand."

The elevator doors slide closed, without me.

"Do you?" I say.

"Mm," she says, gesturing for my umbrella. I hand it to her, and she pops it open, twirls it once over her head. "Where did you find this?" she asks.

"In my closet."

"Right," she says. "Did you know you're not even supposed to open them inside? Bad luck. In fact, Linden is very superstitious." She closes the umbrella, studies it. "And Linden has final say on what's in your bedroom, did you know that? Your clothes, your shoes—this umbrella. If he allowed you to have this, what do you suppose that means?"

"He doesn't want me to get rained on," I say, beginning to understand.

She raises her eyes, smiles at me, tosses the umbrella into my hands. "Exactly. And it only rains outside."

Outside. I never thought the word could make my stomach flip-flop like this. It's one of the small freedoms I've had all my life, and now I'd do anything to have it back. My grip on the umbrella tightens. "But are the elevators the only way outside?" I say.

"Forget about the elevators," Rose says. "Your husband is your only way outside."

"I don't understand. What if there's a fire? Wouldn't we all be killed?"

"Wives are an investment," Rose says. "Housemaster Vaughn paid good money for you. In fact, Housemaster Vaughn is obsessed with genetics, and for those eyes of yours, I'm willing to bet he paid a little extra. If he wants you to be safe, then fire, hurricane, tidal wave—doesn't matter. You're safe."

I guess this is supposed to flatter me. But it only makes me worry. If I'm such an investment, it's going to be that much harder for me to leave undetected.

Rose is looking weary, so I toss the umbrella into my room, and then I help her into her bed. Normally she'll fight the attendants when they tell her to rest, but she allows me because I never try to force any medicine into her. "Open the window," she murmurs, settling into her silky blankets. I do as she asks, and a cool spring breeze rolls in. She breathes deeply. "Thank you," she sighs.

I sit on the window ledge, press my hand against the screen. It looks like a perfectly ordinary screen, one that would pop out of its frame if pushed hard enough. I could jump, although it's several stories up—higher than the roof of my own house, at least—but there are no trees to reach for. It isn't worth the attempt. But still, I think of what Rose said when she found me at the elevator. She said she wouldn't tell on me because she understood.

"Rose?" I say. "Did you ever try to escape?"

"It doesn't matter," she says.

I think of the little girl in the photo, smiling, so full of life. She's been here all these years. Was she bred to be Linden's bride? Or was she once resistant to it? I open my mouth to ask, but she's sitting up in the bed now, and she says, "You'll see the world again. I can tell. He's going to fall in love with you. And if you'd just listen to me, you'd realize you're going to be his favorite once I'm dead." She mentions her death so casually. "He'll take you anywhere you want to go."

"Not anywhere," I say. "Not home."

She smiles, pats the mattress beside her in invitation. I sit beside her, and she gets up to kneel behind me, and begins weaving my hair into a braid. "This is your home now," she says. "The more you resist"—she tugs my hair for emphasis—"the tighter the trap gets. There." She takes a ribbon that was draped over her headboard and ties my hair in place. She crawls across the mattress so that she's facing me, and she strokes a wisp of hair away from my eyes. "You look nice with your hair back. You have great cheekbones."

High cheekbones, just like hers. I can't ignore our resemblance to each other: the thick, wavy blond hair, the pert chin, soft nose. All that's missing in her are the heterochromatic eyes. But there's one other difference between us, and it's significant. She was able to accept this life, to love our husband. And if I have to die trying, I will get out of here.

There's no more talk of escape between Rose and me after that day. She favors me over the other wives, who have never spoken with her at all. Jenna speaks as little as possible, and Cecily has asked me more than once why I bother getting to know Linden's dying wife. "She's going to die, and then he'll focus on us more," she says, like it's something to look forward to. It disgusts me that Rose's life is so meaningless to her, but it's not very different from the things my brother said about the orphan we found frozen to death on our porch last winter.

Tears welled in my eyes when I discovered the body, but my brother said we shouldn't even move it right away, that it could be a warning to anyone else trying to break into our home. "We did such a great job with the locks, they'll die before they get in," he said. Necessity. Survival. It was us or them. Days later, when I suggested we bury the body—a little girl in a threadbare plaid coat—he had me help him haul it to the Dumpster. "Your problem is that you're too emotional," he said. "And that's the kind of thing that'll make you an easy target."

Well, maybe not this time, Rowan. Maybe this time being emotional can help, because Rose and I talk for hours, and I relish our conversations, certain I can use them as an opportunity to learn everything about Linden and earn his favor.

But as the days turn to weeks, I sense a genuine

friendship blossoming between us, which should be the last thing I want from someone who is dying. Still, I enjoy her company. She tells me about her mother and father, who were first generations that died in some sort of accident when she was young; they were close friends of Linden's father, which is how she came to live in this mansion and become his bride.

She tells me that Linden's mother—Housemaster Vaughn's younger, second wife—died in childbirth with Linden. And Vaughn was so immersed in his research, so obsessed with saving his son's life from the start, that he never bothered to take on another wife. He might have been ridiculed for it, Rose says, if he weren't such a capable doctor and so in love with his work. He owns a thriving hospital in the city and is one of the area's leading genetic researchers. She tells me that the Housemaster's first son lived a full twenty-five years and was gone and cremated by the time Linden came along.

This, I suppose, is something I have in common with my new husband. Before my brother and I were born, my parents had two children, another set of twins, who were born blind and unable to speak. Their limbs were malformed and they didn't live past five years. Genetic abnormalities like this are rare, given the perfection of the first generations, but they do happen. They're called malformed. It seems my parents were incapable of making children without genetic oddities, though now I have cause to be grateful for my heterochromia. It may have spared me a gunshot to the brain in the back of that van.

Rose and I talk about happier things too, like cherry blossom trees. I even come to trust her enough to tell her about my father's atlas and my disappointment at having missed the world in its prime. As she braids my hair, she tells me that if she could have lived anywhere in the world, she would have chosen India. She would have worn saris and positively covered herself in henna, and maybe she would have paraded in the streets on an elephant shrouded in jewels.

I paint her nails pink, and she arranges novelty jewels on my forehead from a sticker sheet.

Then one afternoon, as we're lying beside each other on the bed, stuffing ourselves with colorful candies, I blurt out, "How can you stand it, Rose?"

She turns her head on the pillow to face me. Her tongue is deep purple. "What?"

"Doesn't it bother you that he has remarried, while you're still alive?"

She smiles, looks at the ceiling, and fiddles with a wrapper. "I asked him to. I convinced him it will be easier, with new wives already in the house." She closes her eyes and yawns. "Besides, he was starting to get teased in the social circles. Most House Governors have at least three wives, sometimes seven—one for every day of the week." It's absurd enough that she laughs a little, suppresses a cough. "But not Linden. Housemaster Vaughn has been trying to talk him into it for years, and he has always refused. Finally he agreed to it, as long as he had a choice in the selection. He didn't even have a choice with me."

Her voice is cool, and she is so bizarrely serene. It worries me that I've become her favorite new bride simply for my blond hair, my vague resemblance to her. She is such a brilliant, well-read girl, and I wonder if she has figured out that I'll never love Linden, especially not in the way she does, and that he'll never love anyone the way he loves her. I wonder if she realizes, despite all her efforts to train me, that I can never take her place.

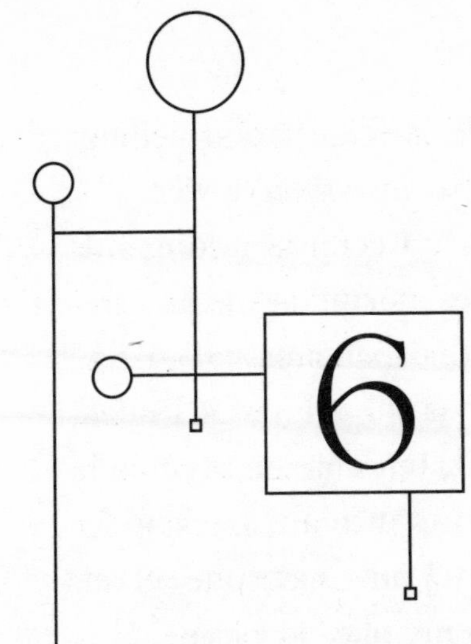

"I WANT TO PLAY a game," Cecily says.

Jenna doesn't look up from her novel. She's strewn languidly on the couch, with her legs dangling over the armrest. "No shortage of those."

"I don't mean the keyboard or virtual skiing," Cecily insists. "I mean a *game* game." She looks to me for help, but the only game I know is the one where my brother and I set noise traps in the kitchen and try to survive the night intact. And when I was taken by Gatherers, I sort of lost.

I'm curled up on the window ledge in the sitting room—a room that is filled with virtual sports games and a keyboard meant to imitate a symphony orchestra—and I have been staring at the orange tree blossoms that flutter like thousands of tiny white-winged descending birds. Rowan wouldn't even believe them, the life they imply, the health and beauty. Manhattan is full of gasping, shriveled weeds that grow from the asphalt. Refrigerator-smelling carnations for sale that are more science than flower.

"Don't you know any games?" Cecily is asking me directly now. I feel her brown eyes staring at me.

Well. There was one game, with paper cups and string, and the little girl who lived across the alleyway. I open my mouth, prepared to explain it, but change my mind. I don't want to whisper my secrets into a paper cup to share with my sister wives. Really I only have one secret that's worth anything, and that's my plan to escape.

"We could play virtual fishing," I say. I can feel Cecily's indignation without even looking at her.

"There has to be something real we could do," she says. "There *has* to be." She paces out of the room, and I hear her shuffling around down the hall.

"Poor kid," Jenna says, and rolls her eyes toward me for a moment. Then she returns to her book. "She doesn't even understand what kind of place this is."

It happens at noon. Gabriel brings my lunch to me in the library—which has become my new favorite place—and stops to look over my shoulder when he sees the sketch of a boat on the page.

"What are you reading?" he asks.

"A history book," I say. "This one explorer proved the world was round by assembling a team and sailing all the way around it on three boats."

"The *Niña*, *Pinta*, and *Santa María*," he says.

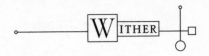

"You know about world history?" I ask.

"I know about boats," he says, and sits behind me on the arm of the overstuffed chair and points to the image. "This one here is a caravel." He begins describing its structure to me—the trio of masts, the lateen rigging. All I truly understand from this is that the style was Spanish. But I don't interrupt him. I can see the intensity in his blue eyes, that he's taken a brief respite from the sullen work of cooking for and catering to Linden's brides, that he has a passion for something.

Sitting in his shadow in the overstuffed chair, I actually feel a smile coming on.

That's when Cecily's domestic, Elle, comes bursting into the room. "*There* you are," she cries at Gabriel. "You need to hurry to the kitchen and bring Lady Rose something for her cough."

I can hear her coughing now, at the end of the long hallway. It's become such a fixture in this place that I don't always notice it. Gabriel hurries to his feet, and I close the book, make a motion to follow him out. "Don't," he says, stopping me at the doorway. "It's better if you stay in here until this passes."

But past his shoulder I can see an unusual chaos. Domestics are scrambling past one another. First generation attendants are coming out of the elevator carrying all sorts of bottles, and a machine that resembles the humidifier my parents put in my bedroom the winter I caught pneumonia. There's an air of futility about it all, and Gabriel senses it too. I can tell by the look in his eyes.

"Stay here," he says. Of course I follow him into the hallway. And it's so frightening out here that I want to follow him into the elevator, which probably isn't allowed, but I'm beyond caring about that. Gabriel swipes his key card, and the doors to the elevator are just opening when it all stops. Simply stops. The domestics freeze in place; the attendants are left holding blankets and pills and breathing machines. Linden is kneeling by Rose's bed with his face buried in the mattress. He's holding the long white stem of her arm, and I follow it up to her body, which doesn't move and doesn't breathe. Her gown, her face, is splattered with blood she must have been coughing up as she made those horrible sounds. But now an eerie silence fills the floor. It's the silence I imagine in the rest of the world, the silence of an endless ocean and uninhabitable islands, a silence that can be seen from space.

Cecily and Jenna come out of their bedrooms, and it's so quiet that we hear the strangled noise in Linden's throat. "Go away," he murmurs. Then louder, "Go away!" It's not until he smashes a vase against the wall that we all scatter. I end up on the elevator with Gabriel, and when the doors close behind us, I'm grateful.

There's nothing for me to do but follow Gabriel to the kitchen; I'd get lost going anywhere else. I sit on a counter, nibbling on grapes while the cooks and the attendants talk as they go about their work. Gabriel leans against the counter beside me, polishing silverware. "I know you were fond of Rose," he whispers to me, "but you won't find much love for her down here. She gave the staff a hard time."

As if in affirmation, the head cook shrieks, "My soup isn't hot enough! Oh, now it's too hot!" and makes dramatic spitting noises as a few others burst into a riot of laughter.

I won't deny that this is painful to hear. I have witnessed Rose's wrath on the help, but she never once raised her voice to me. Here in this place of syringes, sullen Governors, and looming Housemasters, she has been my only friend.

I say nothing, though. Our bond was a private thing, and none of these people, laughing at her expense, would understand anyway. I begin to pick grapes from the vine and turn them in my fingers one at a time before setting them back into the bowl. Gabriel steals glances at me as he works, and for a while it's like that, with the rest of the kitchen chattering loudly, a million miles away. And upstairs, Rose is dead.

"She always had those candies," I say wistfully. "They make your tongue change colors."

"They're called June Beans," Gabriel says.

"Are there more of them?"

"Sure—tons," he says. "She'd have me order them by the crate. Here . . ." He leads me to a pantry between the built-in refrigerator and the wall of stoves. Inside there are wooden crates overflowing with the shimmering wrappers in every color. I can smell their sugar, the artificial dyes. She ordered them, and here they wait to be poured into her crystal bowl and savored.

My longing must be all over my face, because Gabriel is putting some of them into a paper bag for me. "Have all you want. They'll only go to waste."

"Thank you," I say.

"Hey, you, blondie," the head cook calls to me. She's a first generation with greasy hair tied into a graying bun. "Shouldn't you get upstairs before your husband catches you down here?"

"No," I say. "He won't know I'm gone. He doesn't notice me."

"He notices you," Gabriel says. I look at him, unbelieving, but he has turned his blue eyes away from me.

One of the cooks opens the door and tosses out a pot of water, because the sink is in use by the muttering head chef. A gust of cold air pushes the hair from my face. I see a flash of blue sky and green earth, then it's gone. There are no key cards, no locks. So this is why the wives aren't allowed to leave their floor; not every part of the mansion is meant to keep us trapped.

"Do you get to go outside?" I ask Gabriel in a low voice.

He gives me a rueful smile. "Just to do yard work or take in deliveries. Nothing terribly exciting."

"What's out there?"

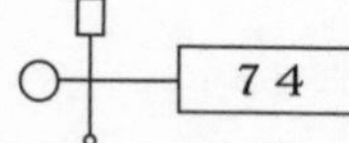

"Eternity," he says with a small laugh. "Gardens. A golf course. Maybe a few other things. I've never been in charge of the yard work, so I don't know. I've never seen the end of it."

"A whole world of trouble is what's out there for you, blondie," the head cook says. "Your place is up on that frilly floor of yours, lounging in satin sheets and painting your toenails. Now go on, before you get us all in trouble."

"Come on," Gabriel says. "I'll take you back up."

Back on the wives' floor, Rose's door is shut, and all the attendants and domestics have gone. Cecily is sitting alone in the hallway, playing some sort of game with yarn entwined around her fingers. She was singing to herself, but when I step out of the elevator, she stops and watches me cross to my room.

"What were you doing with that attendant?" she asks, once Gabriel is gone.

She hasn't seen the paper bag of candies, and I tuck it into my nightstand along with my ivy leaf, which I've pressed between the pages of a romance novel I took from the library. There are so many books that I don't think anyone will miss this one.

I turn just as Cecily appears in my doorway, waiting for an answer. We're sister wives now, and whatever that may mean in other mansions, I don't feel as though I can trust her. I also am not fond of her demanding tone, always impatient, always asking questions.

"I wasn't doing anything with him," I say.

I sit on my bed, and she raises her eyebrows, perhaps waiting for me to ask her to join me. Sister wives can't enter one another's bedrooms without permission. It's one of the few privacies I have, and I won't relinquish it.

There's nothing to stop her from talking, though. "Lady Rose is dead now," she says. "Linden is free to visit us anytime."

"Where is he?" I can't help but ask.

Cecily examines the yarn entwined around her fingers, looking displeased with it or the situation. "Oh, he's in her bedroom. He made everybody else leave. I knocked, but he won't come out."

I go to my dressing table and begin to brush my hair. I'm trying to look busy so that I don't have to make conversation, and there isn't much else to do in this room but stare at the wall. Cecily lingers for a while in the doorway, idly twisting in ways that make her skirt ripple. "I didn't tell our husband that you went off with that attendant," she says. "I could have, but I didn't."

And then she skips away, a trail of bright red yarn following after her.

That night, Linden comes to my bedroom.

"Rhine?" he says softly, just a shadow in my doorway.

It's late, and I have been lying alone in the darkness for hours, steeling myself against what I knew from the start would be a long awful night. Though she's gone, I have been listening for the sound of Rose at the end of the

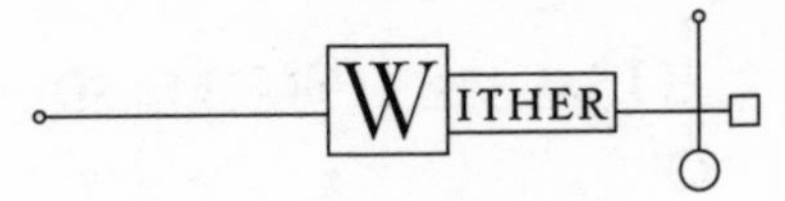

hall, yelling at an attendant, calling for me to come brush her hair and talk to her about the world. The silence is maddening, and perhaps that's why, rather than feigning sleep or denying him, I open the sheets for Linden.

He closes the door and climbs into my bed. I feel his cool, slender fingers encase my cheeks as he settles beside me. He advances for what will be my first kiss, but his lips fail. He sobs, and I feel the heat of his skin and his breath. "Rose," he says. It is a choked, frightened sound. He buries his face in my shoulder and loses himself in tears.

I understand grief. After my parents' death many of my nights resembled this. So just this once, I won't resist him. I allow him to find sanctuary in my bed, and I let him cling to me as the worst of it comes up.

His screams are muffled by my nightgown. Terrible sounds. I feel them vibrating deep in my bones. This goes on for what feels like hours, and then his breathing becomes ragged but even, his grip on my nightgown eases, and I know he's asleep.

I spend the remainder of the night drifting in and out of a fitful sleep of my own. I dream of gunshots and gray coats and Rose's mouth changing color. Eventually I fall into a more substantial sleep, and when the turning of the doorknob awakens me, it's morning. Soft light and the sounds of early birds fill the room.

Gabriel comes in, holding my usual breakfast tray, and stops in his tracks when he sees Linden in my bed.

Sometime in the night Linden turned away from me, and he is now snoring softly with his arm dangling over the mattress's edge. I silently catch Gabriel's eyes and bring a finger to my lips. Then with the same finger I point to my dressing table.

It's impossible to read Gabriel's expression as he sets my breakfast where I've indicated; he somehow looks as wounded as the day when he was limping and bruised. I'm not sure what's causing him to look that way until I imagine how this must seem to him. Rose is dead not even a day and I've already replaced her. But what does that matter to him? He said himself none of the attendants really liked Rose anyway.

I mouth a silent thank-you for the breakfast, and he nods and leaves. Later, perhaps when he sees me in the library, I'll explain what happened. Rose's death is starting to sink in, and I have a feeling that very soon I'll need someone I can talk to.

I'm careful about getting out of bed. Best to let Linden sleep. He's had such a rough night, and I've had better ones myself. I quietly slide the drawer of my nightstand open and retrieve one of the June Beans from the paper bag and head to the window. It still won't open, but the ledge is wide enough to be used as a seat.

I sit and watch the garden as I suck on the candy, which is as green as the mowed lawn beneath my window. From here I have a perfect view of the pool, and I see someone in an attendant uniform cutting into the water with a long net. The water catches the sunlight and breaks into diamond shapes. I think of the ocean that can be seen along the piers in New York. Long ago there used to be beaches there, but now there are concrete slabs that stop where the ocean begins. You can put five dollars in a rusty telescope and see all the way to the Statue of Liberty or one of the gift shop islands beaming with bright lights and key chains and photo opportunities. You can take a double-deck ferry along the pier while a tour guide talks about all the changes to the cityscape over the centuries. You can slip beneath the railing, take off your shoe, and stick your bare foot into the bleary water that's ripe with salt, and fish that aren't safe to eat—fishermen catch them for sport and throw them back.

I have always been fascinated by the ocean, to dip a limb beneath its surface and know that I'm touching eternity, that it goes on forever until it begins here again. Somewhere beneath it lie the ruins of colorful Japan, and Rose's favorite, India, the nations that could not survive. This lone continent is all that's left, and the darkness of the water is so mysterious, so alluring, that I find this bright pool water to be too frivolous. Clean and sparkling and safe. I wonder if Linden has ever touched the ocean. I wonder if he knows that this colorful paradise is a lie.

Did Rose ever leave this place? She talked about the world as though she'd seen it for herself, but how much farther than the orange groves did she go? I hope that now she's someplace with thriving islands and continents, with plenty of languages to learn and elephants to ride.

"Good-bye," I whisper, turning the candy around with my tongue. The taste is like peppermint. I hope she has plenty of June Beans, too.

There's a gasp from the bed, and Linden flips onto his back, propped up by his elbows. His curls are disheveled, his eyes puffy and confused. For a moment we look at each other, and I can see him struggling to focus. He looks so far away that I wonder if he's still asleep. In the night there were times when he opened his eyes wide and looked at me, and then he'd drift off again, muttering about pruning shears and the danger of bees.

Now there's a weak smile coming to his lips. "Rose?" he croaks.

But then he must wake a bit more, because he looks devastated. I stare out the window, unsure what to do with myself. A part of me feels sorry for him, but stronger than my pity is my hatred. For this place, for the gunshots that haunt my dreams. Why should I console him, simply because I have his dead wife's blond hair? I've lost the people I love too. Who is there to console me?

After a long pause he says, "Your mouth is green."

He sits up. "Where did you get the June Beans?" he asks.

I can't tell him the truth. I don't want to risk getting

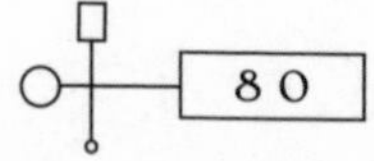

Gabriel into trouble again. "Rose gave them to me. The other day, from the bowl in her room."

"She was fond of you," he says.

I don't want to discuss Rose with him. The night is over, and I won't be his solace any longer. In the night when we were both vulnerable, I was more forgiving, but now in the daylight everything is clear again. I'm still his prisoner.

But I can't be completely cold. I can't let my contempt show if he's ever to trust me. "Do you swim?" I ask.

"No," he says. "You like the water?"

When I was a child, safe in my parents' care, I would swim in the indoor pool at the local gym, diving for rings and trying to best my brother in somersault competitions. It's been years since I last went. The world has become too dangerous since then. After the city's only research lab was bombed, destroying jobs and hope for the antidote in one fell swoop, things deteriorated rapidly. There was once a time when science was optimistic about an antidote. But years turned to decades, and new generations are still dying. And hope, like all of us, is dying fast.

"A little," I say.

"I'll have to show you the pool, then," Linden says. "You've never experienced anything like this one."

The pool doesn't look very special from here, but I think of the effects the bath soaps have on my skin, and the glitter that surrounded Cecily's dress without falling, and I understand that not everything in Linden Ashby's world is as it seems.

"I'd like that," I say. This is the truth. I would very much like to be out there where the attendant is skimming the water. It's not freedom, but I bet it's close enough that I'd be able to pretend.

He's still watching me, though I'm acting interested in the pool.

"Would it be asking too much," he says, "for you to come sit with me for a while?"

Yes. Yes, it would be too much. It's too much that I'm here at all. I wonder if Linden is aware of the unfair power he has over me. If I express even a fraction of my disgust, I'll never leave this floor again in my life. I have no choice but to oblige.

I find a comfortable in-between by carrying my breakfast tray to the bed. I set it between us, and I sit cross-legged before him. "Breakfast came in while you were asleep," I say. "You should try to eat something." I lift the lid over the food, and there are waffles dotted with fresh blueberries, far bluer than the ones in the grocery stores back home. Rowan would say not to trust anything so bright. I wonder if these berries were grown in one of the many gardens, if this is what fruit used to look like before it started being harvested in chemical soil.

Linden picks up a waffle in his hand and studies it. I know that look in his eyes. When my parents died, I stared at my meals the same way. Like food was paste, like there was no point to it. Before I can stop myself, I pick up a blueberry and bring it to his lips. I just can't stand to be reminded of that pitiful sadness.

He looks surprised, but he eats it, smiles a little.

I bring him another blueberry, and this time he puts his hand on my wrist. It isn't a forceful grip, like I'd expected. It's tenuous, and it lasts only as long as it takes him to swallow the blueberry in his mouth. Then he clears his throat.

We've been married for nearly a month, but this is the first time since our wedding that I've been able to look at him. Perhaps it's the grief, the pink swollen skin around his eyes that makes him seem harmless. Even kind.

"There. That wasn't so bad, was it?" I say, and take a blueberry for myself. It tastes sweeter than the ones I'm used to. I take the waffle out of his hand and break it in half—a piece for each of us.

He eats, taking small bites and swallowing like it's painful. It's like that for a while, with only the sound of the birds outside and us chewing.

When the plate is cleaned, I hand him the glass of orange juice. He takes it in the numb way he's taken the rest of the meal, gulping methodically, his heavy eyelashes pointed down. All this sugar will be good for him, I think.

I shouldn't care how he feels. But it will be good for him.

"Rhine?" There's a knock at my door. It's Cecily. "Are

you up? What's this word? A-M-N-I-O-C-E-N-T-E-S-I-S."

"Amniocentesis," I call back, pronouncing it for her.

"Oh. Did you know that's how they test babies for defects?" she says.

I do know. My parents worked in a laboratory that analyzed everything about fetuses and newborns.

"That's nice," I say.

"Come out," she says. "There's a robin's nest outside my window. I want to show you. The eggs are really pretty!" She's rarely interested in seeing me, but I've noticed she doesn't like when doors are closed to her.

"After I get dressed," I say, and listen for the silence that means she's left. I pick up the tray and bring it to my dressing table, wondering how long Linden is going to stay. I busy myself by brushing my hair, fastening it back with clips. I open my mouth and see that the green is gone from my tongue.

Linden leans back on his elbow, picking at a stray thread on his cuff and looking pensive. After a while he gets up. "I'll be sure someone comes for the tray," he says, and leaves.

I take a warm bath, soaking in the layer of pink foam that floats on the water. I've gotten used to the crackling sensation the bubbles leave on my skin. I dry my hair and dress in jeans, and a sweater that feels like heaven to touch. All Deirdre's work. I am always shimmering in the things she makes me. I roam the hallway for a while, expecting Cecily to find me and lead me to her bird's nest, but she's nowhere to be found.

"Governor Linden took her out to one of the gardens," Jenna says when I find her, thumbing through the catalog cards in the library. Her voice sounds clearer today, less sullen. She even looks at me after she speaks, purses her lips like she's deciding whether to say more. Then she looks back to the cards.

"Why do you call him Governor Linden?" I ask her. During our wedding dinner Housemaster Vaughn explained to us that he was to be addressed as Housemaster, because he was the highest authority in the house. But we were expected to call our husband by his given name as a sign of familiarity.

"Because I hate him," she says.

There's no malice in the words, no dramatic outburst, but something in her gray eyes says she means it. I look around us to be sure nobody heard her. The room is empty.

"I understand," I say. "But maybe it'll be easier to humor him. Maybe we'll get more freedom."

"I won't do it," she says. "I don't care about freedom now. I don't care if I die here."

She looks at me, and I can see the severity of the bags under her eyes. Her cheeks are hollow and sharp. A few weeks ago in her wedding dress she had been forlorn but pretty. Now she seems emaciated and years older. The smell on her is like cinnamon bath soap and vomit. But she's wearing her wedding band, a symbol that we're sister wives, that we share this hell just as we shared that long nightmare in the van. She may be one of the girls who curled up beside me in the blackness. She may be the one who screamed.

Whatever she was looking for in that card catalog, she finds it. She mouths the number of the aisle, committing it to memory, and closes the drawer.

She wanders down one of the aisles, and I follow her as she runs her finger along the spines of books, taps one of them, eases it out of its place. The book is dusty, the cover eaten away, the pages yellow and brittle as she flips through them. All of these books are from the twenty-first century or earlier, which isn't very strange. The television also airs old movies, and most shows are set in the past. It has become a form of escapism to visit a world in which people live a long time. What was once real and natural has become a fantasy. "There are lots of love stories here," she says. "They either end happily, or everyone dies." She laughs, but it sounds more like a sob. "What else is there, right?"

She stares at the open pages, and looks like she's going to fall apart. Tears are brimming in her eyes, and I wait for them to escape, but they don't. She holds them in place.

This aisle smells overwhelmingly dingy—dirty pages and mold, and something else, something vaguely familiar. It smells like the earth in the backyard the night my brother and I buried our possessions. And I know my sister wife Jenna is not like Cecily, who grew up in an orphanage and now feels honored to be a wealthy Governor's bride. No. She's like me, who has lost something precious, who has buried things of her own.

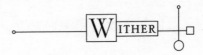

I hesitate, unsure if I can trust her with my plan to earn Linden's trust and escape. She seems resigned to rotting in this mansion, but maybe it never crossed her mind that there could be a way out.

If I'm wrong, though, what's to stop her from betraying me later?

I'm still debating this when Cecily enters the library and huffs indignantly as she falls into a chair at one of the tables. "Well, that was a waste," she says. And then, in case we haven't heard her, "A complete waste!"

As she says this, Gabriel enters the room with a tray of tea, with lemon wedges in a small silver bowl.

I take a chair opposite Cecily, who is holding up her cup, impatiently waiting for Gabriel to fill it. Jenna joins us silently, holding her book open at length from her face. Without looking up, she takes a lemon wedge and begins sucking on it.

"Linden invited me out to the rose garden," Cecily says, taking a sip of her tea. She crinkles her nose. "There's no cream or sugar," she snaps at Gabriel, who promises to be right back with some. "Anyway," she says, "I thought *finally* he was going to start acting like a husband, you know? It's about time. But all he did was show me the sunflower trellis that was imported a hundred years ago from Europe or something, and go on and on about the North Star. About how old it is, how it helped explorers find their way home. It was a total letdown—he didn't even kiss me!"

I think back on the brief time I spent alone with Linden in the same garden, at sunrise. He talked about the Japanese koi and the way the world used to be. It occurs to me now that he likes to lose himself in faraway places, just like his dead wife did. I wonder if that's what they loved about each other, or if growing up within the groomed walls of these gardens instilled in them a love of things they never had cause to see.

The same thing is happening to me, isn't it? All I've done to console myself in this place is get lost in the ghost of how the world used to be. A pang of something rushes through me—what is it? Pity? Sympathy? Understanding?

Whatever it is, it's unwelcome. I have no cause to identify with Linden Ashby. I have no cause to feel anything for him at all.

Jenna is sucking the meat from the lemons, setting the empty rinds on the table when she's done. She turns a page. She loses herself in fiction. In that way I suppose she and I are both lost here.

"Linden won't touch me," Cecily tells me. "But he's kissed you." It's an accusation.

"Excuse me?" I say.

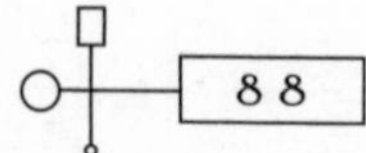

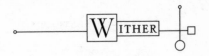

She nods excitedly, like it's the most natural thing in the world. Her brown eyes are suddenly bigger and brighter. "I saw him come out of your bedroom this morning. I know he spent the night with you."

I'm not sure what to say to this. I'm not sure what boundaries are walled between sister wives. "I thought what happened in our own bedrooms was supposed to be private," I manage.

"Oh, don't be such a prude," Cecily says. "So did you consummate?" She leans in. "Was it absolutely magical? I bet it was."

Gabriel returns and sets a pitcher of milk on the table. Cecily takes the sugar bowl from him and dumps nearly half of it into her cup. She takes another sip of tea, and I can hear the grains grinding between her teeth. She's waiting for my answer, but the only sound is of Jenna sucking the life out of those lemons, and Gabriel clearing his throat as he turns to leave.

I feel waves of heat rushing to my cheeks. I can't decide if it's embarrassment or anger. "That is completely none of your business," I cry.

Jenna looks out from behind her book, curious and maybe amused. Cecily is beaming, asking me all sorts of personal questions that spin and spin around in my head until I can't stand to look at her. I can't stand to look at either of these girls, who offer no friendship, no solace, and who would never appreciate the things Linden was talking about anyway. What do they care about the

North Star? One has dug a safe little grave for herself in centuries-old tomes, and the other is perfectly happy to remain trapped. I am nothing like them. My legs can't carry me away fast enough as I run from the room.

Out in the hallway the library smell becomes the smoky wood-and-spice aroma of the incense sticks that burn from little indents along the wall. Gabriel is just stepping onto the elevator and the doors are about to close, when I say "Wait!" and rush into the car with him. The doors close, and I'm holding my knees, gasping like I've just sprinted a mile. Gabriel presses a button, and we begin moving down.

"You know, you're going to get caught if you keep sneaking off your floor like this," he says, but there's no real danger to his tone.

"I can't do this," I say, catching my breath. But it isn't the brief sprint that's winded me. My chest is tightening. My vision blurs around the edges. "I hate it here. I hate everything about this place. I—" My voice breaks. I recognize what is happening to me. My body is doing the one thing it's been desperate to do since the moment I was shoved into the back of that van; only I was too stunned then, and too angry when I awoke in this place.

Gabriel can sense it too. Because he reaches into his breast pocket and hands me a handkerchief just as the first sob comes up.

When the elevator doors open, it's to the hallway that is loud with noises from the kitchen. It smells of lobster steam and something sweet and freshly baked. Gabriel pushes a button and the doors close, only this time the car doesn't move. "Want to talk about it?" he says.

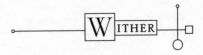

"Don't you have to get back to the kitchen?" I say, blowing my nose. I do my best not to look sniveling and pathetic, but it's hard when the handkerchief is already too damp and slimy to dry the rest of my tears as they come.

"It's all right," he says. "They'll think I got held up catering to Cecily." Sassy, demanding little Cecily is quickly taking Rose's place among the help as least favorite wife. Gabriel and I sit cross-legged on the floor, and he waits patiently for me to stop hiccupping so I can speak.

It's nice in the elevator. The carpet is worn but clean. The walls are cranberry red, inlaid with Victorian patterns that make me think of my parents' bedspread, how protected I felt inside of it. Distantly my mind registers the memory of that long-gone security. I'm safe here, too. Somewhere in the back of my mind I wonder if these walls have ears—if at any moment Housemaster Vaughn's voice will come booming through an overhead speaker, threatening Gabriel for allowing me to make it this far. But I wait, and no voice comes, and I'm so upset that I'm beyond caring anyway.

"I have a brother," I say, starting at the beginning. "Rowan. When our parents died four years ago, we had to leave school and find jobs. It was easy for him to find factory work that paid well. But I had so little skill, I was practically useless. He didn't think it was safe for me to go out alone, so we tried to stay near each other, and I always wound up with phone jobs in the factories that paid next to nothing. We had enough to get by, but not the way we used to, you know? I wanted to do more.

"A few weeks ago I saw an ad in the paper, offering money for bone marrow. Supposedly they were conducting a new screening for causes of the virus." I turn the handkerchief in my hands, studying it through unreliable vision. In one corner there's a crimson embroidery of what appears to be a flower, but it's unlike any I've ever seen, with an abundance of spear-shaped petals crowded together. It blurs and doubles. I shake my head to clear my vision.

"I realized it was a trap as soon as I stepped inside the lab and saw all those other girls," I say, my fingers automatically curling like claws. "I fought. I scratched, bit, kicked. It didn't matter. They herded all of us into a van. And I don't know how long we were riding. Hours. Sometimes we'd stop, the doors would open, and more girls would come in. It was so awful in there."

I remember that blackness. There were no walls, there was no up or down. I could have been living or dead. I listened to the other girls as they breathed around me, above me, inside me, and that was the whole planet earth. Just those terrified hiccups of breath. I thought I'd gone mad. And maybe I am mad, because I think I hear one of the

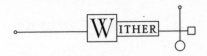

Gatherer's bullets now, and I jump. Sparks fly around me.

Gabriel raises his head just as the lights begin to flicker. There's another loud boom, not a gunshot but something mechanical-sounding. Our car begins to shake, and then the doors slide open, and Gabriel is tugging me to my feet and we're hurrying into the hallway. But it's not the cooks' hallway. This one is darker and sterile-smelling. Neon lights are struggling on the ceiling, and in the floor tiles I can see the dim reflection of our shoes before each step lands.

"We must've gone down a floor," Gabriel says.

"What? Why?" I say.

"Storm," he says. "Sometimes the elevators all move to the basement as a precaution."

"Storm? It was sunny outside just a minute ago," I say, relieved to find the fear isn't present in my voice. The sobs have stopped too, leaving only the soft, infrequent hiccups in the aftermath.

"We get a lot of them on the coastline," he says. "Out of nowhere sometimes. Don't worry, if it was a hurricane, we would have heard the alarm. It's not uncommon for strong winds to mess with the electricity and take out one of the elevators."

Hurricane. From somewhere deep in my mind comes a television image of wind spinning angrily, destroying houses. It's always the houses that go, sometimes bits of a fence or an uprooted tree, a shrieking heroine in a prairie dress, but always the houses. I imagine a hurricane smashing into this mansion and tearing it apart. I wonder if I'd be able to escape then.

"So this is the basement?" I say.

"I think so," Gabriel says. "I mean, I've never been down this way. I've only been to where the storm shelter is. Nobody's allowed without authorization from Housemaster Vaughn." He looks nervous, and I know Housemaster Vaughn is the reason. I can't stand the thought of Gabriel limping to my room, melancholy and bruised because of my transgressions.

"Let's go back up before anyone catches us," I say.

He nods. The elevator doors have closed, though, and they don't open when he swipes his key card across the panel. He tries several times before shaking his head. "It's not working," he says. "It'll be back up eventually, but in the meantime, there's got to be another elevator we can try."

We begin walking down this long hallway, with unreliable lighting that cuts out at times and hisses at us. The main hallway branches off to other, darker hallways and closed doors, and I'm sure I don't want to know where they lead. I never want to see this floor again. It's triggering something very bad in my memories, in the place of nightmares, where the murdered girls in the van reside, where the Gatherer thief cups his hand over my mouth and presses a blade to my throat. Something about being here makes my palms sweat. And then I realize it. This is where the doctor was, the afternoon before the wedding.

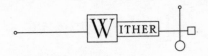

Deirdre brought me to this hallway, led me to a room where a man stuck me with a needle and I blacked out.

My skin becomes gooseflesh at the memory. I need to get out of here.

Beside me Gabriel presses forward without looking at me. "About what you told me," he says in a low voice, "I think it's terrible. And what you said earlier, about hating this place? I understand."

I'll bet he understands.

"It's Housemaster Vaughn, isn't it?" I say. "He's the one that hurt you? It was my fault, because I got out of my room."

"You shouldn't have been locked in a room to begin with," he says.

I realize all at once that I want to know him. That I've begun to see his blue eyes and coppery brown hair as the signs of a friend, and have for a while now. I like that we're speaking, finally, about things more important than what's for lunch or what I'm reading or if I want some lemons with my tea. (I never do.)

I want to know more about him, and I want to tell him more about myself. My real, unmarried self, my self from before I ever saw the inside of this mansion—when I lived in a dangerous place but I had my freedom and I was happy with it. I open my mouth, but immediately he stops me by grabbing my arm and yanking me into one of the dark side hallways. I don't have a chance to protest before I hear the clatter of something approaching.

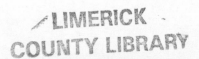

We press ourselves against the wall. We try to be the shadows that cover us. We will the whites of our eyes to be dim.

There are voices getting closer. "—cremation isn't possible, of course—"

"Shame to destroy that poor girl." A sigh; a tsk tsk.

"It's for the greater good, if it will save lives."

The voices are unfamiliar. If I spent the rest of my life in this house, I might never know all its rooms, all the attendants. But as the voices approach, I can see that the people aren't dressed like attendants. They are dressed in white, their heads protected by the same white hoods that my parents wore to work, with plastic covering their faces. Biohazard suits. They're wheeling a cart.

Gabriel grabs my wrist, squeezes it, and I don't understand why. I don't understand what's happening at all until the cart gets closer to us and I can see what's on it.

A body covered by a sheet. Rose's blond hair trailing out around the edges. And her cold, white hand, with fingernails still painted pink.

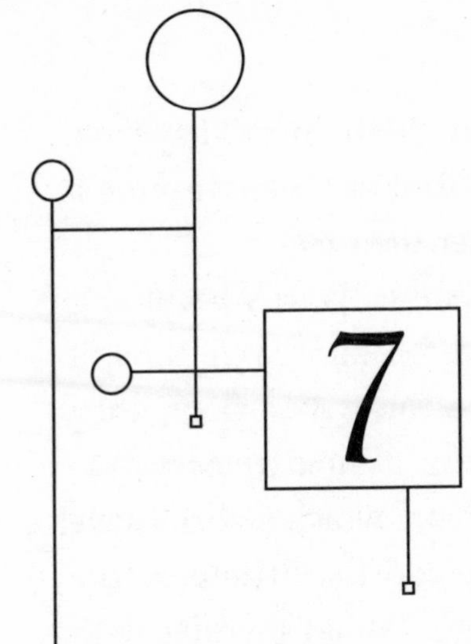

7

I HOLD MY BREATH as they pass. Eternity is the crisp footsteps, the rickety wheels getting farther away. We wait in silence for a while just to be sure it's safe, and then I splutter like coming up for air.

"Where are they taking her?" I gasp.

Gabriel's sad expression becomes evident in the near-darkness. He shakes his head. "Housemaster Vaughn must be planning to study her," he says. "He's been looking for an antidote for years."

"But," I croak. "That's Rose."

"I know."

"Linden would never allow this."

"Maybe not," Gabriel says. "We can't tell him. We never saw this. We were never here."

We find the elevator and make it back to the cooks' hallway, where there's a cacophony of metal against metal, plate against plate, the head cook shouting that someone is a lazy bastard. A riot of laughter. They have no idea that the wife they so disliked has been weaving a cold path through hallways under their feet.

"Hey, blondie's here!" someone calls. It's becoming the kitchen's official nickname for me. Even though brides aren't supposed to leave the wives' floor, they don't seem to mind my hanging around their workspace. I don't ask anything of them, which Gabriel says is more than Linden's last wife and the little one (the brat, they call her) could manage. "What's wrong with your face, blondie? You're all red."

I touch the tender skin under my eyes, remembering my tears. They seem like they happened a million years ago now.

"I'm allergic to shellfish," I call back, stuffing the damp handkerchief into my pocket. "The stink traveled all the way up to the wives' floor, made my eyes all puffy. Are you trying to kill me or what?"

"She insisted on coming down here to tell you herself," Gabriel says obligingly.

As we head toward the kitchen, I do my best to seem disgusted, when really the smell reminds me of home, coaxes an appetite back into me.

"We've got bigger problems than your diet needs," the head cook says, brushing a strand of hair from her sweaty face, nodding out the window. The sky is a bizarre shade of green. Lightning flashes through the clouds. Less than an hour ago there was sunlight and birdsong.

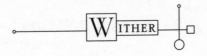

Someone offers me a little cardboard box of strawberries. "Shipped in fresh this morning." Gabriel and I each take a handful as we stand at the window. Like the blueberries, their color is more vivid than what I'm used to. Their juice floods my mouth with sweetness, and the seeds get lodged in my molars.

"It's that time of year already?" Gabriel says. "It seems a little early."

"We might get a good storm this year," says one of the cooks as he kneels at the oven and furrows his brow at something that's baking. "Maybe even a category three."

"What does that mean?" I ask, popping the next strawberry into my mouth.

"Means you three princesses will be locked in the dungeon," the head cook hisses, and I'm just about to believe her when she claps a hand on my shoulder hard and laughs. "The House Governor takes every precaution with his wives," she says. "If the winds get bad, you'll all have to wait out the storm in the storm shelter. Don't worry, blondie, I bet it's comfy cozy, and the rest of us'll be up here cooking and bringing you your meals."

"You just work through the storm?" I say.

"Sure, unless the power's out."

"Don't worry," Gabriel says. "The house won't blow away." His small laugh suggests he knows that's what I'd been hoping for. We exchange a look, and his tentative grin blooms into the first real smile I've seen on him. I allow myself to smile back.

But a few minutes later, a pall hangs over us, as gloomy as the thundering clouds, as we take the elevator back to the wives' floor. There's a pushcart of lunch trays between us. Lobster bisque for the others and a small glazed chicken for me, since I'm supposed to be allergic to shellfish. We don't speak. I try not to think of Rose, but can see nothing but her lifeless hand dipping out of the sheet as she passes. A hand that just the other day was weaving my hair into a braid. I think of the sadness in Linden's eyes; what would he say if he knew his childhood love, the little girl who fed sugar to horses in the orange grove, is being dissected in this very house?

Alone in my room, I don't touch my lunch. I soak in a hot bath and wash Gabriel's handkerchief in the bubbles and then hold it up in front of me. I try to imagine another place, another time, when flowers might have looked like its embroidery. It's such a powerful thing, sharp and dangerous and lovely. It rests on what appears to be a lily pad. I commit the image to memory and then research it in the library. The closest match I find is the lotus flower, which existed in Eastern countries and may have originated in a country called China. All I have to go by is a fraction of a page in an almanac of aquatic botany; the almanac would rather tell me about water lilies, perhaps a close cousin, but not the same. Not as rare. And after hours of research, I still can't find a decent match.

I ask Gabriel, and he says the attendants take the handkerchiefs from a plastic bin where the cloth napkins are kept. He doesn't know who ordered them or where they came from, but I can keep it because there are dozens more.

In the days to come, Gabriel begins bringing breakfast while the other wives are still asleep. He hides June Beans in rolled napkins or under the plate or, once, between the pancakes. He arranges the strawberry slices into Eiffel Towers and boats with spear-shaped masts. He leaves the tray on my nightstand, and, if I'm sleeping, I feel his presence as I dream. I feel warm ribbons reaching into my subconsciousness, and I feel safe. I open my eyes to the silver cover on the breakfast tray, and I know he was nearby. On the mornings that I'm awake, we talk in low voices, barely making out each other's faces in the darkness. He tells me that he's been an orphan for as long as he can remember, that Housemaster Vaughn bought him at an auction when he was nine. "It's not as awful as it sounds," Gabriel says. "In orphanages they teach you skills like cooking, sewing, cleaning. They keep a sort of report card on you, and then the well-to-do can bid. That's how we got Deirdre, Elle, and Adair, too."

"You don't remember your parents at all?" I say.

"Hardly," he says. "I barely even remember what the world outside of this place looks like." And my heart sinks. Nobody, he tells me, not even the help, leaves the property. They order shipments of food and fabric and anything imaginable, but they never visit stores themselves. The only ones to leave are the delivery truck drivers, Housemaster Vaughn, and sometimes Linden if he has a mind to. I've seen House Governors and their first wives on TV at social events—political elections, ribbon-cutting ceremonies, things like that—but Gabriel tells me that Linden is not the social type. He's something of a recluse. And why not? You could take an entire day and still not walk from one end of this place to the other. But I haven't lost hope. Linden took Rose to parties all the time, and she said herself that if he plays favorites with me, he'll take me anywhere I want to go.

"Don't you miss it?" I say. "Being free."

He laughs. "It wasn't much freer in the orphanage, but I suppose I do miss the beach," he says. "I used to be able to see it from my window. Sometimes they let us go there. I liked watching the boats go out. I think if I could have done anything, I would have liked to work on one. Maybe build one. But I've never even caught a fish."

"My brother taught me how to fish," I say. We would sit on the concrete slab that stopped at the ocean, our feet dangling over the edge. I remember the strong pull on the fishing line, the reel spinning out of my control and Rowan catching it for me, showing me how to bring it in. I remember the silver body, all muscle, like a tongue thrashing on the hook, eyes open wide. I freed it from the hook and tried to hold it, but it leapt from my hand. Hit the water with a splash. Disappeared, off to visit the ruins of France or maybe Italy to send them my regards.

I try relaying this experience to Gabriel, and even though I think I'm doing a poor job of imitating the pulling motion of the fishing rod and my pathetic attempts to reel in the fish, he's paying close attention. When I imitate the splash of the fish hitting the water, he even laughs, and I laugh too, quietly, in the darkness of my room.

"Did you ever eat any of the catches?" he asks.

"No. The edible catches are farther out, and then they're hauled in by boat. The closer you get to land, the more contaminated the water. This was just for fun."

"It sounds fun," he says.

"It was kinda gross, actually," I say, remembering the cold slimy scales and bloodshot eyes. Rowan deemed me the worst fisherman ever and said it was a good thing these fish were inedible, because if we needed them for food, we would starve with me in charge. "But it's one of the few things my brother likes to do that doesn't involve work."

The homesickness that comes with my brother's memory is not so bad. Not with Gabriel for company and a tray of pancakes and the June Bean he's hidden in the napkin.

Linden ignores us in the daytime, but begins inviting all three of his wives to dinner each night. He tells us about his father's research, how optimistic the scientists and doctors are about finding an antidote. He says that his father is attending a convention in Seattle, where he will compare notes with other researchers. Secretly I wonder if the Housemaster's notes are about Rose. I wonder if he has named her Subject A or Patient X. I wonder if her fingernails are still painted. Cecily is, as always, very interested in everything our husband says. Jenna still looks disgusted at the sight of him, though she has started eating. I'm getting better at acting interested in what he has to say. And all the while, the windstorms make the electricity flicker, and interrupt with strange infrequent bouts of rain what would otherwise be beautiful afternoons.

And then one evening when Linden is in unusually high spirits, he announces that, in honor of our two months of marriage, he thinks there should be a celebration. A big one, with colored lanterns and a live band. He'll even let us decide which garden to throw it in.

"How about the orange grove?" I say. Gabriel and two other attendants collecting our plates go pale and exchange grave looks. They know the magnitude of what I've said. They brought Rose many meals and cups of tea as she frittered endless days away in the orange grove. It was her favorite, where she and Linden were married, and where—she told me wistfully one afternoon, twirling a June Bean around her tongue—they first kissed. And it was there that Linden found her a week after her twentieth birthday, unconscious and pale in the shade of an orange tree, gasping, her lips blue. That was the day he was faced with the tragedy of her mortality. His inability to save her. All the pills and potions in the world couldn't buy more than a few fleeting months.

A party in the orange grove. The pain on Linden's face is immediate. I am unwavering. He has cost me more pain than I will ever be able to repay.

Cecily, oblivious, says, "Yes! Oh, Linden, we've never even seen it!"

Linden dabs his mouth with a napkin, sets the napkin on the table. "I thought along the pool would be more entertaining," he says quietly. "The warm weather's nice for swimming."

"But you said we could pick," says Jenna; it is perhaps the first time she's ever said a word to him. Everyone looks at her, even the attendants. She glances briefly at me and then at Linden. She bites a piece of steak from her fork daintily and says, "I vote for the orange grove."

"Me too," says Cecily.

I nod assent.

"It's unanimous, then," Linden says into his spoon. The rest of the meal is very quiet. The dinner plates are all cleared. Dessert is served, and then tea. Then we're dismissed, because Linden has a headache and needs to be alone with his thoughts.

"You're something else," Gabriel whispers to me as he escorts us to the elevator. Just before the doors close between us, I smile.

Once upstairs I immediately retreat to my bedroom.

I lie on the bed, sucking a blue June Bean and thinking about how the Atlantic Ocean lapped under my and Rowan's bare feet. I think about the ferry along the pier that I would watch slice a path toward the horizon, and how secure I would feel in my small piece of the world, how lucky to be alive if only for a short while. That's where I want my body to be cast when I'm dead. I want to be ashes in the ocean. I want to sink to the ruins of Athens and be carried off to Nigeria, and to swim between fish and sunken ships. I'll come back to Manhattan frequently, to smell the air, to see how my twin is doing.

My twin, however, does not like to discuss what will happen in four years, when I'll be dead and he'll have five years of life in him. I wonder what he's doing now and if he's okay. I wonder how long it will take me to break free of this place, or at least communicate to him that I'm alive. But somewhere, in a place in my heart that's darker than that awful basement, I worry that my corpse will become part of Housemaster Vaughn's research, and my brother will never even know what's happened to me.

For that, I am not sorry that Linden Ashby is off somewhere being sad because of something I said at dinner.

It's been so hard to keep track of the days in this mansion, when they all look the same, when I'm nothing more than Linden's prisoner. I've never been apart from my brother for so long; from the time we were toddlers, our mother fit my hand in his and told us to stay together. And we did. We were together on our walks to school, clinging to each other in case of dangers lurking in the ruins of an old building, in the shadow of an abandoned car. We were together on our walks to work, and our voices kept each other company at night, in a dark house once filled with our parents' presence. Before now I'd never been away from him a day in my life.

I thought that as twins we would always be able to reach each other, that from far away I would still hear his voice as clearly as I heard him in the next room of our house. We would talk to each other as we moved about the rooms—him in the kitchen, me in the living room—to keep the silence of our parents' deaths away.

"Rowan," I whisper. But the sound doesn't travel farther than my bedroom. The cord between us is severed.

"I'm alive. Don't give up on me."

As though in answer, there's a soft knock at the door. I know it's not Cecily because it's not followed by a question or a demand. Deirdre doesn't knock, and it wouldn't be Gabriel at this hour. "Who is it?"

The door cracks open and I see Jenna's gray eyes. "Can I come in?" she asks in her wispy voice.

I sit up on the bed and nod. She purses her lips in the closest I've seen her come to a smile, and takes a seat on the edge of my mattress.

"I saw the way Governor Linden looked at you when you brought up the orange grove," she says. "Why?"

My instincts caution me to be wary of this somber

bride, but I'm in just the right stage of grief to pull down my defenses—to lower the mast, I suppose Gabriel would say, and allow myself to drift into uncertain waters. And she seems so timid and harmless in her white nightgown that's like mine, with her long dark hair in a veil around her shoulders. Something about all this makes me want to see her as a sister, as a confidant.

"It's because of Rose," I say. "He fell in love with her in the orange grove. That was her favorite place, and he hasn't been able to stand it since she became sick."

"Really?" she says. "How do you know that?"

"Rose told me," I say, and I stop myself from adding that Rose told me all sorts of things about our husband. I want to keep some of his frailties to myself, such as the infection that nearly killed him as a boy and that caused him to lose several teeth, hence the gold ones. These things make him seem less menacing somehow. Like someone I can overpower or outsmart when the time is right.

"So that's why he looked so sad," she says, picking lint off her hemline.

"That's what I wanted," I say. "He had no right to bring us here, and I guess he'll never realize that. So I wanted to hurt him like he hurt me."

Jenna looks at her lap, and her lip quirks in what I think will be a smile or a laugh, but her eyes well with tears and her voice is broken when she says, "My sisters were in that van."

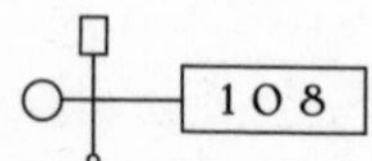

Her skin pales, and mine flourishes with gooseflesh as her little sobs wrack the bed. The room is colder, and the nightmare is growing into so much more than I thought it could be. It only gets worse in this mansion of sweet smells and extra-bright gardens. I think of the gunshots that have haunted me since I arrived. How many of those were Jenna's sisters, and which ones? The first shot? The fifth? The sixth?

I'm too stunned to speak.

"When you brought up the orange grove, I didn't know what it was, but I saw that it was hurting him," she sobs, swipes her nose with her fist. "And I wanted him to hurt, so I agreed with you. He has no idea, does he? What he's taken away?"

"No," I agree softly. I offer her Gabriel's handkerchief, which I've been keeping in my pillowcase, but she shakes her head, apparently hating this place too much to even blow her nose on its cloths.

"I only have two years left," she says. "There's nothing for me out there now, and maybe I'm trapped here, but I won't let him have his way with me. I don't care if he murders me, he won't have me."

I think of her cold stiff body being pushed into a basement laboratory. I think of Housemaster Vaughn dissecting his daughters-in-law one by one.

I'm not sure what to say, because I do understand her anger. I am a good liar, but lies won't help me here. Jenna is a girl who has no illusions about what will happen to her; she knows it will never be okay. Am I the one in denial?

"What if you could get out?" I say. "Would you?"

She shrugs, snorts incredulously through her tears. "To what?" she says. "No, might as well go out in style." She waves her wrist, exaggerating the ruffles on the cuff of her sleeve. Then she wipes her nose with them, and she looks so defeated. A skeleton, a ghost, a very pretty girl who's already dead. She turns to me, and her eyes still have traces of life. "Did you really spend the night with him?" she asks, but her tone isn't invasive like Cecily's. She's not being crass; she just wants to know.

"He spent the night in here when Rose died," I say. "He just fell asleep, that's all. It was never more than that."

She nods, swallows a hard lump in her throat. I touch her shoulder, and she starts but doesn't pull away. "I am really sorry," I say. "He's an awful man, and this is an awful place. The only one who likes it here is Cecily."

"She'll learn," Jenna says. "She reads all those pregnancy books and Kama Sutra stuff, but she has no idea what he will do to her."

This is also true. Jenna, who is as quiet as a shadow, has been paying attention to her sister wives all this time. She has given us a lot of thought.

For a while she sits there, choking down the last of her sobs, pulling herself together. I offer her the glass of water that's been sitting on my nightstand, and she takes a few sips. "Thank you," she says. "For sticking up for yourself at dinner. For showing him how it feels."

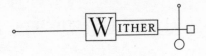

"Thank you for backing me up," I say. I think that's a smile on her lips when she turns to look at me one last time before disappearing into the hallway.

I fall asleep and have horrible dreams of sad girls with exquisite eyes, gray vans erupting with butterflies, windows that won't open. And everywhere girls, tumbling from trees like orange blossoms and hitting the earth with sickening thuds. They crack open.

Sometime in the night my mind enters a deeper dimension of dreaming. The sound disappears and something obscures my vision. There's whiteness, the smells of decay in soil and surgical gloves. Then Housemaster Vaughn in a biohazard suit yanks the sheet from my face. I try to scream, but I can't because I'm dead, eyes frozen wide. He brings his knife between my breasts, ready to cut. The pain is just about to register when a sound comes bursting into my dreams. "Rhine," the voice says.

"Rhine."

I open my eyes, gasp. My heart is thudding in my chest, and all at once I'm bursting with the life I didn't have in my nightmare. In the early morning darkness I can just make out Gabriel's blue eyes. I say his name both to test my voice and to be sure he's really there. I can see the silver gleam of the breakfast tray on my nightstand.

"You were thrashing around," he whispers. "What was it?"

"The basement," I whisper back. I bring the heel of my hand across my forehead, and it comes back damp with sweat. "I was trapped; I couldn't get out." I sit up and turn on the lamp. The light is too much, and I shield my eyes and then blink wildly as Gabriel comes into focus, sitting on the edge of my bed where just hours before, Jenna sat and told me about her own nightmare.

"It was an awful thing to see," Gabriel agrees.

"But you've seen worse," I say. It's not a question.

He nods, his expression darkening.

"Like what?" I say.

"Lady Rose had a baby," he says. "It was over a year ago. It didn't make it. Strangled by the umbilical cord, I think. The House Governor and Lady Rose scattered its ashes in the orange grove, but I wonder about those ashes, if they were really the baby. When people die here in general, I wonder what happens to them. I've never seen any kind of graveyard; it's either ashes or they just disappear."

Rose had a child. I never knew. It, or something like it, is scattered among the orange blossoms.

"Gabriel?" There is true fear in my voice. "I want to get out of here."

"I've been here for nine years," he says. "That's half my life. I can't even remember, most days, that there's a world other than this one here."

"Well, there is," I say. "There's the ocean, and boats leaving harbors, and people jogging on sidewalks, and streetlights that come on in the evening. That's the real world. This isn't."

But I understand where he's coming from. Lately I almost forget these things myself.

The party happens in the orange grove, as promised. Cecily spends the afternoon working poor Elle to the bone with dress adjustments and makeup redos. Her hair is styled, washed, and styled again, and again. She calls me over to see each attempt, and they all make her look beautiful but young. A child in her mother's too-big heels, trying to be a woman.

For me, Deirdre has constructed a soft orange frock that she says will make me look dazzling in the evening light. She leaves my hair untouched, long and wavy and many shades of blond. She doesn't say it, but I know that as she stands beside me in the mirror, she's thinking I look like Rose. And when Linden sees me, I suspect he will not be seeing me at all, but some reincarnation of the girl he lost. I can only hope it earns me his favoritism.

We arrive in the orange grove by early evening, and even with the stage set up and the band tuning its instruments and the crowd of people I've never met, I can see that this place is not like the rest of the mansion. It's wild, with uneven lengths of grass as high as my uncomfortable heels or my knees. It reaches into my dress like thin rubbery fingers. Ants crawl around the rims of crystal glasses and make lines up trees. All the greenery hums and rustles.

I don't recognize most of the faces here. Some are attendants setting up heaters for the food or perfecting the paper lanterns. Others are well-dressed, polished to the point of being borderline greasy, all first generations. "They're Housemaster Vaughn's colleagues," Deirdre whispers to me, standing on a foldout chair and adjusting my bra strap so it will stop sliding down my arm. "The House Governor doesn't have friends of his own. When Rose took ill, he stopped even leaving the property."

"What did he do before then?" I ask, smiling like she's saying something delightful.

"Designed houses," she says, and fluffs my hair around my shoulders. "There! You look so pretty."

My sister wives and I start the night as wallflowers, which is what our domestics have coached us to do. We hold hands with one another, share a cup of punch, look pretty, and wait to be introduced. One at a time the strangers, first generations, steal us for dances. They put their hands on our hips and shoulders, getting too close, forcing us to smell their crisp suits and aftershave. I find myself looking forward to the moment when they'll release me, when I can catch my breath beneath the oranges. Jenna stands beside me, all danced out. Despite her ever-present resentment for her captivity, she is a fantastic dancer. Fast or slow, her body moves like a flame or a ballerina in a music box. She smiles at our husband as she moves, and he blushes, overcome by her beauty. But I know what her smile really means. I know why she's enjoying this night. It's because his dead wife still lingers here, and he's in agony, and she wants him to know that his pain will never go away.

Her smile is her revenge.

Now she stands beside me and plucks an orange from its branch. She turns it in her hands and says, "I think we'll get off easy tonight."

"What do you mean?" I ask.

She nods ahead of us, to where Cecily is slow dancing in Linden's arms. Her white teeth can be seen beaming even from here. "She's captured his heart for the moment," Jenna says. "He hasn't let her go for a second."

"You're right," I say. He has given all of his dances to Cecily. He has spent the rest of his time staring in awe at Jenna. He hasn't looked at me at all.

Jenna is plucked away for another dance, having gained many admirers with her versatility and charming smile. I'm left alone to nurse punch from a crystal glass. A cool breeze washes through my hair, and I wonder where Rose fell ill. Was it where the attendants are arguing over not making enough chicken for the occasion? Where Cecily and Linden have snuck away from the dance floor to giggle in the tall grass? And where did the scattered ashes fall? And what were those ashes, and what really became of Linden and Rose's dead child?

As the night presses on and the guests thin out, Jenna and I sit in the grass while Adair and Deirdre comb the tangles from our hair. Linden and Cecily are nowhere to be found, not even when we slip away to bed much later.

The following day, Cecily stumbles into the library sometime after noon, looking pale and dazed. There's a hazy smile on her lips that won't go away, and her hair is a mess. It's like a brushfire filled with casualties.

Gabriel brings the tea, and Cecily pours in too much sugar as usual. She doesn't talk to us. There are pillow creases on her face, and she cringes whenever she moves her legs.

"It's a pretty day," she finally says, long after I've moved to my overstuffed chair and Jenna has begun pacing the aisles.

She doesn't look right. Not right at all. Her usual verve is subdued, and her voice is gentle like wind chimes. She seems like a wild bird that has been tamed and is surveying its captivity in a daze in which captivity doesn't seem so bad.

"Are you all right?" I ask her.

"Oh, yes," she says. Her head cants to one side, then the other, and then she gently rests it on the table. Across the room Jenna shoots me a look. Her mouth doesn't move, but I understand what she's telling me. Now that Cecily has finally gotten what she wanted of our husband, this means Linden has tucked Rose safely inside his memories, and he's ready to visit the beds of his remaining wives.

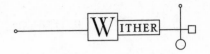

Cecily looks so small and helpless, as happy as she may be, that I say "Come on" and gently bring her to her feet. She doesn't object, and in fact wraps her little arm around my back as I guide her to her room.

Linden is a monster, I think. He's a vile man. "Can't you see she's still a little girl?" I murmur.

"Hm?" Cecily raises her eyebrows.

"Nothing," I say. "How are you feeling?"

She climbs into the bed, which is unmade and looking as though she just left it, and as her head reaches the pillow, she stares at me with cloudy eyes. "Brilliant," she says.

I tuck her in, and I notice the small bit of blood on the sheets.

I sit with her for a while as she drifts back to sleep. I listen to the robins that have nested in the tree below her window. She'd wanted to show them to me before, just a child looking for an excuse to talk to me. I haven't been very kind to her, or fair. She can't help that she's oblivious, that she's so young. She can't help that she grew up in a world without parents, in an orphanage that allowed her to be taken for either a bride or a corpse. She doesn't know how fragile she is, how close she came to death in that van.

But I do. I push some tangled hair from her face and say, "Have sweet dreams."

It's the best thing anyone can hope for, in this place.

I'm so angry with Linden that I can't stand the sight of him. He comes into my bedroom that night, and without asking he advances to my bed. I don't open the sheets, and so he stops. I turn on the light and act as though I'm just waking, when in fact I've been expecting him.

"Hello," he says softly.

"Hello," I say, and sit up.

He touches the edge of my mattress but doesn't sit. Could he be waiting for an invitation? Did Cecily give him one? Jenna never will. If he isn't going to force himself on us, then Cecily is the only one who will ever allow him.

He says, "You looked beautiful last night, in the orange grove."

"I didn't think you noticed me," I say. Even now, he doesn't look at me. He looks out my window that doesn't open. The winds have picked up again, howling like the dead. Oranges and roses must be flying from the greenery and getting mangled in the air.

"Can I come to bed?" he says.

"No," I say, folding the blanket neatly across my lap.

He looks at me, raises a delicate eyebrow. "No?"

"No," I affirm. I mean to sound angry, but somehow it doesn't come out right. There's tight silence between us, and then I say, "But thank you for asking."

He stands rigidly and seems to be trying to decide where to put his hands. His pajama pants don't have pockets. "Then how about a walk?" he says.

"Now?" I say. "It looks like it's a cold night." Florida has proven thus far to have strange weather.

"Wear a coat," he says. "Meet me at the elevator in a few minutes."

Well, I suppose there's no harm in a walk. I go to my closet and put a light knit coat over my nightgown, and a pair of thick socks that make it hard for me to wriggle my feet into my shoes.

When I meet Linden at the elevator, I see that my coat is the feminine cut of his, and I wonder if this is coincidence. Deirdre, hopeless little romantic that she is, may have designed it specially to match. I suppose she means for me to learn to love him. But she's young yet. She has plenty of years to learn what true love is, or at the very least what it isn't.

The elevator moves down and I'm haunted by images of my mother twirling in her billowy dresses, my father dipping her over his arm, music filling the living room. *You want to know about true love?* my father the geneticist said to my brother and me as we watched them dance. *I'll tell you something about true love. There's no science to it. It's natural as the sky.*

Love is natural. Even the human race can't claim to be natural anymore. We are fake, dying things. How fitting that I would end up in this sham of a marriage.

Outside it's bitter and cold. There's a burned, leafy smell like autumn. I think of Windbreakers and rakes and new kneesocks for school. Things that are a world away, but lingering still. My nose is frozen; I pull the collar of my coat up around my ears.

Linden hooks his arm in mine and we begin to walk, not through the rose garden but toward the orange grove. All traces of the party are gone, and now I can see it for what it really is: straggly and natural and pretty. A place where I would want to lie on a blanket and read. I can see why Rose spent so much time here, and I wonder if she knew she was ill that day she collapsed. I wonder if she thought she might slip away quietly, shaded by soft white blossoms, so that her pain would not be prolonged.

The wind rustles everything, and I feel her serenity everywhere. I feel peaceful, not so angry anymore.

"She's here," Linden says, like he was reading my mind.

"Mm," I agree.

We walk for a while, along a vague path of well-trod grass and dirt. There are no man-made ponds here, no quaint little love seats or benches. The wind comes in such loud bouts that when we open our mouths, all hope of words is sucked from our throats. But I sense there's something Linden wants to say, and when it's calm, he stops walking and takes my hands. The cold has chapped my knuckles, but his palms are smooth and moist over them.

"Listen to me," he says. His eyes are bright green in the moonlight. "I will share this place with you. Anywhere you wish to go, just ask and I'll allow it. But this place is sacred, all right? I will not let you use it as a weapon against me."

There's nothing forceful about his tone, but he squeezes my hands and lowers his head so our eyes are even. So he knows, then. He knows that my party suggestion was malicious, and yet he didn't raise a hand to me. He didn't abuse me for my defiance like his father abused Gabriel. Why? Why would a man who stole three girls from their homes show me any kindness?

I purse my chapped lips, fighting the desire to tell him that if I can go anywhere, I want to go back to Manhattan. I can't let him know my dreams of escape, because then he'll never let me go. Truth doesn't factor into my escape plan.

"I didn't mean to hurt you," I say. "I suppose I was just jealous. You haven't paid any attention to me, and I thought that if we could have the party here, you would feel better. It would be like a funeral for Rose. You could celebrate your new marriages and move on."

He looks so taken aback, so touched by my lie, that I almost feel bad about it. I am sorry that his dead wife is being dissected in the basement, her beauty ruined and raped, while I use her name against him. One afternoon, as Rose lay in a sweaty daze, teetering on the edge of consciousness, she made me swear that I would look after Linden, and I promised I would. I didn't expect to keep that promise, but maybe my lie will at least do him some good in the meantime.

"I wanted to bury her," he says, "but my father didn't think it was a good idea. He says we don't know if the virus she had—" His voice catches, and he takes a moment. "If it would affect the soil. So he gave me her ashes."

I wait for him to mention the child that was scattered here, but he doesn't. That is a privacy he means to keep. Or maybe it's just too painful.

"Are you going to scatter her?" I ask.

"I did," he says. "Last night after the party. I thought it was time to say good-bye."

After his tryst with Cecily, I suppose. Even Cecily's adoration can't subdue his heartache. But I don't say anything. Now is not the time to talk about Cecily. Instead we turn, arm in arm, husband and wife, and head back to the sprawling mansion that is covered in ivy. I think of the ivy leaf I've hidden for myself in a romance novel that will end happily or tragically, and all the while I wonder whose ashes were really scattered last night.

For the next few nights Linden invites all three of us to dine with him. And on most nights he stays in my bed. All we do is talk and sleep. He lies in the blankets and watches me rub lotion on my hands, brush my hair, close the curtains, and sip my evening tea. I don't mind his presence so much. I know it would be too much for Jenna, and I would prefer that he leave Cecily alone, because she will let him do anything to her, and her sudden frailty worried me that morning after the party. I know she's jealous that he's coming to me now, and I think it's none of her business, so I answer none of her questions. But Linden and I don't even touch, except for sometimes when I feel his fingers in my hair sending ripples into my dreams.

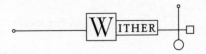

He will talk to me until I succumb to exhaustion. Gabriel starts bringing my breakfast at the same time as my sister wives, and he brings extra food for Linden, who will ask for unpredictable things such as a cup of syrup or grapes, which he will eat by dangling the vine over his lips. Gabriel stops hiding June Beans for me, and I miss them. I miss talking to him. We don't have many chances to so much as look at each other because Linden begins taking me for walks in the daytime.

On warm days he brings all three of us down to the pool. Jenna sunbathes; Cecily somersaults from the diving board with screams of delight that suggest a childhood and freedom she will never have. I spend much of my time underwater, where there are holograms of jellyfish and the ocean floor. Sharks speed toward me and then cut through me, clearing the path for schools of bright yellow and orange fish, whales as big as the pool itself. Sometimes I forget that none of these things are real, and I dive deeper and deeper, searching for Atlantis, and then finding only the bottom of the pool.

There are whole days like this. And it's nice, I think. Like having freedom. Like having sisters. Even Jenna will dip her toes into the water, give me a little splash.

One afternoon Cecily and I conspire to each grab one of her ankles and pull her in. Jenna screams indignantly, and clings to the edge, swearing that we're awful and she hates us. But eventually she comes out of it. She and I hold hands as we go under; we try to catch holographic guppies.

Linden doesn't swim, though sometimes he asks us how we're enjoying the holograms. He's pale and thin in his swim trunks. He reads architecture magazines while sitting on a damp towel, and I think it means he's getting ready to work again. Maybe he'll start to leave the property. Maybe he'll attend a party. And I will be on his arm. I know my escape will have to be carefully planned and that I won't be able to simply vanish into the crowd on my first night out. But maybe there will be a televised event. Maybe Rowan will be watching and he'll see that I'm alive.

One afternoon I run inside to get an extra towel from the cabinet by the door, and I almost careen into Gabriel, who is holding a tray of orange juice in stem glasses. "Sorry," I say.

"Sounds like you're having fun," he says, not quite meeting my eyes. "Excuse me." He steps around me.

"Wait," I say. I glance over my shoulder to be sure none of the others, lounging and splashing at the pool on the other side of the glass door, are watching. Gabriel turns to face me. "Are you mad at me for something?" I ask.

"No. I just didn't think you had time to speak to an attendant anymore," he says. I am not liking the darkness in his normally gentle eyes. "Now that you're the wife of a House Governor."

"Hey, wait a minute," I say.

"There's nothing to explain, Lady Rhine," he says. That's technically what the help is supposed to call me, but I guess I don't have the right air to carry it, because around the house I have always been Rhine. Or blondie. Though Gabriel is right, I haven't been able to speak to anyone but Linden and my sister wives for days. I miss sitting on the kitchen counter and talking to the cooks, and I miss talking to Gabriel. I miss the June Beans, and I'm running low on my supply in the drawer. But these are hardly things I can say in Linden's or Housemaster Vaughn's presence, and I never see Gabriel anymore unless at least one of them is nearby.

"What is it?" I say. "What did I do?"

"I guess I just didn't expect you to fall for the House Governor so easily," he says.

It's such an absurd thought that I laugh and choke on the word "What?"

"I live in the same house, you know," he says. "I bring you breakfast every morning."

He's wrong, so horribly wrong. And I am so offended that I abandon any intentions to correct him. "You didn't expect me to share a bed with my own husband?" I say.

"I guess I didn't," he says. And then he opens the sliding glass door and steps out into the sunshine, leaving me to stand there, dripping wet, teeth chattering, wondering what the hell this place has made me become.

At dinner I am silent. Linden asks me if the food is all right, and I wait until Gabriel has finished pouring my sparkling water before I nod. I really want to pull Gabriel aside and talk to him. I want to explain that he's wrong about Linden and me. But Housemaster Vaughn is sitting at the table, and his presence makes me keep my head down.

In the elevator after dinner, Gabriel escorts us to our floor. I try to catch his gaze, but he seems to be deliberately avoiding me.

Cecily stands beside me and rubs her temples. "Why are the lights so bright?" she says.

The doors open, and Jenna and I get out on our floor, but Cecily doesn't move.

"What's wrong?" I ask.

And that's when I notice how pale she is. Her face glistens in a sheen of sweat. "I don't feel right," she says. As soon as the sentence is uttered, her eyes flutter up into her head, and Gabriel just catches her as she collapses into a lifeless heap.

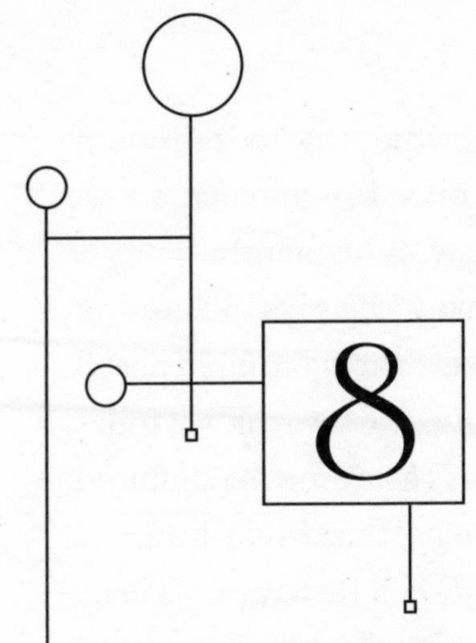

THE ATTENDANTS arrive in abundance. All of them rushing into and out of Cecily's room like in a busy anthill. Housemaster Vaughn is there, and Linden is pacing back and forth over the threshold. Jenna and I are herded into our bedrooms, and I sit at my dressing table, too stunned and worried to try for sleep.

Should I have told Linden how awful she looked the morning after the party? He would have listened to me. I should have reminded him that she's only a child. He doesn't realize these obvious things, and I should have intervened.

Is she bleeding? Is she dying? Earlier today she was fine.

I press my ear to my door, trying to overhear something other than the incomprehensible mutterings across the hall. When the door opens, I almost fall over. Gabriel is peering into the room. "Sorry. Didn't mean to scare you," he says softly. I move out of the way to let him in, and he closes the door behind him. It's unusual to see him in my bedroom without a tray in his hands.

"I wanted to see if you were okay," he says. There's no bitterness in his tone. His eyes are their familiar peaceful blue, with none of the resentment I saw earlier today. Maybe he's just set all that ugliness aside for the moment, but I'm so relieved by his familiarity that I hug him.

He tenses at first, stunned, and then he wraps his arms around me, and I feel his chin rest on the top of my head.

"It's been awful," I say.

"I know," he says, and I feel his arms shift. I've never been this close to him before. He's taller and sturdier than Linden, who is a few pounds from blowing away. And he smells like the kitchen, like all the noise and energy and things boiling and baking.

"You don't know," I say, inching away just enough to look at him. A sort of gentle haze has taken over his face; he looks flushed. "It's not just Cecily. All of us are suffering in this marriage. Jenna hates him, you know. And I know how Linden looks at me—like I'm Rose. It's my only defense to play along, but it's so exhausting at night to have him lying beside me, muttering her name in his sleep. It's like he's erasing me, a little more every day."

"He couldn't erase you," Gabriel assures me.

"And you," I say. "Don't you ever call me Lady Rhine. I heard how it sounded for the first time today, and I hate it. It's not right at all."

"Okay," he says. "I'm sorry. Anything you and the House Governor do is none of my business."

"It's not that!" I cry, and put my hands firmly on his shoulders. I lower my voice, just in case anyone might be standing in the hall outside. "It will be the very coldest day in hell before Linden Ashby has his way with me, all right?" I almost keep talking. I almost tell him about my plan to escape, but I decide against it. For now that will remain my secret. "Do you believe me?" I say.

"I never believed otherwise," he says. "But I saw him in your bed and—I don't know. It got to me."

"Yeah, well, it gets to me, too." I laugh a little, and he follows my lead. I break away and sit on the edge of my mattress. "So, what's happening with Cecily?"

He shakes his head. "I don't know. Housemaster Vaughn is in there with a few of the house doctors." He watches my face drop. "But, hey, listen. I'm sure she's all right. If it was very serious, they would have moved her to a hospital in the city."

I look at my hands in my lap and sigh.

"Can I get you anything?" Gabriel says. "What about tea? Or some strawberries. You hardly ate at dinner."

I don't want tea or strawberries. I don't want Gabriel to be my attendant right now. I want him to sit here with me and be my friend. I want to know he won't be punished for it later. I want us both to be free.

Maybe if I ever work out a plan to escape, I can bring him with me. I think he would like the harbor.

But I don't know how to say all of this in a way that won't make me seem weak, so all that comes out is, "Tell me about yourself."

"Myself?" He looks confused.

"Yes," I say, patting the mattress.

"You know all there is to know," he says, sitting beside me.

"Not true," I say. "Where were you born? What's your favorite season? Anything."

"Here. Florida," he says. "I remember a woman in a red dress with curly brown hair. Maybe she was my mother, I'm not sure. And summer. What about you?" The last part is said with a smile. He smiles so infrequently that I consider each one a sort of trophy.

"Fall is my favorite," I say. He already knows about Manhattan, and that my parents died when I was twelve.

I'm thinking up another round of questions when there's a knock at the door. Gabriel stands and smoothes out the wrinkles in the comforter where he sat. I grab the empty glass on my nightstand in case I need to pretend I was asking him for a refill. "Come in," I say.

It's Elle, Cecily's domestic. Her eyes are wild with excitement. "Guess what I've come to tell you," she says. "You'll never guess. Cecily is going to have a baby!"

In the weeks that follow, Linden devotes so much time to Cecily that I become the invisible bride again. I know this lack of attention is bad for my escape plan, but I can't help feeling a little less burdened without his constant presence, at least for now. When Gabriel brings breakfast to my room, he and I are free to talk once again. He's the only attendant bringing meals to the wives' floor, so he brings me breakfast early, while my sister wives are asleep, although Cecily's sleep pattern has become more erratic as her pregnancy progresses.

Spending time with Gabriel is nothing like the obligatory time spent with my husband. I can be honest with Gabriel. I can tell him that I miss Manhattan, which had once seemed to me like the biggest place in the world, but now feels as distant as a star.

"There used to be more boroughs dividing the city—Brooklyn, I think, and Queens, and a few others. But they called it all Manhattan after they added the lighthouses and new harbors, and they labeled the boroughs by their purpose. Mine is factories and shipping. To the west is fishing, and to the east is mostly residences."

"Why?" Gabriel asks, biting into a piece of toast from my breakfast tray. He's sitting on the ottoman, by the window, and the morning light brightens the ring of blue around his pupils.

"Don't know." I roll onto my stomach and rest my chin on my arms. "Maybe it got too confusing trying to keep all those boroughs straight; they're mostly industrialized, aside from the residences. Maybe the president couldn't bother to learn the difference."

"Sounds stifling," he says.

"A little," I admit, "but the buildings are hundreds of years old, some of them. When I was little, I used to pretend I was leaving my front door and stepping into the past. I used to pretend . . ." My voice trails off. I trace my finger along the seam of my blanket.

"What?" Gabriel asks, leaning toward me.

"I've never said it out loud before," I say, just now realizing it. "But I used to pretend I was going out into the twenty-first century, and I'd see people who were all different ages, and I'd get to grow up and be just like them." There's a long silence, and I keep my eyes on the seam because suddenly it's difficult to look at Gabriel. But I can feel him looking at me. And after a few seconds he comes to the edge of my bed; I feel the mattress dip slightly under his weight.

"Forget it," I say, trying to manage a laugh. "It's dumb."

"No," he says. "It's not."

His finger trails after mine, along the blanket, making a straight line up and down, our hands not quite touching. A flood of warmth rushes through me, creating a smile I can't avoid. There will be no adulthood for me, I know that, and it's been a long time since I've even pretended. I could never share this fantasy with my parents; it would have saddened them. Or with my brother; he would have called it pointless. And so I kept it to myself, forced myself to outgrow it. But now, watching Gabriel's hand move alongside my own as though we're playing a game with a set rhythm and method, I let the fantasy return. One day I'll step outside of this mansion, and there will be the world. The healthy, thriving world, with a beautiful path to the rest of my long life.

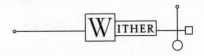

"You should see it," I say. "The city, I mean."

His voice is soft. "I'd like that."

There's a knock at my closed door, and Cecily's voice asks, "Is Linden in there with you? He was supposed to bring me some hot chocolate."

"No," I say.

"But I hear voices," she says. "Who's with you?"

Gabriel stands, and I smooth out the blankets as he picks up my breakfast tray from the dressing table.

"Try paging the kitchen," I tell her. "Maybe someone there knows where he is. Or try Elle."

She hesitates, knocks again. "Can I come in?"

I sit up, quickly throw the blankets across the mattress, and smooth out the wrinkles, fluff up the pillows. I haven't done anything wrong, but now I suddenly feel strange about her discovering Gabriel in my room. I cross the room and open the door. "What do you want?" I say.

She pushes past me, stares at Gabriel, sizing him up with her brown eyes.

"I'd better get these dishes to the kitchen," he says awkwardly. I try to give him an apologetic look over Cecily's shoulder, but he won't acknowledge me. He'll barely even look up from his shoes.

"Well, then, bring up some hot chocolate," Cecily says. "Extra, extra hot, and don't put marshmallows in it. You always do that, and they get all melted and gross because it takes you so long to bring it upstairs. Put marshmallows in a bowl on the side. No, bring a whole bag."

He nods, moves past us. Cecily peers out into the hallway until the elevator doors have closed behind Gabriel. Then she spins to face me. "Why was your door closed?"

"None of your business," I snap. I realize how suspicious that sounds, but I can't help it. Talking to Gabriel is one of the few luxuries I have. My sister wife has no right, and yet every right, to take it away.

I sit on the ottoman and pretend to arrange the hair accessories in the top drawer, fuming.

"He's just an attendant," Cecily says, walking the length of my room and tracing her finger along the wall. "And he's stupid, anyway. He never brings enough cream or sugar with the tea, and it takes him so long to bring my meals that the food's always cold by the time—"

"He's not stupid," I interrupt. "You just like to complain."

"Complain?" she splutters. "Complain? *You're* not the one throwing up breakfast every morning. *You're* not the one trapped in bed all day because of this stupid pregnancy. I do not think I'm asking for too much when I expect the stupid attendants to do their job, which is to bring me whatever I want." She drops onto my mattress and folds her arms in defiance. Point made.

From this angle I can see the slight bump coming up under her nightgown. And vaguely I can smell something like vomit under whatever perfume she's wearing. Her hair is disheveled, her skin pale. And, loathe as I am to admit it, I understand her sour mood. She's going through more than a girl her age should.

"Here," I say, reaching into my drawer and handing her one of the red candies Deirdre gave me on my wedding day. "This will settle your stomach a little."

She takes it and pops it into her mouth with an "mm" of satisfaction.

"And giving birth is going to hurt, you know," she says. "I might even die."

"You won't die," I say, forcing away the thought that Linden's mother died in childbirth.

"But I might," she says. All the challenge has left her voice. She sounds almost afraid as she looks at the candy wrapper in her hand. "So they should get me whatever I want."

I sit beside her and put my arm around her. She settles her head against my shoulder. "Okay," I agree. "You should get whatever you want. But you catch more flies with honey than with vinegar, you know."

"What does that mean?"

"It's something my mother used to say," I tell her. "It means that if you're nice to people, they'll be happier to do things for you. Maybe even do a little extra."

"Is that why you're so nice to him?" she says.

"Who?"

"That attendant. You're always talking to him."

"Maybe," I say. I feel my cheeks starting to burn. Thankfully Cecily isn't looking at me. "I'm just being nice, I guess."

"You shouldn't be so nice," she says. "It gives the wrong impression."

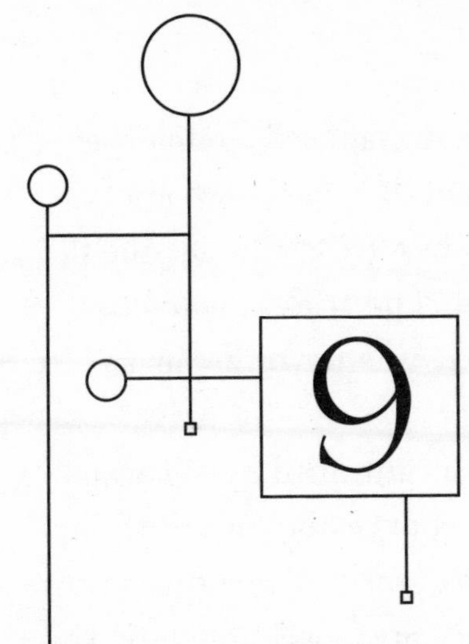

LINDEN is so delighted about the pregnancy, and the mood of the house is so bright, that he offers all of us the freedom to tour the house and the gardens. When I'm alone, I look for the road through the trees to the outside world, but I can never find so much as a path. Housemaster Vaughn leaves the property sometimes to do work at his hospital, but the lawn must be treated somehow to resist tire marks because I've never seen any leading out of the garage. Gabriel called this place eternity and I'm beginning to think he's right. No beginning, no end. And no matter where I go, I always somehow end up back at the mansion.

My father used to tell me stories of carnivals. He called them celebrations for when there was nothing to celebrate. When he was a child, he could go to a carnival and pay ten dollars to walk through a house of mirrors. He described it many times—warped mirrors that made him too tall or too short; mirrors juxtaposed so that they looked like infinite portals. He said that the house always looked like it went on forever, when from the outside it was really as small as a toolshed. The trick was looking past the illusion, because the exit was never as far as it seemed.

I hadn't understood what he meant until now. I wander the rose garden, the tennis courts, the labyrinth of shrubbery, trying to channel his spirit. I imagine him looking down on me, watching my speck of a body searching aimlessly when all the while the exit is just beyond my fingertips.

"Help me figure this out," I tell him. The only answer is a wind through the tall grass as I stand in the orange grove. I've never been good at solving puzzles; my brother is the one who solved the Rubik's Cube on the first try. He's the one who took an interest in the science of things, asking our father questions about the destroyed countries while I was busy admiring the pictures.

I imagine my brother emerging from between the orange trees. "You shouldn't have answered that ad," he'd say. "You never listen to me. What am I going to do with you?" He'd take my hand. We'd go home.

"Rowan . . ." His name spills out of me with a hot wave of tears. Nothing answers me but the breeze. He isn't coming; there's no path on earth that would lead him to me.

When my failed plights become too disheartening, I take a break and succumb to the things that make my prison more enjoyable. I dive into the artificial sea within the pool. An attendant shows me how to use the dial that changes the hologram, and I can swim beneath arctic glaciers or navigate the sunken *Titanic.* I meander alongside bottlenose dolphins. Afterward, dripping wet and smelling of chlorine, Jenna and I lie in the grass and sip colorful drinks with pineapple slices on the rims. We play mini-golf on a course that I suppose was built for Linden when he was a child, or maybe his dead brother before him. We don't keep score, and it's a joint effort to defeat the spinning clown at the last hole. We try playing tennis but give up and make a game of shooting tennis balls at the wall, since that's all we seem to be good at.

In the kitchen I can eat all the June Beans I want. I sit on the kitchen counter, helping Gabriel peel potatoes, and listening to the cooks talk about the weather and how they'd like to serve the bratty little bride a dirty sock. Gabriel, as good-natured as he is, agrees that Cecily has been particularly awful lately. Someone suggests frying up a rat for her lunch, and the head cook says, "Watch your tongue. There are no rats in my kitchen."

Linden feels that he's neglecting Jenna and me, and he asks if we'd like anything—anything at all. I almost ask for a crate of June Beans, because I heard the kitchen staff complaining about early-morning deliveries, and since then I've been fantasizing about escaping on a delivery truck. But then I think of all the progress I've made earning Linden's trust, and how easily it would be destroyed if I were caught, which is highly possible, considering Vaughn knows everything that happens in this place.

Jenna says, "I'd like a big trampoline." And the next morning there it is in the rose garden. We jump until our lungs hurt, and then we lie in the center of it and watch the clouds for a while.

"This isn't the worst place to die," she confesses. Then she props herself on her elbow, which causes my body to slide more toward her, and she asks me, "Has he come to your bed at all lately?"

"No," I say, and fold my hands behind my head. "It's nice to have it to myself again."

"Rhine?" she says. "When he came to you, it wasn't . . . for children."

"No," I say. "It was never that. He hasn't even kissed me."

"I wonder why," she says, lying back down.

"Has he come to you at all?" I ask.

"Yes," she says. "A few times, before all his attention started going to Cecily."

This surprises me. I think back to Jenna's reliable morning routine of taking tea in the library and burying her nose in romance novels. There hasn't been a single morning when she has seemed rumpled or out of sorts, especially not the way Cecily was. And even now, she seems very cool about the whole thing.

"What was it like?" I ask, and immediately a hot blush spreads across my face. Did I really just ask that?

"Not terrible," is Jenna's nonchalant reply. "He kept asking if I was okay. Like he thought I'd break or something." She laughs a little at the thought. "If I was going to break, he wouldn't be the one to do it."

I'm not sure how to respond to that. The very thought of Linden kissing me sets my nerves on edge, puts my stomach in knots. And yet both of my sister wives have done much more than kiss him, and one is even carrying his child.

"I thought you hated him," I finally say.

"Of course I do," she says. Her voice is a gentle hum. She crosses her ankle over her pointed knee and swings her foot casually. "I've hated all of them. But this is the world we live in."

"All of them?" I say.

She sits up and looks at me, her face a mix of confusion, pity, and maybe amusement. "Really?" she says, and cups my chin in her hand, inspecting me. Her skin is soft, and it smells like the lotions Deirdre lays out for me on the dressing table. "You're so pretty, and you have such a nice figure," she says. "How were you earning money?"

I sit up too, as I realize what she's asking me. "You thought I was a prostitute?" I say.

"Well, no," she says. "You seemed too sweet for that. But I just assumed—how else could girls like us get by?"

I think of all the girls who dance in the park at New Year's parties, how some of them will slip into a car with a wealthy first generation. And all the brothels in the scarlet district with blacked-out windows. Sometimes a door would open as I passed by, and I'd hear the burst of pulsing music, see a flicker of rainbow lights. I think of how deftly Jenna danced that night in the orange grove, and how charismatic she was to these men she despised. Her life was in one of those dark and secret places I'd barely had the courage to walk past on the sidewalk.

"I thought the orphanage would have provided you with enough to get by," I say. But I realize immediately that that can't be true. Rowan and I deterred enough orphans from stealing from us. We wouldn't have had to if orphanages had provided for them.

Jenna lies back down, and I lie beside her. "You're serious?" she says. "So you've never . . ."

"No," I say, a tad defensively. In my mind Jenna begins to materialize in a new light. But I don't judge her. I don't blame her. Like she said, it's the world we live in.

"Well, I don't know why he hasn't come to you," she says. "I get the sense there's a reason for everything that happens here."

"I don't get it," I say. "If you hate him so much, why not refuse? Linden is so mild, I can't imagine him forcing himself on any of us."

Though, it has worried me more than once that Linden has not pressed the issue of consummating our marriage. Has he sensed my hesitation and allowed me the luxury of time? How long before his patience is gone?

She turns to face me, and I can swear there is fear in her gray eyes for a moment. "It's not him I'm worried about," she says.

"Who?" I blink. "Housemaster Vaughn?"

She nods.

I think of Rose's body in the basement. All those ominous hallways that could lead to anywhere. And I sense that Jenna, who is such a keen observer, has found her own reasons in this place to be afraid. The question hangs heavy on my tongue: Jenna, what has Housemaster Vaughn done to you?

But I'm too afraid of the answer. The image of Rose's hand under that sheet sends a cold ripple up my spine. There are ugly, dangerous things lurking beneath the beauty of this mansion. And I'd like to be far away from here before ever knowing what they are.

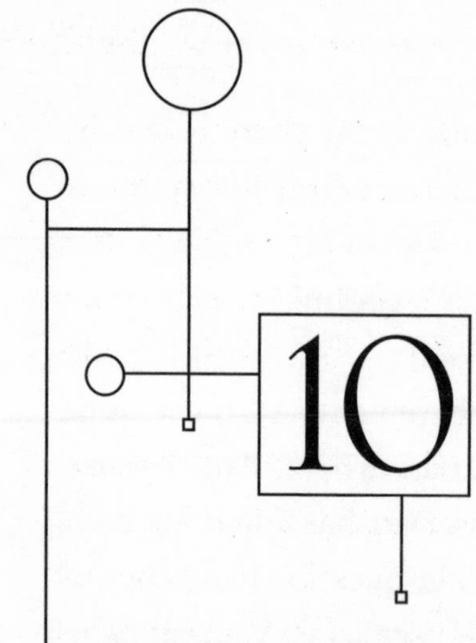

IT SEEMS THAT leaves are always bursting with new colors. I've been here for six months. I avoid Housemaster Vaughn when I can. And at dinner when he regales me in banter about the meal or the weather, I try to smile like his voice isn't sending cockroaches up and down my spine.

Linden finds me one afternoon while I'm alone in the orange grove, lying in the grass, and I'm not sure if he was looking for me or if he meant to be here alone. I smile at him and tell myself I'm glad he's here. Now that most of his attention goes to my younger sister wife, I've had little opportunity to earn his favor. We're alone in his dead wife's favorite place, and I sense an opportunity to bond with him.

I pat the ground beside me in invitation, and he lies in the grass. We're both silent as a breeze moves over us.

Rose still lingers in the trees; the rustling leaves are

her ethereal laughter. Linden follows my gaze to the sky.

For a while we say nothing. I listen to the rhythm of his breaths, and ignore the nearly imperceptible flutter in my chest brought on by his presence. The back of his hand just barely brushes mine. An orange blossom falls over us on a perfect diagonal.

"I'm dreading fall. It is a terrifying season," he says finally. "Everything shriveling up and dying."

I don't know how to answer. Fall has always been my favorite season. The time when everything bursts with its last beauty, as if nature had been saving up all year for the grand finale. I've never thought to be frightened of it. My greatest fear is another year of my life passing by while I'm so far from home.

Suddenly the clouds seem very high above us. They're moving over us in an arch, circling the planet. They have seen abysmal oceans and charred, scorched islands. They have seen how we destroyed the world. If I could see everything, as the clouds do, would I swirl around this remaining continent, still so full of color and life and seasons, wanting to protect it? Or would I just laugh at the futility of it all, and meander onward, down the earth's sloping atmosphere?

Linden takes in another breath, and he musters up the courage to put his hand over mine. I don't resist. Everything in Linden Ashby's world is fake, an illusion, but the sky and the orange blossoms are real. His body beside me is real.

"What are you thinking?" he asks me. For all of our marriage I have never allowed myself to be honest with him, but here, now, I want to tell him what's on my mind.

"I was wondering if we're worth saving," I say.

"What do you mean?"

I shake my head against the ground, feel the back of my skull rolling along the cold, hard earth. "It's nothing."

"Not nothing," he says. "What did you mean?" His voice isn't intrusive. It's gentle, curious.

"It's just all these doctors and engineers are looking for an antidote," I say. "They've been at it for years. But is it really worth it? Can we even be fixed?"

Linden is quiet for a while, and just when I'm sure he's going to condemn me for what I've said or, I don't know, defend the work of his madman father, he squeezes my hand. "I've asked myself the same question," he says.

"Really?" We turn at the same time and meet each other's eyes, but I feel my cheeks starting to burn, and I look back to the sky.

"I thought I was going to die, once," he says. "When I was young. I had a high fever. I remember my father gave me an injection that was supposed to cure it—something experimental he'd been working on, of course, but it only aggravated things."

Vaughn could have been pumping any number of his twisted experiments into his son's veins, for all I trust him, but I don't say this. Linden continues, "For days I was in some halfway land between reality and delirium. Everything seemed so frightening, and I couldn't wake myself up. But from someplace far away I could hear my father and some of his doctors calling me. 'Linden. Linden, come back to us. Open your eyes.' And I remember that I hesitated. I didn't know if I should go back. I didn't know if I wanted to live in a world of certain death. Of fevers and nightmares."

There's a long silence, and then I say, "But you came back."

"Yes," he says. And then, very quietly, "But that wasn't my decision."

He weaves his fingers through mine, and I allow it, feel the clammy warmth of his palm against mine. Flush. Alive. Eventually I realize that I am holding on to him just as tightly as he holds on to me. And here we are: two small dying things, as the world ends around us like falling autumn leaves.

Cecily's little stomach begins to swell. She's often bedridden, but she's louder than ever, according to the attendants.

I'm eating an ice cream cone and watching the koi in the pond one afternoon when an attendant comes running for me. He stops and puts his hands on his knees, doubling over to catch his breath. "Come quick," he gasps. "Lady Cecily is asking for you. Some kind of emergency."

"Well, is she all right?" I say. To look at him you'd

think somebody had died. He shakes his head in response. He doesn't know. I think I hand him my ice cream cone as I run for the door. Gabriel is already waiting at the elevator with his key card. Upstairs I run into her bedroom, thinking it will be Rose all over again, thinking I will find her coughing blood or fighting to breathe.

She's propped upright on pillows, her toes separated by pieces of foam while the nail polish dries. She smiles at me with a straw in her mouth. She's sipping cranberry juice.

"What's the matter?" I say, panting.

"Tell me a story," she says.

"What?"

"You and Jenna are having all the fun without me." She pouts. Her stomach floats in front of her like a little quarter-moon. She isn't very far along—four months—but what I know and she doesn't is that Linden does not want to risk losing another baby. He will spare no precaution. She may be well enough to play mini-golf or even swim in the pool, which is heated and treated to repel leaves and insects this time of year, but she has become the greatest captive here.

"What do you do all day?" she asks.

"We have lots of fun," I snap, because she worried me for nothing. "We eat cotton candy and somersault in midair on the trampoline. Shame you can't come out."

"What else?" She pats the mattress beside her, her eyes eager. "No, wait. Tell me about another place. What was your orphanage like?"

Of course she would think I grew up in an orphanage. That's all her short life has showed her of the world.

I sit cross-legged on her mattress and push the hair from her eyes. "I didn't grow up in an orphanage," I say. "I grew up in a city. With millions of people, and buildings so tall you'd get dizzy trying to see the tops of them."

She's dazzled. And so I tell her about the ferries and the toxic fish that are caught for sport and returned to the sea. I remove myself from the stories and instead tell her about a pair of twins, a brother and a sister, who grew up in a house where someone was always playing the piano. There were peppermints and parents and bedtime stories. The blankets all smelled like mothballs and, vaguely, their mother's best perfume, from when she'd lean in to kiss them good night.

"Are they still there?" she asks me. "Did they grow up?"

"They grew up," I tell her. "But a hurricane came one day, and they were each blown to a different side of the country. And now they've been separated."

She looks doubtful. "A hurricane blew them away? That's dumb."

"I swear it's true," I say.

"And it didn't kill them?"

"That part may be a blessing or a curse," I say. "But they are both still alive, trying to find their way back to each other."

"What about their mom and dad?" she says.

I take her empty juice cup from the night table. "I'll go get you a fresh drink," I say.

"Don't. That's not your job." She pushes the blue button over her night table and says, "Cranberry juice. And waffles. With syrup. And an umbrella toothpick!"

"Please," I add, because I know they're all rolling their eyes at her, and it really is only a matter of time before someone blows their nose into her napkin.

"I liked that story," she says. "Is it really true? Do you really know those twins?"

"Yes," I say. "And their little house is waiting for them to return. It has a broken fire escape, and it used to be covered in flowers. But that city isn't like this place. The chemicals from factories make it very hard for things to grow. Only their mother was able to grow lilies, because she had a magic touch, and when she died, they all wilted. That was that."

"That was that," she echoes in agreement.

I leave her when it's time for her ultrasound. Gabriel catches my arm in the hallway. "Was the story all true?" he says.

"Yes," I say.

"So how long do you think it'll be?" he says. "Before the next hurricane comes along to take you home."

"Can I tell you my biggest fear?" I say.

"Yes. Tell me."

"That it will be a very windless four years."

It isn't windless, though. By late October we have

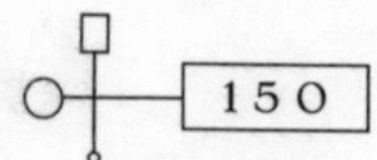

severe weather patterns. In the kitchen there are bets on what category the first hurricane will be. Three is most popular. Gabriel thinks two, because it is a weird time of year for such a thing. I just agree with him because I have no idea what I'm talking about. We don't have very dramatic weather in Manhattan. Whenever the wind is bad, I ask, "Is this a hurricane? Is this?" and the kitchen laughs at me. Gabriel assures me I'll know.

The pool water thrashes, and I think it might get sucked into the air. The trees and bushes convulse. Oranges roll as though being kicked along by ghosts. There are leaves everywhere, red, and brown-splattered yellow. When nobody is around, I gather the leaves into piles and bury myself. I breathe in the dampness of them. I feel like a little girl again. I stay hidden until the wind takes them away in spiraling ribbons. "I want to go with you," I say.

One afternoon I return to my bedroom and find that my window has been opened. A present Linden left for me to find. I test it—it opens and closes. I sit on the sill and smell the wet earth, the cold wind that strips everything clean, and I think of stories my parents told me about their childhood. At the turn of the new century, when the world was safe, they had a holiday called Halloween. They would go out in groups of friends dressed as hideous things and ring doorbells, asking for candy. My father's favorite kind, he said, looked like little traffic cones with yellow tips.

Jenna, whose window remains locked, comes to my room and presses her nose to the screen and breathes deeply, traveling to kind memories of her own. She tells me that on days like this the orphanage would serve hot chocolate. She and her two sisters would share a mug, and they'd all have chocolate mustaches.

Cecily's window is also left locked, and when she objects, Linden says the draft will be too much for her in her fragile state. "Fragile state," she mutters to me once he has left. "I'll put him in a fragile state if I can't get out of this bed soon." But she does like the attention. He sleeps beside her most nights, and he helps her improve her reading and writing. He feeds her éclairs and rubs her feet. When she coughs, there are doctors tripping over themselves to check her lungs.

But she is healthy. She's strong. She's not Rose. And she's restless. On an afternoon when Linden isn't doting so heavily on her, Jenna and I close Cecily's bedroom door, and Jenna teaches us to dance. We don't have Jenna's grace, but that's part of the fun. And in that fun, I can forget how Jenna became such an adept dancer.

"Oh!" Cecily cries, cutting short her clumsy pirouette. I think she's going to collapse again, or start bleeding, but she bounces on her heels and says, "It kicked, it kicked!" She grabs our hands and presses them to her stomach, under her shirt.

As though in response, a terrible wailing alarm fills the room. A red light we didn't know existed begins to flash from the ceiling, and I look out the window and notice that the tree with the robin's nest has fallen over.

Our domestics come to hustle us into the basement, with Cecily in tears because she doesn't want to be in a wheelchair when her legs work just fine. Linden isn't hearing what she's saying, partly but not entirely due to the alarms, and he holds her hand and says, "You're safe with me, love."

The elevator opens to the basement, and everyone steps out. Linden, Housemaster Vaughn, Jenna, Cecily, and our domestics. But not Gabriel, and he's the only one who knows how frightened I am of this place. And the alarms are so loud. I imagine the noise rattling the cold metal table where Rose's body lies. I imagine her being shaken back to life, stitched and rotting and a sickly shade of green. I imagine her dragging herself toward me, hating me, knowing I'm plotting to escape. She'll bury me alive if that's what it takes to keep me here by Linden's side, because he's the love of her life and she will not let him die alone.

"Are you okay?" Jenna says, and for some reason her soft voice in my ear is clearer than the alarms. I realize she's holding my hand, which is full of sweat. I nod dazedly.

Once the elevator doors close behind us, the alarm stops. The silence says that everyone is safe. Well, everyone that Linden thinks is important. The kitchen staff and all the attendants, as promised, are still working about the mansion. If the worst happens and they're sucked into the ether, they can be replaced. Housemaster Vaughn can put in a low bid on good orphans.

As we're walking down the hallway of horrors, I ask, "When will dinner be served?"

What I'm really asking is: Where is Gabriel?

Housemaster Vaughn chuckles. It's such an ugly sound. He says, "All this one can think about is food. I suppose if we're all in one piece tonight, dinner will be at seven as usual, darling."

I smile charmingly, blush like his teasing makes me feel like a happy little daughter-in-law. I want him to get blown away. I want him to stand alone in the kitchen while knives and pans spin around in the hurricane winds and plates smash at his feet. And then I want for the roof to be ripped away, and for him to be pulled up, getting smaller and smaller until he's nothing.

We come to a room that is warmly lit, with overstuffed chairs like the ones in the library, and divans and canopy beds with gauzy lilac and white netting. Comfy cozy. There are windows with images of fake tranquil landscapes. The air comes in through vents in the ceiling. Cecily harrumphs and gets out of her wheelchair, brushing Linden off as she explores the chess table. "Is it some kind of game?" she asks.

"You mean a bright girl like yourself has never been taught the cultural art of chess?" Housemaster Vaughn says.

If Cecily wasn't interested in playing a moment ago,

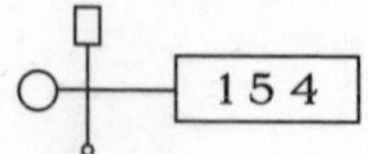

she is now. She wants to be cultured as much as she wants to be sexy and well read. She wants to be all the things a young girl is not. "Teach me?" she asks as she takes a seat.

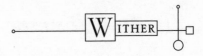

"Absolutely, darling."

Jenna, who hates Housemaster Vaughn even more than she hates our husband, pulls the netting closed around a bed and takes a nap. The domestics are talking dresses and sewing notions; they can't do much for us down here, but I suppose Housemaster Vaughn thinks they will be handy if the mansion is destroyed and we still need someone to knit our blankets and darn our socks. Linden sits on the divan surrounded in papers and architecture magazines he's brought along to amuse himself, with a pencil in his hand.

I sit next to him, and he doesn't notice me until I ask, "What are you drawing?"

His dark eyelashes are downcast, like he's considering whether what's on the page is worth my time. Then he holds it up to show me, and it's a delicate pencil sketch of a Victorian house flourishing with flowers and ivy. But under all that, there's a stable structure. Solid beams on the porch, strong-looking windows. I can even see inside to outlines of floors, and doors with clothes hanging on the knob. I can see that a family lives inside. There's a pie on the window ledge, and a woman's hands are either placing it there or retrieving it. The house is at an angle, so I can see two of its outer walls. A swing in the yard looks like it has just been in motion; its child has leapt off the edge of the page. There's a bowl in the grass, where a dog will take a drink after it returns from a walk around the neighborhood, or a nap in a neighbor's flower bed.

"Wow," I exhale, without meaning to.

He brightens a little, and then clears the papers away so I can sit closer to him. "It's just an idea I had," he says. "My father thinks I shouldn't draw families inside the houses. He says nobody will want to buy a design unless it's clean and they can only see themselves living there."

As always, his father is wrong.

"I would live there," I say. Our shoulders are touching; this is closer than we've ever come outside of my bed.

"It helps me to draw someone inside the house," he says. "It gives it a kind of, I don't know, soul."

He shows me more of his houses. A flat one-story ranch with a sleeping cat on the porch, towering office buildings with gleaming windows that make me think of home, garages and gazebos, and a lone store that pops out of a blurry strip mall. And I'm stunned, not just by the precision of his lines, but by the immediacy of him beside me, excitedly pointing to things and explaining his process. I would not have imagined that he had this kind of energy. This kind of deftness and talent.

He's always seemed too sad to do anything but wallow. Not everything in his world is what it seems. His designs command attention. They are beautiful and strong. Meant to last a natural lifetime, like the home where I grew up.

“I used to sell lots of designs before . . . ,” he says, not finishing the thought. We both know why he stopped designing. Rose fell ill. “I used to oversee the construction, too. Watch the drawings come to life.”

“Why don’t you go back to it?” I say.

“There’s no time.”

“There’s plenty of time.”

Well, four years. A meager lifetime. The look in his eyes makes me think he’s had the same thought.

He smiles at me, and I can’t read what it means. I think, for just a second there, he looked up and saw heterochromatic me. Not a dead girl. Not even a ghost.

He brings his hand to my face, and I feel his fingertips brushing my jaw, his fingers uncurling like something coming to bloom. He looks serious and soft. He’s closer than he was a second ago, and I feel myself being pulled into his gravity, and for some reason I feel like I want to trust him. I’m in his house-building hands, and I want to trust him. My lower lip goes slack, waiting for his to catch it.

“I want to see your drawings too!” Cecily says, and my eyes fly open. I draw my hand away from the crook of Linden’s elbow, where it had somehow become wedged. I look away from him, and there is Cecily, pregnant and sucking on a piece of caramel that fills her whole left cheek. I scoot over and let her sit between us, and Linden patiently shows her his designs.

She doesn’t understand why the rope on the tire swing

is broken, or why there's a solstice wreath on the front door of the empty shop. And soon enough, she's bored with the whole thing, I can tell, but she keeps making conversation about his designs because she has his attention and won't relinquish it.

I climb into the canopy with Jenna, closing the gauze behind me.

"Are you asleep?" I whisper.

"No," she whispers back. "Do you realize he almost just kissed you?"

As always, she has been observing. She turns to face me, and her eyes search me over. "Don't forget how you got here," she says. "Don't forget."

"No, never," I say.

But she's right.

For a moment I almost did.

I fall asleep, and the voices of the storm cellar become far away. I dream of everyone I hear. Cecily is a little ladybug in a plaid skirt, and Housemaster Vaughn is a large cricket with cartoon eyes. "Listen to me, darling," he tells her, wrapping his fuzzy arm around her shell. "Your husband has two other wives. Your sisters. You must not interrupt them."

"But!" Her cartoon eyes well with petulance and sorrow. She's sucking on a caramel.

"There, there," he says. "Jealousy looks so ugly on your pretty face. How about you and your father-in-law play some chess?"

She is his pet. His pregnant, faithful little pet.

Bishop to F5. Knight to E3.

Outside, the winds are roaring, and over and over I hear the words: *It will be the very coldest day in hell . . .*

The very coldest day in hell . . .

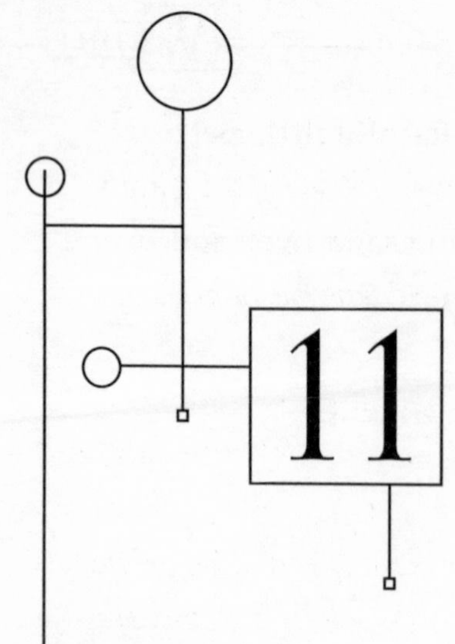

11

THE HOUSE doesn't blow away. Aside from a few broken trees, the world returns to normal.

Gabriel finds me lying in a pile of leaves. I sense his presence standing over me and open my eyes. He's holding a thermos. "I brought you some hot chocolate," he says. "Your nose is all red."

"So are your fingers," I say. Red like the falling leaves. His breath comes out in clouds. In all this autumn, his eyes are very blue.

"There's a bug," he says, nodding toward my head. I look and see some little winged thing jump and crawl along my blond hair. I blow gently, and it's gone.

"I'm glad you didn't get blown away," I say, and as I'd hoped, he takes this as a cue to sit beside me.

"That house is something like a thousand years old," he says, uncapping the thermos. The lid becomes a cup and he pours me some hot chocolate. I sit up and accept it, inhaling the sugary warmth for a while. He drinks straight from the thermos, and I watch his Adam's apple move under his skin. "It's not going anywhere."

I look at the brick mansion in the distance, and I know he's telling the truth.

"So did you win the bet?" I say, sipping my hot chocolate. It burns my tongue and turns a patch of it to sandpaper. "Was it a category two?"

"A three," he says. His lips are chapped, like mine, nothing like Linden's, and I think we are two unwitting prisoners out here in this barren garden. This garden that's gone to sleep for the coming winter.

"I don't love him," I say.

"What?" he says.

"Linden. I don't love him. I don't even like to be in the same room as him. I just wanted you to know that."

He won't look at me, suddenly. He takes another sip, and this time he throws his head back to get the final dregs of hot chocolate. There's a little arch of chocolate left over his lip.

"I just wanted you to know," I say again.

"It's good to know," he says, and nods.

When our eyes meet, we both grin, and then we laugh, tentatively at first, like peeking out to be sure it's safe, and then more confidently. I snort, and throw my hand over my mouth, too hysterical to be embarrassed. I don't know what's funny or if anything even is. I just know it feels really good.

I wish we could spend more time like this, even if all we can do is walk and kick up some dead leaves as we go. But when we get up and start walking automatically toward the house, I remember that we're both prisoners. He can only talk to me if he's bringing me something, and then it's back to the kitchen, back to polishing the woodwork, back to vacuuming the infinite rugs. I guess that's why he brought the hot chocolate.

The closer we get to the house, the more faint the sweet taste becomes. The burned sandpaper part of my tongue spreads. The soft cloudy sky begins to look ominous. The dead leaves scuttle away as though in fear.

Just as Gabriel reaches for the doorknob, the door opens. Housemaster Vaughn greets us with a smile. The kitchen behind his shoulder is quiet, aside from the necessary sounds of things being prepared and cleaned. None of the usual chatter.

"I asked him to bring me hot chocolate," I say.

"Of course, darling," Housemaster Vaughn says. "I can see that." He looks like a kind geriatric when he smiles at us. I feel Gabriel tense up beside me, and I am fighting a strange impulse to hold his hand, to let him know I'm just as afraid even if I don't show it.

"Why don't you return to your duties, then," Housemaster Vaughn tells Gabriel. He doesn't need to be told twice; he melts into the kitchen and becomes part of the work noise.

I'm left to face this man alone. "It's such a nice cool

day. The air is refreshing on these old lungs of mine," he says, patting his chest. "I don't suppose you'll take a walk with your father-in-law?" It's not really a question. We walk away from the house and between the ponds in the rose garden. Jenna's trampoline is covered in dead and dying leaves.

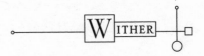

I do my best to ignore this man who has threaded his arm through mine, who smells like tweed and aftershave and the basement I so fear. I leave Florida for a while. I think about the leaves in Manhattan in the fall. There aren't very many trees—the chemical factories have taken their luster. But on a windy day, the scant leaves gather into crowds and fall all at once, giving the illusion of more. The memory helps me to make it through the rose garden without hyperventilating.

Just when I'm thinking I'll be able to get through this without having to speak, we come to the mini-golf course and Housemaster Vaughn says, "There's an expression we old people have. 'The apple of one's eye.' Have you heard it?"

"No," I say. I am intrigued. I am fearless.

You're a good liar, Rhine. You can get through this.

"Well, you, darling, are the apple of Linden's eye." He gives my shoulders an affectionate squeeze. I feel my heart and lungs constricting. "You're his favorite, you know."

I am demure. "I didn't think he noticed me," I say. "He's so fond of Cecily." Though, truthfully, Linden's attention has started to shift toward me. Especially in the basement when he almost kissed me. I still haven't figured out if it's my resemblance to Rose that interests him, or something else.

"He adores Cecily, as do I. She's eager to please. It's charming, really." Cecily is a little girl who never had a childhood, who wants so badly to fit into this role that she'll do anything our husband asks. "But she's young. She has much to learn. Wouldn't you agree?" He doesn't wait for me to answer. "And the older one, Jenna, she fulfills her duties, but she doesn't have an ounce of your charm. She's something of a cold fish, isn't she? If I had my way, we would just toss her back into the water." His fingers flutter dramatically in the air. "But Linden insists we keep her. He thinks she'll come around and conceive a child. He always was a little too compassionate."

Some compassion. He killed her sisters.

"She's just a little shy," I say. "She cares for him. She's afraid of saying the wrong thing. She tells me all the time she can't work up the courage to speak to him." None of this is true, but I hope it will keep Vaughn from tossing her back into the water. Whatever he means by that, I'm sure it's not something I want to happen to her.

"And then there's you," Vaughn says, not seeming to have heard me. "Intelligent. So lovely." We stop walking, and he strokes my chin between his thumb and index finger. "I've seen the way he brightens when you're near him."

I blush, which wasn't supposed to be part of the act.

"He's even thinking of joining the human race again. He's talking about returning to work." Housemaster Vaughn's smile seems almost sincere. He puts his arm around me again, and we walk through the golf obstacles. Grinning clowns, giant ice cream cones, spinning windmills, and a big lighthouse with a working light that shoots out into the trees.

"I had a son, many years ago, before Linden. Strong as an ox—that's another expression us first generations used to have."

"Really?" I say.

"Healthy every day of his life. This was before we realized the poisonous bomb ticking away in our children. He succumbed just like the rest of them. Just as you believe you will."

We stop, and I follow his lead and sit down on the giant gumdrop that is the seventh hole. "Linden isn't the strongest child, but he's all I have." His kind geriatric face is back. If I didn't know better, I'd pity him. But when I put my arm around him in comfort, I'm fully aware that he's not to be trusted.

"From the day of his birth, I've been working tirelessly on an antidote. I have an ever-rotating medical staff that's working in a laboratory as we speak. I will find an antidote within four years."

And if not, then what? I try to fight off a thought that Cecily's baby will become his new guinea pig after Linden and his wives are gone.

He pats my hand. "My son is going to have a healthy lifespan. And so are his wives. You will have a real lifetime. You're bringing Linden out of the darkness that Rose left him with, don't you see that? You're restoring his life. He's going to become successful again, and you'll be on his arm at every party. You'll have everything you can dream of for years and years."

I don't know why he's saying these things to me, but his presence is starting to nauseate me. Is this a concerned father looking out for his son? Or has he somehow read into my intention to escape? He's looking right into my eyes and I can't recognize him. He seems less menacing than usual.

"Do you understand what I'm saying?" he asks.

"Yes," I say. "I do."

When our parents died, our basement became hopelessly infested with rats. They were coming up from the sewers and chewing our wires and destroying our food. They were too smart for the traps we'd laid out, and so Rowan got the idea to poison them. He mixed flour, sugar, water, and baking soda and left it in puddles on the floor. I didn't think it would work, but it did. While it was my turn to keep watch one night, I saw a rat run in strange circles and then collapse. I could hear its little whinnying noises, could see its feeble twitching. This went on for what felt like hours before it died. Rowan's experiment was a gruesome success.

Housemaster Vaughn is giving me a choice. Here I

can live in this house where he's dissecting Linden's dead wife and child for an antidote that doesn't exist. Here I can die in four years and our bodies will all be experiments. But for four brief years I'll be the dazzling wife at ritzy parties, and that will be my reward. I'll still die like the rat, in agony.

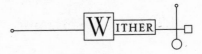

I think of Vaughn's words for the rest of the day. He smiles at me across the dinner table. I think of the dead rat.

But by nightfall I force Vaughn's menacing voice out of my mind. Lately I have been promising myself that once I'm in bed, I will think only of my home—how to return to it, and what it looks like. What my life was before coming to this place.

Nobody in this mansion is allowed into these thoughts, except for when I remind myself that Linden, even with his mild manner, is the enemy. He has stolen me from my twin, my home, and he keeps me for his own.

So at night, when I'm alone, I think of my brother, who from the time we were children had a habit of standing in front of me, as though any terrible danger would have to hit him before it could reach me. I think of how he looked, gun in hand, after he shot that Gatherer and saved my life; the terror in his eyes at the thought of losing me. I think of how we have always belonged to each other, our mother fitting our young hands together and telling us to hold on.

These thoughts build night after night, when I'm

most alone in this mansion of spouses and servants, and for a few hours I'm able to separate myself from this fake life. No matter how lonely it makes me, and no matter how wide and horrific the loneliness, at least I remember who I am.

And then one night, while my mind is fading into sleep, I hear Linden close my bedroom door after coming in. But he's a thousand miles from me. I'm with Rowan, setting the kite string. My mother's light laughter fills the room, and my father is playing a Mozart sonata in G major on the piano. Rowan casually unravels the string that's tangled around my fingers, and he asks me if I'm still alive. I try to laugh like what he's saying is crazy, but the sound doesn't come, and he won't raise his eyes to me.

I won't stop looking for you, he says. I won't ever stop. If it kills me, I'll find you.

"I'm right here," I say.

"You're dreaming," he says. But the voice doesn't belong to my brother. Linden has buried his face into the curve of my neck. The music is gone; my fingers fumble for string that isn't there. And I know the truth, that if I open my eyes, I'll see the dark bedroom in my lavish prison. But I don't try to free my mind of its hazy state, because the disappointment is too much to take.

I feel the dampness of Linden's tears on my skin, his shuddering gasps. And I know he has been dreaming of Rose; like me, his nights are often too lonely. He kisses my hair and wraps an arm around me. I allow it. No, I want it. Need it. Eyes closed, I lay my head to his chest for the forceful *thud-thud* of his heart.

I want to be myself, yes. Rhine Ellery. Sister, daughter. But sometimes it's too painful.

My captor pulls me toward him, and I fall asleep enveloped in the sound of his breathing.

In the morning I awaken to Linden's breath at the nape of my neck. I'm facing away from him, and he's pressed to my back with his arms around me. I lie perfectly still, not wanting to wake him, ashamed with myself for my vulnerability last night. At what point does this good wife act stop being an act? How long before he tells me he loves me, and expects me to carry his baby? And what's worse, how long before I agree?

No. That will never happen.

I try to fight it, but Vaughn's voice floods into my brain.

You'll have everything you can dream of for years and years.

I can have this. I can be Linden's bride, in Linden's mansion. Or I can run, as far and as fast as I can. And I can have a shot at dying with my freedom.

Three days later, when the next hurricane alarm begins to scream, I break through the screen in my bedroom window.

I just manage to grab on to the tree near my window ledge, and that gives me the leverage to fall into a shrub a few feet down. It hurts, but I'm unbroken. I untangle myself and I run, with the house screaming behind me, and the wind a strange shade of gray. Leaves and hair are in my eyes. I don't care. I run. The clouds are throbbing. There are sick flashes of white in the sky.

My sense of direction is gone. All I can see is dingy, angry air. And there's so much noise, and it doesn't get quieter no matter how fast or far I move. Dirt and bits of grass are rising and dancing chaotically as though enchanted.

I don't know how much time passes, but I hear my name being cried, once and then several times, like gunshots. And this is right about the time I crash into a giant ice cream cone. The golf course. Okay. I can navigate better now that I know where I am.

I don't know how far the exit is. I have been to every garden, the golf course, the tennis courts, the pool. I've even passed the horse stables, which have been abandoned since Rose's illness. But I've never seen an exit.

I press my body against the giant chocolate scoop as branches fly past me. The trees are waving and howling. The trees! If I could climb one of them, it would be easier to see farther. There has to be a fence or at least a shrub I've never seen before. A hidden door. Something.

One step, and I'm shoved back against the scoop. The air is sucked from my lungs. I drop to the ground and try to turn myself away from the wind so I can breathe, but it's everywhere. It's everywhere and I'm probably going to die right here.

I turn, gasping, to the storm. I won't even get to see the world one last time before I die. I will only see Linden's strange utopia. The spinning windmills. The strange flashing light.

Light. I think my eyes are playing tricks on me, but the light persists. It spins, shooting toward me and then continuing on its circular path. The lighthouse. My very favorite obstacle because it reminds me of the lighthouses off the Manhattan harbor, the light that brings the fishing boats home. It's still going even in this storm, throwing its light into the trees, and if I can't escape, I at least want to die beside it, because it's as close as I can get to home in this awful, awful place.

Walking is impossible now. There are too many things flying, and I actually think I might be blown away. So I crawl, jamming my elbows and toes into the Astroturf of the golf course for traction. I move away from my name being called, away from that ongoing siren, away from a sudden stabbing pain that hits me somewhere. I don't look to find out what the injury is, but there's blood. I can taste it. I can feel it pooling and dripping. I only care about not being paralyzed. I can keep moving, and I do, until I'm touching the lighthouse.

Its paint is chipped; the wood is splintered. Even though I've reached my goal, there is something about this marvelous little structure that is telling me I'm not ready to die. To keep going. But there's nowhere to go. My hands grope for a solution, for a path up to the light.

I am clinging to a ladder. Not the kind that's meant to be climbed. It's clearly for decoration, flimsy and nailed to the lighthouse's side. But it can be climbed, and my body is able to do it, and so I go. Up and up and up.

Now my hands are bleeding too. Something drips into my eye and stings. The air is being sucked out of me again. Up and up and up.

I feel as though I've been climbing forever. All night. All my life. But I make it to the top, and the light greets me by searing into my eyes. I look away from it.

I almost fall.

I'm higher than all the trees.

And I see it, far, far in the distance. Like a whisper. Like a timid little suggestion. The pointed flower from Gabriel's handkerchief, constructed into an iron gate.

It is the exit, miles from me.

It is the end of the world.

And I realize what the lighthouse was trying to tell me. That I am not supposed to die today. I am supposed to follow the path it's lighting for me—like Columbus with his *Niña*, *Pinta*, and *Santa María*—to the end of the world.

The gate in the distance is the most beautiful thing I've ever seen in my life.

I'm just starting to climb down when I hear my name again. It's too loud and too close to ignore this time.

"Rhine!"

Gabriel's blue eyes and his bright brown hair, and his

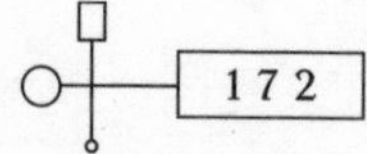

arms that are so much stronger than Linden's, are coming toward me. Not all of him, not a whole body, but pieces of him, disappearing and flickering in the wind. I see the fierce, angry red of his open mouth.

"I'm getting out!" I scream. "Come with me! Run away with me!"

But all he says is "Rhine! Rhine!" with increasing desperation, and I don't think he hears what I'm saying. He opens his arms, and I don't understand why. I don't understand what he's shouting at me until an incredible pain comes crashing to the back of my head, and I'm falling right into his open arms.

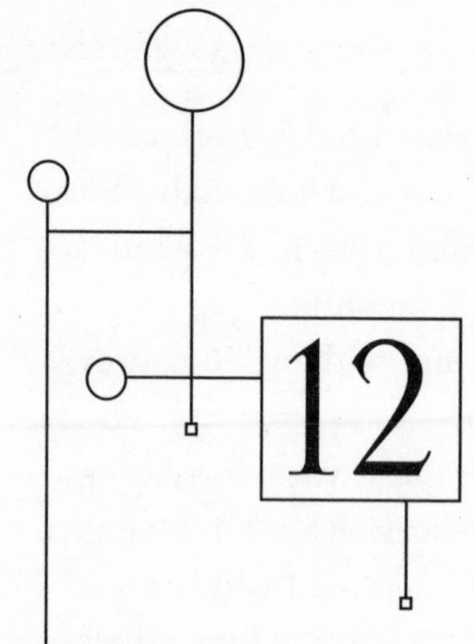

12

THE AIR IS STILL. It's quiet. I can breathe without the wind to steal air from my lungs. It's sterile and antiseptic. "Don't," I say, or try to say. I can't open my eyes. Vaughn is here. I can feel his presence. I can smell his cold metal scalpel. He's going to cut me open.

There's something warm rolling through my blood. I feel my heart beating with loud, intrusive beeps.

He asks if I can open my eyes.

But it's the smell of tea that truly rouses me. Despite something telling me it's not right, I think Rowan is here, and he's waking me for my shift with a cup of Earl Grey. Instead I'm met with Linden's eager green eyes. His lips look redder, cut up, bloody. Strange purple welts make spreading circles on his face and throat. My hand is in both of his, and when he squeezes, it hurts.

"Thank goodness," he says, and hides his face in my

shoulder and convulses with a sob. "You're awake."

I vomit, and I'm still gagging when the world goes black again.

I open my eyes many, many years later. The wind is still howling like the dead. It pounds against my bedroom window, trying to break in, to steal me away. I look for the lighthouse gleam, but I can't find it.

Linden is asleep beside me, his head on the same pillow as mine. His breath against my ear, I realize, is the wind that has been howling in my dreams. There's a slight wheeze to it.

As I lie here, coming back to myself, I realize that no years have passed at all. His face is still smooth and young, though rather bruised, and I'm still wearing his wedding ring, and I'm still in this centuries-old mansion that will never be blown away.

But there are new strange things to observe also. There's a needle jabbing into my forearm, and it leads up to a bag of fluid hanging on a metal rack. There's a monitor steadily relaying the rate of my pulse. Calm, methodical. I try to sit up and there's pain in each of my ribs, one by one, like a xylophone breaking as it plays. One of my legs is elevated on some kind of sling.

Linden feels me stir beside him, and he makes muttering sounds as he awakens. I close my eyes and pretend to be asleep. I don't want to see him. It's bad enough that

I'll have to see him every day for the rest of my life.

Because no matter where I go or how hard I try, I will always end up right back here.

When I can remain comatose no longer, there's a constant stream of visitors to my bedroom. Linden is always by my side, fluffing my pillow, working on his designs, and reading library books to me. I find *Frankenstein* to be unnervingly ironic. Deirdre, Jenna, and Cecily hardly get more than a few seconds with me before Linden tells them I need my rest. Housemaster Vaughn, the doctor, the concerned father-in-law, gives me a repertoire of what I've broken or sprained or fractured. "You've really done a number on yourself, darling, but you're in the best possible hands," he says. In my medicated delirium he has transformed into some kind of talking snake. He tells me I won't be able to put weight on my left ankle for at least two weeks, and it's going to hurt to breathe for a while. I don't care. It doesn't matter. I have the rest of my life to lie in this miserable room and recover.

Time has lost all meaning; I don't know how long I've been lying in this bed. I drift in and out of consciousness, and something different awaits me each time I open my eyes. Linden reads to me. My sister wives huddle in the doorway, frowning over my condition; I stare at them until the frowns melt from their faces and their eyes turn black. There's pain everywhere, and heavy numbness on top of that.

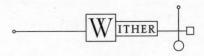

"I must admit, a hurricane is more extreme than an air vent." Vaughn's voice is floating over me. I struggle to open my eyes, but all I can make out is a smear of color. His dark slicked-back hair. Something warm rushes through my veins, and I shudder with relief as the pain in my ribs disappears. "Did you know that's what your dead sister wife tried? The air vents! And she made it all the way down the hall in that air duct before she was discovered. Such a clever little girl she was, and only eleven at the time."

Rose . . . The word won't reach my lips.

I feel Vaughn's papery hands brushing over my forehead, but I can't open my eyes anymore. His hot breath spirals into my ear with his echoing words. "Of course, who could blame the girl; it was how she was raised. Her parents were colleagues of mine, very well-respected surgeons, in fact. But then they lost their minds. They traveled state to state spreading some crackpot conspiracy that if we couldn't find an antidote, there had to be some surviving country out there in that wasteland of water that would help us. They taught her all about the destroyed countries, as though any of that matters."

Another surge of warmth through my blood. More medicated numbness. What is he injecting me with? I will all of my strength to my eyelids, and I manage to raise them. The room doubles, then materializes just enough for me to see that Linden isn't beside me, and my sister wives are no longer standing in the doorway.

"Shh, it's all right," Vaughn says, and lowers my eyelids with his thumb and index finger. "Listen to my bedtime story. It doesn't have much of a happy ending, I'm afraid. They toted that girl with them everywhere they went, spouting their nonsense. And do you know what happened to them? A car bomb in a parking garage. And she was orphaned, just like that. The world is a dangerous place, isn't it?"

A bomb. I have heard those in Manhattan, a distant *boom!* telling me that people have just died. The memory is not something I care to relive, and instinctively I try to move, but whatever courses through my veins has made moving impossible.

"There are people out in that world who don't want an antidote. People who think the world is ending and it's best to let the human race die out. And they'll kill those who try to save us."

I know! I know this. My parents received so many death threats for their lab work. There are two warring sides: pro-science, which favors genetic research and the pursuit of an antidote; and pro-naturalism, which believes that it's too late, and that breeding new children and subjecting them to experimentation is unethical. In short, pro-naturalism believes that it's natural to let the human race end.

"But lucky you," Vaughn says. "You're warm and safe in here. And you wouldn't want to jeopardize the good thing you have here. You're more special than you realize;

if Linden were to lose you, it just might destroy his spirit. You don't want that."

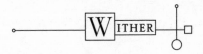

And suddenly it makes sense that Rose tried to deter me from escaping. It wasn't simply because she wanted Linden to have a companion after she was gone. She was trying to warn me, to spare me whatever punishment she faced for her own escape attempt. It's her voice, not Vaughn's, that whispers the final words into my ear.

"If you value your life, you won't run again."

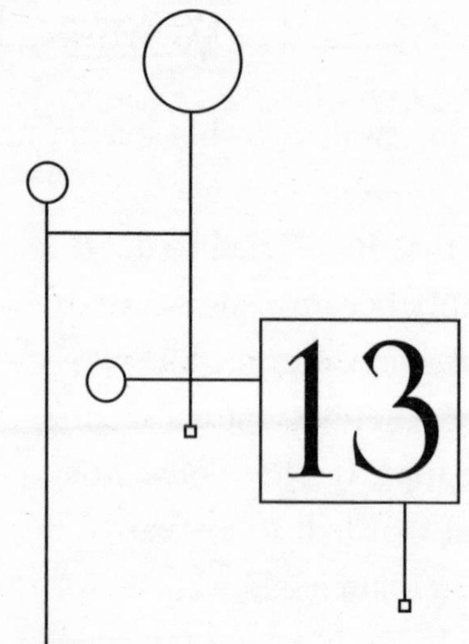

13

LINDEN SEEMS to have no idea that I sustained these injuries trying to run away from him.

"I told him you were in the garden when the storm came," Jenna whispers one afternoon, while Linden sleeps with his arms wrapped protectively around my elbow. "I saw you go out the window. What were you doing?"

"I don't know," I say. "Whatever it was, I failed."

She looks like she wants to hug me, but she can't because it's painful enough for me just to lie there and be looked at. "Did he believe you?" I ask.

"Governor Linden did, despite the broken window. I don't know about Housemaster Vaughn. Everyone in the kitchen said they saw you out in the garden before the storm, and that you were trying to get back inside when you heard the alarm. I think that might have convinced him."

"They did that?" I say.

She smiles a little, tucks my hair behind my ear. "They must like you. Especially Gabriel."

Gabriel! His blue eyes stabbing through the frenzy. His arms opening up. I remember crashing into him. I remember feeling safe, before the world disappeared into nothingness.

"He came after me," I say.

"Half the house went after you," she says. "Even Governor Linden. He took a few hits from some flying branches."

Linden. Bruised and sleeping at my side. There's a little blood dribbling from the corner of his lips. I brush it away with my finger.

"I thought you were dead," she says. "Gabriel carried you into the kitchen and it looked like every bone in your body was broken."

"Pretty close," I say.

"Cecily was screaming her head off, and it took three attendants to drag her up to her room. The House-master told her she was going to miscarry if she didn't quiet down. But she's fine, of course. You know how she gets."

"What happened to Gabriel?" I say. I haven't seen him since waking up. I still don't know how much time has passed.

Linden mumbles in his sleep, startling me. He nuzzles his face against my shoulder, and I wait for his eyes to open, but his breathing remains deep and even with sleep.

Jenna, whose eyes are suddenly serious, leans close to me. Although we're already whispering, she wants to be extra sure nobody will hear us. "I don't know what's going on between you two, but be careful. Okay? I think Housemaster Vaughn suspects something."

Vaughn. Just mention of him makes my blood go cold. I haven't spoken to anyone about what he said about Rose, partly because the memory is so fuzzy that I can't delineate fact from dream, but also because I'm afraid of what he'll do. I force him out of my mind.

I don't know how to answer Jenna, because I don't know what's going on between me and Gabriel. And now all I can think of is the fear that makes Gabriel go rigid when Vaughn is nearby. Is it because he's been threatened? I swallow something painful. "Is he okay?"

"He's fine. Just a little scratched up. He's been in a few times, but you were asleep."

I can always trust Jenna to know what's happening in this house. She's quiet, a background fixture, but she misses nothing. I think of what Vaughn said about casting her back into the water. I think about her sisters being shot in that van, and tears are filling my eyes and I can't stop myself from sobbing, and she says "Shh, shh" and kisses my forehead. "It's okay," she whispers. "I'll look out for him. It's okay."

"It's not okay," I choke. But I can't say more than that, because Housemaster Vaughn might overhear. He already knows everything. He's already everywhere, this awful man who controls us all. And he's right. I'm going to die here, so I might as well get comfortable. I'm starting to think he's my real captor, and that this man sleeping beside me is as much a prisoner as his own brides.

Jenna stays with me until I exhaust myself and the pain in my ribs and my legs and my head becomes too much to stay conscious for.

In the morning I awaken to Cecily standing uneasily in the doorway. She is noticeably more pregnant. She's becoming skinny arms and legs and a full moon of a stomach. "Hi," she says. It's a child's voice.

"Hi." My voice is like broken glass, but I know it will hurt to clear my throat. I think of what Jenna said, about Cecily screaming her head off when she saw my body.

"How are you feeling?" she asks. And before I can answer, she takes her hands out from behind her back and shows me a vase of white star-shaped flowers. "Lilies, like in your story," she says.

And they are just like my mother's lilies, with pink-red streaks running from the stamens like spilled ink. Cecily puts them on my nightstand and then touches her hand to my forehead. "You're running a slight fever," she says.

She's a little girl playing mother. Playing house. And maybe it's all the painkillers in my system, but I just adore her. "Come here," I say, and open my IV arm to her, and she doesn't hesitate. She's mindful of my ribs when she hugs me, but she grips my nightgown, and my neck is damp with her tears.

"I was so scared," she says. This mansion is her perfect dream house. Nobody is supposed to be hurt. Everything is happy ever after.

"Me too," I say. I still am.

"Is there anything I can do?" she asks, once she's had a little cry and is rubbing her cheeks dry.

I nod my head to where Linden is sleeping beside me. "Get him out of here for a little while," I say. "It's no good for him to be cooped up in here, worrying about me all day. See if you can get him to play a game with you or something that's fun."

She brightens and nods. She's good at lifting our husband's mood, and she knows she can do this for me. Besides, she seizes any opportunity to have Linden's undivided attention.

By late morning she has convinced Linden that she's starved for attention and if he doesn't help her practice chess, she's going to cry. He doesn't want her to cry, because he thinks she'll miscarry.

And I am granted my limited form of freedom.

I enjoy the quiet for a while, drifting in and out of summery dreams. All warmth and light. My mother's hands. My father playing the piano. The little girl next door's voice humming in a paper cup in my hands.

And then there's another voice, and my eyes fly open so fast that the room spins.

"Rhine?"

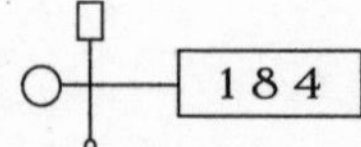

Gabriel's voice can reach me anywhere. Even in a hurricane.

He's standing in my doorway now, scratched and bruised, holding something I can't quite make out. I struggle to sit up, but I'm doing a lousy job of it, and he comes and sits beside me. He opens his mouth to speak, but I beat him to it.

"I'm so sorry," I say.

He sets whatever he was holding on the bed, and takes my hand in both of his, and the security I feel is exactly like the moment I crashed into his arms.

"Are you okay?" he says.

It's a simple question. And for him, because he saved my life, for whatever that is worth, I give him the truth. "No."

He looks at my face for a while, and I can't imagine how pathetic I must look, but he doesn't seem to even be seeing me. The sight of me is taking him someplace far away.

"What is it?" I say. "What are you thinking?"

He doesn't answer me for a while. Then he says, "You were almost gone." He doesn't mean I almost escaped.

I open my mouth to, I don't know, apologize again maybe. But he takes my face in his hands and presses his forehead to mine. And he's so close that I can feel his little warm breaths, and all I know is that when he draws his next breath, I want to get sucked in.

Our lips touch, almost as soft as not touching at all.

Then they press closer to each other, draw back uncertainly, touch again. There is warmth shooting through my broken body where there should be pain, and I put my arms around the back of his neck and I hold on to him. I hold on because you never know in this place when something good will be taken away.

It's a noise in the hallway that rips us apart. Gabriel gets up, looks out into the hallway. Then out the window. We're alone, but shaken. So much for being careful.

My heart is hammering in my ears, and it's something euphoric, not the pain or an angry wind, that makes it a little hard to breathe. Gabriel clears his throat. His cheeks are warm pink and his eyes have taken on a sleepy haze. It's difficult for us to look at each other. "I brought you something," he says, his eyes averted. He holds up the thing he was carrying a moment ago. It's a heavy black book with a red earth ingrained on the cover.

"You brought me Linden's atlas?" I say, skeptical.

"Yes, but look." He opens to a page that is all brown and beige maps with blue lines on them. The text at the top says *Rivers of Europe.* There's a key on the side that lists landmarks and rivers. Gabriel points to the third one down. *Rhine.* He traces his finger along the length of a blue line. "Rhine is a river," he says.

Well, it was a river, before everything got destroyed. But I never knew this. My parents must have. They so loved to be mysterious scientists, and there are so many things they never had a chance to tell my brother and me.

My finger trails after Gabriel's, along the vein of a river that no longer exists. But still I think it's out there. I think it has flooded over and freed itself into the ocean, somewhere beyond the pointed flower on the iron gate to freedom.

"I had no idea," I say. "I didn't think my name meant anything."

Was this what Rose meant, when I told her my name and she said it was a beautiful place?

"It says it was a freight river," Gabriel says. "There isn't any other information about it." He sounds disappointed.

"That's okay!"

I laugh a little, and put my arm behind his neck to bring him closer, and I kiss his cheek with gratitude. He turns a wild shade of red, and so do I.

He has no idea what this means to me, but by the look in his eyes I can tell he knows it must be something good. He brushes the hair from my forehead and looks at me. Rhine. The river that, somewhere out there, has broken free.

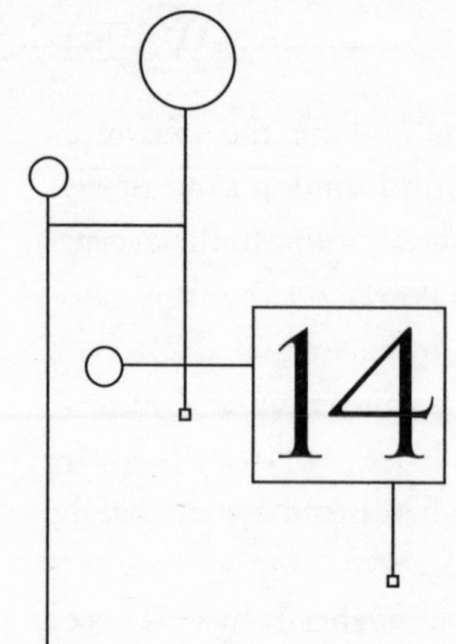

14

ALL NIGHT I dream of rivers, and beneath the water, brilliant sharp-leafed flowers.

"You were smiling in your sleep," Linden says when I open my eyes. He's sitting on the window ledge with a pencil in his hand and a drawing in his lap; sheets of paper are stacked beside him, and I can tell he's been working for a while. I think of what Vaughn said about how I coaxed Linden back into his designs. I still don't understand Vaughn's intentions in telling me, but it's true. Linden has been working a lot lately, and I just might be the one inspiring him.

"I dreamt we lived in that house you drew, with the pie in the window and the swing in the yard," I say, faking everything but this luscious feeling of happiness that comes out in my voice. The view from the window is showing me a lovely day.

Linden smiles at me, relieved but unsure. He isn't used

to seeing me like this, and he might think the painkillers are to thank. I try moving and find it's not so agonizing as before. I'm able to sit upright and lean against the pillows for support.

"I heard you went after me, in the storm," I say.

He sets down his work and joins me on the bed. The cut on his lip is healing. He looks like a pristine boy who got into a school-yard fight. I try to picture his fragile, thin body braving the hurricane, but I can't see him getting far. I can only see him being swept up or rescued or killed.

"I thought I'd lost you," he says, and I can't tell if that's a smile or a frown on his lips.

"I got lost when the wind picked up," I say. "I couldn't find my way back. I tried so hard."

"I know you did." He pats my hand, and there's such sadness in his eyes that I hate myself for lying. Linden seems to have that effect on me.

He says, "I want to show you something."

He tells me that I was mostly unconscious for a week. The thing that hit the back of my head was a blade from one of the windmills. The various other injuries came from debris that stretches from as near as the tennis courts to as far as the stables, but he wants me not to worry, because his father has hired people to clean it up, and they're doing a fantastic job. He says the real damage was done to me. He tells me that in between long stretches of silence, I muttered about rats and sinking ships and explosions, always explosions, and trying to stop the bleeding.

Mercifully I remember none of these nightmares.

But he heard everything. He stayed by my side, and since he couldn't reach me, he tried to draw what I was seeing. He hesitates a moment before showing me the first paper, like it's going to be a crime scene photo or something.

And then he shows me. He's drawn heavily shaded houses that are tilting to one side, or bursting with branches from a tree that takes up the building's insides. There are windows dripping blood, a yard filled with upturned rats. I've been married to this man for nearly nine months, and I thought he knew nothing about me, but he has captured my fears. All that's missing is Rowan, and even still I think he might be beneath the full moon in one of the drawings. He's in that bleeding house, looking at the moon, and I'm here in this frilly mansion looking at the same moon. And we're both wondering if our twin is okay.

I feel nauseous and dizzy, like my dreams have been spilled out into my hands. The last drawing is our wedding gazebo, overrun with cobwebs and bloody fingerprints, and what appears to be a piece of the windmill wedged into the roof. "That one wasn't you," he says. "That's how I felt while you were gone. When I wasn't sure if you'd wake up."

I'm staring at a ruined marriage in the rubble of that

gazebo. Linden's greatest tragedy was losing his first wife. The night before I ran away, he climbed into my bed, and I could feel the heat of his grief for Rose as he cried into my nightgown. Even though it's been my goal to earn his favor and become first wife, I had no idea I was as precious to him as my dead sister wife. Why? Is it because I look like her?

I say nothing for a while, flipping through the same drawings over and over again, taking time to look at each. His usual detail rings true. I can see inside these houses. One room is flooded with June Beans; another room seems to be made up of road maps.

"Are you angry?" Linden asks. "Maybe I shouldn't have showed you." He reaches to take them back, and I tighten my grip.

"No," I say, blinking at a house that's full of fish. It's an exact replica of my favorite pool hologram, but the sharks are swimming with limbs in their mouths—bleeding arms and legs. "These are . . . horrifying. I had no idea you could see things like this."

"I—I shouldn't." Linden goes pale and looks away from me. "My father says I should design things that are more—"

"Forget what your father says, he's wrong," I say. Linden looks at me with as much surprise as I feel. I hadn't meant to say that out loud, but now that I've got his attention, I might as well finish. "You shouldn't keep these things to yourself. You're talented. Okay, maybe nobody wants to live in a house full of trees or sharks or blood, but the other ones."

"I didn't mean anybody would want to live in these houses," he says, indicating the stack of nightmares in my hand.

"Clearly," I say.

"That was my point. Maybe someone would have lived in these houses once." He points to the careful detail around the threshold of the shark house, how there's even a door knocker and decrepit shutters that were once clean and new. And the house with rats in the yard has a trellis of dead roses that once thrived. "But something went wrong. They went bad."

I can see it. I can see the beautiful house where my mother was born, in a beautiful city that later succumbed to all the chemicals, until even flowers couldn't grow. I can see a whole world that used to be full of countries. Linden is searching my face for understanding, and his eyes are a little misty, and I nod because I do understand. I understand what these drawings mean, and I understand why he'd want to cry about them.

"I know," I say. "I know exactly."

The houses went bad like the world went bad.

Linden begins drawing more. He draws more viable houses and asks me for my opinion. He says he's going to start trying to sell them soon. It amazes me that a boy who has spent all of his life living in one place, and who hardly ventures into the world, can create such convincing places to live.

Cecily comes in the afternoons to take him off my hands. I appreciate this because I want time to myself. But I also think it's good for Linden to leave my bedside. Sometimes it's as though he's the one who's incapacitated.

And then one afternoon Cecily comes looking for Linden, and I say, "I thought he was with you."

Neither Gabriel nor Jenna knows where he is, and neither do any of our domestics. Housemaster Vaughn is nowhere to be found either, and sometime after lunch, Cecily is restless. She climbs into the bed with me, holding a big hardcover book with an ultrasound image on the cover. "What's this word? G-E-S-T-A-T-I-O-N."

I pronounce it for her, and she tells me what it means, though I already know. For a while she shows me diagrams and describes what her baby is doing right now, how it's big enough to suck its thumb, how fetuses can hiccup. Twice she presses my hand to her stomach and I feel the baby kick. It reminds me that all of this is real, as though I'd managed to forget. I worry about Cecily being in labor. I worry about the baby being born dead, like Linden's first child. I worry that, living or dead, this baby will end up in Vaughn's basement on a rolling cart.

Cecily is in the middle of describing how the placenta is delivered when Linden appears in the doorway. He's dressed in a suit, and his curly hair has been slicked back in a less menacing replica of Vaughn's style.

"Where have you been?" Cecily frowns.

"With a contractor interested in my designs," he says, looking at me. His eyes are bright. "There's a company that wants me to work with them designing a new strip mall that's opening up."

"That's great!" I say, and I mean it. Linden sits on my bed, Cecily between us. He even smells like he's been in the real world. Car exhaust and polished marble floors. "I was thinking that in a month or two, when you're feeling more up to it, we could go to an architecture expo. They're a little dry, but it's a great opportunity to show off my designs. And my beautiful wife, of course." He pushes the hair from my face, and for some reason I find that I'm flattered. And excited. I'm going to leave this mansion!

"That's sort of stupid," Cecily interjects. "Who cares about shopping? There were no malls where I come from."

"They aren't malls in the traditional sense," Linden says patiently. "They're more like wholesale warehouses, not open to the public but to invested companies. They mostly carry medical equipment, sewing machines—things like that."

I know exactly what he means. I've taken phone orders for wholesalers and tagged along with my brother on several of his deliveries.

"Do they televise the expos?" I say.

"These, no. They aren't as exciting as the ribbon-cutting ceremonies or the christening parties."

"What's a christening party?" Cecily says, reasserting her presence between us.

Linden explains that with the state of the world (he means that we're all dying), it's a cause for celebration when a new building goes up. Like a hospital or even a car dealership. It's a sign that people are still contributing to society and that we haven't given up hope that things will improve. So there are christening parties, usually held by the person or company that put up the building, where everyone involved in its construction can celebrate. "Like a New Year's party," Linden says. "But it's a new building."

"Can't I go to a christening party?" Cecily says.

Linden puts his hand on her stomach and says, "But your job is here, love. And don't you see how important it is?"

"Once the baby is born," she says.

He smiles and kisses her. She lets him, and it's clear that they've been this familiar for a while. "Then you'll have the baby to look after," he says.

"Elle can care for the baby sometimes." She's starting to get upset, and Linden says this is something they can discuss privately later, and she says, "No, now." There are tears in her eyes, and she's forgotten all about the pregnancy book and has discarded it on my lap.

"Cecily . . . ," I say.

"It's not fair!" She turns to me. "I've given him everything, and I deserve to go to a party if I want to. What have you done? What have you given up?"

So many things, Cecily. More than you know.

Anger is burning inside of me, making my bones hurt. She's pushing me, and I'm trying so hard to keep quiet. I have to. I have to, because if I say the truth now, then I'll forever be a prisoner. And I won't give her this expo or any of the parties to follow, because they are mine. My only chances to show my brother that I'm alive, to find a way out of this place. I deserve this. Not her.

Her eyes are big and full of tears. Her sobs are wet and full of hiccups, and Linden picks her up—her small, swollen body in his arms—and he carries her away. I can hear her wailing across the hall.

I sit in the bed, fuming, staring at the lilies she brought me a few days ago. They're starting to come apart. Petals have fallen around the vase and shriveled into scraps of tissue paper. It's like looking at the open eyes of a pretty corpse.

Cecily's good intentions never last long.

Gabriel and I have been very careful about how we interact. I could spend a whole morning thinking about our one kiss, and when he shows up to bring me lunch, all we'll do is talk about the weather. He tells me it's getting colder and he thinks there'll be snow.

"Did you bring Cecily her lunch yet?" I ask him as he's fitting the tray onto my lap. Being confined to my bed makes it hard for us to see each other. I can't follow him as he works or steal a moment with him in one of the gardens.

"Yes," he grumbles. "She threw a gravy boat at me."

I laugh in spite of myself. "She didn't."

"Because she wanted a twice baked potato, not once baked. Surprisingly good aim for a girl in her condition." He says that last part sarcastically. We all know that Cecily isn't nearly as delicate as Linden or Vaughn thinks. "She's in a lovely mood."

"That may be my fault," I say. "Last night Linden told me he's thinking about taking me to some kind of party for his building designs, and she had a fit because he didn't ask her instead."

He makes a face, and sits on the edge of my bed. "You're interested in a christening party?"

"Gabriel," I say softly, "it may be my only way out."

He looks at me for a while, face unreadable, and then he looks at his lap. "I guess it's not the worst escape plan you've had, is it?"

"Hard to argue. I'm sitting here in four different casts."

"Is it really so bad here?" he asks. Then panic fills his eyes. "Is the House Governor forcing you to do anything—you know—in bed?" His cheeks are on fire.

"No!" I say. I reach out and put my hand over his. "It's

nothing like that. Gabriel, I can't stay here for the rest of my life."

"Why not?" he says. "What has the free world got that you can't get here?"

"My brother, for starters," I say. "My home." I squeeze his hand; he stares at it uncomprehendingly. "What's the matter?"

"I think it's dangerous," he says. "I think you should stay."

I don't recognize this look on his face. It's not cold or angry like that day by the pool. He's not bitter. It's something else. "What if I asked you to come with me?"

"What?"

"That night, in the hurricane. I stood on the lighthouse, and I saw you coming toward me, and I said 'Run away with me,' but you didn't hear. I saw the fence. I was going to try and make it."

"Right before a giant piece of windmill knocked you unconscious," he says flatly. "Rhine, it's dangerous. I know you're not talking about running off into another hurricane, but what do you expect to do? Do you think he'll take you to a party and you'll just walk out the door?"

"Actually, yes, maybe," I say. It sounded better in my head.

Gabriel moves the tray from between us, and takes both of my hands and leans close. This is a big risk with my door being wide open and everyone home, but for the moment it doesn't seem to matter. "Whether it's a hurricane or a party, it's the same," he says. "It's dangerous. The House Governor is not going to let you just walk away, and neither is the Housemaster. It was months before he'd even let you open your window or leave the mansion, and guess what? Housemaster Vaughn is talking about revoking those privileges."

"How do you know that?" I say.

"He told all the attendants that if you or Cecily or Jenna wants to use our key cards for the elevator, we have to clear it with him."

"When was this?"

"While you were hooked up to five different machines fighting for your life," he says.

"I wasn't fighting for my life," I say, squeezing his hands. "If I'd had my way, I would have died right there and it wouldn't have mattered. But do you know what keeps me going every day? That river. Rhine. I think my parents gave me that name for a reason. I think it means I'm supposed to go somewhere. *This* is me fighting for my life."

"Go where?"

"I don't know!" It's so frustrating to have logic thrown at me now. It's making all my plans seem so hopeless. "But not here. Anywhere but here. Now, will you come with me or not?"

He raises an eyebrow. "You'd leave without me?"

"No," I say. "I'll drag you kicking and screaming." I'm grinning, and eventually he breaks down and flashes me his rare smile.

"You're insane, you know that?" he says.

"It's the only thing keeping me afloat," I say. He leans toward me, and I feel that rush of exhilaration telling me we're about to kiss. My eyes are just closing, and his hand brushes across my cheek, when a knock on the door frame interrupts.

"Sorry to intrude," Deirdre says, indicating the tray in her hands. "Housemaster Vaughn asked me to bring you some aspirin."

Gabriel withdraws, but I can see in his eyes that he wants to touch me. All he says is, "See you later."

"See you."

Once he's gone, Deirdre hands me two white pills and a glass of water. "You weren't intruding," I say, once I've downed the pills. "Nothing was going on between Gabriel and me—I mean—"

My cheeks burn as I fumble for the right words, but Deirdre only smiles. "It's all right," she says. "Housemaster Vaughn isn't even here. After he asked me to bring you the aspirin, he was called to the hospital." She moves to my dressing table and returns with a tube of lip balm, which she smears across my chapped lips. Then she moves on to fluffing my pillow. "It's a nice day. Would you like me to open the window?"

"I'm all right," I say. She stops fussing over me long

enough for me to see the concern in her eyes. My faithful little domestic. "Really, I'm okay."

"What did the Housemaster say to you?" she whispers, startling me.

"What?"

"While you were sleeping—at least I thought you were sleeping. I came to bring you a new pillow, but Housemaster Vaughn was in here and he told me to leave." She looks guiltily at her feet. "I stayed in the hallway. I tried to listen in. I'm sorry; I know I shouldn't have. It's just . . ."

There are tears welling in her eyes. It's so unlike her that at first I think my fever is back and I'm hallucinating. "It's just that I thought he was going to hurt you."

I reach for her hand, which is trembling. "Why would you think that?"

"Oh, Rhine," she sobs. "If you were trying to run away, you can't try it again. You'll never get out, and he'll make life here miserable for you."

"I wasn't trying to run away," I say.

She shakes her head. "But if he thinks you did, that's what matters. You don't understand. You don't understand what he's like when he doesn't get his way."

"Deirdre." I gently pull her toward me. "What are you trying to tell me?"

Tears are streaming down her face. She hiccups. "Lady Rose never wanted a baby—she never did. She and Housemaster Vaughn used to argue all the time. She didn't believe he was going to find the antidote, and she didn't want another child to be born just so it would die. He called her a pro-naturalist. I could hear them screaming at each other. Once, I had to hide in the closet while I was putting away her laundry, I was so afraid to get in the middle of it."

She sits down on the edge of my bed, swipes the tears from her eyes, but more come. "And when she got pregnant, even though she hadn't planned on it, she was excited. She asked me to teach her to knit, and she made a blanket for the crib." The memory makes her smile, but that smile is quickly gone. "When Lady Rose went into labor, Linden was away at an expo. And her pain was so extreme that Housemaster Vaughn kept her heavily sedated. When she came out of it a few hours later, and he told her the baby girl didn't make it, she didn't believe him. She said she'd heard the baby cry. He told her she was delirious, that the baby was born dead."

The room suddenly seems darker, colder. Deirdre says, "But I was changing the incense in the hallway, and I heard it cry too. Housemaster Vaughn told Lady Rose, 'You want the human race to die, and it looks like you got your wish.'"

I can hear Vaughn's voice in the words, and my heart breaks as though the words were meant for me. I can see Rose, alive and bereft, touching her stomach where hours earlier her child had moved inside her. I wish she'd

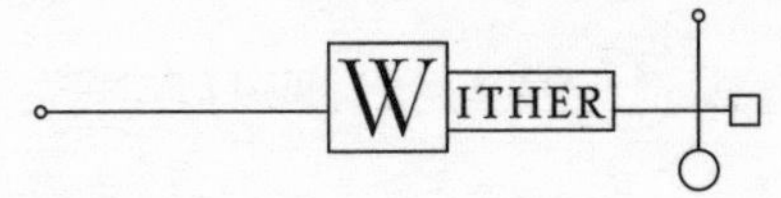

told me this story herself when she was alive, because now I feel an overwhelming need to hug her and tell her how sorry I am that it happened. I sense that the fire she felt toward Vaughn is as strong as mine. Maybe the only reason she endured him at all was her love for Linden. And maybe she was hoping I'd learn to love our husband so I'd learn to endure Vaughn as well.

"Oh, it just destroyed her," Deirdre continues. "She was never the same after that. She had her own domestic, Lydia. But it was too much for Lady Rose to have a young girl around reminding her of the daughter she would have had. Eventually she convinced House Governor Linden to have her sold off. She couldn't even look at Elle and me."

"Does anyone else know about this?" I say.

"No. They all believe the baby was a stillbirth. Or if they don't, they keep it to themselves. Please don't tell."

"No," I say, handing her a tissue from my nightstand. "No, this will stay between you and me."

She dabs at her nose, folds the tissue, and tucks it into her skirt pocket. "I've never told that to anyone before."

Even through the tears, I can see that some of the weight has been lifted from her shoulders. It's a terrible secret for such a young girl. In this place—no, in this world—it's impossible for a child to be just that. I put my arm around her, and she grants herself an uncharacteristic moment of weakness and collapses onto my chest, hugging me.

"He always gets the final say. So whatever he asks of

you, please, for your own good, listen to him."

"Okay," I say. But it's a lie. If anything, this story has reinforced my need to escape, to be like the river in Linden's atlas. Because things here are more frightening than even I could ever have imagined. Life is much different from the days when there were lilies in my mother's garden, and all my secrets fit into a paper cup.

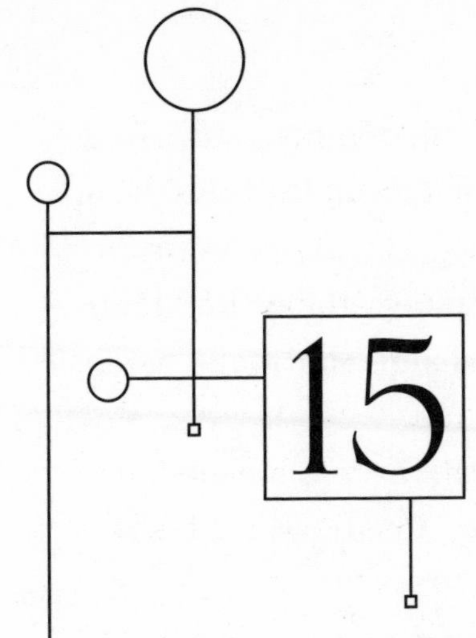

15

WHEN CECILY finishes playing her song, and the illusion shrinks back into the keyboard, she stretches her arms up over her head and cracks her knuckles.

"That was beautiful, love," Linden says. He sits on the couch with his arm around me. Jenna is curled on the armrest, and Linden's other hand absently traces patterns on her thigh.

"We have a little concert pianist," Jenna agrees, and works one of Linden's curls around her finger.

"Maybe not a *concert* pianist," Cecily says, laying the dustcover over the keys.

"No," I agree. "A concert hall is too sterile. Didn't you tell me you wrote that song while you were out in the rose garden?"

"The hedge maze, actually," Jenna says.

"You're both wrong," Cecily says, climbing into Linden's lap. "I wrote it in the orange grove."

"You wrote that by yourself?" Linden says, surprised. Jenna is still toying with his hair, and Linden's head cants absently toward her.

"Yes. In my head. I remember them for later. Although . . ." Her voice trails off. She looks aside, sighs sadly.

"What is it, love?" Linden says.

"Well. It's sort of an older song," Cecily says. "I haven't been outside in such a long time."

"None of us have, Cecily," I say. "It isn't just you. It's been so dangerous with the hurricanes. You saw how injured I was. I'm only just now getting back on my feet."

"But we haven't had any hurricanes in weeks," Jenna says. "The weather's been quite nice. Wouldn't you agree?" She's looking at Linden, whose cheeks have become flushed. The adoration of three wives at once is more than he can handle.

"I—I suppose it has."

"But Housemaster Vaughn is only trying to keep us safe," I say. "That's why he escorts us outside."

"He escorts you everywhere?" Linden asks.

"It does get depressing," Jenna admits. "We adore our father-in-law, of course. You know that. But sometimes a girl needs some time alone."

"To channel her creativity," Cecily says.

"To think," I add.

"And for girl talk," Jenna says. "And Rhine and I haven't been able to play a game of tennis or jump on the

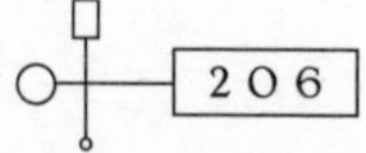

trampoline. The virtual games are all right, but we don't get any exercise at all, really."

"I wasn't going to say this," Cecily says, "but they're both gaining weight."

Jenna narrows her eyes. "Look who's talking."

Linden is looking a little red in the cheeks already, but when Cecily cups his face, kisses him, and asks if he thinks pregnancy has made her unattractive, it's just about all he can stand. "Y-you're beautiful," he says. "All of you are. But if you think some time outdoors will pick up your spirits, I'll talk to my father. I had no idea you were feeling so—uh—stifled."

"Really?" Cecily cries.

"Do you mean it?" I say, cozying up to his side.

"You're so sweet," Jenna says, and kisses the top of his head.

He bristles and gently slides Cecily off him, squeezes himself out from between Jenna and me. "I'll talk to him as soon as he's back from the hospital tonight."

My sister wives and I listen until we hear the elevator doors close behind him. There's a moment of silence, and then we collapse against one another on the couch, bursting with laughter.

"That was amazing," Jenna says.

"Even better than we planned," I say.

"Did I do all right?" Cecily asks.

"Forget music," Jenna says, ruffling Cecily's hair. "You should be an actress."

We hug one another in celebration of our small victory. And I can't help enjoying this camaraderie. It's the closest I'll ever get to feeling like I'm in a marriage.

The night we're supposed to attend the expo, Cecily starts having contractions.

"They're only Braxton Hicks," Housemaster Vaughn assures her. "It's not the real thing."

But she is in real pain. She's kneeling by the bed, clinging to the mattress, and I can see the terror in her eyes, and I know she isn't just doing this out of spite.

"We should stay home," I tell Linden. I've been back on my feet for well over a week, which is about how long it took Deirdre to design and sew the beautiful red dress I'm wearing. And after enduring an hour of being buffed and waxed and polished by an overeager group of attendants, I was determined to make tonight worth it. Linden stands beside me in Cecily's doorway, his mouth in a tight, worried line.

Housemaster Vaughn and Elle are helping Cecily into the bed. "Go on," Vaughn says. "She's got another two months yet before the baby comes."

I don't trust him. I imagine Cecily being rolled through the basement on a gurney, screaming in agony as the baby is born dead, and Vaughn going to work dissecting it for an antidote. He's a merciless beast; there's no humanity in his eyes as he cuts the infant apart.

Cecily whimpers, and Elle dabs her face with a wet

cloth. Cecily opens her mouth, and I think she's trying to form the word "stay," but Vaughn grabs her hand and says, "Darling, if your husband secures any buyers tonight, that means one of his drawings will become a new house. Or maybe a store. And wouldn't you like to visit it? Wouldn't that be nice?"

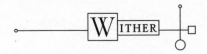

She hesitates. She and Vaughn have some kind of weird bond I can't figure out. It's like she's his favorite, or she thinks of him as the father she never had. And she'll do anything he says.

"You should go to the expo," she says. "I'll be fine here. This is my job, after all. I'm happy to contribute." Strangely, there's no malice in the way she says it.

"That's a good girl," Vaughn says.

I don't want to leave her alone with him. I don't. But when will I have another chance to prove to Linden that I'm first wife material, the one who should be on his arm at parties?

While Linden is saying good-bye to Cecily, promising he'll be back soon, I find Jenna in the library and ask her to keep an eye out. "I don't trust Housemaster Vaughn with her," I say.

"Me either," she says. "They've got all kinds of secrets together. I don't know what he tells her. It makes me nervous."

"I don't want him alone with her."

"No," she says. "Of course not." She's already a step ahead of me. She's found a chessboard in the sitting room, and she's going to ask Cecily to teach her how to play.

"Just try to have fun, okay?" Jenna tells me. "Tell freedom I said hello."

"If I happen to see it, I will," I say.

Of all things, Linden leads me to the same limousine that brought me here in the first place. He opens the door for me and doesn't even understand my hesitation. "Can we open the windows?" I ask.

"It's snowing," he says. I'd always thought Florida was a temperate state, but so far it's proven to be sporadic.

"The cold air is good for our lungs." I heard this from Vaughn, so it might not be true, but Linden just shrugs.

"If that's what you want," he says.

I climb into the back of the limo, and despite the bottle of champagne waiting for us in a bucket of ice, and the heated leather seats, I keep expecting something awful to happen. I open my window right away, and I breathe in the frozen air, and don't mind when Linden puts his coat around my shoulders. We haven't started moving yet, and I am still unconvinced this is safe. Knowing Vaughn, he's probably arranged for me to be knocked out just so I won't find my way to the gate.

There's a window in the roof. But it's tinted dark and I can't see the night sky beyond it. "Does that one open?" I ask.

Linden laughs and rubs my arms to generate warmth. "Are you trying to turn yourself into an icicle? Sure the sunroof opens."

After it opens, I stand, almost losing my balance because we've started moving. Linden grabs my waist to keep me from falling, and I don't mind at all because I've got the sunroof open, and I rest my arms on the roof of the car. There's snow falling into my hair, and it seems to melt as it reaches the light of the limo. I watch the trees pass, the repaired mini-golf course, the orange grove, Jenna's trampoline. I watch as all these things that have been my entire world for these past months get smaller when the car pulls away. They seem to be saying good-bye to me. Good-bye, enjoy your night. I smile, look ahead to see what's coming up next.

There's nothing but trees for a while. I've never gone this far before. I didn't even know there was a road this way. We drive for what feels like eternity. I begin to watch the stars through the trees, and the three-quarter moon that hurries to keep up with me.

Then we come to the gate, with the pointed flower that breaks open as the gate parts to allow us through. Just like that. And then we're off the property. There are more trees, and then suddenly there's a city. Bright lights and blurs of people laughing and talking. It's a wealthier place than where I come from, by the looks of it, and money has given these people the illusion of time. Maybe they're hoping for an antidote to save them, or maybe they're just happy to have a comfortable home to return to. There are no traces of desperation, no panhandling orphans. Instead I see a woman in a pink dress doubled over with laughter in front of a cinema that's displaying its movie titles on a giant illuminated marquee. I can smell fast food and fresh concrete and the stench of an irrigation pipe somewhere far off.

It's a shock. It's like landing on Mars, but also like coming home.

We drive past a harbor, and it's not exactly like the one in Manhattan. There's a sandy beach dissolving into the water, and plenty of docks where sailboats are tied for the night, swaying to the rhythm of the sea.

Linden is guiding me back inside, telling me I'll catch pneumonia. For a second I don't care, but then I think if I get pneumonia, he'll never let me leave the house again. I'm already lucky to be out now, given how worried he was while my broken bones healed. Vaughn had to convince him that I was as strong as an ox (like his dead son, I thought when I heard the comparison) before Linden considered taking me out tonight.

I settle back in the heated seat and let Linden close the windows, and I watch the city through the subdued tint of the glass. This isn't so bad. Linden pours me a glass of champagne and we clink our glasses together. I've had alcohol once before, a few years ago when I fell off the roof while Rowan and I were trying to repair a leak. I dislocated my shoulder and Rowan gave me a dusty bottle of vodka from the basement to help with the pain as he set my shoulder back in place.

But this is different, bubbly and light. It warms my stomach, where the vodka had burned.

I let Linden put his arm around me. It's something a first wife would do. He's rigid for a while, and then he seems to relax a little. He picks up one of my curls—all over-sprayed and conditioned and treated to last the evening—and winds his finger around it. I wonder how Rose wore her hair when he took her out.

We finish the last of our champagne, and he takes the empty glass from my hand and tells me there will be more at the expo. He tells me there will be lots of toasts and attendants carrying glasses of wine on trays. "After the alcohol came to be too much, Rose would only pretend to take sips. I think she was getting an attendant to serve her empty glasses to help the illusion." He looks away, to the traffic outside the window, looking like he regrets what he said.

I put my hand on his knee and gently say, "That's good. What else would she do?"

He purses his lips, ventures a glance at me. "She laughed at everything anyone said, and she looked at their eyes when they spoke. And she was always smiling. At the end of the night, when it was just us, she said her cheeks hurt from all the smiling."

Smile. Look interested. Pretend to drink. *And shine like a star,* I add to the list, because it also seems like something Rose would have done. As we get closer to our destination, I feel myself entering her world. I feel like her replacement, which is what she said to me on the day we met, and I hadn't wanted to believe it then. But now, with the warmth from the leather seats and the smell of Linden's aftershave, being her replacement doesn't seem so bad. Though this is only temporary, of course.

I take a moment to remind myself that the vibrant city outside is not *my* city, that these people are strangers. That my brother isn't here. He's alone somewhere, waiting for me. While I'm gone, there's no one to keep watch while he sleeps. And the thought brings up a bitter wave of anxiety sloshing in the champagne in my stomach, but I force myself to calm down before I vomit. The only way I can return to him is if I pull this thing off, however long it takes.

We come to a tall white building with a large velvet bow over the double doors. As we step out of the limo, I see the same velvet bows on streetlights and storefronts. There's a man dressed as Santa Claus ringing a bell while people drop money into a red bucket at his feet.

"They're getting ready for the winter solstice early this year," Linden says casually.

I haven't celebrated a solstice since I was twelve. Rowan thought spending money on gifts and wasting time decorating was too impractical. When we were children, our parents would decorate the house with red bows and cardboard snowmen, and all through December there was always the smell of something wonderful and sweet baking in the kitchen. My father would play sheet music from a centuries-old book entitled *Christmas Classics*, even though nobody has called it Christmas since before his time. And on the solstice, the shortest day of the year, our parents would give us gifts. Things they'd made, mostly—my mother was an excellent seamstress and my father could make anything from wood.

Without them our little tradition died. Winter for my brother and me was nothing more than the worst season for beggars in Manhattan. We would have boarded up the windows by now to discourage any orphans who might try to find respite from the blustery cold. The cold there is brutal and violent. Snow piled up to our doorknob, and we'd be up at dawn some mornings carving our way to freedom so we could make it to work. We'd drag the cot closer to the furnace and still be able to see our breath in front of our faces.

"Don't be upset if they all want to kiss your hand," Linden whispers in my ear as he takes my arm and we venture up the steps.

After Linden called these expos dry and boring, I didn't expect much. But inside there is a large and well-dressed crowd. There are holograms suspended around the room, with images of houses that spin and swivel. Windows open, and you're taken inside for a sweeping tour of the rooms. Architects stand beside their holograms and eagerly explain them to anyone who will listen. Even the walls and ceiling of the expo room are a sweeping illusion of a blue sky with meandering clouds. The ground looks like swaying grass full of wildflowers, and I can't help stooping to touch the floor to be sure the grass isn't real. I feel the cold tiles, though it looks like my hands are digging into the soil. Linden chuckles as I reattach myself to his side. "They always try to present an atmosphere in which a house could be built," he says. "It's better than the last expo I attended—it looked more like a desert. All it did was make everyone thirsty. And the year they made it an empty sidewalk to encourage businesses was just depressing. It looked postapocalyptic."

The dessert table is set up like a cityscape. There's a bio-dome cake that's already been cut into. There's a wobbly gelatin swimming pool with chocolate chip concrete, a chocolate fountain. Frosting flowers have been swiped, mutilated, and it's like Dorothy's Oz after someone has bitten into it.

We've barely taken a few steps before someone has snatched my hand and kissed it. The hair on the back of my neck stands up. I smile beamingly. "And who is this lovely young thing?" a man says. To even call him a man seems wrong, because he's probably younger than I am, though he's dressed in a suit that would cost more than a month of electricity in the mansion.

Linden proudly introduces me as his wife, and I keep my smile, but I drink the entire glass of wine that comes my way, and the next, because I find it makes all these kisses and hellos easier to endure. There are other wives, but they all seem happy with their husbands. They compliment my bracelets, ask how long it took to style my hair, and they complain about their own attendants and domestics being incompetent with zippers or pearls or whatever. After a while it all blurs into white noise and I just nod and smile and drink. One is pregnant, and she makes a big production of yelling at an attendant who offers her a glass of wine. They call me sweetheart and honey and ask me when I'm going to have a baby of my own. I say, "We're trying."

None of the wives mention the security guards by the door, who will probably tackle us to the ground if we try to leave without our husbands.

I do enjoy the spinning house holograms, though, and when Linden sets up his own hologram, I'm mesmerized by his drawing that's been colored and brought to life. It's not exactly something I've seen before; it's more like a collaboration of many designs. It's a Victorian house with tendrils of ivy that grow up the walls, retract, and grow again. Inside I can see the outlines of people moving, but when the image enters the window, the people step back, showing me the hardwood floors and billowing curtains, and I think I even smell Rose's potpourri. One of the bedrooms is filled with vases of lilies. There's a library full of nothing but atlases, with an unfinished game of chess in the middle of the room.

The sweeping tour makes me dizzy. I cling to Linden's arm, and he keeps me steady, places a light kiss on my temple. And after all the strangers handling and kissing me, I find myself relieved that he's the only one who's touching me now.

"What do you think?" he asks.

"If nobody wants to live here, they're all crazy," I say. We smile at each other, and take synchronized gulps of wine.

By the end of the night, my mouth is filled with alcohol and heavy bakery frosting that somehow makes the world smell sweeter. My curls have not wilted, even though there's sweat pooling on the back of my neck. I'm in a daze, smiling always, laughing, putting my hands on the shoulders of strange men and saying "Oh, stop" when they compliment me over and over on my eyes. Half of them ask if they're real, and I say, "Of course. What else would they be?"

One man asks, "Where did you get such incredible eyes?"

I say, "My parents."

And Linden looks startled, like my having parents never even occurred to him, much less that I might have known them.

"Well, you sure are gorgeous," the man persists, too drunk to see the concern on Linden's face. "Better keep this one close to you. Don't know where she comes from, but I bet there's not another like her."

Linden answers with a subdued, stunned, "No, there isn't . . ."

What's more, I think his surprise is genuine. "Come on, sweetheart," I say, searching for a term of endearment that doesn't belong to Vaughn or Cecily. I tug his arm. "I want to look at that house over there." I smile at the man, who is cackling, lost in his inebriation. "Excuse us."

We linger. We flatter architects. I leave Linden's side for a while because he's started to talk sales with one of them. He finds me a few minutes later as I'm nibbling on a strawberry and trying to recover from the commotion.

"Ready to go?" he says. I take his arm, and we manage to escape unnoticed.

Once outside, I can see that the snow has faded away. I realize that the sunny afternoon inside the building was not reality. The cold air hits me with a force. We move toward the limousine, and I think, *I could run.* The security guards are inside, not outside. There's only Linden to overpower, and he's so frail that I could just push him and he'd be out of my way. I could do it. I could go. I would never see the inside of that iron gate again.

But when Linden opens the door, I climb inside the limousine, where there's warmth and light. It's offering to take me back home. *Back home*, I think, and it feels strange but not that strange. I slump tiredly and begin unbuckling my painful black heels. It's more difficult than I remember. The limo starts to move, and I lurch forward, and Linden catches me, and for some reason I laugh.

He takes my shoes off for me, and I sigh in gratitude. "How did I do?" I ask.

"You were beautiful," he says. His nose and cheeks are red. He traces my cheek with the back of his finger.

I smile. It's the first smile I haven't forced since the expo began.

It's late when we make it back to the mansion. The kitchen and all the hallways are empty. Linden goes off to check on Cecily, whose light is still on. She'll be waiting for him. I wonder if she'll notice that he's a little bit drunk, which I guess is my fault, because he was following my lead. I wonder if Rose used to take the glasses from his hand and tell him when he'd had too much. I wonder how she endured these things with her sobriety in check.

I retire to my bedroom and unpeel the sweaty red dress from my body. I put on my nightgown and sweep my hair—still durably curled—into a clumsy ponytail and open my window and take gulps of the cold air. The window is still open when I climb into bed and begin to drift off, my eyelids full of spinning houses and pregnant bellies and glasses of wine floating to me on trays.

Sometime in the night the air gets warmer. I hear the sound of the window being closed, and whisper-quiet footsteps on the lush carpet, and Linden's voice saying, "Asleep, sweetheart?"

He remembers what I called him at the expo. Sweetheart. It sounds nice. Soft. I allow it.

"Mm-hm," I answer. The darkness is swimming with glittery fish and spreading ivy. The room is also spinning a little.

I think he asks if he can get into bed with me. I think I

mumble in the affirmative. I feel his slight weight beside me, and I'm an orbiting planet and he's the warm sun. I can smell the wine and the party on him. He gets close to me, and my head rolls right toward his.

It's silent and dark and warm. I feel the tendrils of ivy leading me into a lavish dream, and then Linden says, "Please don't go."

"Mm?" I say.

He's breathing against my neck, putting little kisses there. "Please don't run away from me."

I'm back from my dream, but barely. He tilts my chin with his finger, and I open my eyes. I can see a strange glaze in his eyes, and a small droplet hits my cheek. He's just said something, something important, but I'm so tired and I can't remember. I can't remember anything, and he's waiting for my response, so I say, "What is it? What's wrong?"

And he kisses me. It isn't a forceful kiss. It's soft, his lower lip gathering mine with a gentle lapping motion. His taste fills my mouth, and for a moment it's not so bad. Just like everything else about this night was not so bad. In a drunken, hallucinogenic kind of way. A small noise escapes my throat, like a baby gurgling into its bottle. He draws back and looks at me. I'm blinking wildly.

"Linden . . ."

"Yes, yes, I'm here," he says, and tries to kiss me again, but I draw back.

I put my hands on his shoulders to push him away, but

I can see the strange pain in his eyes that makes me think he was dreaming of Rose for a minute before I materialized back into Rhine.

"I'm not her," I say. "Linden, she's gone, she's dead."

"I know," he says. He makes no more advances, so I release his shoulders and he lies beside me. "It's just, sometimes, you—"

"But I'm not her," I say. "And we're both a little drunk."

"I know you're not her," he says. "But I don't know who you are. I don't know where you came from."

"Didn't you order that van full of girls?" I say.

"My father did," he says. "But before that, what made you want to be a bride?"

I choke on my next breath. What made me *want* to be a bride? And then I think of the surprise in his eyes tonight when that man asked where I'd gotten my eyes from.

He really doesn't know.

And I know who does. Vaughn. What did he tell his son? That there are bride schools where eager women devote their childhoods to learning to please a man? That he's saving us from a destitute orphanage? That may be true for Cecily, but even she is so dangerously unprepared for what's to come when this baby is born.

I could tell him right now. I could tell him that Jenna's sisters were executed in that van, and that the last thing I'd ever wanted to be was a bride. But would he believe me?

And if he believed me, would he let me go?

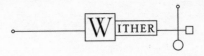

I ask, "What do you think happened to the girls you didn't choose? The others."

"I suppose they went back to their orphanages and homes," he says.

I stare at the ceiling, stunned, a little nauseous. Linden puts his hand on my shoulder. "What is it? Are you sick?" I shake my head.

Vaughn is more powerful than I thought. He keeps his son in this mansion, away from the world, and he makes up a reality for him. He gives Linden ashes to scatter while he hoards the bodies in the basement. Of course I would want to run away. Anyone who's been free can understand wanting to be free again. But Linden has never been free. He doesn't even know freedom exists, so how could he want it?

And Gabriel has been captive for so long that even he is beginning to forget how much better it is out there than in here.

It is better out there, isn't it? I lie still for a while, comparing the New York harbor to the voluminous ocean within the pool. I compare a city park to these infinite golf courses and tennis courts. I compare my Manhattan lighthouse to the one at the ninth hole amidst giant gumdrops. I compare my blood sibling, Rowan, to Jenna and Cecily, who have become my sisters. And in this blurry, somewhat inebriated state, I can almost see what Gabriel meant when he asked, *What has the free world got that you can't get here?*

Almost.

I give Linden a small kiss, my lips tightly closed until I withdraw. "I've been thinking, sweetheart," I say. "I haven't been a very good wife, have I? I'll try to be better."

"Then you weren't running away from me that night, with the hurricane?"

"Don't be silly," I say. "Of course not."

He sighs happily, and puts his arm around my waist and drifts off to sleep.

Freedom, Gabriel. That's what you can't get here.

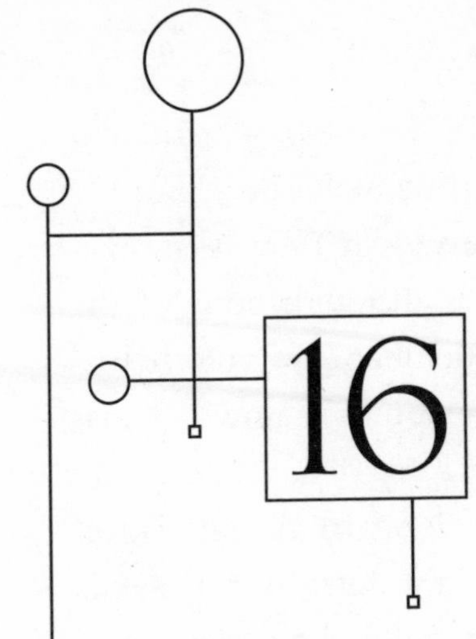

I DON'T SEE GABRIEL the next day. My breakfast is waiting for me when I wake up, even though it's past noon, but there are no June Beans, no evidence that he's been here. I page the attendants for permission to use the elevators, and Gabriel is not standing in the elevator to escort me when the doors open.

Vaughn is.

"Good afternoon, darling," he says, and smiles. "You're looking a bit rumpled, but lovely as ever. Late night last night?"

I put on my charming smile, and Rose is right, it does make my cheeks hurt. So much for Linden convincing his father to give us more freedom. Vaughn has the final word around here, even if he lets his son pretend otherwise. "It was incredible," I say. "I don't see how Linden can call those expos dry and boring at all."

I get into the elevator beside him, and the doors close,

and I try not to choke. He smells like the basement, and I wonder who he was dissecting this morning.

"So where would you like to go today?" he asks.

I'm wearing my coat because, although none of the snow stuck to the ground, I remember how cold it was last night. And I can't afford pneumonia now. "It just seems like a nice day for a walk," I say.

"Have you seen the repairs done to the mini-golf course?" Vaughn says, pressing the button that sends us down. "You really should. The crew did a marvelous job."

He makes words like "marvelous" sound ominous. But I smile. I am charming. I am fearless. I am Linden Ashby's first wife, the one he comes to in the night, the one he wants on his arm at parties. And I adore my father-in-law.

"I haven't seen it," I say. "I'm just getting my bearings back after my accident. I'm afraid I'm not very up to date."

"Well, then." Vaughn hooks his arm around mine, and it's so much more invasive than the way Linden does it. "How about a game, then?"

"I'm not very good," I say. I am demure, coy.

"A bright girl like yourself? I don't believe you for a minute."

And for once, I think he's telling the truth.

We play the entire course, and Vaughn keeps score. He praises my swing when I get a hole in one, and patiently helps me when I botch a shot. I hate the feel of his papery hands over mine as he guides my golf club. I hate his hot breath against my neck.

And I hate that he's standing beside me when we come to the lighthouse—the final hole in the course—which is still casting rays to freedom. While Vaughn goes on about the beautiful new Astroturf, I look for the path to the iron gate. I'm sure the limo drove through a path in the trees somewhere around here.

Just after I've taken my swing, Vaughn says, "So tell me what you thought of the city last night."

"I was really impressed by all the designs. There's real talent—"

"I'm not asking about the designs, darling." He's standing too close to me. "The city, how did you like your first glimpse of the city?"

"I didn't get a very good look," I say a little stiffly. What's he driving at?

"But you will." He gives his geriatric smile and taps my nose with his finger. "Linden is already talking about all the upcoming parties. You're really doing it, darling."

I blow warmth into my hands, watch him land a perfect hole in one. "What have I done, exactly?"

"Brought my son back from the dead." He puts his arm around me, kisses my temple right where Linden kissed me last night. But while Linden's lips had been warm, and his gesture one of comfort, Vaughn's lips send millions of insects crawling along my spine. This father and son look so eerily alike, and yet I can't imagine two more different people.

But I'm a good wife, a good daughter-in-law, and I blush. "I just want for him to be happy," I say.

"You should," Vaughn says. "Make that boy happy, and he'll give you the world on a string."

"On a string" being the operative words.

Vaughn wins the game, but my score isn't much worse than his. I wasn't letting him win. He did that on his own. "You're a much better player than you give yourself credit for," he laughs as we walk back to the mansion. "Not good enough to best me. But good."

I look everywhere for the path the limo took, but it's nowhere to be found.

It's very clear that I won't be allowed outside unless I'm accompanied by Vaughn. At least not today. So I find Jenna, who's curled up in my favorite overstuffed chair, her nose in a paperback with young seminude lovers on the cover; the man is saving the woman from drowning. "I haven't seen Gabriel," she tells me before I've even opened my mouth.

"Do you think that's strange?" I ask, taking the chair next to her.

She purses her lips and looks at me over the top of her book. She nods sympathetically. She has never been one to sugarcoat things.

I say, "Has lunch come yet?"

"No . . ."

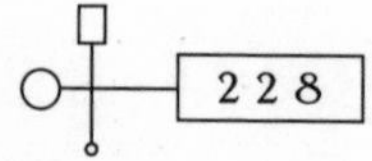

"Maybe we'll see him then." Gabriel is the only one who brings meals to our floor, unless Cecily throws a tantrum that requires more than one attendant to cater to her.

But we don't see him. An attendant we've never seen—a first generation—brings us our lunch, and he doesn't even know to look for us in the library. He has to ask Cecily where we are, and she's in such a lousy mood after being woken from her nap that we hear her yelling at the poor man from down the hall.

"Will you quiet down?" I say as Jenna and I gather in her doorway. The attendant looks frightened of this small pregnant fireball of a girl. But when I look at her, I can only see the bags under her eyes, the purple swollen ankles propped on pillows. "You're going to hurt the baby if you get yourself all worked up."

"Don't lecture me," she growls, gesturing wildly to the attendant. "Lecture him for being incompetent!"

"Cecily . . . ," I begin.

"No, she's right," Jenna says. She has lifted the lid off one of the dishes, and she's making a face. "This looks disgusting. What is it, pig slop?"

I look at her, shocked, and she looks right into my eyes. "I think you should go down to the kitchen and complain."

Oh.

"I'm sorry, Lady Jenna," the attendant begins.

"Don't apologize," I say. "It isn't your fault. It's the

head cook who should be overseeing these things, and she knows we all hate mashed potatoes." I lift another lid and crinkle my nose. "And pork. The smell alone will give Jenna hives. I'd better go down and get this straightened out."

"Yes, of course," the attendant says, and I think he's shaking a little as he begins rolling the cart of lunch trays back to the elevator, with me in tow.

"Don't mind them," I say, and give him a reassuring smile once we're in the elevator and the doors have closed. "It's nothing personal. Really."

He smiles back, glancing nervously at me in between staring at his shoes. "They said you were the nice one," he says.

The kitchen has its usual verve, which means Vaughn isn't nearby. "Excuse me," the attendant says, "but Lady Rhine is here with a complaint."

They all turn to look at me standing in the doorway, and the head cook snorts without missing a beat, and says, "This one, she doesn't complain."

I thank the attendant for bringing me down here, and someone takes the trays away, and I'm sad to see perfectly good food go to waste, but I came here for a more important reason. I make my way through the steam and the chatter, and I lean against the counter where the head cook is standing over her giant boiling pot. In all the commotion I know she'll be the only one to hear me ask, "What happened to Gabriel?"

"You shouldn't be down here asking about him," she says. "Only going to make more trouble for that boy. The Housemaster's had his eye on him since your botched escape."

A fierce chill rushes up my spine. "Is he okay?"

"Haven't seen him," she says. And she looks at me with such a sad expression. "Not since this morning when the Housemaster called him down to the basement."

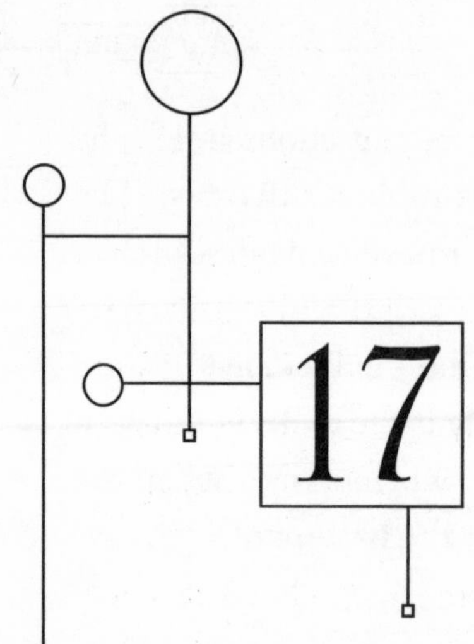

17

I'M SICK for the rest of the afternoon. Jenna holds my hair back while I retch into the toilet, but nothing comes up.

"Maybe you had a little too much to drink," she says gently.

But it isn't that. I know it isn't that. I back away from the toilet and sit on the floor, my hands dropping hopelessly into my lap. Tears are welling up behind my eyes, but I don't release them. I won't give Vaughn the satisfaction. "I have to talk to you," I say.

I tell her everything. About Rose's body in the basement, and about the kiss with Gabriel, and about Linden having no idea where we came from, and the absolute control Vaughn has over our lives. I even tell her about Rose and Linden's dead child.

Jenna kneels beside me, dabbing my forehead and the back of my neck with a damp cloth. It feels good, despite everything, and I rest my head on her shoulder and close my eyes. "This place is a nightmare," I say. "Just when I think it might not be so bad, it gets worse. It gets worse and I can't wake up. Housemaster Vaughn is a monster."

"I don't think the Housemaster would kill his grandchild," Jenna says. "If what you say is true and he's using Rose's body to find an antidote, wouldn't he want his grandchild to live?"

I keep my promise and don't tell her what I learned from Deirdre—that the stillbirth was no stillbirth at all. But the thought haunts me. I want to think Jenna is right. What reason could Vaughn have for murdering his grandchild? It's true that he's only ever had sons—maybe he prefers them—but a granddaughter would at least be useful to him as a child bearer. The daughters of wealthy families even get to choose whom they marry sometimes, and take priority over their sister wives. And Vaughn is all about finding a use for things, people, bodies—nothing is wasted.

But I know, somehow, that Deirdre and Rose were right when they heard that baby's cry. And I don't think it was a coincidence that Linden was away when it happened. The thought bubbles up a new wave of nausea. And Jenna's voice feels so far away when she asks if I'm all right and says that I look awfully pale.

"If anything bad happens to Cecily or that baby, I am going to lose it," I say.

Jenna rubs my arm reassuringly. "Nothing will," she

says. It's quiet for a while after that, and I think of all the horrible things that could be happening to Gabriel in the basement. I think of him being bruised, beaten, etherized. I can't allow myself to think he's already dead. I think of that noise we heard in the hallway when we kissed, and how reckless we were to leave the door open, and the atlas he stole from the library that's still sitting on my dressing table. And I know this is all my fault. I've brought this on him. Before I came here, he was a happily oblivious servant who had forgotten the world. It's an awful way to live, but it's better than no life at all. And it's better than Vaughn's windowless basement of horrors.

I think of the book Linden read to me while I was recovering. *Frankenstein.* It was about a madman who constructed a human out of pieces from corpses. I think of Rose's cold hand with its pink nail polish, and Gabriel's blue eyes, and the stone-small heart of a dead infant, and before I even realize I've moved, I'm vomiting, and Jenna is holding back my hair, and the world is spinning out of control. But not the real world. Vaughn's world.

Cecily appears in the doorway, pale and bleary-eyed. "What's wrong?" she asks. "Are you sick?"

"She'll be all right," Jenna says, smoothing my hair back. "She's had too much to drink."

That's not it at all, but I say nothing. I flush the toilet, and Cecily pours water into the rinse cup and hands it to me. I take it. She sits on the edge of the tub, groaning as she bends her knees. "Sounds like it was a fun party," she says.

"It wasn't really a party," I say, and swish the water in my mouth and spit. "It was just a bunch of architects displaying their designs."

"Tell me everything," Cecily says, a spark of excitement filling up her eyes.

"There isn't anything to tell, really," I say. I don't want to tell her about the dazzling holograms or the succulent dessert selection or the city full of people where I considered running away. It's better if she doesn't know what she's missing.

"You two never talk to me anymore," she says, and she looks like she's going to get worked up again. It's like she gets more emotional with each trimester. "It's not fair. I'm stuck in that bed all day."

"It really was boring," I insist. "There were all these first generations showing me their sketches, and I had to pretend to be interested. And there was an architect who gave a long lecture about the importance of shopping malls, and we had to sit in these uncomfortable foldout chairs for over an hour. I got drunk just for something to do."

Cecily looks doubtful for a moment, but then she must decide I'm telling the truth, because her unhappiness seems to fade, and she says, "Well, okay. But can't you tell me a story, then? What about those twins you used to know?"

Jenna raises an eyebrow. I've never told her about my

twin brother, but she's more intuitive than Cecily and she's probably figuring it out now.

I tell the story of the day the twins were walking home from school and there was an explosion so loud that it rattled the ground under their feet. A genetic research facility had been bombed by first generations in protest of experiments being done to prolong the life span of new children. Cries of "Enough!" and "The human race cannot be saved!" filled the streets. Dozens of scientists and engineers and technicians were killed.

That was the day the twins became orphans.

I wake up to the sound of a dinner tray being set on my night table. Cecily is curled up beside me, snoring in that nasal way she's adopted in her third trimester. My eyes dart to the bringer of the tray hopefully, but it's just the nervous new attendant from this morning. The disappointment on my face must be obvious, because he tries to smile as he's turning to leave.

"Thank you," I say, but even that sounds heartbroken.

"Look in the napkin," he says, and then he's gone.

I sit up slowly so as not to disturb Cecily. She mumbles into a little lake of drool on the pillow and sighs.

I unroll the cloth napkin that encompasses the silverware, and a blue June Bean falls into my hand.

I don't see Gabriel the next day, or the next.

Outside, the snow begins to stick to the ground, and

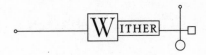

I keep Cecily company while she pouts about not being allowed to go out and make snowmen. The orphanage never let her go out in the snow, either. It would be too easy for the children to get sick in the cold, and the staff members weren't equipped to deal with an epidemic.

She only sulks for a little while, though, before she fades into one of her naps. I can't wait for this pregnancy to be over. My fear over what's to come when the baby is born is surpassed by my fear of what's happening to her now. She's always out of breath, or crying, and her finger is swollen around her wedding band.

While she sleeps, I sit on her window ledge, flipping through the atlas Gabriel brought me. I find out that while my name is a European river, Rowan is a type of small red berry that grew in the Himalayas and Asia. I'm not sure what it means or if it means anything at all. But the last thing I need is another puzzle to try and solve, and after a while I just watch the snow falling outside. The view from Cecily's window is nice. It's mostly trees, and I think it could be just the normal woods out in the real world. It could be anywhere at all.

But then, of course, I see the black limousine driving a path through the snow, and I'm reminded of where I am. I watch it navigate around a shrub and then drive straight into the trees.

Straight into the trees! There's no impact. The limo simply drives straight through them as though they weren't even there.

And then it dawns on me. Those trees *aren't* really there. That's why I couldn't find my way to the gate from any of the gardens or the orange grove. The true path is hidden by some sort of illusion. A hologram, like the houses at the expo. Of course. It's so simple. Why didn't I think of it before? It figures that I'd learn this now, when Vaughn has made it nearly impossible for me to be outside unaccompanied.

For the rest of the day I try to figure out a plan to get outside so I can inspect the tree hologram, but all paths in my mind lead back to Gabriel. If I found a way out, I couldn't leave without him. I told him I wouldn't leave without him, but he was against the idea in the first place. If he's in trouble because of me, will he completely abandon the idea of escaping?

I just need to know that he's okay. I can't even think about leaving until I know that much.

Dinner comes, and I don't eat. I sit at a table in the library with my hand in my pocket turning the June Bean over and over. Jenna tries to distract me with interesting facts she's read in the library books, and I know it's for my benefit, because normally all she reads are romance novels, but I just can't bring myself to pay attention. She coaxes me to try some of the homemade chocolate pudding, but it's like paste in my mouth.

That night I have a hard time falling asleep. Deirdre draws a bath for me with chamomile soaps that leave a layer of frothy green on the water. The soapy water feels

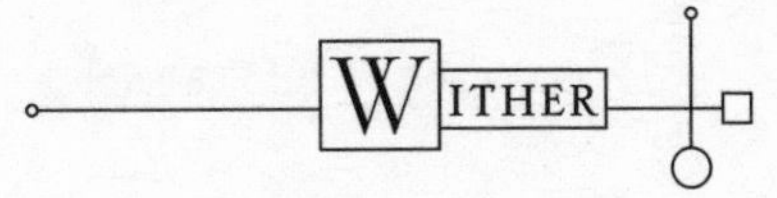

like a deep-tissue massage and smells like heaven, but I can't relax. She braids my hair while I'm soaking, and she tells me about the new fabrics she's ordered in from Los Angeles, and how they'll make lovely tiered summer skirts. And it only makes me feel worse to think I'll still be here next summer to wear them. And the less responsive I am, the more desperate her tone seems to become. She can't understand the cause of my unhappiness. Me. The pampered bride of a soft-spoken Governor who will give me the world on a string. She's my eternal little optimist, always asking how I am or if I need anything and trying to make my day better. But it occurs to me that she never talks about herself.

"Deirdre?" I say as she's replenishing the soaps and adding more hot water to the bath. "You said your father was a painter. What did he paint?"

She pauses with her hand on the faucet, and she smiles in a sad, wistful way. "Portraits, mostly," she says.

"Do you miss him?" I ask.

I can tell that this is a subject of great sorrow for her, but she's got a strength and tranquility that reminds me of Rose, and I know she's not going to break down and cry.

"Every day," she says. Then she presses her hands together in a cross between a clap and a gesture of prayer. "But now I'm here, and I get to do what I love, and I'm very fortunate."

"If you could run away, where would you go?"

"Run away?" she says. She's at the cabinet now, searching through the bottles of scented oils. "Why would I want to do that?"

"It's just a question. If you could be anywhere in the whole country, where would you go?"

She laughs a little, dropping a bit of vanilla oil into the water. The foam sparkles and pops. "But I'm happy here," she says. Then, "Well, there was a painting my father did—of a beach. There were starfish on the sand. I've never held a real starfish. I would have liked to go to that beach, or one just like it." She looks lost in the memory, staring through the bath tiles. Then she comes out of it and says, "How's the water? Are you almost ready to get out?"

"Yeah," I say. I change into a nightgown, and Deirdre rubs some lotion on my feet and calves, and admittedly that does relax me a little. She lights a few candles and tells me the smell will help me fall asleep. The candles are supposed to smell like lavender and something called sandalwood, but as I'm drifting off to sleep, they take me away to a warm sunny beach, and a canvas freshly painted.

I'm up before dawn the next morning. I had a dream that Gabriel came into my room with an atlas on the breakfast tray. It's not awful, as nightmares go, but the loneliness I feel when I awaken is crushing.

I venture into the hallway, which is dimly lit. The incense sticks have stopped burning, and there's a distant smell like charred perfume. I know Jenna and Cecily will be asleep at this hour—especially Cecily, who has taken to sleeping until noon most mornings in her third trimester, but I'm sure one of them will let me get into bed with them. Maybe it will work better than sleeping alone.

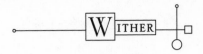

When I knock on Jenna's door, I hear her soft giggle from somewhere in the room. There's a rustling sound, and then she says, "Who is it?"

"It's me," I say.

Another giggle. "Come in," she says.

I open the door to a bedroom that's warm with candlelight. Jenna is sitting up in the bed, running her fingers through her tousled hair, and Linden is tying the drawstring of his pajama pants. His bare chest is pale; his cheeks are flushed. He pulls his shirt on in a hurry, and it's still unbuttoned when he stands and heads for the door. "Good morning, sweetheart," he tells me, not quite meeting my eyes.

There's nothing wrong with this. It's perfectly normal. Jenna is his wife. He's our husband. I should be used to the idea. It was inevitable that I'd eventually catch a glimpse of what goes on behind these doors. But I can't help the painful blush that washes over my face, and I can see that Linden is looking embarrassed too.

"Morning," I say, surprised not to have stuttered.

"It's early; you should try to go back to sleep," he says, and plants a quick kiss on my lips and hurries down the hall.

When I turn my attention back to Jenna, she's walking around the room, extinguishing the candles. Her body shimmers in a layer of sweat; the hair receding from her face is damp; the buttons on her nightgown don't align. I've never seen her this way, so wild and beautiful; Linden must be the only one who usually sees her like this. I push back a wave of jealousy, which is, of course, absurd. I have no reason to be jealous. If anything, she's doing me a favor by keeping Linden's affections away from me.

She says, "Don't these things smell awful? They smell like the inside of a leather purse. Governor Linden thinks they set a mood."

"How long was he here?" I say in a measured tone.

"Ugh, all night," she says, and collapses back into bed. "I thought he'd never leave. He thinks if we do it a bunch of different ways, it'll get me pregnant."

I'm fighting not to blush. The Kama Sutra book, one of Cecily's favorites, is open page-down on the floor.

"Is that what you want?" I ask.

She snorts. "To bloat up like a puffer fish like Cecily? Hardly. But what can I do? And anyway, I don't know why he can't knock me up. I'm just lucky, I guess." She pats the mattress beside her, inviting me over. "So, what's up?"

Without candlelight the room is much darker. I can barely make out her features. Had I really come here a few moments ago expecting to sleep? That seems like an impossibility now.

"I'm worried about Gabriel," I say. I sit on the edge of the bed, where Linden moments ago was adjusting his drawstring, and somehow I can't bring myself to get under the covers.

Jenna sits up and puts her arm around me. "He'll be okay," she promises.

I stare dismally at my lap.

"Okay, that's it, get up," she says, pushing me to my feet and following suit. "I know what you need."

A few minutes later we're huddled under a blanket on a couch in the sitting room, sharing a gallon of vanilla ice cream she ordered from the kitchen, and we're watching an early-morning rerun of yesterday's soap opera. Along with the romance novels, these are another of her guilty pleasures. The actors are all teenagers made up to look much older. Jenna tells me they're constantly changing the actors, since of course the show has been on for more than a decade and the original actors have died by now. The only consistent actors are first generations. And as she's explaining to me who's in a coma and who unknowingly married an evil twin, both of us bathed in the television's glow, I do start to relax a little.

"You two are so loud." Cecily is in the doorway, rubbing her eyes. Her stomach looks like an overblown balloon. She hasn't bothered with the last few buttons of her nightgown, and the skin around her belly button is stretched so far that it shines painfully. "What are you doing at this hour?"

"It's called *This Maddened World*," Jenna says, making room on the couch. Cecily gets between us and retrieves the spoon I stuck in the mound of ice cream. "See, this guy here—Matt—he's in love with the nurse, so he broke his arm on purpose. But she's about to tell him that the X-ray is showing he has a tumor."

"What's a tumor?" Cecily licks the spoon and dips it back into the carton for more.

"It's what used to cause cancer," Jenna says. "This is supposed to be the twentieth century."

"Are they going to have sex on that operating table?" Cecily says, incredulous.

"Gross," I say.

"I think it's sweet," Jenna gushes.

"It's dangerous." Cecily gestures wildly with the spoon. "There's a tray of needles, like, right there."

"He's just been given a death sentence," Jenna says. "What better time to make a move on the love of his life?"

The couple on the screen does, in fact, begin having sex on the operating table. It's censored by strategically placed props and close-ups of the actors' faces, but I still look away. I dig a spoon into the ice cream and wait for the romantic music to stop.

Cecily catches me and says, "You're such a prude."

"I'm not," I say.

"You haven't even consummated with Linden," she says. "What are you waiting for, our golden anniversary?"

Cecily is the only one who believes Vaughn will find his miracle antidote, and that we'll live to see old age.

"What goes on in my bedroom is none of your business, Cecily," I say.

"It's just sex," she says. "It's no big deal. Linden and I do it practically every day. Sometimes twice."

"Oh, you do not," Jenna says. "Please. He thinks you're going to miscarry if he even looks at you funny."

Cecily bristles. "Well, we will, once this stupid pregnancy is over. And if you think I'm having all the babies, you're crazy." She waves her spoon between Jenna and me. "One of you is doing this next. You have no excuse, Jenna. I see how often you two shut the door." Cecily may not be the most observant of us, but she always seems to know what goes on in our bedrooms—or, in my case, what doesn't go on.

Jenna looks uneasy, suddenly, putting a spoonful of ice cream into her mouth. "We've tried. It just hasn't happened."

"Well, try harder."

"Drop it, okay?"

They continue to argue, but I turn my attention back to the television, where there's a much safer scene of two people talking in a garden. I want no part of this conversation. I am more of a sister wife to Cecily and Jenna than I am a wife to Linden. And I can't bring myself to think of him in the way they're discussing. I can't bring myself to think of anyone that way.

Gabriel once again enters my mind. Our kiss after the hurricane, the eager warmth that filled my body, quelling my pain. If we ever manage to escape this mansion, will our connection develop into something more? I don't know, but the beauty of running away with Gabriel is that I'll have the freedom to decide for myself.

A wave of heat rushes up between my thighs. The ice cream in my mouth tastes twice as sweet. And for no reason at all, I sigh.

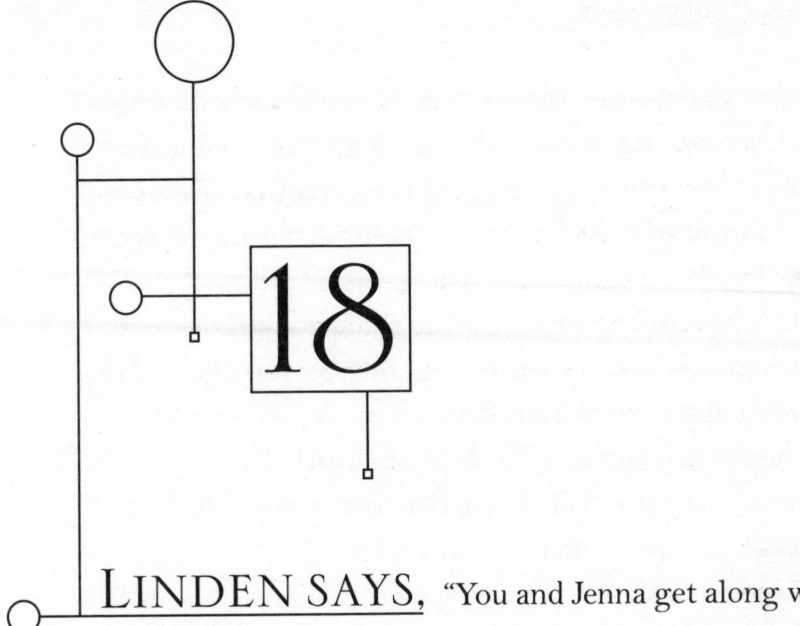

LINDEN SAYS, "You and Jenna get along well, don't you?"

He and I are walking hand in hand through the sleepy winter wonderland that the orange grove has become. Everything around us is white and deeper white, and a path has been carved for us through snowdrifts as high as my head. I didn't know winter could be so extreme this far south.

"She's my sister," I say, and nod into a cloud of my own breath. Linden looks at our joined hands, mine in Deirdre's cable-knit gloves. He brings my hand to his lips for a kiss, and as we press forward, I say, "She doesn't speak to you much, does she?" In the ten months we've been here, Jenna has held on to her resentment for her imprisonment and the murder of her sisters. I can't blame her. And if Cecily has noticed the strain between our sister wife and husband at all, she's probably just glad not to have the competition. If Jenna wanted to, she could become my rival to be Linden's first wife easily. She's beautiful and graceful, and she is very compassionate and loyal when you aren't responsible for the murder of her family.

"Usually, no," he says. "Last night she asked me up to her room, and we spent time together, as you know." He blushes a little. "And we talked."

I furrow my brows. "Talked? About what?"

"You," he says. "She's worried about you. With the stress of the baby coming and everything."

"Linden," I say, "that's not even my baby."

"No," he agrees, "but Jenna says that my father has kept the three of you on a tight lockdown, and that it's been especially difficult for you to try to care for Cecily the way she is, without being able to have a few moments to yourself."

"It does get a little crowded with three wives on one floor all day," I agree, but I'm confused. What was Jenna trying to do?

Linden smiles at me. He looks like a little boy, his nose and cheeks bright red, his dark curls coming out of his knit hat in tangles. He's the child in Rose's photograph. "I think we should change that, then," he says. "I spoke with my father, and—well, here." We stop walking and he reaches into the pocket of his wool coat and extracts a small colorfully wrapped box. "The solstice isn't for another week yet, but I think you deserve this now."

I remove my gloves so I can untie the beautiful bow, and I work fast because my fingers are already going numb. There's a small box under all the paper, and I lift the lid, expecting something impractical like diamonds or gold, but it's something else. A plastic card strung on a silver necklace. I've seen them around the necks of all the attendants.

It's a key card to use the elevators.

It's happening. I'm becoming first wife! And I'm being given the trust that comes with it. I can't help the squeak that escapes my throat. I cover my mouth, and the excitement just fills my eyes. Freedom. Just being handed to me in a little box. "Linden!" I say.

"Now, it won't take you to *every* floor. It will allow you to access the ground floor so you can go outside, and—" I launch myself into his arms, and he stops talking, takes a deep breath into my hair.

"Thank you," I say, even though he has no idea what this means, and he never can.

"Do you like it?" he whispers, a little stunned.

"Of course," I say, and draw back. He smiles at me in that little boy way that makes him so much different from his father. The cold makes his lips especially red, and I think he is exactly the type of portrait Deirdre's father would have painted. So soft and lovely and sweet. He takes my face in his hands, and for the second time in our ten-month marriage, we kiss. And for the first time, I don't draw back.

Back on the wives' floor, I run down the hallway calling Jenna's name, the key card swinging around my neck. Linden's slight taste is still on the tip of my tongue, and it clashes with the incense smell of the hallway flooding my senses, like I'm returning home after a trip to outer space.

I can't find Jenna, and Cecily is sleeping. I can hear her snoring through the closed bedroom door. I page Deirdre, who tells me that Adair hasn't heard from Jenna either, but don't worry, she couldn't have gone far. And it's true, she couldn't have. So I wait in the library, looking for more information on the Rhine River or rowan berries, but there's nothing, of course. Instead I read about the life cycle of hummingbirds until Linden calls me to dinner.

Cecily, heavy and burdened in her eighth month, slumps against me in the elevator, complaining about back pain. The attendant offers to bring a dinner tray to her in bed, but she says, "Don't be stupid. I'm having dinner with my husband like everybody else."

When we enter the dining hall, I see Jenna already seated at the table with Vaughn. She looks pale, and she barely raises her eyes when Cecily and I take our places beside her, according to age. Jenna turned nineteen quietly last month. She told me. One year left. And I asked her to run away with me when I formulate a plan, but she declined. Even if her body becomes one of Vaughn's experiments, she doesn't care. She'll be far away from

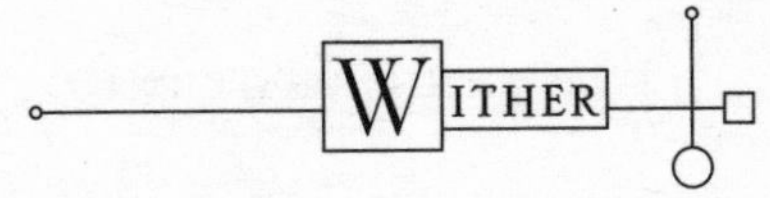

here by then, far beyond, with the family she lost.

I sit beside her now, wondering whose ashes Linden will be given to scatter when Jenna's gone. I've already promised myself I won't be here for that funeral.

Linden joins us, and the meal is very subdued. Cecily isn't feeling well, and she must be out of it, because she hasn't even complained about my having a key card around my neck. Instead she squirms uncomfortably until one of the attendants is asked to bring her a pillow for her back, and she doesn't even yell at him when he props it behind her.

I keep hoping to see Gabriel, but he isn't among the attendants bringing us dinner. I still carry the June Bean in my pocket, and keep his handkerchief in my pillowcase, hoping he's okay, hoping I'll hear from him soon. My concern must be obvious, because Vaughn asks me, "Is everything all right, darling?" and I say I'm just a little tired, and Cecily says she's willing to bet she's more tired, and Jenna says nothing at all, which only makes me worry even more.

I try to keep up a pleasant conversation with Linden, though, because that's the least I can do. And Cecily pipes in occasionally, and Jenna knocks the boiled carrots around with her fork. Vaughn tells her to eat something, and his voice is so frightening despite his smile that she does.

After dessert we're escorted back up to our floor. Cecily goes to bed, and without speaking, Jenna and I retreat to a remote aisle of the library. "You got a key card," she says.

"Thanks to you," I say, thinking back to early this morning when I walked in on her and Linden. "How did you convince him?"

"I didn't really have to," she says, idly tracing her finger over the spines of some books. "He already seemed to want to. I think he just needed a push. It's obvious that I don't want to be first wife, and I'm going to die in a year anyway"—she says this so casually it breaks my heart—"and Cecily may outlast us all, but she could never handle the responsibility. And that leaves you, which is what I told him. Rhine, it should be you. You've already got him convinced you adore him. You do such a good job that I'm almost convinced myself."

My fondness for Linden isn't entirely an act, but I don't know how to explain my feelings for him when I don't even understand them myself, so I only say, "Thank you."

"But listen, be careful," she says, leaning close to me in that intent way of hers. "This afternoon while you were out, I convinced one of the attendants to tell me where Gabriel is."

"What?" I say. "Where is he? Is he okay? Did you talk to him?"

"I tried," she says. "When the attendant brought lunch, I complained again, and while we were in the elevator, I hit the panic button, the one that takes you into the basement."

"The basement?" I say, swallowing a lump in my throat. "Why would you go there?"

"That's where Gabriel has been reassigned indefinitely," she says, and immediately her eyes fill with pity. "I'm sorry. I tried to find him. But as soon as I got into the hallway, I crashed right into Housemaster Vaughn."

I feel as though I've been kicked in the chest. I double over to catch my breath, and end up falling into a sitting position on the floor. "He's stuck there because of me," I say.

"That's not true." Jenna kneels beside me. "And there are plenty of rooms down there. There's the storm shelter, and an emergency infirmary, and supply closets full of biohazard suits, medical supplies, fabric for the domestics. Maybe it doesn't mean anything bad. The Housemaster is always reorganizing the staff here."

"No," I say. "I know this is my fault." I was too reckless. The door was wide open when he kissed me. *Wide open!* How could I have been so stupid! That noise we heard was probably Vaughn, and then he slipped away like the snake that he is before he could be spotted.

Jenna catches my fist after I've punched the ground. "Listen," she says. "I told the Housemaster that I was lost, but I don't think he believed me. I'm probably not going to be allowed out anymore."

"I'm sorry, Jenna—"

"But I'll try to distract him for you. I'll—I don't know. I'll throw a fit, or Cecily will, and it'll create a scene. And that'll be your chance to go down there and find him. Okay?" She pushes the hair from my forehead. "You're going to find him, and you'll see that he's okay."

"You'd do that?" I say.

She smiles, and for once she looks strikingly like Rose smiling on her deathbed. "Sure," she says. "What have I got to lose?"

We sit beside each other in silence for a while, while her question echoes in my head. What *has* she got to lose? And just where was she all afternoon after she crashed into Vaughn in the hallway? That day on the trampoline, she hinted at being afraid, but I wasn't brave enough then to ask her what she meant.

"Jenna," I say, "what did he do to you?"

"Who?"

"You know who. Housemaster Vaughn."

"Nothing," she answers, a little too quickly. "It's just what I said. He caught me in the basement, and he sent me back upstairs."

"You were gone all afternoon," I say. She's looking at the ground, and I tilt her chin with my finger. "Jenna." She holds my gaze for a second. One horrible second, and I can see the pain in her eyes. I can see that something's broken. And then she backs away and stands.

"And how do you know what's in the basement?" I say, following her toward the door. "You've only been to the storm shelter. How do you know about the biohazard suits and the emergency infirmary?"

Jenna and I have an unspoken agreement to keep Cecily out of things. We keep a protective eye on her, but because of her closeness to Linden and Vaughn, we don't tell her everything. It never occurred to me that Jenna would keep any secrets from me as well. But now I think she's been keeping secrets for a while. She stops pacing toward the door and looks at her feet and gnaws on her lower lip. I hear my brother's voice in my head. *Your problem is that you're too emotional.*

But how can I not be emotional, Rowan? How can I not care?

"Please," I say.

"It doesn't matter," she says softly.

"Tell me what he did," I cry, forgetting the low voice I've been using. "What did he do to you?"

"Nothing!" she cries back. "It's what he's going to do to *you.* He knows you tried to run once, and he expects me to convince you to stay, but I'm trying to help you, so just shut up and let me!"

I'm so stunned that I don't follow her when she storms out of the library and slams the door behind her.

The hologram in the fireplace winces.

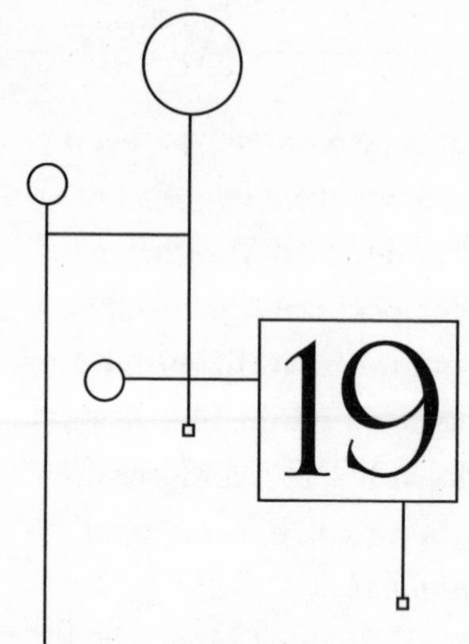

19

I WORRY for the rest of the evening. Deirdre tries massaging my shoulders, but she seems devastated that her efforts aren't consoling me at all. "Isn't there anything I can do?" she asks.

I think for a moment, and then I say, "Could you send up someone to do my nails? And maybe an eyebrow wax, too? Maybe I'll feel better if I can do something about my appearance."

Deirdre assures me that I look lovely, but she happily obliges, and a few minutes later I'm soaking in a warm bath while the chattering first generations massage conditioner into my hair and strip my eyebrow line of both hair and a layer of skin. They're the same women who prepared me on my wedding day, and it's a relief that they're so absorbed in their gossip that they don't notice my distress. It makes what I'm about to do that much easier.

"The day we met, you asked if my eyes were natural," I say. "Can irises be dyed?" It sounds painful and absurd, but I've seen stranger things in my time here.

The women laugh. "Of course not!" one says. "Only hair can be dyed. You change your eye color with contact lenses."

"Little pieces of plastic that go right into your eye," the other says.

I think it sounds as absurd as the dye, but I say, "Is it painful?"

"Oh, no!"

"Not at all!"

"Do we have any contact lenses?" I ask. "I'd really love to see how I'd look with green eyes. Or maybe a nice dark brown."

The attendants are more than delighted to grant this request. One of them disappears and returns with little circular containers that house contact lenses. They look disturbing, like irises peeled from eyeballs, and my dinner threatens to make a reappearance. But I work through it, because if I can survive that van full of girls, I can do this, too.

It takes several tries to get the lenses into my eyes. I keep blinking, or my eyes water and that flushes them out. One of the attendants even gives up and says, "Your eyes are so pretty, honey, I'm sure your husband wouldn't want you to change them." But the other is more determined, and together we work it out, and I'm staring at my newly green eyes in the mirror.

Impressive, I have to say.

The attendants cheer at their success. Before they go, they leave me a bottle of contact solution and some blue and brown lenses to practice with. They warn me not to fall asleep with them in my eyes because they'll stick to the iris and I'll have a hard time removing them.

Once the attendants are gone, I practice putting the green lenses on and taking them off. I think about what Rose said that afternoon when she caught me trying to escape through the elevator. She said that, for my eyes, Vaughn probably paid extra. And earlier this afternoon Jenna said she was worried about what he'd do to me. Not her, not Cecily. Me. Are the two things related? And if they are, what does that mean—that he'll pluck my eyes from my head and run some experiment on heterochromia? Heterochromia for the antidote? I can just see the party he'll hold; Linden could draw up the layout.

I leave the contacts to soak in the solution, and I fall into a deep, dreamless sleep.

In the morning Jenna and I conspire over breakfast. We sit on my bed, talking in low voices, and we finally think we've worked out a plan to distract Vaughn and get me into the basement, when we hear Cecily scream. We rush to her bedroom and find her kneeling on the floor in a watery puddle of blood, with her face pressed against the mattress. Her back convulses in gasps and sobs.

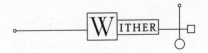

My heart is pounding in my ears, and Jenna and I struggle to help her to her feet. It's difficult just getting her onto the bed, because her body is so tightly locked, so bizarrely heavy, and she's so hysterical with pain. "It's happening," she cries. "It's happening and it's too soon. I couldn't stop it."

We manage to lay her down on the bed. She's gasping and white. The sheets between her legs bloom red with her blood.

"I'm getting Governor Linden," Jenna says, and I move to follow her, but Cecily grabs my arm, and her nails are clawing into my skin, and she says, "Stay! Don't leave me."

Her condition worsens rapidly. I murmur soothing things to her, but she doesn't seem to hear them. Her eyes flutter wildly back toward her skull, and horrible groans spill from her mouth. "Cecily." I shake her shoulders to bring her back to me. I don't know what else to do; she's the one who read all those books on childbirth. She's the expert, and I'm useless now. Useless and terrified.

She's right. It's too early. There's supposed to be another month, and there shouldn't be this much blood. Her legs writhe in her anguish, and the blood is getting everywhere. Her nightgown. Her lacy white socks.

"Cecily." I grab her face. Her eyes stare at me uncomprehendingly. Her pupils are wide and unreal. "Cecily, stay here with me."

She reaches up, touches my cheek with her cold little hand, and says, "You can't just leave me."

There's something strange about the way she says it, some deeper meaning brought on by delirium or something more urgent. There's a fear in her brown eyes I've never seen.

Vaughn comes running into the room with a crew of attendants and a gasping Linden in tow, and they take over. I move out of the way so Linden can take his rightful place beside her, holding her hand. The attendants have brought carts of medical equipment, and Vaughn helps her to sit up. "That's a good girl," he coos, and jabs an enormous needle into her spine. I'm dizzy by the sight of it, but for some reason an eerie calm washes over Cecily's face as the fluid is injected. I back away and back away until I'm in the doorway.

"Now's your chance," Jenna whispers. She's right. In this frenzy I could probably set the house on fire and it would go unnoticed. It's the perfect time to go to the basement and find Gabriel.

But Cecily is so small in a bloody sea of tubes and machines and white rubber gloves. She's gasping and moaning, and suddenly I'm terrified she's going to die.

"I can't," I say.

"I'll look out for her," Jenna says. "I'll make sure nothing happens."

I know she would. I trust her. But she doesn't know the story about Rose's baby, how Rose gave birth with no one but Vaughn to take care of her, and the awful thing he did when she was too sedated to stop him. He did something similar to me, after the hurricane. He's most dangerous when Linden's wives are unable to fight back. And I will not leave this room while his gloved hands are lifting up Cecily's nightgown.

Something else keeps me frozen to that spot too. Cecily has become a sister to me, and I feel it's my place to protect her just as my brother and I protected each other.

It goes on for what feels like hours. Sometimes Cecily is screaming and thrashing her legs, and other times she drifts in and out of sleep, or chews on ice chips that Elle feeds her from a paper cup. Once she asks me to tell her a story about the twins. I'd rather not share my life stories with a room full of attendants and Linden and Vaughn, so I tell her one of my mother's stories instead, and I embellish to make up for the details I don't know. I tell her about a neighborhood where everyone flew kites. They had hang gliders, too, which were giant kites that people could ride. The riders would stand somewhere high, like on a bridge or at the top of a very tall building. Then they would jump, and their hang glider would catch the wind. They would fly. Cecily sighs dreamily and says, "That sounds like magic."

"It was," I say. And on top of everything else now, I miss my mother. She would know what to do; so many babies were born on her watch. Young, expectant mothers would donate their children to research labs; in exchange they were given prenatal care, a few warm months off the street. And my mother was always so careful with the newborns. All she wanted to do was find an antidote so that the new generations would be able to live full and normal lives. When I was little, I believed she and my father would do it, but when they were killed in that explosion, Rowan said it was pointless. He said there was no saving this miserable world at all, and I believed him. And now I'm about to witness the birth of a new generation firsthand, and I don't know what I believe. I just know I want it to be alive.

Cecily's body is seized by another contraction, and her back arches off the mattress. I'm holding one hand and Linden is holding the other, and for a strange moment I feel almost like she's our child. All through my kite story, I noticed him looking at me in gratitude. Now she makes a terrible shrieking, whimpering sound. Her lip quivers. Linden tries to soothe her, but she jerks her face from his kisses, gurgles and screams in response to our cooing voices. I feel tears brimming in my own eyes as I watch the tears stream down her face, and finally I snap at Vaughn, "Can't you do something more for her pain?" Genius that he is, expert on the human form, aspiring bearer of the world-saving antidote.

His eyes meet mine with neutrality. "No need."

The attendants are putting Cecily's legs up on a pair of strange platforms that look like bicycle pedals. I think they call them stirrups. Vaughn leans close and kisses Cecily's sweaty forehead and says, "It's almost done, darling. You're doing wonderfully." She smiles wearily.

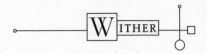

Jenna sits on the divan in the corner, looking pale herself. A little while ago she braided Cecily's sweaty hair back for her, but she hasn't spoken much since then. I want to go and sit with her, to comfort her and be comforted by her, but Cecily won't release her death grip on me. And soon, too soon, Vaughn is telling her to push.

To her credit she has stopped moaning about the pain. She sits upright, propped against the headboard, and a new determination washes over her face. She's ready. She's going to assume control.

When she pushes, the veins in her neck bulge. Her skin is sunburn pink. She grits her teeth and clamps Linden's and my hand. A long, strained whimper gets trapped in her throat and escapes as a spluttering gasp. This happens once, then again, then again, with a few seconds between for her to catch her breath. She's getting frustrated, and Vaughn tells her this next time will be the last time.

It turns out he's right. She pushes, and there's a horrible bloody sound as the baby comes out of her. But worse than that is the silence that follows.

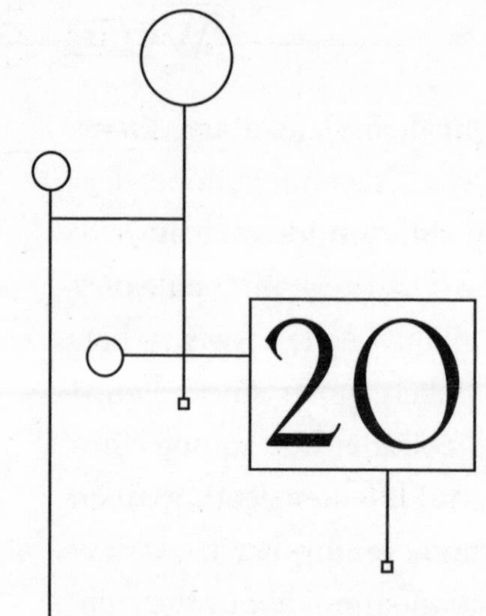

20

WE WAIT, and we wait. I want to look away, and I think Linden does too, as this white infant, bloody and still, is held up by one of the attendants, but we're frozen. All of us are frozen. Jenna on the divan. Cecily clinging to our hands. The attendants like sleeping cattle.

I barely have time to form the thought that Vaughn will let this baby die like his last grandchild, before he goes into action. He takes his new grandchild and sticks some kind of turkey-baster device into its mouth, and in a second the room is filled with a shrill cry, and the baby's limbs begin to thrash. Cecily deflates.

"Congratulations," Vaughn says, holding the writhing child up in his gloved hands. "You have a son."

All at once the room is filled with commotion and noise. The baby, still crying, is taken away to be cleaned and inspected. Linden holds Cecily's face close to his, and they're talking to each other in fast, hushed voices and kissing between the words.

I fall beside Jenna on the divan, and we put an arm around each other. I whisper, "Thank goodness that's over."

"Maybe not," Jenna says.

We watch as the attendants tend to Cecily, who has delivered the placenta, who is still bleeding, who is still too pale for comfort. She is transferred onto a gurney, and I am immediately at her side. This time I'm the one clinging to her hand, and I say, "I'll go with her."

"Go?" Vaughn laughs. "No, she's not going anywhere. We just need to get this mess cleaned up."

Already there are attendants stripping the bed of its sheets. Vaughn oversees this and says, "No, this is no good. The whole mattress is ruined."

"Where's my baby?" Cecily whispers. Her eyes are glassy and distant. Tears and sweat roll down her face. Her breaths rattle in her chest.

"We'll see him soon, love," Linden says, and kisses her. For the moment she looks nothing like a child. If I didn't know either of them, I would almost believe that they were a normal mother and father in a normal hospital under normal circumstances.

But of course, there's no such thing as normal anymore. Any chance of normal was destroyed long ago, like a research lab with my parents inside.

Cecily looks so weak and exhausted, her face drained

of color, and other worries start to take over. What if she loses too much blood? What if there's an infection? What if giving birth was too traumatic for her small frame and there are complications? I wish Vaughn would take her to a hospital, even if it had to be the hospital he owns in the city. Someplace well lit, and full of other doctors.

I don't say any of this out loud. I know it would be futile. Vaughn never lets us leave, and suggesting it might even scare Cecily. I brush the hair from her sweaty face, and instead I say, "You should rest now; you've really earned it."

"You've earned it, love," Linden echoes, and kisses her hand and presses it to his cheek. There's an almost smile on her lips as she fades into unconsciousness.

That night Cecily sleeps deeply and without snoring. Thinking of my encounter with Vaughn after the hurricane, when I was too weak to defend myself, I check in on her periodically. She barely moves, and I'm relieved to see that Linden is faithfully at her side.

Jenna goes to bed even before dinner is served. But Vaughn is constantly arriving at our floor with excuses to check on the mother of his new grandchild. And it's abundantly clear that I won't be able to make it to the basement for a while. It's too risky, and I've only just been given this key card. I don't want to have it confiscated. I try to console myself with thoughts that Gabriel's okay. After all, he was able to get that June Bean to me. Maybe Vaughn knows nothing about that kiss. Maybe Gabriel has only been assigned to clean medical equipment or mop the floors. But still the thought of him alone in that windowless basement sets my stomach doing flip-flops. And on top of that, I haven't seen the baby since it was carted away. And every time I hear Vaughn's insipid voice outside my bedroom, I think he's going to say that it didn't survive.

Gabriel, please look after the baby if you see it down there, okay?

Sometime after midnight, while I'm watching the snow and nursing a cup of Earl Grey, Linden comes into my bedroom. His eyes and cheeks are all lit up, and he's grinning wildly. "I've just been to see him," he says. "My son. He's beautiful. He's strong and he's healthy."

"I'm so happy for you, Linden," I say. And I mean it.

"How are you?" he says, pulling the ottoman near me and taking a seat. "Have you had enough to eat? Do you need anything—anything at all?"

He's over the stars right now, and I admit it makes me feel a little better. Like everything is really going to be okay.

I smile and shake my head, look out the window. "Full moon," I say.

"Must be a sign of good luck." He reaches out and touches a lock of my hair. Then he gets on the ledge beside me, and I curl my knees to my chest to make room for him. He smiles at me, and I sense him advancing. Gently he moves my legs from between us, and my feet land on the ground, and he tilts my chin and kisses me.

I allow it, because I'm first wife—the key card makes it as official as it could get—and because I promised him I'd be a better wife, and it would make him suspicious if I pushed him away. And because, truthfully, it isn't the worst thing in the world to kiss Linden Ashby.

The kiss lingers for a while, and then I feel his fingers starting to unbutton my nightgown, and I draw back.

"What is it?" he asks, his voice as hazy as his eyes.

"Linden," I say, blushing, fixing the one button he'd managed to free. I can't think of a suitable explanation, so I look at the moon.

"Is it because the door is open?" he asks. "I'll close it."

"No," I say. "It's not the door."

"Then, what?" He tilts my chin again, and hesitantly I bring my eyes to him. "I love you," he says. "I want to have a baby with you."

"Now?" I say.

"Eventually. Soon. We only have such a short while together," he says.

Shorter than you know, Linden. But I only say, "There are so many other things I want to do with you. I want to go places. I want to see your houses come to fruition. I want—I want to go to a winter solstice party. There must be one coming up."

The romance is draining from his face, replaced by confusion or disappointment—I can't tell which. "Well,

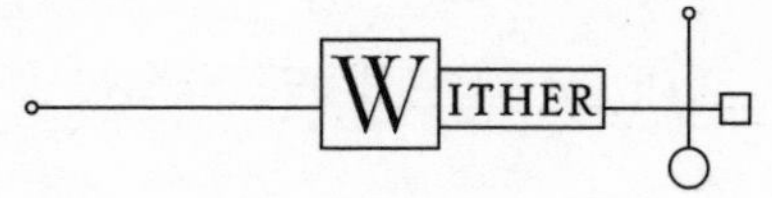

there is probably one coming up. The solstice is next week . . ."

"Can't we go?" I say. "Deirdre has all those beautiful fabrics, and she hardly gets the opportunity to make me a new dress."

"If that's what will make you happy."

"It will," I say, and kiss him. "You'll see. Getting out of the house will do us both some good."

He looks heartbroken, though, so I give in and sit close to him and let him put his arm around me. He loves me, he says, but how can he when we know so little about each other? I admit it's easy to succumb to the illusion. I admit that sitting here in front of the beautiful moon, embraced in his warmth, it does feel like love. A little bit. Maybe.

"You're just overexcited," I assure him. "You have a beautiful new son, and he'll be enough to make you happy. You'll see."

He kisses my hair. "Maybe you're right," he says.

But even though he's trying to agree with me, I know I'm wrong. I know it's only a matter of time before I'll be unable to fend off his restless advances without him suspecting me. However I plan to escape, it will have to be soon.

In Gabriel's absence the nervous first generation attendant brings all of our meals. Jenna and I take lunch at the same time in the library, but she's practically invisible compared to the attention I get.

"I hope you enjoy your lunch," the attendant tells me, pulling the lid off the tray. "Chopped Caesar salad with grilled chicken. If you don't like it, the head cook will make you anything you like."

"It looks delicious," I assure him. "I'm not too fussy."

"I didn't mean to imply that at all, Lady Rhine. Not at all. Enjoy your lunch."

Jenna is grinning at her plate. After the attendant has left, I say, "Did you see that? And that's only a small part of it. This morning I had an attendant asking if I wanted her to brush my hair. Something strange is going on."

"It's not strange." Jenna bites off a forkful of lettuce. "For a first wife."

"They can tell that just by the key card?" I say.

"That," she says. "And other things." She raises her glass, clinks it against mine. "Congrats, sister wife."

I respond with a bittersweet, "Thanks."

While all of the attendants are busy catering to my every need, I worry about what this key card means. At first I thought it would mean more freedom, but now I wonder if Vaughn has concocted a scheme more diabolical than that, because with all this extra attention it's becoming difficult for me to find a minute to myself. I'm allowed outdoors whenever I like, but am often interrupted with attendants bringing me mugs of hot chocolate or tea. They come to my bedroom two, three, four times a night asking if I need extra pillows, if my window has a draft.

I can't help but think Vaughn allowed me the key card

so his staff could smother me with kindness. Maybe he even hid Gabriel away just to mock me.

And for all the places I can go, none of them lead to Gabriel. I know I should have looked for him when there was the distraction of Cecily's labor. Jenna has told me as much since. But I couldn't bring myself to leave her.

I'm still worried about her. She and her son survived the labor, but she's been weary since then. Her room is kept dark and warm, smelling of medications and, faintly, of Vaughn's basement. In her sleep she murmurs about music and kites and hurricanes. She's lost too much blood. That's Vaughn's diagnosis, and I agree, but I'm still uneasy when she's given the transfusion. I lie beside her as she recovers, as the color slowly returns to her cheeks, and I wonder whose blood is coursing through her. Maybe Rose's. Or some unwilling attendant's. I wonder if Vaughn, who I believe is capable of such darkness and destruction, ever truly uses his abilities to heal. But as the days pass, Cecily begins to improve.

When the baby cries, Linden carries him to Cecily's bedside. Sleepily she unbuttons her nightgown and holds her son to her breast. From the hallway I look into her bedroom and see Linden helping her stay awake. He speaks softly to her, pushing the straggly red hair from her face, and his words make her smile. They're perfect for each other, I think, so wide-eyed and sheltered, so content with this little life they've built with each other. Maybe I should stop telling my twin stories; maybe it's better for both of them to forget there are better things beyond this mansion. Things that don't dissolve, things more tangible than the sharks and dolphins in the pool, the spinning houses at Linden's expos. And it's better that their son never knows there's a world out there at all, because he'll never get to see it.

Cecily turns and notices me standing in the doorway. She waves me over, but I fade back into the hallway, pretending there's some way I can be useful elsewhere. I do not want to intrude on their marriage. Sharing a husband with two other wives isn't complicated; being married to Linden means something different for each of us. For Jenna, Linden's mansion is nothing but a luxurious place to die. For Cecily, her marriage is some kind of partnership of "I love yous" and children. For me, it's a lie. And as long as I can separate the three marriages and stick to my plan, it will be easier to leave. Easier to tell myself that they'll be okay once I'm gone.

I'm happy when Cecily is well enough to get out of bed. I follow her to the sitting room and watch as she sets a slide into place on the keyboard and begins to play. Her music brings the hologram to life, like a floating television screen. A green field dotted with poppies, and a cobblestone-like blue sky with moving white clouds. I am sure this is a replica of a painting I've seen in one of the library books, something impressionistic as the artist began the slow descent into madness.

The baby lies on the floor, staring up, the lights from

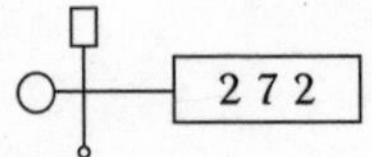

the illusion flickering about his face. The winds thrash the grass and the poppies and the faraway bushes this way and that, until everything is one grayed-over tangle of color. A delirium. Smears of wet paint.

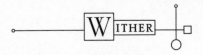

Cecily has lost herself. Her eyes are closed. The music streams out of her fingers. I concentrate on her young face, her small slightly parted mouth, her thin eyelashes. The colors of her song do not reach her where she sits poised over the keys, and I do not think the illusion matters to her. She's the most real thing in this room.

Her son makes uncertain faces and wriggles in place, unsure what to do with all this splendor. As he grows, he will see many illusions. He will watch paintings come to life as music plays for him, and he'll see his father's houses spin, and he'll dive into schools of guppies and great whites in the swimming pool. But I don't suppose he will ever know the ocean lapping up around his ankles, or will ever cast a fishing line, or have a house of his own.

The music fades; the winds calm; the illusion folds in on itself and dies.

Cecily says, "I wish we could have a real piano. Even the dumpy orphanage had a real piano."

Jenna, standing in the doorway with her mouth and hand full of shelled pistachios, says, "'Real' is a dirty word in this place."

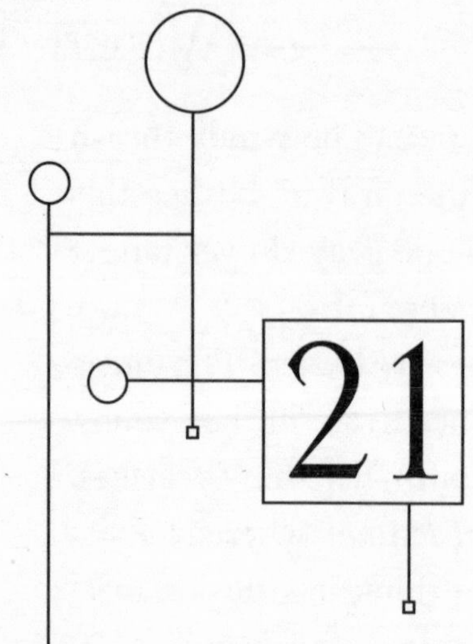

21

ON THE MORNING of the winter solstice, Jenna manages to steal the lighter from an attendant after he lights the incense in the hall. She pretends to flirt with him, and when she drops her stack of risqué romance novels, he's eager to pick them up, and she manages to swipe the lighter right out of his hand. He's so enamored by her smile that he doesn't realize the lighter's gone.

"Bye, bye." She smiles as he leaves, and he nearly catches his tie in the elevator doors as they close. The second he's gone, the seduction leaves her gray eyes and she becomes just a girl again. In my doorway I applaud, and she makes a curtsy with her skirt.

She's sweating a little, as though the effort exhausted her. But she holds the lighter like it's a trophy.

"What are you going to do with that?" I ask.

"Give me one of your candles—I'm going to set the

sitting room on fire," she says matter-of-factly.

"Excuse me?"

"When Governor Linden and the Housemaster and the attendants hear the alarm, they'll come rushing to find out what the commotion is. And that's when you go to the basement."

It's not the craziest plan one could come up with, as Jenna points out, recalling my brush with death on the mini-golf course. But I make her wait until I've put the green contacts into my eyes. "Maybe then I won't be recognized," I say. Even the attendants who have never met me have heard about me. Rhine. The nice one who doesn't complain, who has the unusual eyes.

Jenna is impressed by my cunning. "Look for a biohazard suit," she says. "Then nobody will recognize you for sure. They should be in one of the labs." I don't tell her that the thought of venturing into one of those dark rooms terrifies me. I only nod and give her one of the lavender candles that's supposed to help me fall asleep at night. "You stay in here," she says. "And when the alarm goes off, just try to be invisible." She smiles at me, and then she's gone with a little skip in her step. I think she has wanted to set fire to this place for a long time.

A few seconds later the fire alarm is blaring. The ceiling lights are flashing. Across the hall the baby starts screaming, and Cecily runs into the hallway with her hands over her ears. The elevator opens, and attendants flood out, but Linden and Vaughn don't show up until the car comes back a second time, and by then you can see the smoke billowing out of the sitting room. There's no stairwell leading to the wives' floor, and I've always wondered what would happen if there were ever a fire, but knowing Vaughn, he would let Linden's wives die and replace us later.

It's easy for me to escape. The key card, of course, won't grant access to the basement, and so I have to push the panic button. But in all this commotion and with all these alarms already wailing, it doesn't make a difference. The doors open and I'm in the windowless basement. It's eerily calm down here. There's no indication that there are any sirens, and the ceiling lights lazily flicker.

Green-eyed and anonymous, I stumble along the wall, whispering Gabriel's name and looking for a biohazard suit. I find a closet of them and quickly adjust one over my clothes. There's a harsh plastic smell inside, like being slowly suffocated. I take deep breaths that fog the face covering. It's like being in a nightmare. It's like being buried alive.

"Gabriel!" My whispers are becoming increasingly desperate. I am hoping he will just crash into me, or I'll turn a corner and there he'll be, mopping the floor or organizing storm supplies. And as I'm hoping I won't have to open a door, I won't have to open a door, I won't have to open a door, I hear his voice. At least I think it's his voice. It's so hard to hear in this thing, and my own breathing is amplified in the confined space.

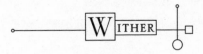

Something touches my shoulder, and I start. "Rhine?" He spins me around, and there he is. Gabriel. In one piece. Not etherized on a table. Not bruised. Not dead. Dead. The word trills through my head like the fire and the hurricane alarms, and I realize that's what I'd feared underneath everything else. I throw my arms around him, and it's awkward, with the helmet in the way, but I don't care. I can feel his sturdy arms around me, and I don't care about anything else.

He eases the helmet off my head, and sounds of the world outside my own breathing enter my ears. He's laughing a little. The helmet falls. He squeezes me, says, "What are you doing?"

"I thought you were dead," I say into his shirt. "I thought you were dead, I thought you were dead."

It feels good to say the words. To relieve myself of them. To know they're not the truth. He can hear the fear coming out of me. And his hand runs up my back, along my spine, and it crashes into my hair and holds the base of my skull. Holds me steady. And it's like that for a while.

When we draw apart, he pushes the hair out of my eyes and stares at me. "What's happened to you?" he says.

"What? I'm fine."

"Your eyes."

"Contacts. I didn't want to be recognized, in case I ran into someone, and—What about you!" I cry, remembering the situation. "I haven't seen you for days!"

He presses his finger to my lips to quiet me, and then leads me into one of the horrifyingly dark rooms. One of the places I most fear. But he's with me, and I know it will be all right. He doesn't turn on a light, and I can smell cold metal, hear water dripping against a hard surface. In the perfect darkness I hold both of his hands and try to decipher his outline.

"Listen," he whispers. "You can't be down here. The Housemaster knows everything. He knows about the kiss. He knows you tried to run away. If he catches us together, I'm out of here."

"He'll kick you out?"

"I don't know. But I have a feeling a body bag will be involved."

Of course. How stupid of me. Nobody leaves this place alive. In fact, I'm not even convinced anyone leaves this place once they're dead. More bodies for Vaughn to dissect. Is that what Jenna was trying to warn me about? I imagine my eyes in a jar in one of Vaughn's medical rooms, and I purse my lips against a wave of nausea. There's a good chance this is all one of Vaughn's traps—the key card, putting Gabriel into the basement where he knew I'd look for him. He could be lurking around a corner, waiting to lock me in one of these rooms. The thought causes my pulse to hammer against my temples, but Gabriel's presence overpowers my fear. I would never have been able to live with myself if I hadn't tried to find him.

"How?" I say. "How does he know?"

"I don't know, but he can't see us together. Rhine, it isn't safe."

"Run away with me," I say.

"Rhine, listen, we can't—"

"I've found a way out," I say, and I grab his hand and bring it to the key card hanging around my neck. "Linden gave me permission to use the elevator. And I found a way out. There's a glitch in the trees that border the property. Some of them aren't real. They're a hologram."

He's quiet, and in the darkness it's the same as disappearing, and I grab at his shirt. "Still there?"

"I'm here," he says. He's silent again, and I listen for his breathing. I hear his lips part, and he utters a fraction of a syllable, and I know, just know, that he's going to use logic against me, and that will never do if I want to get out of this place at all before I die, so I kiss him.

The door is already closed, and in this isolated darkness it's almost like we're not in the basement at all. We're in the infinite ocean with no continents in sight, and there's nobody to catch us. We're free. His hands are in my hair, behind my head, traveling the length of me. The biohazard suit crinkles, making audible record of his movements.

He tries to break away every so often, getting out a "But—" or "Listen to me—" or "Rhine—," but I stop him every time, and he gives up, and I will this moment to last forever. I will the wedding band off my finger. I will us both to be free.

Until one time when we draw apart and I feel his forehead press against mine, and he says, "Rhine. It's too dangerous. The Housemaster will do anything to protect his son. If he catches you running away, he'll murder you and make it look like an accident."

"That's far-fetched even for him," I say.

"I wouldn't put it past him," he says. "His son is all he has. He had you and your sister wives brought here just to console him while Lady Rose was dying. Don't think he wouldn't destroy you before he lets you hurt him again."

If you value your life, you won't run again. That's what Vaughn said to me after my botched escape attempt. But he also said I was more special than I realized, that Linden's spirit would be destroyed if he lost me. And despite all the horrible things I think of Vaughn, I do believe he cares about his son. There's no accident he could stage that would make Linden accept my demise. Linden would never forgive his father if something were to happen to me on Vaughn's watch.

A pang of guilt rushes through me, and with some effort I force it away. I don't belong to Linden. I don't want to hurt him, but that's just the way it has to be.

"It will be okay," I say. "We just won't get caught. That's all."

He laughs, but it's full of disbelief. "Oh, is that all."

"I said I'd drag you kicking and screaming, and I will," I say. "Don't you see what's happened? You've been captive for so long that you don't even realize you want freedom anymore. And don't say it's not that bad here. Don't ask what the world has got that this place hasn't got, because the answer is something I can only show you. You have to trust me. Please. You have to."

I can hear him hesitating. He works a lock of my hair around his finger. "I didn't think I'd ever see you again," he says after a while.

"You can't see me right now," I say, and we allow ourselves to laugh quietly.

"You are insane," he says.

"So I've been told. So, does that mean you'll at least try my plan?" I say.

"And if it doesn't work?" he says.

"I guess we both die," I say. I'm mostly serious.

There's a long pause. His hands finding my cheeks. Then his voice, smooth and clear. "Okay."

We work out the details in hushed voices, pressed close to each other in the darkness. On the last Friday of every month, at about ten p.m., he takes the bio waste out the back exit, to the dump truck that Housemaster Vaughn orders in. He'll watch the truck leave, and then he'll follow its path through the hologram trees and wait for me. I think it's a solid plan, but Gabriel keeps asking how we'll get through the gate, and what if there's security, and I wave him off. "We'll figure it out," I say.

Tonight Linden is taking me to a solstice party in the city. "While we're out, I'll make a note of the roads. I'll look for someplace we could go once we're out."

"It's the last week of December," he tells me as we're saying good-bye. "So I guess I'll see you next year."

We kiss one last time, and then the elevator doors close between us.

On the wives' floor the fire has been successfully extinguished, though we have to bid farewell to the scorched remains of what were the ugliest pink curtains I've ever known. I enter the sitting room just as Jenna is telling Housemaster Vaughn, ". . . and I saw that the flame from the candle caught the curtain, and I tried to put it out, but it was just out of control."

Linden pats her shoulder reassuringly. "It's not your fault," he says.

"We'll get some new curtains," Vaughn says. "But maybe we shouldn't leave candles burning unattended." For some reason Vaughn looks right at me.

Cecily, holding the fussy infant against her shoulder, says, "What's happened to your eyes?"

"My eyes?" I say.

Jenna taps the skin below her own eye, and I realize what she's trying to tell me. I still have the green contacts in.

"I . . . thought I'd try something different," I say. "It was supposed to be a surprise. For the party tonight, Linden. I was trying them on, and then the alarm went off and I suppose I forgot."

I can't tell if Vaughn is convinced by my story, but

mercifully the baby starts screaming and that distracts everyone. When Cecily can't calm him, Vaughn takes him from her arms. "There, there, Bowen, my boy," he says, and this soothes the crying. Cecily stands in Vaughn's shadow, looking like she wants to say something, her hand poised to reach for her son, but for some reason she doesn't move.

"I think he's hungry," Vaughn says.

"I can feed him," Cecily says.

"Now, darling, don't trouble yourself." He taps her nose, like she's a little girl. "That's what wet nurses are for." He leaves the room, baby Bowen in his arms, before Cecily can say another word. Her small, swollen breasts are leaking through her shirt.

It takes an hour for the attendants to get me ready for the solstice party. I'm so relieved to have found Gabriel, and so excited about our escape plan, that I don't mind that they're pulling my hair and spraying it until I'm choking in the perfumed cloud. They discourage the contact lenses, and I pretend I'm sad to take them out. "Your eyes will be the talk of the party, trust me," one says.

"Especially if there are cameras," another says dreamily.

Cameras. Perfect. I don't know what the odds are of my brother watching a televised solstice festival. And there are probably dozens of them airing on the news networks tonight. He wouldn't usually care about these things, but has he been looking for me? Is there still a chance after all this time? I just need one month, and then I'll be able to find my way back home. In the back of my mind I worry that I'll be returning to an empty house, that he has gone to look for me, or, driven to extremes by grief, he has moved away, too pained by the memories to stay. We've seen it happen. Families have moved away once their sisters and daughters have been taken. And Rowan has never been one to sit idly by.

Wait for me, I try to cast my thoughts to him, twin to twin. *I'll be home soon.*

As always, there's no answer.

I was skeptical when Deirdre told me my dress would be pink, but when she unfolds it before me, I am, as always, dazzled by her skill. It's a muted, shimmering pink with a hemline meant to simulate snowdrifts. The shawl glitters with pearls. She does my makeup to match. "I bet most of the other wives will wear blue or white," she says. "For winter. I thought you'd want to stand out a little."

"It's incredible," I say. And she beams and holds a folded tissue to my lips and tells me to blot.

Linden is happy I decided against the green contacts.

"They looked kind of freaky," Cecily says with her arms folded in the doorway. Her hair is tousled, and faint purple bags droop down under her eyes. Her skin is pale and full of veins. "I thought you had some kind of stroke. Don't wear them again, okay?" She shudders at the memory and retreats into her room.

I frown after she's gone. She is hardly the bouncy, winged bride she was less than a year ago. She had her fourteenth birthday shortly before the baby was born, and unlike Jenna who aged quietly, she made a big deal of it. There was a sheet cake covered in frosted leaping unicorns, and the attendants had to sing to her, and Linden bought her a gorgeous diamond necklace she never has cause to wear. She wore it for a while around the house, but I haven't seen it since she gave birth to Bowen.

"She seems so tired," I say to Linden. "Have you been helping her with the baby?"

"Every chance I get," he says, and frowns a little too. We've both lowered our voices. "It's not always easy to wrestle him away from my father. He's so excited to finally have a grandchild." He looks at me, and for a moment I think he's going to tell me what I already know, that he had a baby that didn't live. A little piece of Rose he should have been able to keep. But he only says, "You look stunning," and takes my arm.

It's freezing outside, but Deirdre's shawl keeps my shoulders warm. Linden makes some joke about whether we should open the skylight, but I just snuggle against him and say we should leave it closed. Because of the tinted glass and the darkness of the night, I can't see exactly where the hologram of trees is. But once we're out into the city, I pay attention to the streets. I press myself close to the glass and look for landmarks that will guide Gabriel and me when we break free.

Linden is smiling brightly.

"What?" I say.

"You. You're so excited." He tucks an oversprayed curl behind my ear. "It's just kind of cute."

His comment takes me by surprise. Here he is admiring me while I'm thinking of nothing but how to get away from him and never look back. I feel so guilty that when he kisses my cheek, I reward him with a smile of my own. And I continue to keep an eye out.

The cinema will be the first thing to look for. It should be easy to find from anywhere—the marquee is so bright, and the neon sign on the door boasts that it's open twenty-four hours a day. Then there's what looks like some kind of seafood place, with bright red tables and paper lanterns. And then I remember that we're close to the ocean. I get a good look at it as we're turning a corner, and I see yachts farther out in the sea, full of lights. I can hear their music even with the windows closed. "They have parties on the water?" I say.

"I suppose the yacht clubs do," Linden says, looking out over my shoulder.

"Have you ever been on the water?" I ask him.

"Once, when I was small," he says. "But I'm too young to remember it. My father tells me I was seasick for days. Some kind of condition, he says. I've avoided the water ever since."

"So that's why you never go into the pool or learned how to swim," I say. He nods. I try to hide my horror.

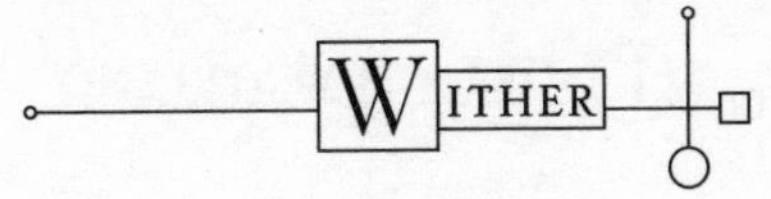

Vaughn so carefully controls his son, that he can't even allow him to enjoy the illusion of a real ocean in the pool. I have my doubts that the seasickness story is even true. In fact, Linden's childhood illnesses and supposed frailty seem like things Vaughn concocted to keep his son from venturing far. I put my hand on Linden's knee and say, "When it gets warm again, I'm teaching you to swim. It's easy. Once you learn, you can't sink even if you try."

He says, "I'd like that."

And then I remember. By the time the weather gets warm, I will be far from this place. I get one last look at the ocean before it disappears behind some buildings. The waves roll on past the yachts and the lights, into the deep night, into forever. It's the one place Linden can never follow me. And Gabriel says he loves boats. I wonder if he knows enough about them to sail us away.

The party is held on the fifteenth floor of a towering skyscraper. There's a dance floor on which shoe prints linger in neon lights for a few seconds before fading. Icicles are suspended in the air, reflecting back the colorful lights. The floor is a snowy hologram, and Deirdre was right, all the wives are wearing blue or white.

Linden is looking a little rigid as we linger by the door. "Do you know anyone here?" I ask.

"A few of my father's colleagues," he says.

The strobe lights make his shadow jump in rainbow colors. I think about what Rose said, about his being a wallflower at parties, about his being an excellent dancer.

He looks a little seasick right now. And I decide to wait for a slow song before asking him to dance, to make it easier.

We stand by the buffet table, sampling filet mignon and soups and the biggest assortment of pastries I've seen since the bakery I used to pass on my way to work in Manhattan. I tell him we have to bring home some of the éclairs for Cecily, who has a weakness for anything with chocolate icing.

When there's a slow song, I drag Linden out onto the dance floor, and though he's bemused at first, it doesn't take long for him to forget about everyone around us. I've never danced a day in my life, but he guides me flawlessly even in these impossible heels. And while we're spinning, floating, and just after he's dipped me over his arm and I've recovered, a camera pans over us. I try to let it get the best possible shot of my eyes.

We mingle for a while, and fewer of the men here want to kiss my hand, because they all have their wives on their arms. The wives are more bearable too. There are first generation wives talking with younger wives, and I join a conversation about rare birds in eastern California. I don't have much to contribute, but it's a welcome change from the wives who asked when I'd let my husband knock me up.

I see Linden joining in on a conversation with a group of men across the room, meeting my eyes occasionally and just barely raising his hand in a wave. I think he's following my lead.

"You're married to Linden Ashby, right?" one of the young wives says, leaning close to me.

"Yes," I say. It seems more natural to admit to it now, somehow.

"I was so sad to learn that Rose died." She presses her open hand over her heart. "She was a friend of mine."

"Mine, too," I say. Across the room I think Linden is actually laughing at something he's heard.

"He looks like he's doing well, though," the young wife says, and her youthful smile reminds me of Cecily before the baby was born. "I'm glad he's opening up again. We all—my husband works with Linden's father at the hospital—we heard about her falling ill, and we haven't seen Linden at any of the parties."

"It's been difficult, but he's doing much better," I say.

"You must have a magic touch," she says.

Linden sweeps my arm up in his, and, still laughing about some secret joke, he begins to introduce me to his father's friends, and their wives, and even some people he's only just met. I've never seen him like this. So happy. So . . . free.

We return home in the early hours of the morning. He had a few glasses of wine and is sagging against me as we take the elevator to the wives' floor so he can check on Bowen, whose crib is in Cecily's room. There's been talk of building a nursery on another floor, and it's become a great source of tension between Cecily and Vaughn. She refuses to part with her son, and Vaughn thinks it's a shame to waste all these infinite rooms. Rose's bedroom door is closed off at the end of the hall, and even Cecily has not been so bold as to suggest converting it into a nursery.

I hand Linden the box of éclairs I've brought home for Cecily. He stares at me a long while and says, "You're so thoughtful," and gives me a quick kiss as he turns into her bedroom.

In my bathroom I scrub off my makeup, rinse my hair out in the sink, and change into my nightgown, but quickly realize I'm unable to sleep. My bones still want to dance, and my mind is all full of lights and music and thoughts of the ocean. If I were truly an orphan like Linden believes, if I had really spent my childhood in a school for brides, I think this would be a nice life to lead. I could see how a girl could get lost in it.

I think about calling Deirdre to rub my stiff ankles, or draw me a chamomile bath (the exact science of which I cannot seem to recreate myself), but I remember how late it is and decide against it. Instead I knock on Jenna's door. She's barely awake, and I ask if I can get into the bed with her. In the darkness I can just make out her nod.

"Did you tell freedom hello for me?" she says as I wrap my arms around a pillow and she tucks the covers over me.

I tell her about the icicles, and the snowy hologram, and the food. "The chocolate-dipped strawberries were worth dying for," I swoon. "They had a huge fountain just bubbling chocolate. I wish you'd been there."

"Sounds nice," she says. Her voice is a little strained, and she coughs. She was coughing earlier today too, and she has looked a little pale for the past few days. I move closer to her and touch my hand to her forehead, but Linden isn't the only one who had a bit to drink, and I can't tell if she's warm.

"Are you feeling all right?" I ask.

"I'm just tired. And a little congested. It's the weather." She coughs again, and I feel something warm land on my cheek. My blood runs cold.

"Jenna?" I say.

"What?"

I want to stay here, in the dark, and not make a move in the direction of this new fear. I want to go to sleep and wake up in the morning and find that everything's okay.

But I don't. I reach over and I turn on the light. Jenna coughs again, and I see the splatter of blood on her lips.

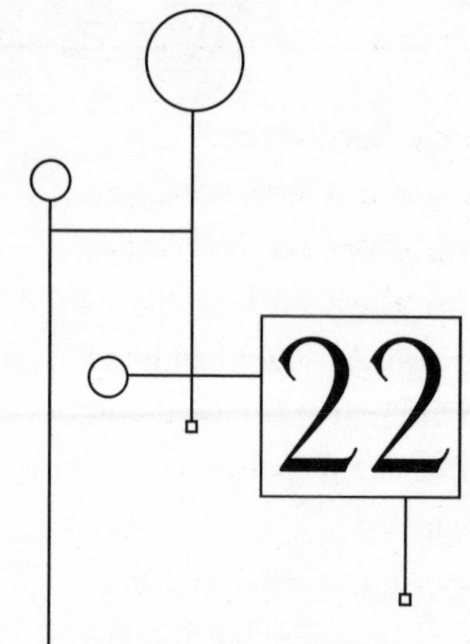

THE BABY will not stop crying. His face is bright red, and Cecily paces and paces with him on her shoulder, murmuring nice things to him, though there are fat tears rolling down her face. She doesn't try to brush them away.

And Vaughn is touching Jenna, feeling the sides of her jaw, holding her tongue under his cruel papery finger to look down her throat, and I can see that she hates having him near her. And she looks so wilted.

Linden takes the baby, and he gurgles for a second, but then resumes screaming. I jam the heels of my hands against my temples and say, "Will you get him out of here please?"

Vaughn is asking Jenna, for the third time, how old she is. And she is telling him, for the third time, that she is nineteen. And yes, she's sure.

Linden brings the screaming baby out of the room, but we can all still hear him.

"What is it?" Cecily says. "What's wrong?"

"It's the virus," Vaughn says. I suppose he's trying to sound remorseful, but all I see is a giant cartoon snake flicking his tongue. Jenna's life is nothing to him.

"No," someone says. And I realize the voice was my own. Cecily touches my arm, and I shrug her away violently. "That doesn't make sense. It isn't possible."

Jenna's eyes are closing. She can barely even stay conscious long enough to hear she's dying. How is it possible that she's gotten so sick so rapidly?

"But you can fix it, right?" says Cecily. Tears are staining the collar of her shirt. "You're working on an antidote."

"I'm afraid it's not there yet," Vaughn says. "But maybe we can prolong her life span until then." He taps Cecily's nose, but she no longer finds his favoritism endearing, and I see her take a step back. She shakes her head.

"What the hell have you been working on, then?" she says. "All this time. All this time you spend down there!" Her lip is quivering, and her breaths have taken on a wet, drowning quality. She believes Vaughn spends all those long hours working on an antidote in the basement, and that soon he'll save us all. I wish I believed that too.

"Now, darling—"

"No. No, you do something and you do it right now."

They get into an argument in low voices. Their voices spin and spin, and her sobs splash around me like waves, and I can't stand it. I want them both to go away. Vaughn and his little pet. I climb into the bed with Jenna and wipe some blood from her lips. She's already begun to lose consciousness. "Please," I whisper into her ear. I don't know what I'm asking. I don't know what I expect her to do.

Vaughn leaves, mercifully, and Cecily climbs into the bed with us. Her dramatic crying is shaking the mattress, and I snap at her, "She's sleeping. Don't wake her up."

"Sorry," she whispers, and lays her head on my shoulder. There's not a sound from her after that.

Jenna falls into an unreachable sleep, while Cecily and I drift in and out of nightmares of our own. I hear Cecily muttering as she stirs beside me, but I can't reach either of my sister wives. Over and over I am running through the trees with no iron gate in sight. Sometimes I'm drowning. The waves spin me over and over until I don't know which way is up.

I wake up gasping. The dampness on my neck is Cecily, pressed against me, sweating and crying and drooling. Her lips are moving, trying to make words. Her eyebrows are pressed together.

Down the hall the baby is crying and crying, and Cecily's shirt is stained with breast milk, but she is never allowed to feed her son. Vaughn takes him away. He hired a wet nurse, and he says it will be healthier for Cecily this way, but she always looks like she's in pain. My sister wives are wilting like my mother's lilies, and I don't know how to revive them. I don't know what to do.

Jenna opens her eyes and looks me over. "You look awful," she says hoarsely. "What's that smell?"

"Breast milk," I say.

At my tone, Cecily begins to stir. She's choking on her drool and complaining about not liking the music. Then her eyes open and register awareness, and she sits up. "What's happening? Are you feeling better?"

The baby is still crying, and Cecily looks to the doorway. "I have to feed him," she says, stumbling and hitting the door frame on her way out.

"Something's not right with her," Jenna says.

"You're just now noticing?" I say, and we both laugh a little.

Jenna manages to sit up, and I coax some water into her. I think she's only drinking it for my benefit. She's pale, and her lips are faintly tinted purple. I try comparing her to Rose, who was still able to act healthy on a good day. I think of how the June Beans dyed her mouth such ridiculous colors, and I wonder if that was part of her concealment. And how her face was always blushed with makeup. I think of how she hated the medicines, how she begged to be left to die.

"Are you in a lot of pain?" I ask.

"I can't really feel my arms or legs," Jenna says. She laughs a little. "So I guess I'm getting out of here before you after all."

"Please don't say that." I push the hair from her forehead.

"I had a dream that I was in the van with my sisters," she says. "But then someone opened the door, and I looked at them and saw you and Cecily in their places. Rhine, I think I've begun to forget what they looked like. Sounded like."

"I forget my brother's voice." I only realize it once I've said the words.

"But you don't forget his face. Because you're twins."

"You figured that out, huh?"

"Your twin stories were too vivid to be fiction," she says.

"But we aren't identical twins," I say. "Boys and girls can't be identical twins, you know. And I do forget what he looks like a little bit."

"You'll see him again," she says, sounding sure about it. "You never told me if you made it into the basement."

I nod, sniffle, and try to disguise it as a cough. "We've figured out a plan. We're leaving next month. But maybe I can stay a while longer."

"I did not light those curtains on fire for nothing. You're getting out of here, and it's going to be amazing."

"Come with us," I say.

"Rhine . . ."

"You hate it here. Do you really want to spend what's left of your life in this bed?" I don't know what I think freedom can do for her. That she'll get to see the ocean. That we'll watch the sunrise as free beings. That we'll bury her at sea.

"Rhine, I'll be gone before you leave."

"Don't say that!"

I rest my forehead against her shoulder, and she brushes her fingers through my hair. Tears are threatening behind my eyes, but I force them away. The effort makes my lip quiver. I'm trying to stay strong for her sake, but she picks up easily on my distress. "It's okay," she says. "It's fine."

"You're crazy to say that."

"No," she says, drawing back so that I raise my head and look at her. "Think about how close you are to finally having what you want."

"What about you?" I say, louder than I mean to. The quivering has spread to my hands, and I grip at the blanket.

She smiles. It is an easy, beautiful smile. "I'll have what I want too," she says.

In the days that follow, Linden starts spending time with Jenna. But it's not like the time he spent with me after my escape attempt, or Cecily while she was in labor. Jenna has never established herself as his wife in any emotional capacity. He sits on a chair or on the divan, never on the bed with her. He doesn't touch her. I don't know what they talk about, this estranged husband and wife who were never even acquainted to begin with, but I can't help but think their conversations are the obligatory terminal discussions you'd expect to find in a hospital. Like he's granting her last wishes. Like he's trying to get some closure before she goes.

"Did you know Jenna had sisters?" he asks me as we're eating dinner. It's just the two of us. Cecily is catching what little precious sleep she can, and Vaughn is supposed to be in the basement working on his miracle antidote.

"Yes," I say.

"She tells me they died, though," he says. "Some kind of accident."

I try to eat, but chewing feels arduous. The food falls down my throat and into an empty pit. I never taste it. I wonder why, with all her resentment, Jenna hasn't told Linden the truth about her sisters. Maybe it isn't worth the energy. Maybe keeping it from him is her ultimate form of spite. She will die, and he will never have known her at all.

"I've never really understood that one," Linden says, dabbing his mouth with a napkin. "But I know how fond you were of her."

"'Were'?" I say. "I still am. She's still here."

"Of course. I'm sorry."

We don't talk for the rest of the meal, but even the sound of his silverware touching the plate is gnawing at me. He is so painfully clueless. When I run away, I bet Vaughn will tell him I died, give him some fake ashes to scatter. And he'll be left alone with Cecily, who wanted this life from the start, who will probably have half a dozen more babies to fill the empty spaces in both of their lives. And then they'll both die, and Vaughn will replace them easily enough, because he's a first generation, and who knows how long he'll live. Our bedrooms will be filled with new girls after we're dead and gone.

Linden and Cecily. They've both been so isolated that they don't even know what they're missing. And that is for the best. They'll say good-bye to Jenna and to me, bury us in some dark place in their hearts, and carry on for the remainder of their short lives. They'll find happiness in holograms and illusions.

In another time, in another place, I wonder who they might have been.

The attendants come to take our plates, and Linden frowns at how little I've eaten. "You're going to make yourself sick," he says.

"I'm just tired," I say. "I think I'll go to bed."

Upstairs Cecily's bedroom door is open, and I can hear Bowen gurgling softly, breathing in that cadenced, raspy, newborn way. The light is off, and perhaps he's lying awake in his crib while Cecily sleeps. I know this routine. Left unattended when he awakens from a nap, he will inevitably start to cry. And when he cries, he doesn't stop.

My plan was to try to get some sleep, but it's better to take Bowen from his crib before he wakes up my sister wives. But when I step into the bedroom, I find Jenna sitting on the edge of the bed, illuminated in a strip of light from the hallway. Her long hair cascades over one shoulder, and her face is tilted down toward the baby in her arms. Cecily is sleeping under the covers behind her in silence.

"Jenna?" I whisper. She smiles without raising her head.

"He looks like our husband," she says softly. "But I can tell by his temper that he's going to be like Cecily. It's too bad none of us will get to see that."

She looks so beautiful like this. The darkness hides her pale complexion, her purpling lips. Her nightgown is tiers and tiers of lace, her hair a perfect dark curtain. And I am struck with the painful realization that she looks like she could be somebody's mother. The caregiver, deft and gentle, with long capable fingers tracing Bowen's half-moon face. I wonder if she cared for her sisters this way before they were murdered, the way she has cared for Cecily. The way she has cared for me.

I swear I've just watched a tear roll from the corner of her eye, but she swipes it away before it gets far.

"How are you feeling?" I ask.

"All right," she says. I force myself to believe her. She looks so strong right now, so young. "Here, take him for a minute, okay?" She stands, and when she walks toward me, I can see that her knees are trembling. She comes closer, and the light from the hallway shows me the beads of sweat on her face, the blue shadows under her eyes.

I let her ease the baby into my arms, and she walks by

me with all the presence of a ghost, sweeping through the spot where she flirted with the baffled attendant, where hundreds of times she paced toward her room with her nose in a romance novel.

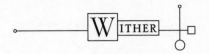

Her hand trails the wall as she makes her way to her bedroom and closes the door. Moments later I hear the mangled sounds of her coughing.

Bowen, unfazed by her absence, has fallen asleep. I envy his complacency. I envy his twenty-five remaining years.

Later, I close my bedroom door. I shut off the lights. I bury my face in my pillow and I scream and scream until I'm so numb that I can't feel my arms and legs, just like Jenna. And the silence throbs. Rowan, my parents, Rose, the Manhattan harbor. Things I miss. Things I love. Things that I have left behind, or that have fallen through my fingers. I want my mother to come and kiss me good night. I want my father to play the piano. I want my brother to keep watch while I sleep, to give me a swig of vodka when the pain is too bad. I miss him. I haven't allowed myself to truly miss him in a long time, but now I can't help it. A floodgate has opened. And I'm so tired and so lost, and I don't know if I'll ever truly be able to escape. I don't know how I'll be able to open the iron gate with its pointed flower. I wipe my tears on Gabriel's handkerchief, which I've kept hidden in my pillowcase all this time. In the darkness I feel the embroidery, and I sob until my throat is raw, and I just hope, hope, hope that I'll make it home.

I dream of being cast into the sea. I dream of drowning, but this time I don't thrash or struggle. I succumb. And after a while, in the quiet of the underwater, I can hear my father's music, and it's not so bad.

In the morning, Cecily wakes me in tears. "Jenna won't open her eyes," she says. "She's burning up."

Cecily tends to be dramatic, but when I stumble, still half sleeping, to Jenna's room, I can see that it's even worse than she described. Our sister wife's skin has paled and taken on a cruel yellow tinge. Bruises are spreading across her throat and arms. No, not bruises; they're more like festering wounds. I touch her forehead, and she makes a pitiful croaking sound.

"Jenna?" I whisper.

Cecily paces, clenching and unclenching her fists. "I'm getting Housemaster Vaughn," she says.

"No." I get onto the mattress and bring Jenna's head into my lap. "Go to the bathroom and get a wet cloth."

"But—"

"There's nothing he can do for her that we can't do ourselves," I say, forcing a calm tone.

Cecily obliges, and I hear her sobbing as she runs the water, but she has composed herself when she returns with the wet cloth. She pulls back the blankets and undoes the top buttons of Jenna's nightgown to help cool the fever, and all the while I can see her struggling to contain the panic that's filled up her eyes. Do my eyes look the same way? I'm sitting here, calmly running my fingers through Jenna's hair, but my heart is pounding, my stomach is sick. This is so much worse than what I saw Rose go through. So, so much worse.

Hours pass, and I think this is going to be the end of my sister wife. She'll never open her eyes again. Even I hadn't expected it to happen so fast.

Cecily puts her arms around me and buries her face in my neck. But I have no words of comfort for her. It takes all my effort just to keep breathing.

"We should get Housemaster Vaughn," she says, for the third or fourth time.

I shake my head. "She hates him," I say.

And then Jenna laughs. "Yep," she says. It's a weak, garbled sound, but Cecily and I snap to attention, and we see the smile on Jenna's purpled lips. Her eyelashes flutter and she opens her eyes. They're not the vivacious things they once were. They're eerie and distant. But there's still life in them. She's still with us.

"Hi," Cecily croons, kneeling at the bedside and taking Jenna's hand in both of hers. "How are you feeling?"

"Great," Jenna says, and her eyes roll back as she closes them.

"Can we get you anything?" I say.

"A tunnel of light," she says, and I think she's trying to smirk.

"Don't say things like that," Cecily says. "Please don't. I can read to you if you'd like. I've gotten much better at it."

Jenna opens her eyes long enough to watch Cecily flip through one of the many books piled on the nightstand, and then she laughs again, and it's more painful to hear than before. "That one's not exactly deathbed appropriate, Cecily."

I can't stand this. I look at Jenna and all I can see is this thing that's killing her. This voice doesn't even sound like hers.

"I don't care," Cecily says. "I'll read it anyway. There's a bookmark in the middle, so I'll start there. You should at least get to see how it ends."

"Skip to the last page, then," Jenna says. "I'm not made of time." And then her chest convulses and blood and vomit spill from her mouth. I turn her onto her side and rub her back while she struggles to cough it all up. Cecily cringes, her eyes filling with tears. I don't know how Cecily has the energy to cry so much. I can barely muster the energy to move. Just being alive feels so arduous that all I want to do is climb under the covers and sleep. It seems impossible that I ever had the strength even to walk.

I slept for days after my parents died. Weeks. Until my brother couldn't take it anymore. *Get up*, he said. *They're dead. We're alive. We have things to do.*

Jenna chokes and gasps. I can see the notches in her spine through her gown. When did she become so thin? There's barely any life left in her when she's through coughing and vomiting. She rolls onto her back, eyes shut, motionless except for her jagged breathing. She doesn't even move when Cecily and I strip the ruined bedsheets from under her.

She sleeps the morning away, barely mumbling when Cecily and I change her soiled nightgown and dab at her with cool cloths. Her skin is bruised everywhere, so translucent and marbled with veins that I hesitate to touch her. Some of the bruises have started to bleed. It's like her body is rotting from the inside out. Her hair has become thin; locks of it fall out at a time. I sweep it away. Cecily reads aloud from the romance novel, which is all about healthy young lovers and summer kisses. She pauses sometimes to clear the sobs caught in her throat.

We dismiss the attendants who come with medications, after Jenna proves too weak to swallow pills, and fails to keep down anything else they try to give her. It gets to be so bad that Jenna, hazy and barely able to speak, starts to hide her face in my or Cecily's nightgown when she hears footsteps approaching. I know what she's trying to tell us. It's the same thing that Rose was begging for. She doesn't want to prolong this misery.

She doesn't struggle with Adair, though, and so we allow him in. Her domestic is light on his feet and unassuming with his touch. He rubs a salve on her chest that takes the creakiness out of her breathing. And he doesn't stay longer than he has to. He always raved about Jenna's beauty, and he understands that she doesn't want anyone to witness her dying in such a hideous way.

By late afternoon, Linden is concerned enough to check on us. Immediately his face changes when he crosses the threshold. He can smell it: the heavy stench of decay and sweat and blood. I can see in his eyes that this is familiar. He spent the final days at Rose's side. But he doesn't approach this wife. I know Jenna always kept an emotional distance from Linden, that their marriage was purely sexual, but I wonder if Linden was partly to blame for that too. After losing Rose, he didn't want to love another woman he would outlive. I have as many years left as he does, and Cecily will outlive us both. But Jenna . . .

Linden looks so piteous and apologetic, standing there. His three wives are huddled together on the bare mattress, one of them dying; when we're together, we form an alliance he can't touch. He's scared to even try.

"I forgot to feed Bowen, didn't I?" Cecily says when she sees her son in Linden's arms.

"It's all right, love," Linden says. "There's the wet nurse for that. I'm more worried about you."

I can't imagine why Linden would bring his son here, unless he's feeling lonely and hoped it would lure Cecily away to spend some time with him. It doesn't work. Cecily buries her face against Jenna's arm and closes her eyes. I close my eyes too. We're in the Gatherers' van all over again, recoiling into the darkness, wanting to disappear in the safety of one another.

"The attendants said you've been turning them away,"

Linden says. "At least let me send someone up with fresh bedsheets."

"No," Cecily murmurs. "Don't send anyone. Tell them all to leave her alone."

"Can't I do anything?" he says.

"No," I say.

"No," Cecily echoes.

I can feel our husband standing in the doorway. The closeness of his wives frightens him, as if one dying wife could be the death of all three.

Eventually he leaves without another word.

Jenna mutters a word I can't understand. I think it's a name. I think she's looking for her sisters.

"It's not safe for you here," she says. I don't know if she's talking to her sisters, or to us.

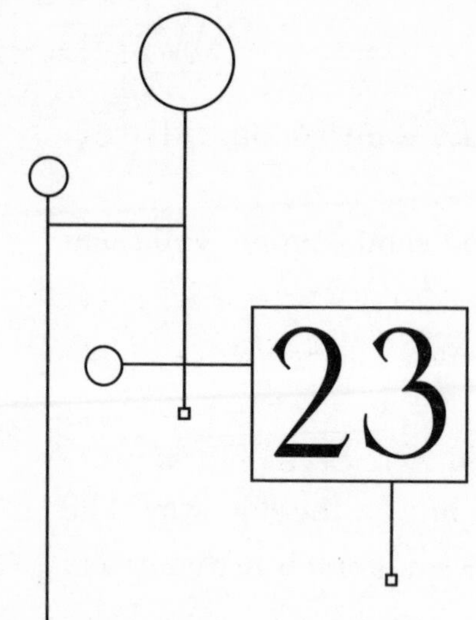

23

JENNA WAS RIGHT. She leaves before I do. We lose her on January 1, in the early hours before the sun comes up. It's just Cecily and me at her side, and after days of living in her bed, all that was left was for us to talk to her for a while as her eyes fluttered open and shut. We wanted her to know she wasn't alone. For all our months together as sister wives, I should have had something meaningful to say to her, but in the end I could only bring myself to talk about the weather as I watched her die.

And now she's gone. Her eyes are still open, but they've taken on a deeper shade of gray. Hollow. Like a machine that's been unplugged. I lower her eyelids with my thumb and index finger, and then I kiss her forehead. She's still warm. Her body still looks like it's about to draw a breath.

Cecily stands and begins to pace. She touches her

forehead, her chest. "I don't understand," she says. "It happened so fast."

I think of how happy she was when Rose died, how she immediately asserted herself as the one willing to bear Linden's child. They've already talked about having more.

"Housemaster Vaughn should have been able to prolong—"

"Don't mention his name," I say fiercely, but I don't know why I'm getting upset with her. I haven't been able to stand the sight of her since Jenna became sick, and I'm not sure why that is. But now isn't the time to dwell on it.

I tuck Jenna's long hair behind her ears and try to comprehend her stillness. She's like a wax figure, when only a minute ago she was a human being. Cecily gets into the bed with her and buries her face in Jenna's neck and says her name. Jenna, Jenna, Jenna. Over and over, like it will do any good.

It isn't long before Vaughn comes to check on Jenna's vitals. He doesn't even have to approach the bed. He can see in Cecily's tears, in my distant gaze out the window, that our sister wife is gone. He says it's a pity but when he checked on her last night, he knew she wouldn't be long for this world.

When the attendants and their gurney come for Jenna's body, Cecily is still holding on. But she's too distraught to protest when Jenna's hand is pulled from her grasp. "Be brave," is all Cecily says.

I hear her a short while later. She's in the sitting room, playing an angry Bach in D minor. The keys are like the footsteps of death storming down the hall.

I listen to it as I lie on my bedroom floor, too bereft even to move toward my bed. I imagine this great music pouring out of Cecily's small body, notes hovering around her in reds and blacks, like a dark genie awoken from its slumber.

I wait for her music to stop. I wait for her to appear in my doorway, teary-eyed, asking if she can lie beside me for a while the way she always does when she's upset.

But she doesn't come. Instead my doorway is filled with her angry, fearless song.

Be brave, it seems to say.

I want to be away from here. I want to escape now. I can't stand to be in this mansion, with Vaughn doing who knows what to my sister wife's body while the rest of us are expected to eat our dinner and drink our tea. Cecily carries Bowen around like he's her little rag doll, and the two of them are red from crying. He's the most discontent baby on the planet. Probably means he's intuitive.

Within hours Vaughn gives us the ashes to scatter, and Cecily clings to the urn. She asks if it would be all right for her to keep Jenna's ashes on a shelf in her room. It will make her feel better. I say that's fine by me, and quietly I resent her ignorance.

In bed that night I hear a soft knock at the door, but I

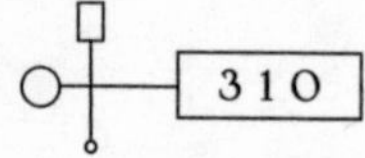

don't answer. Partly because I don't want to see anyone, but mostly because I am a million miles from earth. I have been lying in the dark for what seems like forever, listening to the distant sobs of a girl who has possessed my skin. I am floating in space.

When I do coast back to my senses, the wailing sounds coming from me are terrible and inhuman.

The door opens, filling my bedroom with light, and I curl away from it, just like I did in the van. I feel all at once how heavy my body is, how raw my throat is from all the screaming. My vision is blurry and wet.

"Rhine?" Linden says. His voice is barely familiar. I don't want to see him, and I try to tell him to go away, but when I open my mouth, there are only these unintelligible sounds. He sits on the edge of the bed and rubs my back. I try to shrug him away, but I don't have the strength.

"Sweetheart, you're scaring me. I've never seen you like this."

That's right. I'm Rhine, the orphan who trained to be his bride, who is happy to be here. Maybe in his mind I should even be happy because one dead sister wife means more of his time can be devoted to me. But I was always more of a sister wife than an actual wife. I can't imagine being in this marriage with him alone.

"What can I do for you?" He kneels by the bed, pushes the hair from my face. I stare at him through a mess of tears. *Set me free*, I think. *Send me back to last year. Give Jenna her sisters back.*

I just shake my head. I cover my face with my fists, but he moves them away, and I don't put up any kind of a fight.

"It's a new year now," he says softly. "There's a party tomorrow night. Would you like that?"

"No," I choke out.

"Yes, you would," he says. "Deirdre is already working hard on your dress, and Adair is even helping her."

Adair. What's to become of him now that Jenna is gone? He worked for her, and her alone. Though, there wasn't much to do—Jenna was so self-sufficient, and she rarely had any cause to wear new clothes. Maybe it makes him feel useful to help with my dress. I can't just throw it back in Adair's face. I swallow a lump in my throat and nod assent.

"There, that's better," Linden says. But I can see in his eyes that he knows I'm in pain. Maybe as much pain as he felt when he lost Rose. When she died, he threw things, screamed for all of us to go away. So doesn't he understand that I want to be alone too?

But he's not having it. "Move over," he says softly, and lifts up the blankets and climbs into the bed with me. When he pulls me to his chest, I don't know if it's meant to comfort me or him. But I crumple in his arms and succumb again quickly to tears. I try to float into outer space, to disappear from this miserable world for a while, but all night I'm kept firmly in place by his fragile bones. Even as I phase in and out of a restless sleep, I feel him there, holding me with more strength than I thought he had.

As I expected, Deirdre and Adair parade into my room the following afternoon with a stunning dress. In Manhattan there's not much cause to attend a New Year's celebration. It's an occasion reserved mostly for first generations who have the wealth and longevity to celebrate. It's also an opportunity for orphans to break into unattended houses in more well-to-do areas. Rowan and I would spend the first nights of the new year ramping up security and making sure the gun was loaded. It's also something of a free-for-all for Gatherers. There are all those drunk, gorgeous, motherless girls who dance and sell sparklers in the park. Rowan won't even let me leave the house to go to work, it's so unsafe.

Rowan. I worry about how he's doing, alone in that house with only the rats to help him keep watch.

The first generation attendants buff and wax me to a shine, and then Deirdre goes to work on my makeup while Adair winds my hair around a curling iron. It's always curls. "They open up your eyes," Adair says dreamily. Deirdre coats my lips with red and tells me to blot.

Cecily comes in for a while and sits on the divan to watch. Vaughn has taken Bowen off somewhere to draw his blood or analyze his DNA, or whatever it is he's doing to that poor child in the name of an antidote, and Cecily seems lost without the baby to care for. Over the course of several months I watched her go from a giggling teenage bride to a swollen stomach, and I could never have imagined that she'd be any kind of mother. And now, suddenly, it seems she doesn't know how to be anything else.

"Do her makeup," I tell Adair, who is busying himself by inspecting my dress, which is already perfect. "Don't you think she would look nice in purples?" I have no idea what I'm talking about. I just can't stand to see Cecily looking so sad.

"Earth tones," Deirdre cries, while she pins fake baby's breath to my hair clip. "With that hair and those eyes? You need browns and greens for sure." She winks at me in the mirror.

I make room for Cecily on the ottoman, and we sit back-to-back while the domestics make us sparkle. Cecily threatens to hurt Adair if he stabs her in the eye with the mascara wand, but she relaxes a little when she realizes he knows what he's doing. And then it's kind of nice. Like we're really sisters, and like there isn't the promise of an early death hanging over us.

"What do you think the party will be like?" Cecily asks me, blotting her lipstick into a tissue Adair holds out for her.

"Nothing fancy," I say, still not wanting to entice her with something she won't get to see. Maybe once I'm gone, Linden will take her out. She would love the chocolate fountains, and something tells me she would like the attention of the House Governors and architects kissing her hand and telling her how pretty she looks. "It's just a bunch of rich drunks all dressed up, talking business."

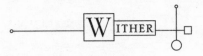

"Will you bring me some éclairs?" she asks.

"If they have them, sure."

She takes my hand, and it's small and warm. A child's hand. She was so eager to abandon her youth, in this world that has stolen the luxury of time, and I wonder who she would have been if only she could have had more years to live. When I'm gone, will she assume first wife? Will she embrace womanhood entirely? I feel like I've failed her somehow. It was hard enough to watch Jenna slip away, and here I am planning to leave the sister wife I have left. I worry about how she'll handle losing me.

But if not now, it would be later. In less than four years she would be at my bedside, watching me die.

I squeeze her hand. "Doing okay?" I ask.

"Yes." I can hear the smile in her voice. "Thank you."

My dress is a short strapless number, in a shimmering aqua with black pearls sewn into vaguely floral firework shapes up one side. A black pearl choker wraps around my throat, and black leggings and gloves will keep me warm against the biting January cold. Deirdre tops if off with a black ribbon for my hair, to go over the baby's breath, and a light coat of glitter that reminds me of Cecily's wedding gown. Cecily seemed so happy then, fluttering ahead of me to the gazebo.

Now she stands back and admires my completed

ensemble. She suddenly looks so grown-up with her face artfully colored in earth tones. Her hair is curled like mine, and she's beautiful even in her rumpled nightgown. "You look great," she says. "You're gonna kill tonight."

I don't tell her that, dress or not, I have no desire to go to this party. I would much rather crawl into that bed and pull the covers over my face and cry. But these are not the actions of a first wife. And Deirdre, Adair, and Cecily are watching me, so I smile in that way that my mother reserved for my father.

It scares me how easily I can pretend to be in love with this life, and the husband who comes with it.

Linden shows up in a simple black tuxedo—standard dress attire for all of the House Governors, I've noticed, but his lapels are the same aqua as my dress. I catch our reflection in the metal elevator doors, arm in arm, a perfect match. The doors open. We step inside.

"Have fun!" Cecily says.

When the doors have closed, Linden says, "Has she been a little strange lately?"

I'm not sure how to respond, because I have noticed a change in Cecily. Even since before Jenna's death, she has been oddly forlorn. But I think it might have something to do with Vaughn's constantly taking Bowen from her. And who knows what he's doing to him. It's common knowledge that new babies are the test subjects for wealthy households seeking the miracle antidote, but Vaughn has been so secretive and Bowen looks unscathed. I also can't find a nice way to tell Linden that I think he was selfish and wrong to impregnate such a young girl in the first place. And maybe I'm worried he'll start pressing me for children again. At sixteen I'm practically an old maid.

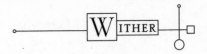

"She's just tired," I reply. "You should help her with the baby more."

"I'd love to," Linden says. "Between Cecily and my father, I'm lucky I even remember what my own son looks like."

"Linden," I venture cautiously. "What do you suppose your father is doing with the baby all the time?"

"Monitoring his heart rate, drawing his blood to be sure he's healthy, I suppose." He shrugs.

"And that seems normal to you?" I say.

"What's normal?" he says. "The first generations didn't even realize their children were dying until twenty years later when it started happening. Who knows what will happen to our children?"

He has a point. I stare at my glittery heels. Here I am in a pretty dress while the world falls apart. I can hear Jenna's voice saying, *Don't forget how you got here. Don't forget.*

Linden grabs my hand. At times like these I think he's as frightened as I am. I give him a small smile, and he bumps his shoulder against mine. The smile grows. "That's better," he says.

In the limo he pours us each a glass of champagne, but

I don't finish mine and I stop him from finishing his also. "There will be plenty more at the party," I say.

"Spoken like a true first wife." He laughs and kisses my temple. I blush in spite of myself. It's the first time he's said the words out loud. First wife. It's only for a few days longer, but I can pretend, for his sake, that isn't so.

"Do you suppose there will be cameras?" I ask.

"Tons," he says. And he looks a little worried. "Maybe I should have asked you to wear those green contacts," he says. "I don't want the whole world knowing just how extraordinary you are."

I straighten his tie. "Are my eyes what make me special to you?"

"No," he says. His voice has become soft and dreamy. He pushes the curls from my face. "They are only a ripple on the surface."

I smile. For a moment I think this is the way my father felt about my mother, and I could almost swear this marriage was real. A stranger passing by would think we had been together for years, that we planned to live the rest of our lives together. I always knew I was an excellent liar; I just didn't know I had it in me to fool myself.

We enter the party with our arms linked together, and with the music blasting it's easy for us to be unnoticed. The party is being thrown in an upscale bar that has platforms and a spiral staircase. The top two platforms are made of some sort of one-sided glass, so that we can see the people below but not the people above us. I'm relieved, because this means nobody can look up my dress. And something tells me some of these House Governors would try.

It takes approximately two minutes for one of Vaughn's colleagues to approach us, with two giggling brunettes on his arms carrying neon glasses. They look barely older than Cecily. They're dressed in matching fuchsia dresses that look like plastic wrap wound around their angular bodies. He introduces them as his wives—twins, each of them pregnant—and when he kisses my hand, both women stare at me with contempt.

"They're jealous of your beauty," Linden whispers when they've gone. "You look stunning, by the way. Stay close so nobody snatches you up."

Right. Being snatched once is enough for a lifetime.

I do stay close to him, though, because I don't trust any of these men, and because most of the other wives my age seem to already be drunk. This is a post–New Year's party, and Linden explains that at midnight they'll replay the countdown to the new year. When I ask him why, he says, "Who knows. But we only have so many new years left in life. What's the harm in adding a few more?"

"Good point," I say, and he pulls me onto the dance floor.

I do better with slow dances, which barely involve any motion at all, but one look at the flickering strobe lights tells me there will be no slow music tonight. I try to keep up with Linden, who patiently guides me along, and all I can think of is Jenna. How she taught Cecily and me her dance moves on that afternoon before the hurricane hit. She would love this party, even if she wasn't fond of Linden. She would be breaking hearts and crushing them under her heels as she whirled about the platform. I have an urge to tell her about the party when I get home, and then I remember that she's gone.

Linden dips me over his arm. He's in high spirits, considering how little he's had to drink. When I'm swept back to my feet, he plants a quick kiss on my lips.

"Mind if I cut in?" a man asks. And perhaps "man" isn't even the right word. He can hardly be any older than I am. He's short and pudgy, and his carrot hair is reflecting back the rainbow of lights. His pale skin is so washed out I can barely make out his features. There's a tall blonde on his arm in a bright red dress that matches her lips. She looks sober as she looks Linden up and down.

Linden hesitates and looks at me.

"Come on!" the man says. "Just for one dance. We'll swap wives."

"All right," Linden says, taking the red dress's hand and passing me over to the carrot-head. "But I'm rather fond of my Rhine. Don't get too attached."

I feel nauseous. The man smells like an unfortunate assortment of all the meats on the deli platter, and he's had too much to drink. He steps on my black shoes more than once, marring them with dirty footprints. He's so short that I can see right over his head, and I'm watching Linden dance with this man's wife, and she seems to be having the time of her life. She's probably relieved to be with a husband who knows what he's doing. But he isn't her husband! He's mine.

The thought stops me in my tracks. The pudgy carrot-head crashes into my breasts and laughs. "You sure are clumsy, baby," he says. But I barely hear him. Mine? No. Linden is not mine. It's all an act. These parties, the key card, this first wife business—it's insubstantial. In a few days Gabriel and I will run away, and this whole life will be a distant memory. What was I thinking?

I force myself to look away from Linden and the blonde, who is clearly enjoying dancing with a man her own height. And when this dance ends, I disappear to the dessert table and scoop up some éclairs and chocolate mini-cakes for Cecily before the good ones are taken. One of the attendants offers to refrigerate them for me until I'm ready to leave.

I hang back and watch the bodies dancing in the chaotic lights. Red, green, blue, white, orange. Images of colorful stars spin around the walls. I am floating on this glass plate. Below me, more bodies, more lights, more music rattling the floor. And as I watch them, I become more appreciative of Deirdre's fashion sense. Most of these other wives look as though they're wearing tinfoil. Lots of silvers and metallic pinks and greens and baby blues. Platform shoes with six-inch heels and exaggerated pearl necklaces that look like they weigh a ton. Most of the women wear so much makeup that the lights make them appear radioactive. Their teeth are glowing.

A few of the wives pull me into their dance circle, and I allow it. It's a good opportunity for the cameras to film me. And it's better than dancing with their husbands, at least, and actually it's pretty fun. Most of them, like me, don't have any idea how to dance. Their jewelry clatters together, and we twitch like we're dying, and we hold hands, and our laughter disappears in the music. I've always had cause to fear New Year's celebrations because of the Gatherers; I've always had to worry about who would be breaking into my home. But I'm safe here, able to enjoy the food and this dress and the music, and able to giggle at my clumsy dance steps. Attendants carry trays of drinks in throbbing neon cups, and, still moving, I swipe one and down it in seconds. The alcohol spreads warmth to my extremities. And I have to admit the party is making me feel better.

There's comfort to the repetitiveness of these parties. Whether it's a fake New Year's bash or a christening party, the theme is the same: life. Enjoy it while it lasts.

Then the lights stop flickering and the music dies down, and a voice announces through the speakers that there's one minute until midnight. The wives all scurry off to find their husbands, and I'm alone for a few seconds before Linden grabs my wrist and I feel his familiar chest pressing against my back. "There you are," he says. "I've been looking for you all night."

"Where's your girlfriend?" I say, before I can stop myself.

"What? What are you talking about?"

"Nothing," I say as he turns me to face him. "I just forgot you have a weakness for blondes."

"Oh, her?" he says. "Her husband's father is a contractor I've been working with. I thought it would benefit me to stay on his good side."

"Okay," I say, watching as a giant screen on the wall counts down the seconds to midnight. Twenty . . . nineteen . . .

"Don't be mad," Linden says, squeezing my hands. They're sweating in the black gloves. "I didn't like watching you dance with him, either. In fact I wanted to apologize the moment the music stopped, but you'd disappeared."

Ten . . . nine . . .

He tilts my chin, forcing me to look at him. Of all the Governors and Housemasters here, he's the only one I would allow to touch me in this way. He's familiar, like it or not. The closest thing I have to home this far down the coast.

"You're the only blonde I have a weakness for," he promises. And it's so pathetic that I have to laugh, and he laughs too, and takes my face in his hands. "I love you," he says.

Three . . . two . . . one.

He kisses me, amidst a sea of fake fireworks and fake stars. And we ring in this fake new year together. And it only seems fitting that, in this moment of illusion, the words just come out of me. "I love you, too."

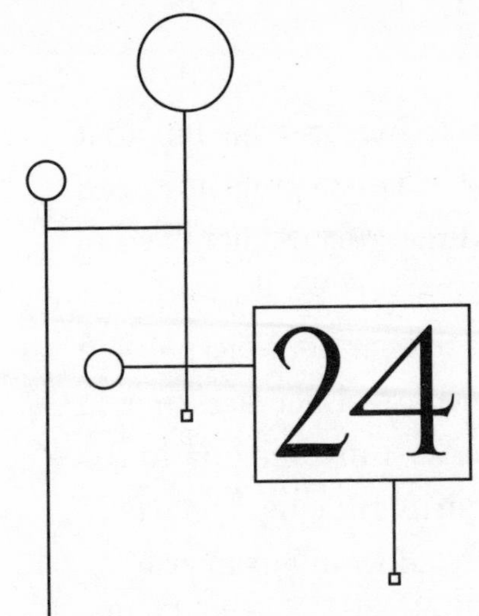

24

WE RETURN from the New Year's party in the early hours of morning, and my bedroom window lets in a smoggy blue light. Across the hall from my bedroom, Cecily's door is open, and I can hear her breathing, the rustle of her body moving in the satin sheets. Next to her door there's an empty bedroom, and no sound at all. And somehow that silence is what makes it impossible for me to sleep. I toss and turn for a while, and then I cross the hall to Jenna's bedroom.

Her door creaks open. In the morning light I can see that her bed has been made. One of her paperback romances remains on the nightstand. It's the only bit of her that lingers. From here I can see the candy wrapper marking the last page she ever read.

Even her smell is gone. That light, airy collaboration of perfumes and lotions that made attendants blush. In her final days it was overpowered by the heavy salve

Adair rubbed on her chest to help her breathe, but that medicinal smell is gone as well. The vacuum has been swept over her footsteps, erased the gurney marks from when her body was taken away.

I wait. To be haunted by her, to hear her voice. When Rose died, I could still, for months, feel her presence in the orange groves. Even if it was just my imagination, it was something. But if Jenna's spirit still exists on earth, it isn't here. There's not even a shadow in her mirror.

I peel back the blankets, climb into her bed. The sheets smell brand-new, and maybe they are, because I don't recognize them—white with little purple flowers. This isn't her satin comforter, either, which had a cherry juice stain in the corner. She's gone. Not a trace, aside from the paperback. I'll never know what happened to her that afternoon when she disappeared into Vaughn's basement. She'll never run away with me and see the ocean. She'll never dance or breathe again.

I bury my face in the mattress, the spot where she died, and I pretend her fingers are brushing through my hair. It takes a lot of effort before I'm able to conjure up a clear memory of her voice.

You're getting out of here, and it's going to be amazing.

"Okay," I tell her.

After a while I fall into a mercifully dreamless sleep.

It is my last dreamless night. After that, Gabriel is always on my mind, alone somewhere in that awful place beneath my feet. I think of his skin made gray by those flickering lights, his breath coming out in clouds. I close my eyes at night and begin dreaming of him lying on a cot to sleep, with my dead sister wives in a freezer beside him.

I worry about Vaughn discovering our plan and harming him. Killing him. Vaughn says he began working on his antidote the day Linden was born, and even if I don't believe that he means to do good things, I do believe that much. I also believe that Linden's is the only life he cares about saving. And Bowen is Vaughn's backup if he can't cure his son in time.

I have a horrible dream one night. Bowen, tall and willowy like his father, pressing his lips to the mouth of some hesitant bride who lives in what was once his mother's bedroom. He tells her that he loves her, and she holds a knife behind her back, spiteful and beautiful, waiting for the right moment to end him. There is nobody to warn him. No mother to love him. All he has ever known is Vaughn, who pries Linden's body apart in the basement, frantic for a cure. And me? I am long dead, frozen and perfectly preserved with my sister wives, our eyes open in stunned expressions, our hands not quite touching. In a row of four, icicles on our eyelashes.

Something touches me, and I scream before I can stop myself. My heart is hammering in my chest, and immediately I struggle to break away from my sister wives' corpses, desperate to be out of Vaughn's basement.

"Hey," a soft voice whispers. "Shh—hey, hey. It's all

right. You had a bad dream." I roll over, and there's Linden beside me in my bed; I can just barely make him out in the moonlight. He pushes the hair from my face. "Come here," he says, and draws me to him. I don't resist. My hands are trembling when I grip his shirt. His cheek against mine is warm, melting away the frozen skin of my dream.

Across the hall I hear the baby hiccup and then start wailing. I move to get out of bed, but Linden pulls me back down.

"I have to go," I say. "It's my fault. I woke him."

"You're shaking," he says. He touches the back of his hand to my forehead. "And you might be a little warm. Do you feel sick?"

"I'm not sick," I assure him.

"Stay in bed," Linden says. "I'll go."

I want to go. I want to confirm that Bowen is still just an infant, that the willowy boy in my dream isn't real. At least not yet. I get out of bed, and Linden follows me across the hall to Cecily's room. She's trying to drag herself out of her bed, hair disheveled, eyes half-open.

"I've got him," I whisper. "Go back to sleep."

"No," she says, and pushes me aside just as I'm reaching into the crib. "You aren't his mother. I am." Bowen whimpers and hiccups as she brings him into her arms. She shushes him, hums sweetly, and settles in the rocking chair. But when she undoes the top buttons of her nightgown, Bowen thrashes away from her breast, whining.

Linden comes up behind me and puts his arm around my shoulders. “Maybe we should try the wet nurse, love,” he says to Cecily.

She looks at him, and there are tears brimming in her eyes. “Don’t you dare,” she spits. “I am his mother. He needs *me*.” Her voice breaks, and she turns her attention back to her son. “Bowen, please . . .”

“My father says this is normal for the first few weeks,” Linden tries. “Newborns don’t take to the breast easily.”

“He used to,” Cecily says. “Something’s wrong.” She buttons her nightgown and stands, holding her son to her chest and pacing back and forth. This settles him; he’s asleep in seconds.

“He just wasn’t hungry,” I say.

Cecily says nothing more as she sets Bowen back into his crib, stooping to kiss his forehead. She did not see my dream—a world in which her son has grown into a motherless young man with unwitting brides of his own—but has she had nightmares too? Has it occurred to her, even once, that she will only be a very small part of his life, and that one day she’ll be nothing more to him than the distant memory of red hair and the sullen, elegant chords of a keyboard? If he remembers her at all.

“My parents used to work in a lab that had a nursery,” I tell her, ignoring my own rule about not letting Linden hear about my life. These words aren’t for him anyway. “All of the babies were orphans, and there were so many of them that they couldn’t get one-on-one care sometimes. So the technicians played a recording of a lullaby to soothe their crying. But the ones who were held always seemed more alert. Those were the ones who laughed and learned to reach for things sooner than the others."

Cecily was staring into the crib as I spoke, but now she raises her head toward me. "What does that mean?"

"I guess it means babies understand human contact. They know when they're being cared for."

"I don't remember anyone," Cecily whispers. "I grew up in an orphanage, and I don't remember anyone ever caring for me. I just want him to know I'm his mother. That I'm here and I'll take care of him."

"He knows," I whisper back, and I put my arm around her.

She wipes her hand across her eyes. "He doesn't have to listen to recordings. He has a mother. He has me."

"He does," I agree.

She covers her mouth to hold in another sob. Cecily has always been emotional, but giving birth to Bowen and losing Jenna have taken their toll. Every day she's more withered. I've been hoping Linden will be able to comfort her, so that it will be easier for her once I'm gone, but there are times when he can't reach her, when her sorrow comes out too irrationally or is too heavy for him to comprehend. Times like this, when she slips her hand into mine and holds on tight, and our husband becomes just a shadow in the doorway.

"Come on," I say. "You should get back to sleep." She lets me guide her to her bed. I tuck the covers in around her. Her eyes are already closed. She's always so weary.

"Rhine?" she says. "I'm sorry."

"Sorry for what?" I ask. But she has drifted off to sleep.

I turn for the door and realize that Linden is gone. He probably slipped away while I was trying to console Cecily, afraid he might make things worse. Cecily's temper is a fragile thing, especially now that she's grieving over Jenna. Her intensity terrifies him; I think it's because her grief reminds him of losing Rose.

I stand in the doorway for a while, listening to the cadenced breathing of my sister wife and her son, their forms barely visible in the moonlight. And a terrible sense of mortality washes over me. Very soon, Cecily will lose her remaining sister wife, and in less than four years, she'll lose her husband, too. And one day this floor will be nothing but empty bedrooms, with not even a ghost to keep Bowen company.

And then he'll be gone too.

It doesn't matter how much his mother loves him; love is not enough to keep any of us alive.

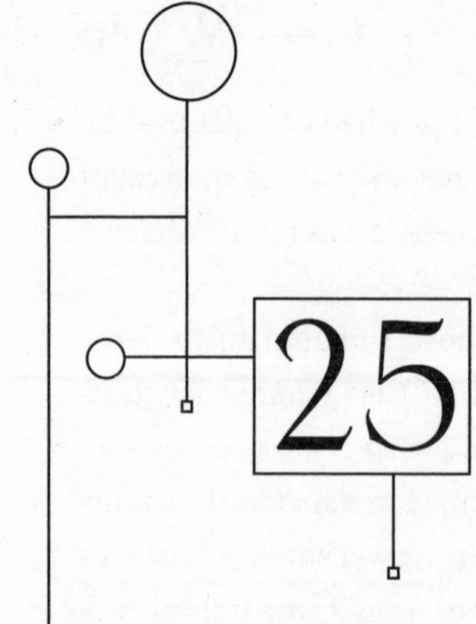

25

IN THE MONTH before my escape, I spend all of my time outside. There's still some snow on the ground, and I wander the orange groves. I play minigolf alone. And bit by bit, the month passes by.

On the morning of my planned escape, I lie on the trampoline and listen to the coils creaking as my body moves. This was Jenna's favorite place to be, her own island.

It's here that Cecily finds me, her red hair catching some snowflakes as they fall. She says, "Hey."

"Hey."

"Can I come up?" she asks. I pat the empty space beside me, and she climbs up.

"Where's your little tagalong?" I ask.

"Housemaster Vaughn," she says, a little unhappily. It's the only explanation necessary. She settles beside me and wraps both of her arms around my elbow and sighs. "What now?" she says.

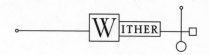

“I don’t know,” I say.

“I really didn’t think she was going to die,” she blurts out. “I thought she had another year, and by then there’d be an antidote, and . . .” She trails off. I lie on my back and watch her breath and mine fade into the cold air.

“Cecily,” I say. “There is no antidote. Get that through your head.”

“Don’t be so pro-naturalism. Housemaster Vaughn is a brilliant doctor. He’s working very hard. He has a theory that the problem is that the first generations were *conceived* artificially. So if a baby is born naturally, that baby can be fixed through”—she pauses, trying to remember the words, then she says them carefully, like she might break them—“external intervention.”

“Right.” I laugh cruelly. I don’t tell Cecily that my parents devoted their lives to finding an antidote, and that I have a hard time believing Vaughn could possibly have the same motives that they had. I don’t tell her about Rose’s body in the basement, and that Jenna is probably down there too, locked up in a freezer or dissected into unrecognizable pieces.

“He’ll find an antidote,” Cecily repeats firmly. “He has to.” I understand her denial. Her own son’s life depends on Vaughn’s imaginary antidote, but I am in no frame of mind for pretending. I shake my head, watching snow tumble and swirl from an all-white sky. The world seems so clean if you only look up.

“He has to,” Cecily says again. She sits over me, her

face blocking my view of the clouds. "You have to stay here and let him cure you," she says. "I know you're planning to run away. Don't think I don't know."

"What?" I say, sitting up.

She grabs my hand in both of hers and leans closer to me in earnest. "I know all about you and that attendant. I saw him kiss you."

That noise in the hallway. "That was you?" I say. My voice sounds strange and far away, like I'm overhearing a conversation between two people I don't know.

"He was distracting you from your duties as a wife. I thought that once he was gone, you'd realize what a good husband Linden is. You would see things more clearly. And you have, haven't you? You've been having fun at those parties?"

It hurts to breathe, suddenly. "You're the one who told Housemaster Vaughn."

"I did it to help you," she insists, squeezing my hand. "He and I were only looking out for your best interests. That's why Housemaster Vaughn had the attendant reassigned to another part of the mansion."

I rip my hand out of hers, and I want to back away. I want to get as far from her as I can, but for some reason I can't move from this spot. "What else did you tell him?"

"I know more than you give me credit for," she says. "You and Jenna had your little club that I was never a part of. You never told me anything, but I'm not stupid, you know. I know she was helping you to see that attendant.

And that's no good. Don't you see? Linden loves you, and you love him! He's *good* to us, and Housemaster Vaughn is going to find the antidote and we'll be here for a long, long time."

Her words tumble around me like the snowflakes, which have multiplied in amount and intensity. My breath is coming out in cloudy, frantic gasps. I hear Vaughn's voice in my head. *She's something of a cold fish, isn't she? If I had my way, we would just toss her back into the water.* "Do you have any idea what you've done?" I say.

"I've helped you!" she cries.

"You've killed her!" I cry back. I press the heels of my hands against my eyes, and I want to scream. I want to do a lot of things I'm likely to regret, so I just sit like that for a long while trying to catch my breath.

But I can't stay unresponsive forever, because Cecily is saying, "What?" and "What do you mean?" and "What are you talking about?" And finally I've had enough.

"You killed Jenna! That's what! You told Housemaster Vaughn that she was snooping around, and he killed her! I don't know how, but he did! He was looking for a reason to do her in, and you gave it to him. And Gabriel is stuck alone in that . . . awful basement, and it's all your fault."

Disbelief and then fear fills Cecily's brown eyes, and I can see her struggling to deny what I've told her. "No," she says, averting her gaze, nodding with certainty. "Jenna died of the virus, and—"

"Jenna was only nineteen," I say. "She was dead in a week. Yet Rose was alive for months. If your Housemaster Vaughn is such a brilliant doctor, explain to me why she was gone so quickly on his watch."

"E-every case is different," she stammers. And then she says, "Wait! Where are you going?" because I can no longer look at her and I've jumped to the ground, and I'm running. I don't know which way I'm going, but she follows me. I hear her shoes crunching the snow. She manages to catch up to me and grabs my arm, and I push her off me so hard she falls into a snowbank.

"You're just like him!" I say. "You're a monster just like him, and your baby is going to grow up to be a monster too! But you won't even get to see him grow up, because in six years you'll be dead. You'll be dead and Linden will be dead, and Bowen will be Housemaster Vaughn's new toy."

Her eyes are red with tears, and she's shaking her head, saying, "No, no, no" and "You're wrong." But she understands that I'm right. I can see the regret all over her face. I run away from her, before I can lose control and do something awful to her. As I go, I hear her screaming my name in a brutal, bloody way, like she's being murdered, which maybe she is. But slowly. It will take her six years to die.

My last day in Linden's mansion. Or maybe it's Vaughn's mansion. He's the one who made it what it is, and Linden is just a pawn like his brides. It would be easier if I could maintain my original hatred for Linden, to escape his cruel tyranny without ever looking back. But I know in my heart he isn't an awful person, and the very least I can do is say good-bye to him. In the morning he'll wake up and I'll be gone. He'll think I'm dead, and he'll scatter my ashes. Or maybe Cecily will keep them in a vase beside Jenna's memory.

Cecily. My last remaining sister wife. I take great care to avoid her for the rest of the afternoon, but I don't have to try very hard. She's made herself scarce. She doesn't even come down to dinner, and Linden is, of course, starting to get concerned that she's missing so many meals. He wants to know if I've noticed anything strange about her behavior lately, and I say she's doing as well as can be expected, under the circumstances. Linden has not been able to understand his wives' grief over Jenna's passing, not truly. So when I use it as an excuse for Cecily's erratic behavior, it shuts him up.

Linden hardly knew Jenna, and I no longer think Vaughn captured three brides for his son's benefit. I think he just wanted an extra body for his antidote. Jenna was the disposable one. Cecily is the baby factory. And I was supposed to be the apple of his eye.

After dinner, at about eight p.m., I call Deirdre to draw one of her chamomile baths for me. She's somber, though. After Jenna's death, Adair was sold off in an auction. So I'm not the only one who has lost a friend. Deirdre keeps busy, though, organizing and reorganizing the makeup in my dressing table as I soak. I wonder what will happen to her once I've gone, if she'll be sold to another mansion. Maybe she'll be reassigned as Bowen's caregiver. She is a little younger than Cecily, and she'll live at least until he's an adolescent. Maybe she can soothe his crying and be sure to tell him nice things about the world, like the beach her father painted.

"Come and talk to me for a while," I say. She sits on the edge of the bathtub and tries to smile a little. But the overall feeling of sadness on the wives' floor has even spread to her.

I'm trying to think of something I can say to her. Some way of saying good-bye without actually saying good-bye, but to my surprise she's the one to say, "You aren't like the others, are you?"

"Hm?" I say.

My head is resting against a rolled-up towel on the edge of the tub, and Deirdre begins to braid my wet hair. "It's just your demeanor," she says. "You're . . . like a paintbrush."

I open my eyes. "What do you mean?"

"It's a good thing," she says. "Good things have happened since you arrived." She waves her hand as though painting a picture. "Things are brighter."

That's a joke. Gabriel is confined to the basement and Jenna is dead. "I don't see what you mean," I say.

"The House Governor is so much stronger. Happier.

He used to be so fragile before. And things are just . . . better."

I still don't see it, but I can tell by her tone that she means it, and so I give her a smile.

Is it true? I don't know. I think of what I said on the way to the party, about coaxing him into the pool when the water is warm. Maybe something like that would have made him happy, like Deirdre says. I'll have to add it to my list of failed promises, right up there with my promise to take care of him. But when Rose asked me to do that, she hadn't anticipated Cecily. She and Linden are better suited for each other anyway. Cecily is so devoted to him that she would rat out Jenna and me to Vaughn, and she's the one who was so eager to carry his child, and they are both so painfully oblivious, that maybe they'll be good for each other. Two caged lovebirds. I'm no good for Linden. I'm full of atlases and maps. So what if I look like Rose? I'm not her, and even she had to leave him.

"Ready to get out?" she says.

"Yes," I say. As I change into my nightgown, she begins to turn down the covers on my bed, but I sit on the ottoman and say, "Can you do my makeup?"

"Now?" she says.

I nod.

And one last time, she works her magic.

I page one of the attendants and ask him to find Linden. A few minutes later Linden shows up in my doorway. "You were looking for me?" he says. He's going to say more, but he stops when he sees me, all made-up with my hair falling naturally, unsprayed or primped, the way it's supposed to. I'm wearing one of Deirdre's cabled sweaters that's as fluffy as a cloud, and a billowing black skirt that glitters with black diamonds.

"You look very nice," he says.

"I was just thinking how I've never seen the verandah," I say.

He holds out his arm for me. "Come on, then," he says.

The verandah is on the ground floor, off a dancing hall that doesn't get much use. All the tables and chairs in the hall are covered in sheets, as though ghosts have fallen asleep after a spectacular party. We navigate through the darkness of it, arm in arm, and stop before the sliding glass doors. Against a deep black sky, snow is falling in a dizzying fury like millions of pieces of broken stars.

"Maybe it's too cold to go out," he says.

"What are you talking about?" I say. "It's a beautiful night."

The verandah is a simple porch with a love seat and wicker chairs that face the orange groves. Linden dusts away the snow, and we sit on the love seat together. The snow falls around us, and for the longest time we don't talk.

"It's okay that you miss her," I say. "She was the love of your life."

"Not the only love," he says, and wraps his arms

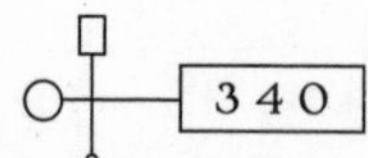

around me. I can smell the cold wool of his coat. We watch the snow fall for a while. And then he says, "It feels wrong to think about her as often as I do."

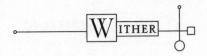

"You should think about her," I say. "Every day. You shouldn't try to look for her anywhere else, because you'll never find her. You'll see her walking away in a crowded street, and when you reach for her, she'll turn around and be somebody else."

I did this for months and months after my parents died. Linden is looking at me intently, and I tap my finger over his heart. "Just keep her here, okay? It's the only place you'll always be able to find her."

He smiles at me, and for a moment I see the glint of gold in his teeth. When I first met him, I thought they were a symbol of power and status. But they are just scars, the result of a fragile little boy whose teeth succumbed to an infection. He's not menacing at all.

"You seem to know a lot about loss," he says.

"I know a thing or two," I say, and rest my head against his shoulder. There's warmth radiating from his neck, and the distant clean scent of soap.

"I still don't know where you came from," he says. "Some days it's like you just fell from the sky."

"Some days I feel like I did," I say.

He weaves his fingers through mine. Through our matching white gloves I think I can feel his pulse. Our hands are so deceptive, and yet not. They look like they belong to a husband and wife; you can see the line of my wedding ring. And the way our hands fit together, it's like he can't have me close enough.

There is nothing in those hands to indicate the finality of this moment. Soon we will never touch each other again. We will never attend another party, or have a baby, or die together in the same anguish.

Will we die at the same time, at our own places along the coast? I hope Cecily will be there to hold his head in her lap. I hope she'll read to him, and say nice things. I hope that by then I will be far from his mind and he'll be able to find peace.

I hope Vaughn is not as heartless as I think, and that he'll commit his son's body to ashes unmarred, whole, and that Linden will be scattered in the orange grove.

As for myself, I try not to give my own death a lot of thought. I just know I want to spend my final years at home, in Manhattan, with my brother, in the house that our parents left us. And with Gabriel, maybe. I'll try to teach him as much as I can about the world, so he's able to find a job, maybe at the harbor; so he'll have something to do with himself after I'm dead.

"Sweetheart, what is it?" Linden says, and I realize there are tears in my eyes. It's so cold that I don't know how they haven't frozen.

"It's nothing," I say. "I was just thinking about how little time there is."

He's looking at me the way he does when he asks for my thoughts on his building designs. Like he wants to

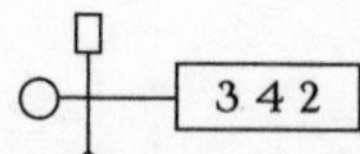

cast himself into my mind. He wants to understand, and be understood.

In another time, in another place, I wonder who we would have been to each other.

And then I realize how ridiculous that is. In another time and place I wouldn't have been kidnapped to be his bride. And he wouldn't be trapped in this mansion. He would be a famous architect, and maybe I would live in one of his houses, and have a real marriage, and children who would live a good, long time.

I laugh, trying to be reassuring, and squeeze his hand. "I was thinking how little time people will spend in your beautiful houses."

He presses his forehead to my temple, closes his eyes. "When the weather gets nicer, I'll show you some of them," he says. "It's nice to see the changes people make, the pets and swing sets and evidence of life. It's enough to make you forget sometimes."

"I'd like that, Linden," I say.

We don't talk after that. I let him squeeze his arms around me. The snow and the cold get to be too much for him after a while, and he brings me back to my room. We kiss, his frozen nose touching mine, one last time.

"Good night, sweetheart," he says.

"Good-bye, sweetheart," I say. And it's so casual, so innocent, that he doesn't suspect a thing. The elevator doors close between us, and he's gone from my world forever.

The door to Cecily's bedroom is ajar, and I see her on the rocker in her bedroom. She's got her nightgown open and she's offering her bare breast to Bowen, but he's thrashing and whining. "Please, please take it," she's sobbing in a hushed tone. But he won't. Vaughn was lying about there being a wet nurse. I saw him giving Bowen a bottle, and once a baby has the sweet taste of formula, it never returns to the breast. This is something I remember my parents telling me, when they worked in the lab. But Cecily has no idea. Vaughn is taking her son away slowly, beginning to control him the way he controls his own son. Vaughn wants Cecily to think her own child doesn't love her.

I stand in the hallway for a long time, watching her. This excited little bride who has become so haggard and pale. I remember the day she tumbled from the diving board, and we swam through the tropics and reached for imaginary starfish. That's my best memory of her, and it's an illusion.

No, maybe that's not the best memory. When I was bedridden, she brought the lilies to my room.

I can't think of a way to say good-bye to her. Eventually I walk away, as quietly as I came, and leave her to the life she was so eager to have. I know that someday I'll stop hating her. I know that she's only a child, a silly, naive little girl who fell victim to Vaughn's lies. But when I look at her, all I see is Jenna's cold body in the basement, under a sheet and awaiting the knife. And that is Cecily's fault. And I do not forgive her.

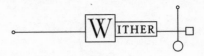

My last stop is Jenna's room. I stand in her doorway for a long, long time. I look at the placement of things. The brush on the dresser could belong to anyone; her paperback romance is gone. Only the lighter she stole from the attendant remains of her, in plain sight, because nobody paid enough attention to even know it was there. I take it now, put it in my pocket. This one small piece of her I'll keep. There's nothing left of any sentimental value. The bed has been stripped, cleaned, made up as though it expects her to come and rest her head on its pillows. She won't, but maybe another girl will soon.

There's nothing here to say good-bye to. There's no dancing girl. No mischievous smile. She's gone, off with her sisters, broken free, escaped. And if she were here now, she would say, "Go."

The clock on her night table is showing me the time—9:50. It's like she's pushing me out the door.

I don't say good-bye. I'm just gone.

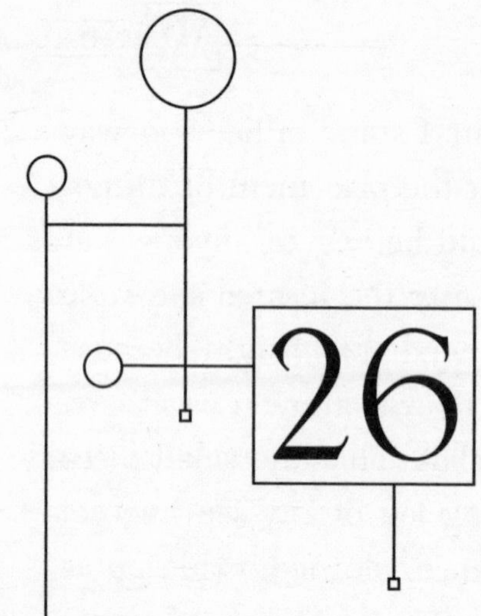

I TAKE the elevator to the ground floor and cross through the kitchen, expecting it to be empty. But as I'm putting my hand on the doorknob, a voice stops me with, "Bit cold for a stroll, isn't it?"

I spin around, and the head cook is emerging from the hallway, brushing the greasy hair from her face.

"It's just going to be a short walk," I say. "I couldn't sleep."

"Be careful out there, blondie," she says. "In this kind of snow, you go out for a short walk and you might just get lost and never return." A sly smile creeps across her face. "Nobody wants that, right?"

"Of course not," I say cautiously. What does she know?

"Well, just in case, here's something to keep you warm." As she approaches, I see that she's carrying a thermos. It's so warm that I can feel it through my gloves when she presses it into my hands.

"Thank you," I say.

She opens the door for me, and slaps me on the shoulder. "Careful," she says. "It's cold out there."

I step outside, and by the time I've turned around to thank her again, she's closed the door.

The snow has gotten heavier. It takes me a long time to trek through the drifts because I'm trying to cover my tracks. When I'm far enough from the house, I start whispering Gabriel's name, but the wind is stealing my voice. It's like the hurricane all over again, but full of snow. I stumble into a tree, and I feel my way along the edge of the woods as I go, calling his name a little louder and a little louder. Eventually I find the hologram. I reach for a tree and fall right through it. I'm far enough from the house now that I can call his name loudly.

"Gabriel! Gabriel!"

But he doesn't come, and he doesn't come. And I know that soon I'll have a decision to make. I can run to the ocean without him, or I can go back into the maelstrom of snow and look for him. Either way I am leaving this mansion tonight. Even if Gabriel has never sailed a boat, he knows more about boats than anyone else I know, and I know next to nothing. And, more important, I fear what Vaughn will do if Gabriel is left behind. Vaughn will know that Gabriel helped me escape. That settles it. Just as I'm realizing I can't leave him behind, that I need to go looking for him, someone grabs my wrist.

"Rhine."

I turn, and I'm careening right into his arms. For the second time, in a second storm, he's come to hold me steady. And there's so much I want to tell him about what's happened in this whole horrible month without him, but there's no time. The wind has picked up, and we can't make out each other's words, so we just start running, hand in hand, into the darkness.

The wind sounds like voices. It sounds like my father and mother laughing, and Rowan waking me up for my shift, and Cecily's baby crying, and Linden saying I love you. I don't stop to listen. I don't respond. But sometimes we trip on twigs and snowbanks, and we pull each other back up. We are unstoppable. And then we make it to the gate, which is, of course, locked.

There's a panel, but my key card doesn't work on it. Did I really think it would? "What now?" Gabriel shouts to me over all the wind. I start walking the length of the fence, looking for the place where it ends, but it soon becomes abundantly clear that there is no end to it, that it must wrap all the way around the property in a circle that's miles and miles wide.

What now?

I don't know. I don't know.

Escape is so close. I can reach through the bars and touch the free air. I can almost grasp at a tree limb on the other side. Frantically I survey our surroundings. The trees would be impossible to climb; the branches are too high; the fence is too icy. I try scaling the iron bars and fail every time. But I try and try until eventually Gabriel grabs me and holds me back. He unbuttons his wool coat and brings me to his chest, and wraps it around the both of us. We kneel together against a snowbank, and I think I know what he's trying to tell me. There is no way out. We're going to freeze to death.

But I don't feel the acceptance I felt in the hurricane. I was so sure that night that I was going to die, and yet something told me to keep going and keep going, and when I climbed the lighthouse, I saw the exit. I don't believe that was for nothing.

I feel Gabriel kiss my forehead. But even his normally warm lips have gone cold. I draw back a little, pull his collar up around his ears. He slides his hands under my hair, on either side of my neck, and we bring warmth back to each other that way.

I take Jenna's lighter from my pocket, and with the wind it's almost impossible to spark a flame. I have to wriggle free of Gabriel's coat, and he cups his hands around the flame so that the wind won't steal it. It calls to mind a story I read in Linden's library about a dying girl who lit matches to keep warm. Each new little flame brought a different memory of her life. But right now the only memory is Jenna, her little glowing life flickering in our hands. It's the only light in all this darkness, and I think I'd like nothing more than to light this place on fire. To watch it burn like those ugly curtains. Light one tree and watch the fire spread to them all. But the wind is too strong. I feel like Vaughn has somehow brought on this blizzard. I'm afraid that tomorrow morning he'll find Gabriel's and my body frozen and dead, so hopelessly close to our escape.

It can't happen. I won't give him the satisfaction.

Just as I'm considering trying to ignite one of the trees, I hear a voice on the wind. I think I'm imagining it again, but Gabriel looks too. We can just make out a shadowy figure running toward our little light.

I hurry to my feet, pulling Gabriel with me. It's Vaughn. It's Vaughn coming to finish us off, or worse, to drag us into his basement to torture us, mutilate us, strap us to operating tables in the same room as Rose's and Jenna's corpses. I start to run, but Gabriel stops me. The man gets closer, and it's not Vaughn at all.

It's the nervous attendant who took Gabriel's place. The one who said I was the nice one; the one who told me to check my napkin for the June Bean.

He's waving something over his head. A key card. His mouth is moving, but with all the wind and snow, I can't hear his words. So we just watch, Gabriel and I, as he swipes the key card across the panel. The gate hitches a little, trying to dig through the snow, but it opens.

For the longest time I just stand there, not sure what to make of this. Not sure if I should trust it. I am still expecting Vaughn to—I don't know, pop out from behind a tree and shoot us or something.

But the attendant is waving us along, and I think he's saying, "Go, go!"

"Why?" I say. I move close to him so that I can hear him better. I'm shouting over the wind. "Why are you helping us? How did you know we were here?"

"Your sister wife asked me to help you," he says. "The little one. The redhead."

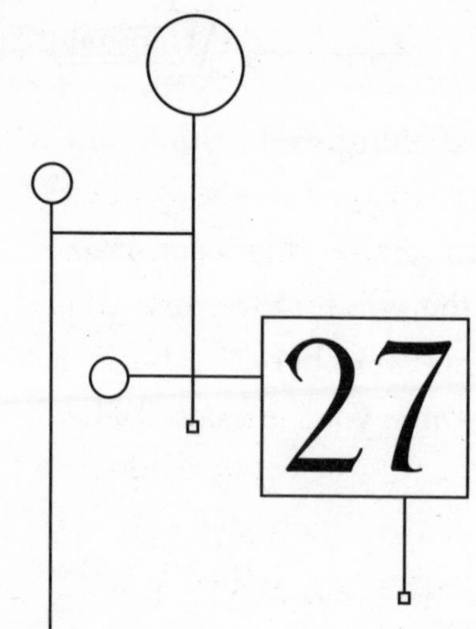

27

WE RUN for what feels like all night. It feels like the world could have ended and there's nothing left but this path, and these trees, and this snowy darkness. We stop to catch our breath, but the frozen air offers little relief to our gasping lungs. We are cold and exhausted, and still the wind rages.

In the library I read a book called *Dante's Inferno* about the many circles of a place called hell, in the after-life. In one of the circles were two lovers who were for-ever punished for their adultery by being trapped in a windstorm, unable to speak, unable to hear each other or have a moment of stillness.

That could be us, I think. And the sad part is that we've never even had the chance to become lovers. We are just a servant and an unwilling bride who haven't been granted one moment of true freedom to explore how we feel about each other. I'm even still wearing my wedding band under Deirdre's cabled glove.

When we're far enough from the iron gate, we relax our pace and go slowly. I can't understand why this road is so long. In the limousine it was only minutes that we were on it. Did Gabriel and I take a wrong turn? There's so much snow that I can't even be certain we're on the road at all. Right about the time I'm deciding that the world has ended, or that we're in our own circle of hell, there are lights. There's a rumbling sound, and then a big yellow truck sweeps past us, plowing up the snow along the city street.

And we've made it. We're here. The lights and buildings all reveal themselves as though a curtain has just been parted for us. There are more plows, and even a few people meandering beneath the streetlights. The cinema's marquee is advertising an all-night zombie-fest.

While we were in that barren wasteland, contemplating certain death, the world was peacefully going on just a few miles away. I laugh, somewhat hysterically, and I'm shaking Gabriel and pointing and saying, "See? See what you were missing?"

He says, "What's a zombie?"

"I don't know. We could find out, though. We can do anything we want."

We go into the cinema, where it's warm and it smells like hot butter and carpet cleaner. Neither of us has any money. Even if I'd thought to steal some, I wouldn't have known where to look. There's no use for it in the mansion; even Linden doesn't carry it around.

But the cinema is crowded, and we're able to sneak into one of the theatres unnoticed. We huddle together in the darkness, surrounded by strangers. We're anonymous, and in that anonymity there's safety. The movies are horrifying, the special effects tawdry and silly, and I feel a rush of exhilaration. "This is what Manhattan is like," I whisper to him.

"People crawl out of their graves in Manhattan?"

"No. They pay to see movies like this."

The marathon runs all night, one grotesque movie after another. I drift in and out of sleep. There's no sense of time, no sense of night or day. I hear the screams and howls in my subconscious, but my mind registers that the horror is fake. I'm safe here. Gabriel holds on to my hand. I wake up at some point to him tracing my wedding band with his finger. It has lost its meaning now; I am no longer Linden Ashby's wife, if I ever even was. I was always led to believe that for two people to truly be married, the bride would have to speak on her own behalf at some point.

"My real last name is Ellery," I say sleepily.

"I don't have a last name," Gabriel says.

"You should make one up, then," I say.

He laughs, and there's his smile again, shy and toothy and brilliant. His face is washed over by the flickering white screen, and I turn and realize the movies are over and the seats around us are empty. "Why didn't you wake me?" I ask.

"You looked cute," he says. He looks at me for a while, considering. Then he leans forward to kiss me.

It's a fantastic kiss, with neither of us worrying about open doors. His hand is under my chin, and my arms move slowly around his neck, and we're lost in this world of flickering darkness, in a sea of empty seats, and we are absolutely, unequivocally free.

It's the creak of the swinging door that breaks us apart, and the theatre employee—a first generation with a broom—saying, "Hey, the shows are all over. Go home."

I look at Gabriel. "Shall we go, then?" I say.

"Go where?"

"Home, of course."

It's such a long way home that I have no idea how we'll get there. There's no phone at the house, no way to call Rowan and let him know I'm all right. But once we get out of Florida, I'll track down a pay phone and call the factory where he was working when I last saw him. There's a good chance he's still there. I have to hold on to that thought, though a sinking feeling in my gut is telling me he's already moved on, lost in his search for me.

Outside, the city has settled into the hazy, fleeting moment between falling asleep and waking. It's subdued, though not entirely silent. There are still cars and plows mashing up the muddy sludge that's become of the snow. People are still walking here and there, but with less excitement and urgency. The sky is beginning to take on pink and yellow hues, and I know we don't have much time. It's nearly morning, and Vaughn will realize Gabriel and I have gone. That's if he doesn't know already, if Cecily has covered for us somehow.

Cecily. She sent that attendant out to help us last night. I didn't trust it. How could I? But there are no flashing police cars chasing us down. There's no wild hunt. Gabriel and I stand here, hand in hand, staring at a peaceful city.

Why did she help me?

Yesterday afternoon on the trampoline, she used that word. "Help." *I've helped you*, she cried. And there was such horror on her young face when she realized the opposite was true.

"What now?" Gabriel says, bringing me out of my thoughts.

"Come on," I say, and pull him along the sidewalk. Fat grains of salt crinkle under our shoes. At least a dozen people pass us, one or two nodding hello, most ignoring us completely. We are just two people in wool coats, on our way home.

We make it to the harbor, and it is different up close from how it looked in the limo. It's more vibrant. We can really smell the salt, hear the tide turning, the gentle knocking of boats against the dock. I'm eager to get going, to find a boat worth stealing before we're discovered, but I see the awe on Gabriel's face and I allow him this moment. This bewildered joy.

"Is it anything like you remember?" I say.

"I—" His voice catches. "I thought I remembered the ocean, but I didn't remember it at all."

I sidle up against him, and he puts his arm around me and gives an excited squeeze.

"Think you can steer us out of this place on one of those boats?" I say.

"Oh, absolutely."

"You sure?" I say.

"Well, if I'm wrong, I guess we die."

I laugh a little. "Fine by me," I say.

There isn't much time to be particular. I let Gabriel choose the boat because he's the expert. He's only ever seen pictures, and most of these models are much newer than the ones you can read about in Linden's library, but his expertise is still greater than mine. We settle on a small fishing boat with an indoor steering panel—I'm not sure of the technical name, and Gabriel has no time to explain—but it will protect us from the cold winds. It's surprisingly easy to untie the rope, to cast ourselves off. And even if Gabriel isn't familiar with these newer models, he's impressively deft. I try to help, but I only make it worse, and eventually he tells me to just be the lookout. That much I can do.

And then we're moving.

Gabriel works the steering unit, looking so serious and important, such a contrast to the uncertain little attendant pushing lunch carts around on the wives' floor. He watches the horizon, and his eyes are blue like the water, and I know he's right where he's meant to be. Maybe his parents were sailors. Or maybe a hundred years ago, when people were natural and free, his ancestors looked just this way.

We're finally free, and I have so much to tell him. Jenna. Cecily. And I know he must have things he wants to tell me, too. But for now those things can wait. I stand at a distance, admiring, letting him have his moment. I let his capable hands steer us into the forever, over sunken continents, until Florida disappears. Just disappears, as though swallowed.

Maybe, I think, we'll end up on the beach Deirdre's father painted. Maybe we'll touch real starfish that we can hold in our hands, that don't fall right through our grasp. Either way we'll have to find a shore somewhere. We'll have to stop and ask for directions to Manhattan; only, when we stop, it will be in a place where nobody knows us, where I'm not Linden Ashby's bride and he's not an attendant, and nobody has ever heard of Vaughn Ashby or his sprawling mansion. We're traveling up the coastline, and the wind has picked up.

Gabriel puts his arm around me, and I rest my hand on his, feeling the sturdy resistance of the steering wheel. "Look," he says in my ear.

In the distance I see a lighthouse. The light washes over us and continues on its rotation. This time, I don't know where the light will guide us.

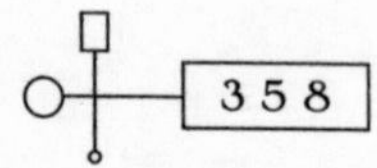